the
...orld of escorts. With ...
alongside the exploitation, and a brave, intelligent,
unapologetic crusader of a heroine, this book is unlike
anything I've read before. I loved every word. Grace
will stay with me for a long, long time'
**Elizabeth Haynes, author of INTO THE DARKEST
CORNER and BEHIND CLOSED DOORS**

'*Untouchable* is the stiletto of crime books – sleek,
deadly and sexy as hell'
**Eva Dolan, author of TELL NO TALES and
LONG WAY HOME**

'Imagine if Belle du Jour and Martina Cole teamed up to
write a thriller together: the result would be *Untouchable*,
a dark and sexy thriller with a flawed but likeable
heroine. It is fast-paced, compelling and deserves to be a
huge hit. I can't wait to see what Ava Marsh writes next'
**Mark Edwards, author of THE MAGPIES
and BECAUSE SHE LOVES ME**

'A gritty, no-holds-barred thriller, with a flawed,
uncompromising heroine – it had me racing through its pages'
Ruth Ware, author of IN A DARK, DARK WOOD

'Beautifully observed, eye-opening and exhilarating.
A compelling read. It took me out of my comfort
zone and I'm glad it did'
**Steven Dunne, author of DEITY and
A KILLING MOON**

'Dark, gritty and very sexy – a thrilling story
of greed, intrigue and revenge'
Mel Sherratt, author of the DS Allie Shenton series

Also by Ava Marsh

UNTOUCHABLE

and published by Corgi

EXPOSURE

AVA MARSH

CORGI BOOKS

TRANSWORLD PUBLISHERS
61–63 Uxbridge Road, London W5 5SA
www.penguin.co.uk

Transworld is part of the Penguin Random House group of companies
whose addresses can be found at global.penguinrandomhouse.com

Penguin
Random House
UK

First published in Great Britain in 2016 by Corgi Books
an imprint of Transworld Publishers

Ava Marsh ... ... and
Paten ... Act 1988 to be ... ...

This book is ... work of fiction ... ... , any
resembla ... ... al.

Every effor ... ... with
referen ... ...
We apolog ... ... d to
make th ... ... knowledge ... ...

ISBN 9780552171212

Typeset in 10.5/13.5 pt ITC Giovanni by Jouve (UK), Milton Keynes
Printed and bound in Great Britain by Clays Ltd, Bungay, Suffolk

Penguin Random House is committed to a sustainable future for
our business, our readers and our planet. This book is made from
Forest Stewardship Council® certified paper.

MIX
Paper from
responsible sources
FSC® C018179

1 3 5 7 9 10 8 6 4 2

To J. R.

1

HMP Brakehurst

Sunday, 3 January 2016

Where the fuck is Maxine?

There's no one left in the queue. Everyone's already seated, stripping off scarves and coats, hanging them over their chairs. I glance at the clock on the far wall of the visiting room.

Nearly half past two.

She should've been here thirty minutes ago.

I sit back, legs sprawled, trying to look like I don't care, but catch that new girl – the one in for benefit fraud – smirking in my direction. Ash, I think she's called. A sassy little cow with an annoying face. The kind who reckons she's much hotter than she is.

We lock eyes for a second, then she turns back to a ratty bloke with a pigtail. Her boyfriend, presumably. For now. A few more months in here, and he'll be her ex.

Lovers and friends are lost causes; only blood ties survive the separation of prison. And sometimes not even those.

Hardly a surprise, then, that my best friend is a no-show. Clearly she's had a change of heart.

I get up, raising a hand to let Janice know I'm leaving. Nod at Rita, who's sitting at the next table with her teenage daughter, tossing me a look of sympathy.

Don't bother, I want to tell her. No skin off my nose.

But as I head for the exit, I notice a large woman lumbering towards me, dressed in tight black leggings and an ugly navy puffa jacket. For a second I assume she's here for someone else. It's not till she gives me a hesitant smile that I realize.

Maxine?

Jesus. *What happened to her?*

I sit down again, trying not to stare as she waddles up to my table.

'Hi, Leanne.' Maxine glances around, taking in the other prisoners and their families. 'Sorry I'm late. Roadworks on the motorway.'

'No problem,' I mumble, doing my best to disguise my shock. At least her voice is familiar, though I barely recognize anything else about my oldest friend. Her hair, once long and full of auburn highlights, is now a dull brown. She isn't wearing a scrap of make-up, her skin red and blotchy, eyes piggy without mascara.

But it's her size that really has me thrown. Maxine has put on weight – a lot of weight. Her features lost in the bloat around her face, neck hidden under several folds of fat.

'Wow,' she asks, 'is it always this hot in here?'

I nod, studying her as she strips off her jacket, exposing a short-sleeved T-shirt and arms swathed in pale mottled flesh. My gaze drops to the swell of her belly, and I feel a tightening inside.

She's pregnant. At least seven or eight months gone.

'You OK?' Maxine sinks into the seat opposite, sighing with the effort.

I clear my throat. 'Fine. How about you?'

My friend forces a smile. 'Not fabulous, actually. Gestational diabetes,' she adds, like that explains the extra five or six stone she's carrying. 'They're thinking of inducing me early.'

'Sorry to hear it,' I say, though honestly I've no clue what she's on about. 'Anyway, it's good to see you.'

Her mouth twitches, but Maxine doesn't respond. She shifts her weight on the seat, obviously uncomfortable, and I wonder again what's brought her here; have been wondering since she put in for the visit four weeks ago.

I've not seen Maxine since my court appearance, and even then she sat at the back of the public gallery, keeping her head angled towards the judge, like I wasn't in the room. Which was weird, given I was the reason everyone was there.

So now I'm really curious. Travelling in her condition, all the way from Stevenage, can't be fun. I wonder how she got here. If Gary is waiting in a car outside.

'You haven't changed,' Maxine says, eyeballing me.

Jesus. It's only been eight years – what did she expect? I'd be all shrivelled up? Covered in scars or cigarette burns?

Mind you, those years have worked quite a transformation on her.

'The Taylor Swift of Brakehurst,' Maxine adds, with a laugh that doesn't sound genuine and wobbles the flesh under her chin.

'Who?'

'You know, the pop star.'

'No idea what she looks like,' I mutter, though I remember that chirpy 'Shake It Off' song. Someone's always got the bloody radio on in here.

There's a pause while I consider what to say. Even 'you look well' would be an out-and-out lie. Not that I'm averse to the odd fib – far from it – but Maxine would surely know it was insincere.

'So you can wear your own stuff in here, then?' she asks, before I come up with anything convincing.

'Six tops and six bottoms. That's the allowance.'

My friend smiles, like this confirms something, though fuck knows what. Then uses my own line on me. 'You're looking well, Leanne. Seriously.'

'Thanks. It's the organic food they give us.'

'Really?'

Maxine's frown makes me grin. How gullible can you get?

'So they let you have make-up, do they?' she asks. 'And have your hair done.'

Actually I've made a bit of an effort. Borrowed blusher and mascara off Nadine in the opposite cell. God knows why. The best thing about being banged up is not bothering with all the crap I had to do outside to keep my fans happy, keep people buying my stuff.

'We've got trainee hairdressers,' I explain. 'You know, learning skills for when they get out.'

'Handy.' Maxine adjusts her weight on her seat again, her eyes flitting around the room. She seems exhausted, her chest rising and falling like every breath is an effort. Uneasy – and not just because she's in a prison.

She isn't here for small talk, I sense, or to check how I am. She's here to tell me – or ask me – something.

Something important.

I drop my gaze to the floor, giving her a chance to screw up the courage. And see it scuttle past my foot – not your standard cockroach, but a tiny silverfish. Heading for the tip of Maxine's shoe.

10

'Don't move!' I bend to scoop it up, but it scoots round my hand, streaking away in the direction of Ash and her boyfriend.

At that moment Ash looks up, follows my gaze. Spots the little creature scurrying towards her. Her lips twitch into a smile as she lifts her foot and, with one decisive movement, crushes it into the floor.

I glare at her, my fingers curling into fists. Not now, I tell myself, pushing it down. Later.

'Leanne? You all right?' Maxine is watching me, her forehead creased again.

'Never better,' I lie.

She studies me, clearly deciding how to broach whatever brought her here. Another twinge of emotion – sadness? nostalgia? – as I remember how once we filled our days with talk, gossiping about teachers and other kids at school. Moaning about parents, or homework.

My best friend.

The only one left – at least on the outside.

'So, why are you here?' I prompt, losing patience.

Maxine swallows. Her eyes drift from mine. 'I have to tell you something, Leanne.'

She stops, waiting for me to ask. But suddenly I'm not sure I want to know. Whatever it is, it can't be good – the look on her face tells me that.

Pity.

Under the table my fists clench tighter. In the corner, standing against the wall, I see Janice watching me carefully.

Does she know what this is about, I wonder? Do all the screws?

'It's your mum,' Maxine says, and I swing my gaze back to hers.

11

'Mum?' I repeat, the word foreign in my mouth. 'What about her?'

Maxine clears her throat. Swallows again. 'It's bad news, Leanne. I'm sorry. She's ill . . . cancer.'

I force myself not to move a muscle. Give nothing away. 'OK,' I say, though of course it isn't.

'Breast cancer,' she continues. 'Very advanced.'

Very advanced.

My breathing shallows. The air in the visiting room thickens into something difficult to breathe. 'When?'

'The tumour? They found it last year, but it had spread to her liver. So that means . . .' Maxine stops.

'That means she's *dying*?' I make myself say what she can't.

My friend nods.

'How long?'

'A month or two. Maybe three.'

I try to picture Mum's face, but all that comes is the way she looked at me that last time I saw her – back before it happened. Anger distorting her features, turning them hard.

I barely know who you are any more, Leanne. Impossible to believe you were ever any part of me.

We haven't spoken since. She didn't answer my call when I was arrested. Never showed her face in court.

'Why didn't anyone tell me?' I whisper.

Maxine fidgets, her mouth shifting around as if uncertain what expression to adopt. 'You know how it was, Leanne. How your mum . . . Mike, felt about it all.'

'Only now she's changed her mind?' I can't keep the bitterness from my voice.

My friend shrugs. 'Not exactly. They don't know I'm here. I just thought you should know . . . I don't think it's right not telling you.'

12

A whimper escapes my throat. Heads swivel, then Janice appears, placing a firm hand on my shoulder.

'You OK, Leanne?'

'Yes,' I manage, though my breathing has shrunk to gasps. Like I'm on the verge of something. Something bad.

'Perhaps we'd better call it a day?' Janice glances at Maxine.

'No,' I say quickly, forcing myself to get a grip. 'I'm all right.'

Janice eyes me for a moment longer. 'If you're sure.' She retreats to her post by the wall, her gaze still trained on our table.

I lean across so only Maxine can hear me. 'Does she . . . Mum want me to visit? I could put in a request. They might let me come and see her.' Unlikely, but you never know – maybe Drew, my pet screw, could swing it.

Maxine's face flushes. 'I don't think that's a good idea, Leanne.'

I laugh. A bark of a laugh that isn't about anything funny. 'No deathbed reunion, then? No last-minute forgiveness?'

My friend doesn't reply. I turn away. You chose this, I remind myself. You knew how it was going to be.

The price you'd pay for hiding the truth.

'I'm sorry,' Maxine says, looking like she means it.

'Yeah,' I snap, before I can stop myself. 'Like you give a fuck. It takes a terminal disease for you to drag your sorry arse to see me.'

Maxine goes even redder. Two bright hand-slaps appear on her cheeks. 'Actually I think about you all the time, Leanne. I lie in bed at night, when Gary's asleep, wondering how it ever came to this. You in here.

What you did . . . I go over and over it in my mind . . . wondering.'

'Wondering what?'

'If we somehow drove you to it.'

'How do you mean?'

Maxine inhales. Releases it as a long sigh. 'I don't know . . . if there was anything we should have said, could have done that might have changed things.'

I close my eyes for a second or two. Compose myself.

'It had nothing to do with you, Maxine,' I hiss, low enough to stay under Janice's radar. 'Or Mum or Mike. Nothing to do with any of you, all right?' She flinches at my tone, though I'd have thought I'm doing her a favour, letting her off the hook.

Not that she was ever on it.

But I'm insulted by what she said. Like my life wasn't my own. Like I couldn't screw it up all by myself.

A chirp from Maxine's bag. She opens her legs to make space for her stomach as she bends to retrieve her phone. I watch her read the text. Probably from Gary, asking how long she'll be. Or whether he should get something in for supper.

Jesus.

Snapping the case shut, Maxine glances at the clock. 'I should go.'

A pain in my chest. Out of nowhere, I'm engulfed by a tidal wave of panic. I lean across, grab her arm. 'Wait, Maxine, please. I'm sorry. Give me a minute.'

Suddenly I'm desperate for her not to leave. Like she's everything I have left, my last connection to the outside world.

To my old life – before it all got screwed up.

'How is Mike?' I ask quickly. 'And the twins.'

Maxine stays put. I release her arm. 'Not great, Leanne, to be honest. Mike's finding it hard, what with keeping the pub going and looking after your mum. And the twins, though they seem all right. You know what they're like.'

A spasm like a kick to the stomach. I don't know, actually; have had no news of my half-brothers for ages. I want to tell Maxine that I miss them, even more than Mum and Mike. That I send them a card – one each – every birthday, every Christmas.

Nothing, of course, ever comes back.

Oh God, how will they cope with Mum gone? Tears prick my eyes. I should be there, I think. Should be helping take care of them.

Maxine checks the time again. 'I'm sorry, Leanne. I really have to go.'

'Gary waiting?' I ask, trying to keep the sarcasm from my voice. Good old Gary. I imagine him sitting in the car, radio on, tuned into the football. Older now. A bit paunchy, I'll bet, hair receding at the temples.

'It's a four-hour drive. We've got to get back for the babysitter.'

'Babysitter?' I drop my eyes to her stomach again. 'So this isn't your first?'

'Second. Alex is nearly three.'

A dull ache in my belly as I remember my own child. The one I lost. Probably my only chance; I'll be getting too old by the time I'm released – for men, or babies.

I watch as Maxine heaves herself to her feet, shrugging her jacket back on. It's not hard to imagine, her little family. The road I could have chosen: marriage, kids, an ordinary life. I picture a starter home in

Stevenage. A neat patch of back garden, swing in the corner. Collages decorating the walls of the nursery. Oven chips and fish fingers for tea.

We might as well be from different planets, Maxine and I. Hard to believe we were ever friends.

'Why didn't you bring him?' I ask, stalling. 'Your son. I'd have liked to meet him.'

No mistaking the look that flits across her face. She doesn't want him anywhere near this place.

Anywhere near me.

She doesn't want to be here herself, I realize, only doing this out of a sense of duty. Maxine wants nothing to do with me.

No one does.

Suddenly this feels so terrible I barely know how to survive the next minute. I want to cry and scream. I want to punch myself in the head, pull out my hair. Smash, kick, claw myself into oblivion.

They hate me.

They all wish I was fucking dead.

I reach over, seizing Maxine's hand this time. See her fight the impulse to snatch it away.

'Listen,' I say quickly, before I can change my mind. 'It's not like you think. None of it. I didn't do what . . . what you imagine.' All at once I'm desperate to blurt out the truth.

Keeping it hidden is killing me.

Maxine pulls her hand from mine. 'Leanne . . .' She bites her lip. Pushing down her own emotions. 'Leanne, I—'

Her eyes slide away. She doesn't believe me, I can see that. And there's not time enough to convince her. To explain why I said what I did in court.

Too late.

16

'I can't do this.' Tears glint on her fat cheeks. 'I'm sorry, Leanne, but I can't do this any more.'

She turns and heads for the exit, hips rippling with the effort of movement. I watch her disappear, back to her husband and children and cosy little life.

Without so much as a kiss goodbye.

2

HMP Brakehurst

'You going to tell me what happened?'

We're sitting in the broken shower in B block, backs against the tiled wall, Tanya's hand still fondling my breast. Clearly she's missed me while I've been in isolation.

Drew too, no doubt.

I shrug. 'Nothing much. Ash got on my nerves, that's all.'

Tanya scissors my nipple, pinches it till I twist and swat her away. 'C'mon, Leanne. You don't usually let a silly little bitch like that bother you. What was it all about?'

I consider what to say. What I told the governor, I guess, when I was hauled in front of Harding. After they took Ash off to the medical unit.

Mind your own fucking business.

But I was upset then – a week ago – still reeling from the news about Mum. And Tanya's different. She's been there for me ever since I arrived at Brakehurst.

'I dunno,' I groan. 'I just wasn't in the mood for her crap.'

Ash's face flashes up again, the cut on her lip bleeding heavily. That stupid whining sound she made as she crouched on the floor.

OK, maybe I went a bit too far.

But like I said, I was upset. And she kept goading me. 'Kitty Sweet,' she intoned, drawing out my last name with a sneer. 'Kitty fucking Sweet. Think you're really something, don't you, cos your name's always in the papers.' She got her face up close to mine. Right in my space.

'Sweet as shi—'

That's when I hit her.

'I heard you were in quite a state, after that visit,' Tanya says, not about to let the matter drop.

I feign a blank expression. 'What visit?'

Tanya narrows her eyes. 'Don't fuck with me, Leanne. You *told* me your friend was coming to see you.'

Did I? I can't remember now. Find it hard to keep track of all the things I've said.

'Rita reckons you had an argument, with your friend. Said Janice made her leave. That she was crying.'

I don't reply.

'She heard you call her a silly cow, Leanne.'

I grit my teeth. 'Tell Rita she needs a fucking hearing aid.'

Tanya eyes me steadily. For a moment I think she's going to push it further, but she changes her mind. 'Anyway, Ash won't bother you again. I've had a word. Told her to stay out of your way.'

That pisses me off too. I can take care of myself, when push comes to shove. Not that I often have to. When you're in for double murder, your reputation goes before you; most people steer well clear – except psycho wind-up merchants like Ash.

'Thanks.' I force myself to look grateful. I'm not daft. Tanya's well connected, and I need her onside, watching my back. So I hold my smile and let her believe she's done me a favour.

'You at least going to tell me how it went with Harding?' she persists.

I sigh. Try to come up with some fib to fob her off, then decide it's not worth the bother. 'She wants me to see that new therapist.'

'Therapy?' Tanya raises an eyebrow. 'Wouldn't have thought that was your thing.'

'She reckons it will do me good. You know, to talk about stuff.'

'Like what?'

I hesitate, tempted to confide what Maxine told me about Mum. But the golden rule in here is keep everything that matters to yourself – never give anyone leverage over you, a way to press your buttons.

Not even the people you think you can trust.

'I've no idea.' I shrug. 'I'm not a therapist. Probably the usual crap on anger management and so on.'

Tanya sniffs. Gets to her feet and pulls on her jeans. I check out her expression, worried I've annoyed her. Now Harding has put me on basic, cutting all my privileges, I need to keep her sweet.

Drew too.

'You OK?' I get up, touch her cheek.

She smiles. 'Sure. It was nice.'

'It was,' I agree, though to be honest I wasn't really in the mood. I'd had to fake it, my mind busy grappling with Harding's implication that I was a headcase.

'It's in your interests, Leanne,' she'd said, all solemn and serious. 'Any more of this kind of incident and you'll seriously damage your chances of early release.

You need to start thinking. You could be up for parole in six years – that's not as long as it might seem.'

Isn't it? I wondered. As if Harding would know. A day in here can feel like a year, a year like a century.

It's like being fucking immortal.

'Give it some thought.' Tanya runs the tap and splashes water over her face. 'Therapy, I mean. Might do you good.'

Jesus. She sounds just like Harding.

'Well, it's not as if you haven't got the time, is it?' she adds, catching my expression.

That makes me laugh. One thing we have in here is plenty of time. Sure, we're supposed to spend twenty-four hours a week on 'purposeful activity', but it never works out that way. There's still long spells in lock-up, sitting around your cell. Hours on your hands to remember. To brood.

On how you ended up here, and your hopes of ever getting out.

What will be waiting when you do.

Tanya turns and I study her face – plain, square jawed, brown eyes surrounded by a spider's web of wrinkles – and feel a sudden rush of affection. I like Tanya. It's not just the sex, nor the other perks of being on her good side. She's kind, softer than she looks.

A real friend, perhaps – a rare commodity in this place.

'Do it,' she says. 'What have you got to lose? Maybe she can get you to open up a bit, let people in.'

She leans in to hug me. 'God knows I've tried, Leanne, but always the closed book, aren't you?'

I answer this with another smile.

And this time it's genuine.

3

HMP Brakehurst

Tuesday, 23 February 2016

Most times when people smile at you in prison, you can read anything into it. They're taking the piss. It's a warning, a put-down, a come-on, a challenge.

But sitting here today, staring at Yvonne Conway, I know it's sincere. And my heart droops. She's one of those do-gooders who come into the prison thinking they'll be making a difference; watching their inevitable disillusionment is painful, if amusing.

Give me the seen-it-all, fuck-you types any day.

'So, shall we start with you telling me a little about yourself, Leanne?' The therapist flashes that smile again. You can trust me, it says. You're safe here. I won't judge. I won't use any of this against you.

Yeah, right.

'What do you want to know?' I ask.

Her eyes lock on mine, gazing at me with an earnest expression, the kind clearly meant to encourage you to spill your guts. The kind that is never going to work on me.

'Whatever you'd like to tell me, Leanne. This isn't an

interrogation. The idea is that you have space to talk to someone in confidence about some of the events in your life.'

'In confidence?'

She nods. 'Nothing you say in these sessions will be passed on without your permission.'

I run my tongue over my teeth, look around. We're in a room at the end of the admin block. A pair of worn armchairs, and a large, stained coffee table. Nothing to see here, so I peer out the window at the February landscape. Nothing much to see there either: dull skies and bare trees, the grass around the compound providing the only lift of colour. And even that looks washed out in the low thin fog that settles around this place in winter.

'OK, so let's discuss what you're hoping to get out of our sessions together,' Yvonne says, searching for another way in.

I turn back, pretending to mull this over, but really I'm studying her faded jeans and baggy purple top, the bottle-dyed hair clipped back at each side. She's not wearing much make-up, beyond a smudge of mascara, a clumsy sweep of blusher where her cheekbones should be – if her face weren't drooping with age.

She must be fifty if she's a day.

'I dunno,' I say eventually. 'Harding said it might help.' And as Tanya reminded me, one-to-one therapy isn't something on offer every day. I should make the most of it, she said, so I figured the least I could do is turn up and play along.

'Yes, Sharon Harding mentioned there'd been an incident a couple of weeks ago. That you were very upset following a visit from a friend. Do you want to talk about that?'

23

No, I fucking don't, I think, but keep the words in my head. What the hell is the point of this anyway? It's like the psychologists I saw before my case went to court. Always prying and probing, trying to get to the heart of you. All the way to why.

They could fuck off too. I had nothing to say to any of them.

'OK, Leanne.' Yvonne smiles and sits up straighter. 'I can see you're finding this difficult. Let me go over again what I'm hoping we might do together over the next eight sessions. I'm keen for this to be an opportunity to explore some of the things that have happened to you. What's brought you to this situation, and your hopes for the future. How I might help you achieve some of your goals.'

The usual bullshit, in other words. I've lost count of the number of times I've heard this kind of well-meaning 'positive framing' crap.

I give Yvonne a nod, and she seems pleased, like it's some sort of breakthrough. She glances down at the file on her lap, and I wonder what's in there, what she's read up on me.

Wonder too if she's seen the stuff that came out after my arrest. The pieces in the papers, most of them using pictures nicked off my website; a few of the racier tabloids including stills from my videos – tits and all. The descriptions of me in the courtroom, 'stony-faced and unrepentant', as one of the headlines said.

If only they knew. Grief leaves you numb . . . sort of vacant. It only appears like a lack of emotion.

'Can I make a suggestion, Leanne?' Yvonne says, and I notice she's looking at my hands. I'm clenching them again, I realize, thumb tucked tight beneath my fingers.

'Go right ahead.'

'Would it be easier if you were to get things down on paper? If you find talking hard, I mean. You could write whatever you like and give it to me before the next session. It might take the pressure off when we meet.'

'Write what?' I ask, hoping it won't be one of those tedious lists of 'goals' we're encouraged to set ourselves. Like 'work on our response to stress' and 'develop problem-solving skills'.

'Anything you want,' Yvonne suggests. 'You could start with what brought you here, to prison.'

'I'm assuming you're aware of that already.'

'Only the official side. The court reports, assessments and so on. I'd be interested to hear it from your perspective.'

I'll bet, I think, remembering better offers for 'my story'. The interview requests that came in the early days, reporters wanting my 'perspective' on the industry. No doubt with a view to turning it into more wank fodder.

'I'll give it some thought,' I say.

'Great.' Yvonne looks pleased. Puts the folder into her bag, an ugly fabric sack of a thing. Not even leather. 'Well, I'll see you next week, Leanne.'

She gets to her feet. Hesitates. Seems about to hold out her hand for me to shake, but evidently changes her mind, remembering the injunction never to touch a prisoner.

I should remind Drew of that one, I think, as the guard comes to usher me away.

Give him a good laugh.

'Got you these.'

Drew drops a pile of goodies on the end of my bunk.

A notepad and blue biro, half a dozen books. 'Picked up a selection from the library,' he adds, knowing I can't get there while I'm stuck on basic. 'Wasn't sure what you liked.'

Not this rubbish, I think, studying the paperback on the top. A woman in a black corset and fishnet tights draped across the cover, wearing stilettos so high even a porn star couldn't walk in them.

Christ, the shit people read in here. Stupid stories about damaged men and the women who 'redeem' them; clearly they haven't met a proper arsehole yet or they'd run a mile. And that real-life crap about people's miserable childhoods – if that's all you need for a book, pretty much every woman in this place is sitting on a bestseller.

But I know Drew's gone out on a limb to bring me these, so I offer him my sweetest smile. 'Brilliant. Thanks.'

He studies me for a moment then retreats to the door of my cell, careful not to act too familiar with the other screws around. He looks tired and harassed, his belt pinching at his waist the way it does when his stomach's playing up.

'So how did it go?' he asks.

I keep my expression blank, though I know perfectly well what he's referring to.

'Your session with that new therapist,' he adds, with a trace of irritation.

I pull a face. 'All right.'

Drew gives me a long look. 'You should make the most of it, Leanne. You never know, it might help.'

Jesus. Why does everyone keep saying that? Like I'm some sort of nutter.

And help how? Get my privileges back? Get me out

26

of this shithole? I'd have thought that was the last thing Drew would want – unless he thinks we'll carry on outside. Set up a love nest together.

In his fucking dreams.

Drew lingers for a minute, one hand on the door frame, the other fingering his keys. Peering at me like he wants to ask something. Like there's something he doesn't understand.

I pretend I haven't noticed and he gives up, closing the door to my cell, locking it behind him. I lie back on my bed, stare at the ceiling, at the four walls that contain what's left of my life.

Sod this.

I sit up and grab the notepad, folding it open to the first page, pen hovering.

Still hovering two minutes later.

My mind wanders back to Mum, brooding about her illness. Is she at home or in hospital? Will anyone tell me when she dies? I should try one last time to make contact, I think. Let her know that I know. I could send a card, ask Drew to rustle up some stamps.

But what's the point? Mum's ignored everything else I've sent. I'm pretty sure she won't make an exception just because she's dying.

One thing we have in common, at least – once our minds are made up, nothing will change them.

I push the thoughts away, smoothing my hand over the first blank page. That therapist made it sound so easy, like it was simply a question of picking up a pen, and off you go.

But where to begin? When I was born? While I was growing up?

Why bother? My childhood wasn't fucked-up, or

pervy in any way, though that's what everyone assumes: that women like me were abused, or had druggy parents or whatever.

Not in my case. All in all, my past was fairly ordinary. Happy – at least most of the time. Especially after my father left, and Mum met Mike.

I gaze around my cell, searching for inspiration. The sink, the desk with its single chair. The gap where my TV used to be till Harding had it removed. Then my eyes settle on that passport photo, Blu-tacked on the wall by my bed. Taken that day on the pier in Brighton, when everything was ahead of me, and nothing was spoiled.

Your face grins out at me, reaching across the years. Your brown eyes and dark hair. Those high cheekbones and the little creases that bracketed your mouth.

I'm seized by a stomach punch of sadness.

Joe.

I miss you more than ever, especially without the telly to distract me. You're the only thing stopping me going insane in the endless boredom of lock-up. I go over and over it, savouring our time together. Every instant. Every word. Every glance. Looping from the beginning to the last time I saw you, in that car park in France.

A lift in my heart as I grab the biro, knowing now where to start – at the moment the compass of my life first pointed in your direction.

I'll tell it all, I think, the story of us. Write it down exactly as it happened, from beginning to end. Maybe, if I put it into words, see it there in black and white, I can conjure you back into my life.

And I'll let that therapist read it. Why not? She can't tell anyone, can she? I can say what I like and she has to keep it to herself.

But she'll know the truth – and perhaps even one person knowing will make it easier to bear.

So I turn to the inside cover of the notepad, the bit Yvonne Conway will never see, and write out a dedication in neat capitals.

FOR YOU

4

Balham, London

Monday, 7 June 2004

'Knickers.'

I looked up at the man holding the camera. 'What?'

'Knickers off, darling.' He nodded at my crotch.

'But isn't this just topless?' A pathetic note of protest in my voice. 'That's what the guy at the agency said.' Darryll Crocker. That was his name, wasn't it? Hardly one you'd forget.

The photographer gave me a weary look. 'Darryll's a cunt, sweetheart. I'd have thought even you could work that out.' He grinned at the guy in the baseball cap fiddling with the lighting, who raised his eyebrows in a 'not again' sort of way.

Both of them, naturally, were fully clothed.

I stood there, arms over my breasts, shivering. Though it was warm outside, a day full of blue sky and sunshine, inside this studio it was freezing. There were no windows anywhere, nor any heating.

'Look, Lara, it's the full monty, OK?' barked the photographer. 'If you're not up for that, then fuck off. There's plenty of other girls happy to take your place.'

I remember when I described this to you, my first nude modelling shoot. Your expression. Like you wanted to travel back in time and deck the guy. You, needless to say, never spoke to me that way. You never spoke to any of the girls that way. It was one of the things I loved about you.

But I'm jumping ahead of myself now. This was still months before you came into my life. And back then I was only nineteen – young and green enough to think that this was something I had to take in my stride.

'So you going to take them off or what?' The photographer had his hands on his hips, his camera hanging from the strap around his neck. He was nice-looking, with curly brown hair and pale blue eyes. I might have fancied him if we'd met in any other situation; but somehow, in this one, it only made me feel worse.

I stared back and the tears in my eyes made him go all swimmy. I mentally rewound what Darryll Crocker had told me. A couple of hundred quid for a topless shoot. I'm *sure* that's what he said.

I thought about my ex-boyfriend Ross and the almighty mess he'd left me in. The unpaid rent. Those minus signs on the statement from our joint bank account that made Darryll's advert in the local paper catch my eye.

I'd shown it to Donna, the girl who shared my shift at the wine bar. 'Why not?' she'd said. 'I know a friend at school who did glamour modelling. Made a packet.'

She looked me up and down, smiling. 'OK, you've not exactly got the biggest tits in the world, but your face more than makes up for that.'

All the same, I was surprised when Darryll Crocker had taken me on. And even more surprised when he'd got me this gig a week later, and told me how much I'd earn – just for taking my bra off.

Easy money, or so I'd imagined. Right now, staring back at the photographer, it felt like the worst mistake I'd ever made.

Besides trusting Ross.

My stomach burned at the thought of him. I gritted my teeth, trying to make up my mind what to do. Just this once, I told myself. I'll pay off my debts and be free of him for ever.

I bent down and slipped off my thong. 'What do you want me to do?'

'Sit there.' The photographer indicated a cream leather sofa in the centre of the room. I perched on its edge, still clutching my arms against my breasts. It was so chilly my skin was rough with goosebumps.

'Right.' The man picked up the camera and pointed it in my direction. It felt like an accusation.

'Can we have more light over here, Tom?' He kept looking through the lens then back at me, like something was wrong. Waved a hand at the other man, who pulled a strip of lights to the left.

'OK. Um . . . what's your name again?'

'Leanne,' I said. 'Leanne Jenkins.'

'Right, Leanne. Can you lower your arms and lean back a bit?'

I did as he asked, trying not to look down at my boobs. I could feel my nipples hardening in the cold.

'Not like that. Put your arms up, by your head.' He let go of the camera to give me a demo. 'That's it. Hold it for a moment.'

A series of machine-gun clicks. The photographer circled me, twisting the camera into different angles. 'Raise your left arm more. That's right.'

I tried to relax but I felt stiff and unnatural. My mind was whirring. What were these pictures for, exactly?

Darryll Crocker had said they were going in some magazine, but he didn't say which. He'd been pretty vague about it, now I thought back. I wondered if I dare ask the photographer.

'Relax your mouth, Lara. No, don't smile. I want sultry, a little pouty. Sultry, I said, not sulky.'

I felt a rush of panic. What if Mum saw these photos? I imagined Mike flicking through one of those top-shelf magazines, coming face-to-face with my ... I shuddered. Tried to push it from my mind.

Just get through this, I told myself. Take the money and never do it again. If Mum ever found out, I'd say it was a one-off.

'OK. I want you to lie back, right leg on the floor ... that's it.'

More gunfire from the camera. The lighting man stood watching, his expression blank. I couldn't tell what he was thinking. If anything, he looked slightly bored.

How many girls did he see like this a day? I wondered. Two? Five? A dozen?

'Right, Lara, lift your other leg and lean it against the back of the sofa.'

I hesitated. It was obvious where this was going. Even to me. He was already lining up the camera to take in the length of my body. Seemed to gaze right into the heart of me.

'Yoo hoo? Hello?' A hand waved in front of my face. 'Anyone there?'

I lifted my leg.

'Hands caressing yourself ... that's right. Try to look like you're enjoying this. Imagine I'm your boyfriend ...'

I scowled. If it weren't for Ross, I wouldn't be in this

mess. I wouldn't be lying here, freezing my tits off, a camera peering between my legs.

'Wider, Lara . . . that's good. OK, now use your fingers to spread yourself.'

I sat up, my face a question mark.

He sighed. 'You know, sweetheart. Show me some pink.'

A flush of heat in my cheeks. I lowered my hands, but only to cover myself.

That was it. That was when I should have got up and left, walked out in a cloud of anger and disgust, and then nothing would ever have happened.

Though of course, if I had stormed off, I would never have met you.

The photographer dropped his camera, stood hands on hips. 'Lara, for fuck's sake, shift your fingers out the way. Widen your legs.'

'It's Leanne,' I snapped, but did as he said.

The camera moved in. The lighting guy carried on staring at me vacantly. I'd never felt so exposed in all my life.

I closed my eyes, squeezing back tears, longing for this to end. I just wanted my money so I could leave.

'A bit wider . . .'

I spread my legs as far apart as they would go. A click in my left hip, followed by a hot little flair of pain. The camera edged even closer, like it was trying to get inside me. Like the doctor who used that speculum thingy to look at my cervix, then told me it was only a bad case of thrush.

Darryll Crocker, I thought with a shiver that was either cold or anger. Why didn't he warn me I'd be doing this? I only needed a chance to think about it. A chance to prepare.

Though now I *was* thinking about it, he had asked me to shave – you know, down there. Said they didn't want any 'stragglers' ruining a shot.

Christ, I was naïve.

'Open your eyes, Lara.'

The photographer was standing right in front of me, holding something out. I recoiled. It was a giant dildo, as thick as my wrist, and a lurid shade of pink. It quivered slightly in his hand. Seemed to leer at me it was so obscene.

'Fancy giving it a try?'

I shook my head vigorously.

He smiled. 'An extra hundred quid in it for you.'

I glanced at the lighting guy, arms crossed and openly smirking.

Enough. I got up, grabbed my clothes. 'Fuck you,' I said, marching out into the hallway and pulling them on. I could hear the pair of them laughing back in the studio. I was crying now, trying to squeeze my leg into my skinny jeans, but I kept getting my foot stuck.

'You forgot this.'

I looked up to see the photographer holding out a bunch of twenty-pound notes. For a second, a split second, I was tempted to tell him to stuff them up his arse.

'Your first time?' he asked, studying my face. I must have had mascara tracked halfway down my cheeks.

I nodded.

'Listen, you need to make it clear to Darryll exactly what you're prepared to do and what you're not.' He stuffed the money into the top of my handbag. 'Don't let him push you around.'

I shut my eyes briefly. Then raised my head to thank him, but he'd already gone.

5

Kingston, Surrey

Thursday, 9 December 2004

They say the first time is the worst, and it turned out to be true. I went home, shaken and stirred, but with that bunch of twenties in my bag. Enough to take a chunk out of the debt Ross had left me with. And after a few days, the humiliation and shame of that shoot began to fade, so when Darryll Crocker called the next week with the offer of another job, I only hesitated for a moment.

Once more? How could that hurt?

More money too. Another hundred on top of what I earned before.

This time when I got home, the embarrassment, the sense of self-disgust that made me jump straight into the shower, only lasted a few hours. Amazing, the power of a thick wad of banknotes to soothe the soul. So when Darryll called again, the 'yes' wasn't far from my lips and one shoot led to another, and soon taking my clothes off in front of a camera was second nature.

Weeks went by, then months. A gig a week turned into two then three. I fell into a routine. I'd turn up at whatever address Darryll gave me, strip off, work through all the poses, get dressed again and go home.

Simple as that.

And it was certainly a money-spinner. In six months I'd paid off all the back rent Ross left me with – and even managed to stuff some into a savings account. I was just getting used to being more flush with cash when Darryll called me into his office.

'I'm afraid you're all shot out,' he said, sitting back in his chair and gazing at me with a mournful expression. On his left cheek the place where he'd cut himself shaving was still oozing, a small bright red bead of blood.

'How do you mean "shot out"?'

'Too much exposure, darling. You've done most of the mags now. You're old news, love – people want fresh faces.'

Mine must have fallen because Darryll laughed, revealing the nicotine stains on his teeth. 'I'm not saying you look old, sweetheart. Quite the contrary, you look barely legal.'

He smoothed a hand over the large oak desk between us, caressing it. Clearly he imagined it gave him a bit of class. Otherwise everything about Darryll's office in Kingston was dull and ordinary. A couple of grey filing cabinets. A chunky Sony laptop. White walls, brown carpet, a small window overlooking a supermarket car park.

Like Darryll himself. All a bit worn, over-stuffed.

'What I'm saying is, sweetheart, we've saturated the market. It's harder to find the gigs for you now.'

'Already?' My disappointment caught me off guard. How could Darryll be telling me it was all over? Right when I was getting into the swing of it. 'Everywhere?'

I added, frowning. 'Surely there's other places that want pics?'

In truth, I wasn't entirely sure where my images had gone, apart from some of the larger monthlies. I'd sign the release forms at the end of the shoot and that was the last I ever heard of it. I hadn't been paying much attention, to be honest; if I didn't see the pictures, I could pretend to myself no one else had either.

'What about ordinary modelling?' I asked hopefully. 'You know, catalogues, that sort of thing?'

'You're too short for catalogues.' Darryll sniffed, thought for a moment. 'We could always take you downmarket, I suppose, but I wouldn't recommend it.'

'How do you mean?' Hard to imagine what could be more downmarket than exposing everything I'd got for a load of leery lad mags.

'Phone sex adverts, pictures for escort agencies, stuff that ends up in the small ads at the back of titles. I can get you a few jobs, sure, but I reckon you could do better.'

Christ. Escort agencies? That's all I needed, Mum and Mike thinking I'd gone on the game.

'Of course, you might consider other work.' Darryll leaned forward, eyeing me carefully. I got a heady whiff of aftershave. Something cheap and heavy.

'What *other work*?'

He inhaled, spreading his hands on his desk like starfish. Considering what to say next. 'Well . . . there's other options.'

'Such as?'

'Video, rather than stills.'

'What kind of video? You mean, on my own?' I imagined myself prancing around, like those girls you see on catwalks. Maybe even dancing a bit. Only naked.

Darryll sighed. Ran his fingers over his scalp, where the hair had receded. 'Not on your own, no. Though we could kick off with masturbation, I suppose. But there's not a huge demand for that, not unless you do it live.'

I frowned. 'Live?'

'Webcam. For clients. Men who want to watch you get yourself off.'

I stared at him open-mouthed. 'I can't do that . . .'

'Which is why I'm suggesting video.'

This took a second to sink in. 'You mean porn? Sex on camera . . . with other people?'

Darryll shrugged. 'You're already halfway there, love. Shown everything off. What's the difference?'

I thought about this for a moment or two. It seemed to me there *was* a difference, though I couldn't quite put my finger on it.

Amazing, now, to think I was ever that stupid.

'You'd do well.' Darryll's chair creaked as he leaned back. 'You're pretty, with that whole fresh-faced cute thing you've got going. The point is, you look young. Jailbait, that's always a draw.'

I almost laughed, remembering all the times I'd been ID'd in pubs and clubs. Never occurred to me looking underage could be a bonus.

'So what would I have to do?'

I couldn't believe I was actually considering this. But I'd become used to the money. And I had plans. Moving out of the flat in Hounslow I'd shared with Ross, with its dodgy boiler and draughty single-glazing, and finding somewhere nearer the centre – Ealing, perhaps, or Brent. Get myself a car. See if Maxine wanted to go to Ibiza for a week.

Not to mention Xmas. I was going to get Mum, Mike and the twins something really nice. One of those games consoles maybe, something they could all play on.

I'd assumed the money would keep on flowing in; never imagined it would dry up so quickly.

But porn. No way. The shame of that first photo shoot loomed up again. I shivered, remembering the sensation of standing naked in that studio, under the cold eye of the camera.

This would be even worse, wouldn't it?

And there'd be no going back. Not from that.

'Listen, it's up to you.' Darryll exhaled loudly. 'But I'd suggest starting out slow. Soft core first, build it up gradually. Go for a longer shelf life.' He sucked at one of his teeth, sizing me up. 'We can spin it out even more if we stick to girl/girl for now.'

'Girl/girl?' I looked at him in horror. 'You mean sex with another woman?'

He nodded.

'But I'm not gay.'

Darryll shrugged again. 'Gay for pay, darling. Not the same thing at all.'

'But you said soft core. How the hell is lesbian stuff *soft core*?'

His mouth lifted into a leer. 'No dicks, darling.' That's how Darryll addressed me back then – always luv, sweetheart, honey – though now he knows better. 'It's only hardcore when you can see actual wood.'

I considered this. It seemed insane that sex with another girl could be thought tamer than sex with a guy. But it wasn't about me, I realized. Not about how I felt.

It was all about the people watching. The men. What *they* wanted to see.

So easy to forget where all this was going. The bloke at

the end of it, getting himself off to some image of me. Not me, I reminded myself, just pixels on a page. Though thinking about that made me feel weird, like I'd been replicating myself till there was nothing left of the original.

I swallowed and looked back up at my agent. Allowed myself to ask the question.

It was only a question, after all. Not a yes.

'How much?'

Darryll sniffed again. 'Seven, eight hundred a shoot. I could get you a job right off.'

Blimey. That was way more than I was making with stills.

In my head I felt the same logic kick in. Just this once. Only to get a little more cash behind me, get me set up for something solid. A mortgage and a place I could really call my own. Some more put by so I could go to college.

'OK.' I said it quickly, before I could change my mind.

Darryll's smile widened, and for a moment I wondered if he'd engineered this whole conversation. I felt manoeuvred somehow. Played.

He stuck his hand into a drawer inside his desk and pulled out a sheet of paper, spinning it to face me.

'Fill this in.' He handed me a biro.

I glanced through it. Apart from a space for my name at the top, my age and my measurements, it was basically a list, each option accompanied by a tick box.

☐ Solo hand job
☐ Girl/girl
☐ Boy/girl
☐ Blow job

- ☐ Anal
- ☐ DP
- ☐ Swallow
- ☐ Interracial
- ☐ Cream pie
- ☐ Group
- ☐ Squirt
- ☐ Bachelor parties

I scanned the items, then laughed. 'Is this serious?'

Darryll's brow wrinkled. 'You've lost me.'

'I have to, what, tell you all the stuff I've ever done?'

'Jesus,' he sighed through his teeth. 'You have to tick the ones you're willing *to do*, Leanne. It's standard in the industry. Helps match you up with what people want on a shoot.'

I checked through the options again. Hell. I wasn't even sure what half these meant. I put a tick next to 'boy/girl', 'blow job' and then – reluctantly – 'girl/girl'. Handed it back to Darryll.

'Well, it's a start,' he said, his tone begrudging, 'but you're going to have to pull out a few more stops if you want a proper career.' He wrote something on the back of one of his business cards and passed it to me.

'What's this?' I glanced at the address in Hammersmith.

'A clinic. You'll need an HIV test.'

'But I haven't got—'

'You need a certificate confirming that, honey. You can't work without one. And don't forget to take your passport to shoots – proof of age.'

I stared at the card. HIV test? I was beginning to feel right out of my depth. For a second or two I considered handing it back. Walking out and never returning.

Maybe get a new phone to stop Darryll calling and luring me back in with offers of work.

'Oh, and you'll need a name.'

I frowned again. 'What's wrong with Leanne?'

'A stage name, luv. You know, a porn name.' His eyes went a bit vacant. I could tell he was thinking.

'Cherry?'

I wrinkled my nose. 'Never liked them.'

'Something classy, then . . . Madison . . . or Mercedes.'

'Hmmm . . .' I said, dubious. I never understood the point of names that sound like places. Or cars, for that matter.

Darryll stared at me, his eyebrows knitting with concentration.

'I've got it!' He tapped his desk, looking triumphant. 'Kitty . . . cos, I dunno, you look sort of kittenish. That could be your first name.'

'You need another?'

He nodded.

I closed my eyes for a moment. 'How about "Sweet" . . . Kitty Sweet?'

'Yeah, I like that.' Darryll grinned. 'Pretty much sums you up.'

6

Hackney, London

Wednesday, 15 December 2004

I got lucky with my first scene, though I didn't know it then. Didn't realize how many new girls get sent off to a gonzo shoot with some sleazy director. No script, no storyline. Just walk in, drop to your knees and off you go: BJ, a few positions, then a pop to the face.

Porn without dinner and candlelight, you used to call it. No fuss or foreplay – straight to the fuck and thrust.

But this was different. This wasn't being filmed in a bland semi at the end of the tube line. Pulsar's studios in Hackney were the real deal, housed in what looked like an old factory, though you'd never know it, the building as tarted up as the performers inside.

I pushed through the plate-glass door into a smart reception area. On one side a massive Christmas tree, covered in baubles, tinsel and flashing fairy lights; on the other, boxy leather seating surrounding a huge glass coffee table. The only thing giving the place away were the Xmas cards, strung up on the wall behind the reception desk, girls with massive tits dressed in skimpy elf suits, a cartoon Santa screwing a reindeer.

'Hello.' The receptionist smiled as I approached. 'Can I take a name?'

'Kitty Sweet.'

It was the first time I'd used it since the meeting with Darryll last week. It felt odd in my mouth, hard to get my lips around.

Not too late to back out, said a voice in my head.

I ignored it, nodding as the receptionist pointed along the corridor. 'Down on the left. Set Two.'

I followed her directions. A man bounded up as I entered the studio. He wore a bright Hawaiian shirt covered in palm trees and a pair of cargo shorts that made me shiver to look at him. Didn't he realize it was December?

'You must be Kitty,' he beamed. He stared at me for a second or two, folding my hand in his. 'I'm Gus. The director.'

He waved over two guys, both wearing identical black baseball caps with the peak at the back. 'This is Tony on sound.' He slapped the shorter man on the shoulder, then turned to the other. 'And this is Mark – on lighting.'

I shook both their hands as Gus glanced around. 'Don't know where Joe's got to, but he's our main camera guy. Derek over there is on camera two.' He pointed out a bloke dressed in blue jeans and a white T-shirt, his face hidden as he bent over something on the floor.

The set was bigger than I imagined, filled with lights and equipment and wires. Several large black cameras dominated the space, flanked by a couple of those light-weight folding seats that directors use. In the middle was what looked like an office, if you pictured one with only two walls. On one side a desk and two revolving chairs; against the other wall, a big leather sofa.

45

So ordinary, and yet so strange. An oasis of normal in an unfamiliar world.

'Thanks for standing in at the last minute, Kitty.' Gus placed a hand on my arm. 'Much appreciated.'

Darryll had called just before lunch. Apparently the girl booked in for this morning's shoot was a no-show. He'd persuaded Pulsar to take me instead, and shift their schedule to this afternoon.

'Anyway, it's nice that you're early,' Gus said. 'Rhian will be pleased.'

'Rhian?'

'Make-up,' he explained, steering me towards a room at the far end of the set.

Rhian turned out to be small and blonde, dressed in a white T-shirt and blue leggings. And very obviously pregnant. She air-kissed both my cheeks, then sat me in the chair.

'Kitty, eh?' she said, as she cleaned my face with a wipe then covered my skin with a base coat. 'Cute name.'

I smiled, unable to think of a better response. I was so on edge I could hardly speak. Should I really be doing this? I kept asking myself. I mean, nude pictures were one thing. Not such a big deal. But sex on camera was something I could never take back. I fought the urge to leap out of my seat and run. Kept thinking of the money.

Just this once.

'It suits you,' Rhian said. 'Your name,' she added, seeing my blank expression. 'Did you choose it?'

'Me and my agent. Darryll Crocker.'

Her mouth twitched, but she didn't comment, tilting my chin and smoothing foundation over my skin.

'Look down,' she said, starting on my eyes. 'This your first time?'

'Is it that obvious?' I lifted my gaze briefly to gauge her reaction.

Rhian laughed and picked up a fake eyelash. Tipping my head back, she glued it into place along the edge of my left eyelid. 'You turned up on time. Only the new girls ever turn up on time.'

I waited till she'd applied the other lash then peered in the mirror in front of me. Amazing the effect they had. My eyes looked huge, their impact enhanced by the dark sweep of eyeliner flicking out from each corner.

'You nervous?' Rhian selected a big fluffy brush, using it to dust a cloud of pink blusher over the apple of my cheeks, adding a touch of shimmering highlighter above.

I nodded as she stood back to admire the effect. I had to admit I looked amazing. I'd been made-up for the magazine shoots, of course, but this felt different somehow. More of a make-over.

Leanne Jenkins transformed into Kitty Sweet.

'You'll be fine.' Rhian moved on to my hair, tweaking it with straighteners and adding shine with a spray. 'I remember my first time. I was so anxious I threw up in the bathroom five minutes beforehand. Nearly didn't go through with it.'

For a moment I thought she meant losing her virginity. Finally it clicked. '*You did porn?*' I asked, too late to hide my surprise.

'Only for a year or so. Then I met my boyfriend and, well, being in adult movies puts a lot of strain on a relationship. So I decided to stop.'

'Strain? You mean jealousy and stuff?'

'Yeah. He understood it was my work, but I didn't want to put him through it.' She paused, a comb

47

suspended an inch or so from my face. 'It wasn't just him, to tell the truth. Why I quit.'

'Why else?' I prompted, though I wasn't sure I wanted to hear her answer. Was I about to do something catastrophic? Something I'd always regret?

Rhian sighed, her eyes meeting mine in the mirror. 'It's hard to explain, Kitty. I felt I was losing myself somehow, that every time I did a scene in front of the camera a piece of me went missing.' She cocked her head to one side. 'You know, like those tribes who believe a photograph can steal your soul.'

I didn't know, but said nothing, not wanting to interrupt.

'It's like there's the real you, your ordinary self,' Rhian continued, 'then there's this character you create on-screen, a sort of porn alter ego. The minute the two begin to merge, that's when you need to get out.'

'OK,' I said, not really grasping what she meant, but wanting to ask more. I never got the chance, though. Rhian took a step back, putting her hands on her belly. 'Wow,' she gasped. 'He's kicking a lot today.'

I watched her stomach. A small lump appeared at the side of her T-shirt then instantly disappeared.

'Does it hurt?' I asked, fascinated.

'You mean, being pregnant?' She grinned. 'No. It's just a bit weird. Like being prodded from the inside.' She wrinkled her nose. 'You want a feel?'

I nodded. She took my hand, placing it on the crest of her bump. Underneath the fabric of her T-shirt, the skin was taut, stretched tight as a drum. Nothing happened for several seconds, then suddenly a small, sharp kick. I snatched my hand back in surprise.

Rhian laughed. 'I guess it is freaky, if you're not used to it.'

'Sorry. Honestly, I'm all over the place.'

'That's OK, Kitty. I get it, really. My advice is, do the shoot. See how you go. If you don't like it, well, you don't have to do another.'

Was it that simple? I couldn't rid myself of the feeling that this was a step too far. But how could I back out now? If I walked off the set, they'd probably have to cancel the shoot, and Darryll would go mental. Would likely strike me off his books.

'That's your face done,' said Rhian, as she applied a final coat of gloss to my lips, then stood back again to assess her handiwork. 'Perfect. OK, clothes off, honey.'

Despite my nerves and growing misgivings, I did as requested. Stripped right down and shivered as Rhian rubbed shimmery cream all over me, including my boobs, my back and my legs.

'Nice to see you're not over-tanned,' she said as she blended it into the crease of my arse. 'So many girls come in looking like they've spent a month in Benidorm. Only it's fake. Orange. Like orangutans, but without the hair.'

She giggled and I tried to picture an orangutan. Were they orange? Did they have much hair?

Rhian picked up a lip pencil and carefully drew a line around each of my nipples, filling in with rose-pink lipstick. 'This'll make them look more prominent on camera,' she explained. 'You've such neat little breasts, Kitty. Don't let anyone persuade you to muck about with them.'

'How do you mean?'

'Implants, honey. Trust me, you don't need them. You're perfect as you are.'

I smiled.

'Right, I think we're done.' She gave me a final

once-over then raised her eyes to mine, taking my hand and giving it a squeeze.

'Don't worry. With a face like yours, so fresh and pretty, you'll do well.' She leaned in, voice lowered. 'Keep a sensible head on you, Kitty, and don't let anyone fuck you over.'

I'd been learning my lines since Darryll emailed them over, right before I left the flat. Luckily I didn't have many. I was playing Miss Winston, a secretary in an accounting firm. Mr Archibald was my hotshot boss; Miss Tucker, a colleague working for the same company.

I had scenes with both. This was going to be a first for me today in more ways than one, and despite Rhian's reassurance I was almost faint with nerves.

How did secretaries act, even? I couldn't think. I wasn't sure I'd ever met one, though a friend at school had gone on to do shorthand and typing at college. I'd no idea if she ever became a secretary. We lost touch.

I scrolled through the text on my phone, reading my first bit again, trying to weld the words into my brain.

Miss Winston, approaching desk: 'I can't get these figures to add up, Mr Archibald. I was wondering if you could show me what I need to do.'

Mr Archibald: 'Well, why don't you come round here, Miss Winston, and let's see if we can make those numbers work.'

Even I could tell it was dumb. I mean, who calls each other by their surnames any more?

But at least I looked the part. Sort of. The wardrobe girl had rigged me up in a grey striped pencil skirt and tight-fitting white blouse, and given me a pair of glasses with plain lenses. Only the shoes gave me away. Black stilettos, so high and sexy surely no one would wear them to work? Except hookers – and porn stars.

'Hi.'

I looked up. And there you were, standing right in front of me.

The first time I ever laid eyes on you.

7

Hackney, London

Wednesday, 15 December 2004

'Kitty?'

You held out your hand. You were wearing jeans and a T-shirt with a marijuana leaf on it and the words 'Flying High' underneath. Your black hair was short, lightly spiked with gel. Deep dark eyes. Medium build, a good six inches taller than me.

Cute rather than full-on good-looking. Very boy-next-door – if your neighbours were Asian.

'My name's Joe. I'm the guy on camera one. Welcome to Pulsar.'

I wasn't big on romance back then. Had never believed it, that stuff about love at first sight. A cliché they used in books and films, I'd thought.

But right from that moment, I felt it. That buzz between us when I took your hand. And I'm sure you felt it too, as you looked at me. Into my eyes instead of checking me over, like most guys did, as if I was just a picture on a page, not something real.

'Joe, baby!' cried a girl's voice behind us, and a pair of arms snaked around your waist. 'You gorgeous little hunk,' she murmured into your ear, squeezing tight before letting you go.

I gazed at her. Average height and slim, with long dark hair, wearing low-rise yoga pants and a GAP hoodie. To her side, a tall black guy with a broad handsome face. He grabbed her boobs, then tickled her waist till she folded over, squealing.

'Keep your hands off the crew, young lady,' he said, releasing the girl and slapping you on the back. 'How you doing, Joe?'

'You need to keep that woman under better control,' you grinned.

'Don't I know it!' The man turned his attention to me. 'So this is our lovely new co-star?' He held out a hand. 'Nelson. Aka Nelson.'

I frowned.

'My real name and my screen name,' he said, prolonging the handshake. I could hardly take my eyes off him. Nelson was a god. His hair cut so tight it was almost a shave, and a body that clearly saw the inside of a gym on a daily basis.

A dead ringer for that footballer Maxine had such a crush on.

'Isn't he delicious!' the girl mouthed, stepping forward to give me a hug. 'Pasha Steele,' she said. 'Otherwise known as Esme.'

At first sight Esme seemed quite ordinary, her features small and elfin, her bare skin lightly tanned. Nondescript hazel eyes. But when she smiled, revealing a sexy little gap between her top front teeth, I could see how stunning she'd be once Rhian had finished with her.

'C'mon,' Nelson pulled her away. 'Let's get you sorted out before Gus gets a cob on.'

You turned to me once they'd gone. 'Nicest couple in the business.'

'They're an item?'

You nodded. 'The exception that proves the rule.'

'What rule?' I asked, curious, and you hesitated. 'You know what, this is your first shoot, right? Let me show you around.'

You gave me a quick tour of the building while Esme got ready. There were two other studios, it turned out – one built like a dungeon, the other an ordinary bedroom – small tables either side of a bed, the duvet and pillows dressed in plain yellow covers.

'Nothing to distract from the action,' you explained, steering me off to see the editing suite. A few people looked over and nodded as we entered. I felt embarrassed, teetering around in my tight pencil skirt and ridiculous heels, but no one appeared to notice.

'Better get back,' you said, checking your watch. As we walked in, Esme emerged from the wardrobe room, wearing a smart black trouser suit with a gorgeous red blouse. Rhian had tonged her hair into soft waves, matching Esme's lipstick to her top.

I was right. She looked incredible. Like a proper model, only really sexy too. Next to her I felt dowdy. Mousy and invisible.

'Very corporate,' you laughed, and Esme gave you the finger. Then turned her attention to me, nodding towards the loos.

'So which type are you?' she asked once we were inside. She plonked a Mulberry handbag on the space between the sinks and started rifling through it.

'What do you mean?'

'Which type are you – fucked up or hard up?'

I wrinkled my nose. Thought about it. 'Hard up, I guess.'

'OK.' She nodded. 'Rhian told me this was your first ever shoot.'

'Well, I've done a bit of modelling work. You know, men's magazines and stuff.'

'And now you're trading up, huh?' She pulled a tin from her handbag and opened the lid. Removing a sachet of white powder and a Waitrose loyalty card, she made a couple of lines on the edge of the sink and sniffed them up through a length of straw. First one nostril, then the other.

'Want any?' She held out the tin.

'No thanks.' I'd never actually seen someone do coke before, let alone tried it myself. Though on some of the photo shoots it had been obvious people were high.

Esme put the tin back in her handbag and took out a packet of painkillers. Popped two from the foil and swallowed them with a swig of tap water scooped in her hand. 'Need any?' she looked at me.

'I don't have a headache.'

Esme faced me. Clearly suppressing a smile. 'Not for that, sweetie. To take the edge off, especially with anal.' She turned and touched up her lipstick in the mirror. 'Not that you should be doing that yet. Hold out for a while. Don't let anyone push you into things too fast.'

I studied her, feeling clueless. Out of my depth.

'Relax.' She pushed back a strand of my hair behind my ear. 'You're lovely. You'll do well. Simply follow the golden rules.' She flicked up a finger as she listed each one. 'Show up on time – more or less. Don't scream or make lots of noise – it's annoying. And be nice to the crew – particularly the camera and lighting guys, cos they can make you look like shit if you piss them off.'

I nodded, making a mental note.

'And don't worry, you're in good hands – Nelson's the

king of the jizz bizz. And Gus is a sweetheart. He's living with Derek, by the way – one of the blokes on camera.'

Esme pulled open her shirt and adjusted her bra. I eyed her perfect breasts, full but not huge. Were they real or fake?

Either way they looked fabulous.

'I don't think I'm very sexy,' I said, feeling frumpy by comparison.

'Hey, you don't need to worry about that.' Esme smoothed down her trousers. 'You're gorgeous, and anyway, the guys aren't really fucking *you*, if you know what I mean – most of the talent goes off somewhere in their heads, especially the men. It's how they keep themselves aroused.'

'Nelson too?'

She laughed. 'Well, Nelson's a different matter. Nelson's less man than machine. He doesn't even need Viagra.'

'So you don't mind? Him going with other women?'

Esme leaned against the sink, giving me her full attention. Her pupils enlarging as the coke kicked in. 'Most times it's the other way round – he has to watch loads of other guys screwing me. Besides, you get used to it. You date people in the business and you know the score.'

'OK.'

'Listen.' She placed a perfectly manicured hand on each of my shoulders. 'Stop worrying. You're going to be fine. Have a wee – you don't want to be doing this with a full bladder.'

She pointed at the bidets lining the walls. 'And don't forget to freshen up afterwards – no one likes the taste of piss.'

*

'You two good to go?' Gus looked us over as we emerged from the loos.

'Raring,' grinned Esme.

'Right. Let's get the paperwork out the way, then we'll do the stills before you're all hot and sweaty.'

Esme took an envelope from her bag. Showed him her ID and HIV certificate, and I followed suit. Then Gus handed us both a release form saying Pulsar could use the footage.

'What name should I put?' I asked as Gus went off to prep the crew. 'My real one or my fake one?'

'Whichever you like.'

So I wrote 'Kitty Sweet', in big loopy letters that seemed to suit the name, leaving the form on the desk next to Esme's.

The stills took the best part of an hour. All three of us posing, in various stages of undress, adopting different positions while you prowled around, taking shots from every angle.

But I still managed to fuck it up, distracted by the guy in a Santa hat who kept holding a light meter over my arse. You too. I was aware of your eyes on me through the camera lens, making me self-conscious.

Gus had to give me constant directions on how to pose. 'Not flat on the bed, Kitty. On your elbows. That's right. Twist your head round and smile.'

I felt stiff and awkward and it was actually a relief when at last he said we were ready to start shooting.

Nelson installed himself behind the desk, dressed in what looked like a designer suit, with a striped shirt and red silk tie. Like he'd walked straight out of an investment bank in the City.

'Come in,' he said, as I knocked on the door.

He peered at his laptop screen as I approached, trying to pretend I was in a real office and ignore the camera and the other people circling the set. I trained my eyes on Nelson, as he glanced up and gave me an appraising look.

'Ah, Miss Winston. Take a seat.'

I perched on the chair opposite, praying I didn't look as nervous as I felt. It was like being a virgin all over again – only with an audience.

'I can't get these numbers to add up,' I mumbled, nodding at the empty file I'd been given and hoping that was the right line. I shifted on my seat. The pencil skirt was so tight I was scared it would split at any moment.

'Yes,' Nelson replied in a plummy accent. 'I've been checking your figures.'

Eh? I was sure that wasn't in the script but no one seemed to care, least of all Nelson. He peered over the desk at my cleavage, then wiggled his eyebrows at me until I couldn't help but giggle.

'Cut.' Gus mock-glared at Nelson. 'You going to behave?'

'Sorry, boss,' he saluted, slipping me a wink.

'OK. Let's go at this again.' Gus waited for you to adjust something on the camera, before giving the signal to start filming.

This time it all ran smoothly. 'Why don't you come round here so I can get a closer look?' Nelson beckoned me to his side of the desk. He made a show of tapping on the keyboard, then pointed at the screen. I squinted through my fake glasses and caught sight of Esme and Nelson.

Naked. Screwing on a sofa.

'Oh!' I gasped, not having to feign my surprise. I'd assumed the computer was off.

Nelson pulled me on to his lap and nibbled the side of my neck. 'Do you like it?' He nodded at the video.

'I . . .' Suddenly I couldn't remember my next line. I waited for Gus to shout 'Cut!', but Nelson just hitched up my skirt and peeled off my knickers. Pushing me on to the desk, he dived into my crotch.

'My, Miss Winston,' he crooned, lifting his head to grin at me. 'You taste every bit as gorgeous as you look.'

As he went back down on me, I tried to ignore the cameras moving in. Tried not to imagine what might be going through your mind as you zoomed in for a closer shot. I closed my eyes and focused on the sensation of Nelson's tongue. He was adept, all right – much better than Ross.

Though not you, my love. You were the only person who could get me off in a minute flat.

But before I came even close, Nelson stood up and undid the trousers of his suit. I stared in astonishment, completely unprepared for the size of his erect cock. It was enormous, easily the thickness of a cucumber, and long too. It swayed slightly, as if hardly able to support its own weight.

Nelson's lip curled in brief amusement at my expression, then he cupped the back of my head and inserted himself into my mouth. I tried not to gag, gripping his shaft to stop him pushing too deep, letting my tongue and lips do the work.

But even this was jaw-breaking, and I was grateful when Nelson withdrew. He put a hand under my chin and pulled me to my feet. Stripping off my shirt and skirt, he pushed me back on to the desk. Out of the corner of my eye, I saw you edging around, searching for the best shot.

'Can you shift her leg over a bit,' you said, and

Nelson took my right ankle and held it out of the way as he guided himself inside me, one slow inch at a time. It felt odd when he started to thrust. Not only his size, but the uncomfortable angle – I realized it was to give the clearest view of him penetrating me.

I lay back, trying to relax enough so that it didn't hurt, but a dull ache began to spread up inside. I tilted my hips, attempting to ease the pain, but nothing seemed to work.

Esme was right. I should have taken those bloody pills.

'Kitty?'

There was a lag in my response, till I caught on that Gus was talking to me.

'Kitty, remember to smile,' he said, patiently. 'You're supposed to be enjoying this, OK?'

I fixed my face with what I hoped was ecstasy but I suspected looked more like a grimace. But at the same time I was having fun, in a way. There was something exciting about all this. It was a rush, being watched. The steady gaze of the lens, of the eyes of the other crew. I felt a thrill of adrenalin, the sense of having broken through some boundary.

'Cut,' Gus said, a few minutes later. 'Let's try another position.'

Nelson pulled out, while you angled the camera, setting up the next shot.

'Houston, we have a problem,' I heard Nelson say.

I turned to see him holding out his hand. A girl with a clipboard picked up a box of tissues and gave him several – as Nelson wiped his cock I saw it was smeared with blood.

Has he cut himself, I wondered? Then a split second later my brain caught up with what everyone else had already sussed.

Nelson wasn't bleeding. It was me.

Shit. I must have come on.

Heat rose to my cheeks. 'Oh God, I'm so sorry,' I mumbled, tears of shame pricking my eyes. I felt I might pass out from the humiliation.

I glanced at you. You were looking away, fiddling with the camera, pretending not to have noticed.

Esme appeared out of nowhere. 'Come with me. She handed me a towelling dressing gown. 'Give us five,' she mouthed to Gus as she guided me towards the toilets.

It was then I spotted him. The guy with black hair. Shortish. Tight-clipped goatee. Staring right at me and smirking.

Esme glared at him as we passed, but this seemed to amuse him even more. I heard him laughing as she ushered me into the loos.

'Hey, now. Stop that,' Esme said, as I began to cry. She grabbed more tissues from the box on the nearest sink and handed them to me. 'You'll ruin your make-up.'

I took a deep breath and dabbed at my eyes. 'I'm not due on till next week,' I wailed.

'It happens.' She rooted around in her bag. 'Stress. A big cock. It stirs things up down there.' Finding something, she handed it to me. I assumed it was a tampon but saw it was a small circle of sponge. 'Run it under the tap,' Esme explained, 'then squeeze it out and pop it inside, high as it will go. It'll see you through.'

I stared at it. 'Seriously?'

'Really. It works a treat. All the girls use them to keep shooting through their periods.'

I looked up and smiled. 'Thanks,' I said, pathetically grateful. 'Thank you so much.'

She gazed at me, her expression kind. 'You'll be fine. It's normal. I was a bag of nerves my first time.'

I sniffed. 'So who was that bloke? The one laughing at me?' I was praying it wasn't anyone important.

Esme sighed. 'Oh, ignore him. Victor's an arsehole. Don't worry, he doesn't work here – he makes his own stuff. Probably dropped in to see Gus or one of the other directors.'

Still, I was relieved to find he'd gone when we emerged from the loos. From then on it ran without a hitch. We picked up where we left off, Nelson screwing me doggy style, his trousers round his ankles. No one seemed bothered that I was on my period – including him.

Then it was Esme's turn. She walked into the make-believe office, her mouth dropping in mock indignation at the sight of the two of us fucking on the desk.

'I could report you for this!' she said, looking out-raged, but Nelson merely beckoned her over. 'If you want to hang on to your position, Miss Tucker, I suggest you come over here and get on with some real work.'

He pointed at his erection, and in a flash Esme had stripped to her lingerie and was giving Nelson an eye-watering blow job, half his penis down her throat. An impressive performance. It was beyond me how she didn't gag.

After a couple of minutes Nelson tapped her dis-creetly on the cheek and she immediately pulled away. 'I need a moment,' he said to Gus, grasping the base of his penis. He grinned at Esme. 'Bitch. You know that always tips me over the edge.'

'Right,' said Gus. 'How about we do the scene with the girls.' He turned to me. 'Kitty, you ready?'

I nodded, though in truth I wasn't. In truth I was freaking out.

Esme leaned across and whispered in my ear. 'Easy as falling off a log, sweetpea. Trust me.'

'You're new here, aren't you?' she said, louder. I frowned, then realized we'd started filming.

'Yes. I only got the job last week.'

'Well, I've had my eye on you.' Esme strolled up and grabbed my arm, pushing me on to the sofa. 'Close your eyes,' she whispered again. 'Think of your boyfriend.'

I did as she suggested, keeping my eyes shut as she kissed me, her lips unfamiliar in their softness, the scent of her skin filling my head as she slipped off my bra and dropped her mouth to my nipples, her tongue rotating around them in decreasing circles. I tried to picture Ross – any man – but my mind kept stumbling back to the truth.

Esme was a girl.

I was having sex with a girl.

The shock of her touch gave way to something more disturbing – the growing awareness that my body didn't care. I could sense it responding to Esme, a warmth building in my belly, in my crotch as she worked her way down. I heard myself moan – not in horror, not disgust, but anticipation.

As Esme closed in on me, I realized I wasn't performing any more. I was enjoying this. Getting off on it. All at once I was oblivious to everything around me – Gus, the crew, the cameras, the guy shining a light between my legs.

Even you.

Everything faded till there was just Esme's tongue, and my body's reaction, until I felt that familiar rush of

63

heat, from my crotch up to my chest, and I knew I was coming.

Too late to pretend otherwise.

'Nice work,' I heard Nelson say, and Esme winked at me as I opened my eyes. 'Not so bad, huh?' she murmured, as Nelson slid into her from behind. I saw her wince for a moment, then move her hips in time with his thrusts, making appreciative noises. She dropped her head, laying it on my belly while Nelson fucked her, while I stroked her hair, inhaling the lemony fragrance of her shampoo.

'Let's take another break,' said Gus.

8

Romford, Essex

Saturday, 4 June 2005

Two messages on my mobile. One from Darryll telling me about another booking on Monday. Over in Penge.

The other from my stepfather Mike, sent yesterday.

'Hi, Leanne, Just a reminder that it's your mum's fiftieth tomorrow. Wanted to check that you're coming to the party. Hope you're well.'

Guilt like a punch to the guts. I hadn't been home since Christmas, putting Mum and Mike on a holding pattern, sending the odd text, leaving the occasional post on Facebook. Always vague and lacking in any kind of detail.

Enough to reassure them that I was still alive. That everything was fine.

That's what no one tells you when you start out. How much porn will fuck with your private life. I'd only been shooting for six months, but somehow it had eaten into all my time, all my headspace.

Though in truth, I was enjoying it. I was getting loads of work, and no sign of it drying up. I had friends, I was having fun, in the evenings I wasn't on set, and I had plenty of money. And I was too young and stupid to see that I was running up debts in other areas of my life.

And this one, finally, was being called in.

A banner strewn across the front of the pub in Romford, not quite taut so the message sagged in the middle:

HAPPY 50TH SALLY JENKINS

I handed the driver seventy quid and got out of the minicab, staring up at the big gold letters. My mum. Fifty years old this morning.

Where did all the time go?

I stood outside, long after the taxi had left. Suddenly, being here, the full force of what I'd been doing hit me. I felt like an alien, an imposter, the familiarity of my surroundings bringing home how much I'd changed since that first photo shoot. How far I'd travelled from my old self.

Which I guess is why I'd been avoiding it. Sensing that coming back would be too painful, too challenging.

With a deep breath, I pushed the door open. Mum didn't notice me for a minute. She was standing on one of the bar stools, trying to make some adjustment to the flat-screen TV. Otherwise the place was empty, the twins nowhere to be seen.

I paused, taking it all in. The pub seemed shabbier than I remembered. The fabric on the seats thin and worn. Several large stains on the carpet and the curtains lining the windows beginning to fade. And Mum too, her jeans tight around her legs and bum, digging into her waist, spilling rolls of fat under her T-shirt.

Letting herself go, I thought before I could stop myself.

66

That moment she turned and saw me. Surprise on her face, then a flush of pleasure.

'*Leanne!*'

She climbed down and rushed towards me, folding me into a hug. No hesitation. No hurt or anger in her expression. I felt a swell of relief, releasing some of the tension I'd been holding on the way here.

'I'm so glad to see you.' Mum let me go, standing back to take me in. 'You look well.'

'You too,' I said, untruthfully. Up close, she seemed to have aged ten years over the last six months. There was grey in her fringe, just showing at the roots, the skin under her eyes loose and crêpey.

'Nice do.' She lifted a hand to my hair. 'And the highlights. Where'd you get those done, then?' Mum gave up hairdressing when she had the twins, but she could still recognize a good cut when she saw one.

'Local place,' I fibbed again. 'Up on the high street.' Actually Esme had taken me to a new salon on the Kings Road. With a cut and colour it had cost me over three hundred quid, but no way was I going to admit that to Mum. How could I explain having that kind of money to fling around?

Another thing no one tells you. Porn makes you deceitful. You might be the most honest, truthful person on earth and porn would turn you into a practised liar.

'Where's the twins?' I asked, anxious to change the subject.

Mum patted her own hair self-consciously. 'Gone with Mike to the cash-and-carry. We needed more crisps and sausage rolls.'

I laughed. 'How many people you got coming, then? Five hundred?'

'Ninety-six at the last count. Mike's brother and his kids are driving up from Devon and your Aunty Doreen took the train down from Scotland, with Bill and the girls.'

'Wow.' I hadn't seen my cousins in, what, seven or eight years?

'With you here it'll be a full house,' she beamed, her gaze sweeping across the empty bar. Mike had put a board or something over the pool table, and covered it with a white cloth. It was already loaded with food – quiches, coleslaw, several big bowls of salad, and half a dozen sticks of French bread. A huge trifle.

No sign of a birthday cake. I wondered if Mike had one up his sleeve and felt another sting of guilt. I should have offered to sort that out at least.

'Anything I can do to help?' I glanced around for something to busy myself with.

'You're joking, aren't you?' Mum laughed. 'Dressed like that? Don't be daft, Leanne. Just get yourself a drink.' She leaned in for another hug. 'God, I've missed you.'

No hint of reproach in her tone, although she must be dying to ask. Where the fuck had I been for the last half year?

'Mum, do you mind if I pop upstairs? Freshen up a bit?' My face was burning. I felt hot and sticky though I'd done nothing more strenuous than climb in and out of the taxi.

'Go ahead. I'll finish off in here then I'll come up and get ready myself.'

I climbed the stairs, noticing the grease stain on the paintwork where the twins ran their hands along the wall. Reaching the landing, I stuck my head into the lounge. The TV was on, sound turned low. Toys scattered everywhere. A smell of frying hung in the air.

In the bathroom the bath was ringed with scum and the sink was full of white globs of toothpaste. Cans of shaving foam and shampoo bottles littered the windowsill. Above them, a large patch of mould inching across the ceiling.

Had all this happened since I was last here? Or had I simply not noticed it before? The scruffiness of everything. The air of neglect, of not enough time or money to put things straight.

'Leeeeanne!' The sound of the twins pounding up the stairs. I spun round in time to catch them as they hurled themselves at my knees. I bent down to scoop them up, but they were too heavy and it was difficult in these heels.

'Me! Me!' Tom bounced around my feet, trying to clamber up my legs, while Liam gazed up with his big brown eyes.

I crouched and hugged them in turn. 'It's Mummy's birthday,' Liam said, revealing the card he was hiding behind his back. It was a riot of felt-tip, like he'd used every colour in the pack. 'Happy birthday, Mummy' it said inside, in wobbly, misshapen letters.

'Lovely.' I got to my feet as Mike appeared on the landing.

'Good to see you, Leanne.' He put down the box of crisps he was carrying and came over to give me a hug and a peck on the cheek. 'Glad you could make it.'

'Sorry I didn't let you know sooner. I kept meaning to call. It's just—'

'Don't worry. You're here now, that's what counts.' He gave me a quick once-over. 'Nice dress. Very classy.'

I smiled. 'Thanks.'

'How's work going?' he asked, and my stomach curled with dread.

'Work?' I echoed, blankly.

'At that restaurant. Last I heard you were waitressing at an Italian place over in Richmond.'

I stared back at him. And there it was. Another crossroads. A point at which I could have come clean. Could have told the truth and faced the consequences.

And didn't.

'I gave it up. Got a new job – admin work for an agency.' It was only as the words emerged from my mouth, seemingly off the top of my head, that I realized some part of my mind had been rehearsing this story on the journey here.

Mike's eyes lingered on mine and the twist in my stomach tightened into paranoia. Did he know something? Had someone spoken to him?

'Your mum mentioned what happened with . . .' he stopped. Hesitated. '. . . you know, that lad.' Another rush of relief when I grasped that he meant Ross. I'd told Mum at Christmas that we'd split up, keeping quiet about the mess he'd left me in so she wouldn't ask lots of awkward questions.

'I'm fine,' I said. 'Better off without him.'

The twins retreated into the lounge, bored already. I heard them switching channels on the TV, hunting for cartoons.

'You managing OK, then?' Mum appeared with the empty bag of decorations. 'With the rent and everything. Must be expensive on your own.'

I was still in the same flat. Had been too busy to find anything else, though now I could afford somewhere decent. 'I'm fine, Mum. Don't worry.'

'Maxine's coming,' she said, too brightly, and there in her eyes, I caught it. The disappointment that had dogged me ever since I dropped out of my second year of A-levels to go and live with Ross. Whereas Maxine, my best friend from school, had done everything right: gap year in Australia, marketing degree, the works.

I pushed down a surge of frustration and resentment. I wanted to tell them both how well I was doing. Booked out five days a week, jobs lined up for months ahead. How I could eat out every night at nice restaurants, order whatever I fancied. Shop at Selfridges or Harvey Nichols. Drink champagne. Take taxis wherever I liked – including all the way out here.

I didn't even have to tidy my own flat any more; I paid a cleaner to do that now.

'Be great to see her,' I said, not allowing myself to react. Holding it all in, though the effort made it hard to breathe.

Mum's gaze hovered on my face for a second or two and I felt another twinge of anxiety. Did she know more than she was letting on?

Surely not? Taking my clothes off and having sex on camera was hardly something my mother would ignore.

Not even to keep the peace.

'Here, sit down and open your present.' I dug it out of my handbag, handing her the card first. Let her open it and smile at the message before I passed her my gift, wrapped by the shop in an elegant matt-black paper, topped with a deep-pink chiffon bow.

'That's beautifully done,' said Mum admiringly. 'You are clever.'

I held my smile. 'Go on, unwrap it.'

She tore away the paper to reveal a small pale-blue box. I'd asked for a plain one without the name of the jeweller, not wanting to give the game away. Mum examined it for several moments, then opened the lid and peered inside.

71

Does this make it all worth it? I asked myself, trying to ignore the sense of shame that had hounded me since I'd arrived.

'Oh, how gorgeous,' Mum exclaimed, lifting out one of the earrings, which sparkled and twinkled under the overhead light. 'These are so lovely, Leanne – they look like actual diamonds!'

'Don't they?' I grinned. 'Just like the real thing.'

9

Romford, Essex

Saturday, 4 June 2005

The party was well underway by the time Maxine arrived. I'd already caught up with Aunty Doreen and Uncle Bill, and my cousins Gail and Lucy. I'd chatted to Mike's brother, Kevin, and his wife Julie, as well as most of the regulars I knew from the pub. Even had a dance to the mix tape of eighties music Mike had put together for Mum. I was beginning to think my best friend wasn't coming after all.

But here she was, pushing through the double doors into the main bar. Her height and auburn hair always made her easy to spot. I waved across the room, about to make my way over when I noticed someone following behind.

A bloke. Over six foot and well built, like a rugby player. He put one hand on Maxine's shoulder as she gazed around; in the other, I saw he was carrying a bottle of something fizzy.

'Leanne!' Maxine mouthed, wide-eyed, as she spotted me. She edged through the throng of guests and pulled me into a hug. 'God, I'm sorry we're so late. We got stuck on the motorway. An accident near Harlow – a lorry jack-knifed across two carriageways.'

I looked at her. 'Where've you come from, then?' I thought she was still at university in Brighton.

She frowned. 'Up in Suffolk. I told you – we're staying with Gary's parents now we've done our finals. Gary's hoping to find a job in Ipswich or Cambridge.' She squeezed me again. 'Christ. It's been ages.'

'I know. I'm sorry.' I gave her another hug.

Maxine took a step backwards and looked me over. 'Jeez, Leanne, you look amazing. What have you been up to? Didn't you get my email? And I left you a ton of messages on Facebook. I was starting to think you were ignoring me.'

'Course not,' I said, as her boyfriend appeared behind her. Maxine reached out and pulled him forward. 'This is Gary.' Her eyes glowed. I could tell she expected me to know who he was.

Shit. It must have been in one of her emails. I felt my face flush. I did glance through them, but now it came to it I couldn't remember a single thing my friend had said. Another piece of my old life that seemed to have dropped off my radar.

'Hi, Gary.' I wondered whether to shake his hand, but he bent and kissed me on the cheek.

'Honestly, you look fantastic,' Maxine repeated, pinching the fabric of my dress. 'Where did you get that? It's fabulous. Looks expensive.'

'T. K. Maxx,' I lied. 'Super cheap.'

'What would you two girls like to drink?' Gary asked the pair of us.

'Red, please,' Maxine said.

'I'll have the same.'

She clutched my arm as soon as he was out of

earshot. 'What do you think?' she breathed, her eyes following Gary's back as he picked his way to the bar.

'Seems nice.' I wanted to ask how long they'd been together but I had a feeling I should know. Ditto where she met him. I toyed with the idea of going to the loo and seeing if I could access my emails from my phone.

'Fingers crossed.' Maxine leaned in, a hand on my shoulder. 'I reckon he might be a keeper.'

'You're keen on him, then?'

She laughed. 'You know damn well I am.'

Over in the corner I spotted Mum and Aunty Doreen arm-in-arm. Mum looked a bit pissed, her cheeks glowing scarlet the way they always did when she'd had a few. I was still trying to fathom what I could safely ask Maxine when Gary reappeared with our wine. I downed half of mine in a couple of gulps. It was horrible, sour and thin.

I'd got used to better stuff. Never paid less than ten quid a bottle now – and that's when Esme, Nelson and I weren't drinking proper bubbly.

'So how's Ross?' Maxine asked, and I felt myself flush again. 'We split up,' I said, as matter-of-fact as I could manage. 'A while back.'

She looked shocked. 'When was this? You didn't say anything.'

'A few months ago.' It was actually more like . . . shit, a year now, but Maxine didn't need to know that. Jesus, had it really been that long since I last saw her? I'd missed her at Christmas; had only come home for the day, in a hurry to get back for Esme and Nelson's Boxing Day party.

I caught a flash of hurt on my friend's face, and I wondered why I hadn't said anything about Ross. I'd been meaning to, but at the time had been so busy dealing with the aftermath, discovering the debt he'd left me with. Then seeing Darryll's advert in the paper, and all that led to. It got so if I told her some of it, I'd have ended up confessing everything.

'So what happened?' she asked. Clearly not about to let the matter drop.

'Turns out he was gambling,' I said, surprised how bitter I still felt. 'Emptied our account – you know, the money we'd been saving to buy our own place. Then he got kicked out of his job for taking too many days off sick. Next thing I came in one evening and found he'd packed up his stuff and done a bunk. Last I heard, he was working in a nightclub in Spain.'

'Jesus.' Maxine was clearly astonished. 'Why the hell didn't you mention any of this?'

I shrugged. 'What could you have done?'

'I've no idea, Leanne. Nothing, I guess. But you could at least have told me.'

'Sorry,' I said, meaning it. Being here was driving too many things home. How much I'd neglected the people I cared about. How many ties with the past I'd almost severed.

'Anyway, great bash.' Maxine collected herself and looked around the pub.

'Yeah, great,' Gary agreed, putting his hand on the back of her neck. A small gesture, but there was such tenderness in it, such affection, that it left me feeling hollow inside.

'I hear Mike organized it all.' Maxine turned to me. Was she having a go?

Another flood of self-disgust. This evening was killing me. I almost regretted coming. Should have pretended I was sick. Sent a courier over with Mum's present, made it up to her later.

'Yeah. Mike's done her proud.' I swallowed the rest of my wine, gazing at all the balloons and streamers he'd hung round the ceiling. The vases filled with flowers to brighten up the tables. And there, over near the fruit machine, I spotted it: a large, two-tier chocolate cake with candles shaped like a 5 and a 0 in the middle.

Good for Mike, I thought, making a mental note to thank him before I left. I'll make it up to both of them, I resolved. Come down again soon, take them out for a meal. Or babysit so they can have a night off; God knows, ever since Mum fell pregnant with the twins five years ago, she'd barely spent an evening without them. And it was only now, watching my little brothers dart around the party, stuffing themselves with crisps and cola, that I realized how very much I missed them.

'Where's your mum gone?' Maxine asked, scanning the room. 'We've got a present for her.' She pulled a package out of her bag, a card taped to the front.

I glanced around, and it was at that moment I saw them. Standing over by the other side of the bar, near the fruit machine. A group of blokes – not that old, in their late twenties, maybe, or early thirties. Squaddies, it looked like – probably friends of Mike's, back from when he was in the catering corps.

Nothing unusual about them – ordinary guys in jeans and shirts, short hair and freshly shaved. Several wearing baseball caps. Little to note except one thing.

They were all turned in our direction.

And they were all staring at *me*.

The shortest man clocked my gaze, twisting to say something to the guy on his left, nudging him with his elbow. Their mouths lifted into an open smirk.

I looked away, breath trapped in my chest. In that instant the room became impossibly hot and airless. I felt sweat break out all over me.

'What's wrong?' Maxine asked, her expression concerned.

'Nothing,' I said, too quickly to be convincing. 'I feel a bit sick, that's all. I need some fresh air.'

'Leanne—'

'I'll be back in a mo.' I pushed my way through to the side door and leaned against the brickwork of the pub, gulping in the cool evening air and willing the nausea to recede. My eyes were stinging. I was on the verge of crying.

Fuck.

The look on their faces. That leer of amusement. Unmistakable.

'Shit,' I whispered to myself, pressing my knuckles against my lips. 'Shit, shit, *shit.*'

This was just the start, I grasped. Just the start.

Only a matter of time till someone told Mike – or Mum. And the twins – as they got older, hearing it from another kid. A teacher even.

On its heels another realization. One so awful I could barely put it into words. One that surfaced out of nowhere to ambush me with all the force of something I'd been trying to ignore.

My father.

My father could be watching my videos and never know it was me.

My father could—

I snapped off the thought, pulling out my phone, my hand shaking so much I could hardly dial the number for a taxi.

It would never end. I understood that now as I fidgeted on the pavement, waiting for the cab to arrive. I could give it all up and become a nun, but this would never end.

For the rest of my life, I'd be one thing and one thing only.

Kitty Sweet.

78

10

HMP Brakehurst

Tuesday, 1 March 2016

'So how did it make you feel? This realization, that there was no going back?'

Yvonne lifts her gaze from the pages torn from my notebook, each filled with my neat handwriting, a uniform height on the upstrokes, smooth loops on the curves. I'd spent hours getting it all down, using the torch I'd cadged from Drew so I could carry on after lights out.

'Wretched,' I say, shrugging off a headache from lack of sleep. 'I felt awful. I cried in the cab the whole way home. But what could I do? It was what it was. Like you said, no going back.'

The therapist shifts her weight, crosses her right leg over her left. Today she's wearing loose slacks, cut short to reveal thin calves, the skin scaly and mottled with age.

Last week she wore a wrap-around dress, with a weird psychedelic pattern of intersecting cubes. It was dizzying, distracting, hard to tear your eyes away. Just as well we spent most of the session going over the basics, the 'background stuff', as Yvonne called it. All that early childhood crap I'd been hoping to avoid.

This week, however, we seem to be getting down to it. My story. How I landed up in here.

'You must have known, Leanne, that sooner or later someone would recognize you? That it was inevitable.'

I regard her steadily. 'I'm not an idiot. Of course I knew. But it's like knowing you're going to die one day – not something you want to dwell on.'

In truth, part of me had hoped using an alias would keep me anonymous, that under all the slap and slutty clothes, no one would ever guess it was me. But I'd rather not admit that to Yvonne, because clearly it was stupid.

'I was very young then,' I sigh. 'I was young and shallow and everything was instant. I had no real concept of the future. There was only now – or maybe next week – but that was about as far as it went.'

Yvonne considers this, pursing her lips as she chooses her next words. 'Would you say that's your coping style, Leanne? Not thinking about things?'

'*Is* my coping style or *was*?'

'You tell me.' She leans forward in her chair, her face fixed in an earnest expression meant to show you have her full attention. You used to look at me that way too, like you were really interested in what I had to say; it made a refreshing change from being viewed as a walking set of holes.

But with Yvonne I have doubts. Is it sincere, or practised? I wonder if the moment I return to my cell, she's forgotten all about me.

'I guess it was my coping style,' I agree. 'Definitely. And as you see it all worked out so well.' I use my eyes to indicate the bars on the windows. The sparsely furnished room.

This prison.

Yvonne inhales, frowning slightly. 'So why did you do it?'

'What? The porn?'

She nods.

'I already told you. For the money. To clear up the debt my ex left me with.'

Yet I feel a tinge of embarrassment as Yvonne glances down at my account of that first shoot, and the others following on its heels.

Because of course it didn't stop at one.

It never does.

Not that I've gone into great detail, after describing that first time. After all, these were porn shoots. How much detail do you need? You suck and you fuck. Then you suck and fuck some more. If I wrote it exactly as it happened, it would send anyone to sleep.

Like you always said, nothing duller than a porn flick after the first screw or two. No plot, you explained. No context, or emotion. Just the same old story, with only one possible outcome.

Where's the fun in that?

Nowhere, judging by the look on my therapist's face. She's gazing at me with a sad, almost doleful expression. Like she feels sorry for me. It's annoying the hell out of me, but I'm careful not to show it.

'Yes, I know you needed the money, Leanne. But we're both aware it didn't stop there. I'm interested in what drove you to carry on, after you'd paid off your debts.'

I don't respond. I've no answer for that.

'Did you enjoy acting in porn?' she asks eventually. 'I rather had that impression, from what you wrote.'

I give this some proper thought. 'A lot of the time,' I

admit. 'Actually that surprised me, how much I got off on being filmed.' I pause. Work out what I'm trying to say. 'It made me feel . . . valued. Like I was worth something.'

Yvonne raises an eyebrow. I can't tell if it's surprise or disapproval.

'I liked the idea of all those men sitting there at home, ogling me instead of being with their wives, their girl-friends. I felt . . . desired. Men watched my shoots, wishing they could be doing me. Women watched them too – wishing they *were* me. It was a buzz, a kind of drug. You feel . . .' I pause again, groping for the right word.

'Appreciated?' offers Yvonne. 'Admired?'

'Seen. It makes you feel *seen.*'

The therapist nods, then leans forward again, press-ing the tips of her fingers together to emphasize what's coming. I inspect her open-toed sandals, even though it's only March – her nail varnish chipped and growing out. But I doubt she's even noticed.

Some women are like that. Some women really don't care.

'Leanne, do you feel ashamed, now, about what you did?'

I slide my eyes from her feet to her face. 'Which bit?' I ask.

So much to choose from.

'Appearing in all those films. I'm not saying you *should* be ashamed, I'm simply posing the question.'

'Not really.' I shrug again, knowing I look defensive. 'Sex is everywhere – films, advertising, TV, music vid-eos. It's all around us. Porn is simply more honest, more open about it.'

Yvonne cracks a smile at my little speech. 'So I'll ask

again, why didn't you tell your mum? Your stepfather? If you weren't ashamed, why not be open with them?'

Fair point. I return her smile. Let that serve as my answer.

Yvonne pauses. Regroups. 'Weren't you worried, Leanne? About security, I mean. In the light of what happened to those Eastern European women.'

My stomach tightens at the mention of those girls, but I keep my voice casual. 'I didn't know about them then. No one did. That all came later. Yeah, of course, if I'd been psychic, if I'd known what was coming, I'd have walked away. None of this would have happened.'

Yvonne cocks her head to one side. 'No one would have died, you mean?'

'I mean I wouldn't have got involved.'

Another pause, long enough for me to catch a burst of laughter somewhere outside the window. It's a good sound, comforting. A change, at least, from the usual yelling and screaming.

When I look back, Yvonne's studying me. 'I'm curious, Leanne, regarding those earrings. Why you bought real diamonds for your mother.'

Here it is. A squirm of genuine discomfort.

Do I really want to do this? I wonder again. I know Tanya and Drew said it would help. That when, eventually, I face the parole board, this could make a difference.

Even so, I'm not sure I have the patience – though undoubtedly I've got the time.

'I wanted her to have something nice,' I say finally. 'Something special. It was her fiftieth birthday, after all.'

'But you let her think they were fake.' Her mouth rests in a kind of half-smile that makes her face impossible to read.

'Yeah. Go figure.'

My mother's voice in my head, the last time we actually spoke. *How could you, Leanne? How could you do that?*

'She cottoned on eventually,' I tell Yvonne. 'Had them valued when Mike found out what was going on. Apparently she threw them in the bin.' Twelve hundred quid's worth of Tiffany diamonds and platinum, dumped into landfill.

Like those girls, I think, before I can stop myself.

Something softens in Yvonne's expression. I look away so I don't have to endure her sympathy.

'After a gesture like that, it must have felt very hard what happened at the party. Feeling so exposed.'

Exposed. The word ignites in my mind and with it a thousand feelings. *Exposed*. Where do I even start with that?

At Mum's party?

In front of the camera?

In the courtroom?

In the newspapers?

My life, my body, my actions, my motives – all laid bare for everyone to examine.

People think they know me. They think they've seen everything there is to see.

But they're wrong.

11

Stratford, London

Sunday, 3 July 2005

'OK.' Esme stood over me. 'Let's have a look.'

I leaned back on the bed and opened my legs. Esme peered at my genitals with interest, then sat on the chair opposite, crossing one leg clad in the skinny white jeans we'd found on sale in Harrods a few weeks ago. With her Gucci halter top and big floppy sunhat, she looked like she'd strolled off the beach in Miami or St Tropez.

A small twitch at the corner of her mouth told me she was trying not to laugh.

'What?' I hissed. 'What's so funny?'

'Herpes, sweetheart. Classic first attack.'

'Herpes?' I looked at her, horrified. I felt sick, suddenly. Or rather sicker. I'd been off colour for several days now. Strange aches in my legs and stomach. A seriously bad headache.

Herpes. Oh God. How could this have happened?

'Occupational hazard, babe,' Esme added, reading my expression. 'The wages of sin. Don't worry, the first attack is the worst. It'll settle down.'

'But why?' I stammered. 'I mean, we're tested. We've got certificates.'

This time Esme allowed herself a snort of amusement. 'That's only for HIV, silly. They don't test for everything. Besides, everyone in porn has herpes – and genital warts. It's no big deal. At least you're not pregnant.'

I grimace. No chance of that, thank God. I was religious about taking the pill, made it the first thing I did every morning, before I even had a cup of tea. Not that porn guys ever come inside you – punters want to see the pop shot – but no way was I running the risk.

I inspected the colony of tiny red blisters. Herpes. I'd learned about it from a magazine once – or perhaps a class at school. All I could remember was there was no cure.

Once you had it, you had it for life.

'You'll need to take a week off, though.' Esme nodded at my crotch. 'Let those heal.'

I retrieved my knickers and pulled them on, blinking back tears. Fuck. I was supposed to do a shoot tomorrow. Darryll would go apeshit.

But it wasn't just that. Something shrivelled in the core of me. Suddenly all the good stuff – the money, the attention, the glamorous lifestyle – seemed poor compensation for how degraded I felt.

The sores were a visible sign – what was inside was breaking out.

Esme came over and sat beside me on the bed. Took my hand and gave it a squeeze. 'C'mon, sweetpea, don't let it get you down. You'll be over it in a few days.'

'Shouldn't I see a doctor?' I'd already rung the surgery, but they were shut on Sundays. I'd have to go to A&E to see anyone today.

'You could, but they're only going to give you acyclovir, and all it does is shorten the attack by a day or two.'

I picked up my jeans and stood to get dressed, wincing at the pain in my groin. 'Anyway, how come you're such an expert?'

Esme smiled up at me. 'How do you think?'

Looking back, it's hard to believe I was so floored by this. After all, STDs weren't even the half of it. As the porn mantra went, if it's comfortable, it's boring, and having sex on camera was rough on the body in every sort of way. Backache and neck pain from contorting yourself into unnatural positions. Carpet burns and bruised knees. Colds. Flu. Bladder and throat infections rife amongst the female talent.

Not to mention the eating disorders. At shoots there was always someone puking in the loos. Half the girls turned bulimic after seeing bits of themselves jiggling on camera – high definition being particularly unforgiving.

A peal of rap music from Esme's phone. Her expression clouded as she read the text message.

'Nelson,' she said. 'I have to go soon.'

'Problems?' I flopped on to my bed, exhausted from the effort of getting dressed.

Esme sighed. 'Remember that first shoot you did for Pulsar? You stood in at the last minute for that girl, Anya?'

I nodded.

'We didn't think anything of it. You know how it is, girls don't show up all the time. They're hung over or can't be bothered.'

'Yeah.'

'Well she's disappeared. Everyone assumed she'd gone back home – she's Lithuanian . . . No, Latvian.

Anyway, her parents turned up at Pulsar yesterday, claiming they hadn't heard from her in months. Gus told me. Said they're going out of their minds.'

I shrugged. 'So she's gone off somewhere? Shacked up with someone?'

'Apparently the police have no record of her leaving the country. And she hasn't used her bank account either.'

'Did you know her?'

'Anya? Not well, but we worked together a few times. She was good. Tall, hair same colour as yours, really beautiful. And fucking out there too. We hung out at a few parties, but I couldn't keep up with her.'

That was saying something. In my experience, Esme could keep up with anyone.

'So what's this got to do with you and Nelson?'

Esme picked up her bag, searched inside till she found her tin. 'We said we'd talk to them. I haven't a clue what we can tell them, but you never know, it might help. They've had to save up for ages to come over, it feels the least we can do.'

She did a line on my dresser, wiping her nose on the back of her hand.

'You should go easy,' I said, watching.

Esme rolled her eyes. 'Don't you start. I get enough grief off Nelson.'

'Maybe he's right.'

She gave me a look designed to shut me up, and it worked. No way I wanted to fall out with Esme. She'd taken me under her wing since that first Pulsar shoot, showing me afterwards how to suck in my stomach and push out my tits, how to open up to the camera, pointing your toes and arching your back. It was Esme who'd helped me memorize the positions I looked best in, holding the mirror so I could check out my body from every angle, getting me to practise my orgasms so they looked authentic. She'd explained what pile drive meant, and why reverse cowgirl was considered a great camera shot, though hard on the legs.

She'd even taught me how to make realistic fake spunk with milk and lube – essential for those convincing cream pies. And I don't mean any you might want to eat.

Without Esme, I'd have been screwed – and not in a good way. Washed up in weeks, rather than booked from now until the New Year.

Besides, I liked her. She was kind and generous – and she gave great head.

'You sure there's nothing else?' Esme examined my face as I lay back against my pillow. 'You look really forlorn, Leanne. I'm worried about leaving you on your own.'

I considered telling her about Mum blanking me. Her party was a month ago and I hadn't heard a peep from her since. No reply to the text I sent, apologizing for leaving so suddenly. No response to the message I'd left on Facebook. Not even a thank you for the earrings.

She knew, I was guessing. It must have got back to her. From those guys, probably, the ones who recognized me.

I'd told myself it didn't matter. Threw myself into work. But now, since I'd been ill, I couldn't seem to get it out of my mind.

'Do your parents know?' I asked Esme. 'What you do?'

'Ah. That.' Esme sniffed, wiping the end of her nose again, then sat back on the bed. 'My dad died when I was two, so I've never had to worry about him. And Mum, well, I'm not certain. I hardly speak to her – she moved to Portugal when she remarried. When we do talk she seems happy to maintain the fiction that I work in advertising.'

I grimaced. 'What about Nelson? His parents?'

'Oh, Nelson always lands on his feet,' Esme laughed. 'His family reckon being a porn star is great. His dad's Jamaican – apparently Nelson's quite the celebrity out there.'

I sat up again. Lying down was making my head hurt more. Reaching into the drawer of my bedside table, I groped around for a couple of paracetamol. Swallowed them with water from the bottle beside me.

'I think my mum has found out,' I said. 'But I'm not sure. She's ignoring me.'

Esme pressed her lips into a sympathetic expression. Leaned across and stroked my hair. 'Try not to worry too much, babe. A lot of parents come round, after they've had a chance to readjust. It's like telling them you're gay or something – they need a while to get used to the idea.'

'Yeah,' I sighed. 'You're probably right.'

Maybe I'd played this all wrong, I thought; maybe I should have been more honest from the start.

'You sure you'll be OK?' Esme asked as she got to her feet, looking several inches taller in the gold Versace wedges Nelson had bought for her birthday. 'I could come back later.'

'I'll be fine. I'm going to watch a DVD then get an early night.'

'Sounds like a plan.' She retrieved her handbag from the chair. 'Hey, I nearly forgot. You know that director I told you about, the one who does those kink films. He's having a party in three weeks, in a club on the seafront in Brighton. It'll be a blast. You up for that?'

'I guess.' To be honest, I wasn't really in the party mood. I gazed at my friend. 'Would I be playing gooseberry all evening?' Much as I adored Nelson and Esme, they were sometimes hard to be around. That whole loved-up, perfect couple thing. It left you feeling on the outside. A groupie, a hanger-on.

Always the odd one out.

'You won't be, honey. I was going to invite Joe. You remember him from Pulsar? The cameraman?'

How could I forget? The impression you'd left on me at that shoot was indelible, the sound of your name enough to conjure up your face. Your serious brown eyes, fixed on mine.

'Great,' I say, careful to keep the enthusiasm from my voice. 'Is he a friend of yours?'

'Joe and I have known each other since I got into the business. Before I met Nelson. He's like family.'

Odd, I thought. How come she'd never invited him along to anything before?

'He's at a bit of a loose end,' Esme said, reading my mind. 'Recently broke up with his girlfriend.'

Before I could ask more she bent and kissed my cheek, leaving the lingering scent of her perfume, something sweet and warm. 'I thought that might cheer you up. We'll make a weekend of it. Stay at the Grand or some nice boutique hotel. It'll be fab.'

'Can't wait,' I said, truthfully. 'Looking forward to it already.'

12

Stratford, London

Saturday, 23 July 2005

I was in the bathroom when I heard the horn beeping. Made it to the window in time to see Esme and Nelson pull up in a sporty red open-top car, Nelson wearing his usual shit-eating grin.

Fuck. Where did they get that? They must have hired it for the weekend.

Esme sat in the passenger seat, in a white sundress and the same floppy sunhat, one hand clamped over the top so it wouldn't blow away. She looked up and waved.

'Come on,' she mouthed.

The pair of them so confident, so self-assured. Like the world was their playground.

I grabbed my handbag, locked up and ran downstairs. Clambered into the back of the car. Esme turned for a hug as Nelson slid into the traffic, roaring off towards the main road.

'We're off to the seaside,' she shrieked, like it was the most exciting thing imaginable. 'We just need to pick up Joe first.'

We headed across town, Nelson driving like London was his own personal racetrack. I held on to Esme's seat as we skidded round corners, tyres screeching on tarmac. At this rate we'd be pulled over before we got anywhere near Brighton.

It wasn't long before Nelson was braking hard outside a row of terraced houses in Herne Hill. 'Won't be a minute.' He jumped out, and disappeared inside. Esme touched up her lip gloss in the rear-view mirror, then climbed into the back seat next to me.

'You OK, honey?' She put her hand on my arm.

I nodded. 'Much better, thanks.'

It was true. I'd woken to blue skies and a July heatwave, feeling strong and well – the herpes had cleared up without trace in a couple of weeks, almost like I'd imagined the whole thing.

Esme pulled her drug tin from her bag; with a glance to check if the coast was clear, she crouched in the footspace of the car, working up a line in the fold of a tube map.

'Want some?' She offered her silver coke straw to me.

I waved it away.

'Come on,' she urged. 'Give it a try. We all need the occasional pick-me-up. What's that Jenna Jameson quote? Something about time healing all wounds, but drugs getting it done quicker.'

I don't know why I changed my mind. Maybe it was what Esme said, about drugs taking the edge off things. Mum still wasn't returning any of my texts, nor picking up when I called. I had a feeling this wasn't something that would blow over. Part of me felt abandoned – orphaned – and no way I wanted that part spoiling my good mood.

So I took the straw and sniffed up the line of powder.

A tingly sensation in my nose, followed by a dry taste at the back of my throat.

An instant lift inside.

Nelson reappeared, you following close behind. I remember exactly what you were wearing that day – khaki shorts and a white T-shirt, a brown leather flying jacket slung over your shoulder. You looked lean and fit, and not remotely devastated by your recent break-up.

'Greetings.' You leaned over and kissed Esme on the cheek, got in the passenger seat then turned and held your hand out to me. I became instantly self-conscious, like everything I'd been thinking about you since we met, all my little fantasies, were written right across my face.

'Kitty,' you said. 'Nice to see you again. It's been a while.'

It had. Though I'd done a couple more shoots for Pulsar since that first, you hadn't been working on either.

'How's things?' I asked as Nelson turned the car in a couple of swift jerks and pulled back on to the high street, heads swivelling as he revved at the lights.

'Fine,' you said. 'Same old.'

'Too many cocks and cunts,' yelled Esme, attracting filthy looks from several passers-by and making Nelson snort with laughter.

Once on the M23, he drove even faster. Esme gave up on her hat, stashing it under the front seat, and let the wind mess up her hair. 'Music,' she commanded over the roar of the engine. Nelson punched a button and the radio blasted through speakers in the side panels.

'Oh God, I LOVE this one,' Esme cried. Hanging on to Nelson's headrest, she got to her feet.

'Hey, steady on,' you said, looking alarmed, but Esme ignored you, belting out the chorus from 'Video Killed the Radio Star' at the top of her voice as we gunned our way towards the south coast, her singing almost drowning out the noise of the engine. The look on her face so carefree, so ecstatic, it was infectious.

That was Esme. Loud, impulsive, impossible to resist.

'C'mon, Leanne.' She tugged my arm, and before I could think twice, I undid my own seat belt and joined her. We stood side by side, holding on for dear life, our hair streaking behind like the tail of a comet, the sun golden on our skin. We waved at every car we overtook, pulling faces at the other drivers. Some ignored us. Some turned to stare, smiling, envy in their eyes. Others scowled with disapproval that cracked us up even more.

We joined in with the bits we knew, off-key and probably out of tune, but neither of us cared.

Remember you asked me once, about the happiest time of my life? And I told you it was that evening we lay out and gazed at the night sky – what we could see of it in London.

I lied. This was it. Standing in the back of Nelson's Audi, the world rolling out before us like an endless red carpet. Happiness rushed up at me, sudden and surprising, sweeping away all my worries, my doubts and fears. We were young and beautiful, rich and free, we were having fun and that trumped everything. There were no rules for us. Nothing could touch us.

We were magnificent.

'Video Killed the Radio Star'. That was it. There, in one song, the happiest, most carefree moment of my life. Probably lasted no more than a few minutes.

Maybe five.

*

Nelson parked in a multi-level near the seafront. 'Let's eat,' he said, dragging us into a pub in one of those narrow lanes set back from the beach. It was a weird sort of place, books lining the walls and a big grandfather clock in the corner.

'You do food?' Nelson asked the girl behind the bar. She had black Goth hair and stared at us like we'd beamed down from outer space. Esme stuck out her tits and grinned back at her while I tried to keep a straight face.

Goth girl ignored both of us, nodding at a blackboard across the bar. I chose fish and chips, being as we were at the seaside, though I wasn't really hungry. Esme ordered a steak; you and Nelson had burgers.

'I'm fucking starving,' Nelson said, glancing around. Several of the locals were eyeing us with undisguised hostility. One girl sitting next to the fruit machine leaned across to her boyfriend and whispered something in his ear.

'Ignore them, they're simply jealous.' Esme grabbed my hand, pulling me towards the beer garden. 'If I had a face like that, I'd be fucking jealous too,' she added, brazen, as we passed.

Thankfully there was no one else outside.

'Here.' Esme sat in the corner, out of the wind. Checked no one could see us then offered me more coke.

I shook my head.

'Aww, c'mon. We're on holiday,' she coaxed. 'We're having fun.'

Reluctantly I took it from her. Five minutes later it felt like the best idea in the world. The meals arrived but Esme and I were too wired to eat, picking at our food like it was something we no longer had to bother with. We ordered two more gin fizzes, drank those instead, faces turned up to the sunshine.

I kept watching you out of the corner of my eye. You didn't appear heartbroken, though perhaps you were hiding it well. You seemed happy and relaxed. Laughing at Nelson's jokes, joining in with their banter. Always pulling me into the conversation, making me feel included.

'So, kids, what next?' Nelson asked, once he'd cleared his plate.

'The pier!' Esme squealed, throwing her arms around him. I caught the look on your face. The way your jaw stiffened and you closed your eyes, just for a second.

Like this was something you had to grin and bear.

We spent most of the afternoon on Brighton Pier, wandering around the gift shops, pausing at all the side stalls, selling everything from hot dogs to candyfloss, and every kind of edible rock you could think of. Esme and I held hands as we clattered along the wooden planking in our wedge heels, peering down between the gaps, feeling the ground drop away beneath us until it was like walking on water.

Esme yelped when she saw the arcade, tugging me towards the entrance. She went straight to the kiosk and handed the man a fifty-pound note. 'Pounds and ten pees, please,' she told him, and we all had to hold the bags of change he pushed towards her.

It took us half an hour to spend the lot, Esme meandering around, randomly shoving coins into slots, barely pausing to see if she won anything. The noise around us was deafening, every machine chirping and bleeping, trying to snag our attention.

'Here.' She dumped the remainder of her change into

my hand and strode back to the kiosk. I saw her pass over another fifty.

I went to the game with the miniature racehorses and long green track. 'Place your bets now, please!' the machine commanded, and I shoved ten pence in the slot for the one with the blue jockey. You and Nelson stood beside me, Esme joining us seconds later.

'C'mon,' she cheered, as the blue horse pulled ahead of the others.

'Go on, son!' Nelson waved his fist. 'You can do it.'

And he did. My little horse came in first. Silver coins spilled into the tray below.

'Yeessss!' Esme jumped in the air and whooped and I felt madly pleased, like I'd done something amazing.

By the time we left the arcade an hour later, we'd lost two hundred quid between us.

'I need ice cream,' Esme insisted, spotting a kiosk further up the pier.

She ordered pistachio and mint. Nelson had chocolate pecan and you went for green tea. The girl serving looked at me, her expression a question mark.

'Vanilla,' I said.

Behind me Esme and Nelson burst into howls of laughter.

'Vanilla!' exclaimed Nelson. 'You can't have vanilla, Leanne. You're a fucking porn star.'

The serving girl handed me my cone with a hard stare and I felt my face flush. Nelson gave her a twenty-pound note and walked away.

'Don't you want your change?' she called after him, but Nelson waved his hand. 'Keep it, love. You look like you need it.'

This made Esme snort ice cream up her nose. She

started coughing and spluttering and had to sit on a wooden bench. I licked at mine, trying not to make it look suggestive. Suddenly everything we did felt porny. My short sundress felt slutty, and I was sure everyone was staring at us.

Porn stars.

For the first time that seemed more childish than glamorous. Like we were people who'd grown up too fast and nowhere near enough.

I ate my ice cream slowly, observing the crowds walking past. Older couples strolling along the pier, more interested in the views of the sea and the city than the noise and glitz around them. Families with buggies, wheels clattering over the planking. The odd gaggle of teenagers, shooting us furtive looks and giggling.

I peered at all the men, most with wives or girlfriends, some with kids in tow. One group clearly out on a stag bash, loud and drunk, bantering and yelling friendly insults at each other. The occasional man alone, walking around hands in pockets, minding his own business.

Despite myself, I thought of my father. How old was he now? Mum never said much about him, but I knew he was a few years older than her. Mid-fifties, I guessed.

'Hey, why the long face?' Esme pinched my cheek, then got up and dumped the remains of her ice cream over the side of the pier. She leaned over the railing, watching the waves swallow it up. For a second I pictured her losing her balance, tipping into the sea.

Would the impact knock her out?

Would she drown before anyone could rescue her?

'You OK, Kitty?' you asked, as we headed towards the funfair at the very end. 'You look a bit like the wind's gone out of your sails.'

I turned and smiled. Let myself study you properly, trying to shake off the shyness that had overtaken me since you got in the car this morning. Your dark hair, ungelled today, flat against your scalp. That little bump in your nose. Your eyes, the colour of conkers. You were nice-looking, but in a quiet way – not in-your-face handsome, like Nelson – but somehow more affecting because of it.

'Call me Leanne,' I said. 'Yeah, I'm fine. Just, you know . . .' I couldn't think what to say. You were right. I was deflated, like my batteries had run out.

'They're pretty full on, aren't they?' You laughed as we watched Esme and Nelson, screaming and acting terrified as the little rollercoaster climbed and dived, looking like it might plunge them into the water at any moment. 'Those two can be a hard act to follow.'

I grinned, pleased you understood. It seemed a good sign.

'Don't get me wrong, they're some of the nicest people in the business, but they make me feel a bit drab by comparison.'

'They make everyone feel drab by comparison,' I said, waving as they swooped past.

'Like a force of nature,' you muttered, and that made me smile.

'How about you? Are you all right? Esme mentioned . . .' I stopped. Had she told me about your break-up in confidence?

'It's OK.' You turned to face me. 'It was on the cards really. One of those things that had run its course.'

'Yeah, I know what you mean,' I said, remembering Ross. How that ran its course. I suppose in a weird way, he'd done me a favour – if he hadn't cleaned me out like that, I wouldn't be here now, with you, enjoying this glorious day.

'Everything going OK with the work?' you asked.

'Sure. It's fun. I mean, it's interesting.' I decided not to mention the herpes – obviously – and searched for something to say that didn't make me sound frivolous or a nymphomaniac. I felt tongue-tied, almost nervous around you. 'So how did you get into doing this?'

Even though I'd met you on a shoot, I couldn't imagine you working in porn. You didn't seem to fit in with the other crew, with their stupid jokes and sleazeball attitudes. You seemed above it, somehow. Better than that.

You shrugged. 'I needed the money.'

'That's my excuse,' I laughed.

'That's most people's excuse,' you added, but something passed across your face. Regret? 'Let's say it wasn't exactly my first choice of career, but my options had rather narrowed, so here I am.'

I was wondering what you meant as Nelson and Esme returned from the rollercoaster, Nelson doing a wolf-whistle to get our attention. They dragged us on to the dodgems, and I let you drive. Nelson conceded the wheel to Esme, covering his eyes and laughing hysterically as she lurched and crashed, first into the barrier, then into everyone else. You drove smoothly, evading all the other cars in our path. As the music blasted overhead, my mood began to lift again.

'Let's get some pics!' Esme suggested when the ride ended. She pointed to a photo booth a few yards away. We all squashed into the tiny kiosk, pulling the curtain to block the daylight, heads jostling to line up in shot. I had to sit on your lap, my skin tingling as you rested your hands on my waist.

The flash went off and we spilled out again, Esme wandering away to find postcards while we waited by the machine. A couple of minutes later, it beeped and whirred, and a strip of four little photographs appeared.

There we were, radiant. All smiling.

The perfect shot.

Nelson folded them up, tearing carefully along the join, and handed one to each of us. A memento of that glorious day.

It's the only photo I have of you, my love, though the left half of your face is eclipsed by Esme as she cranes her head into the centre of the shot.

Not that I need a picture. Every moment remains clear in my mind. Feelings, like knives, go blunt in time, but memories stay sharp. Little time capsules, whisking me back, cancelling out all the intervening days.

And everything that happened afterwards.

13

Brighton

Saturday, 23 July 2005

The party, held in a club under the arches on Brighton seafront, was heaving by the time we arrived. Around us a mass of people: porn stars and strippers, hookers and devotees of every fetish imaginable. Men with studs in their skull and girls with split tongues. Black rubber, PVC and bondage gear everywhere.

And plenty of civilians too. I'd already spotted a few famous faces – a couple of premier division footballers, and several people from mainstream TV.

'This is insane.' Esme watched, mesmerized, as bodies writhed and gyrated to the music, many of them half naked. All of them glistening with sweat.

Nelson had snagged us a booth in the VIP area, with views out over the dance floor, but far enough from the towers of speakers to make talking possible. He poured champagne into four glasses, filling each to the brim.

'Bottoms up.' He raised his glass into a toast, downing it in one, then sat back, exuding his air of bullet-proof confidence while Esme nestled against him, her skin glowing from the day's sun.

'Back in a minute.' You finished your drink then disappeared into the crowd – presumably you'd spotted someone you knew. Esme watched you go, her gaze tracking you across the room.

'Do you think he's OK?' I asked.

'Joe?' Esme twisted round to face me.

'Yeah,' I said, trying to look casual. Like I was simply making conversation. 'He doesn't seem that cut up over his break-up.'

Esme shrugged. 'I'm not sure how serious things were with Lila.'

'That's his ex?'

'Lila Rice. She was offered a contract with Wicked in the US. Joe didn't want to move out there, so they split.' She eyed me for a moment, assessing, and I shifted in my seat. Had I given myself away?

I curbed the urge to ask more. Glanced around, wondering where you'd got to. Saw you over by the bar, talking to two women. One of them – blonde, gorgeous – had a hand on your shoulder, leaning in to say something in your ear.

I felt a sharp pang of jealousy. Turned and caught Esme watching you too, her expression unreadable.

'C'mon.' She pulled me up and we weaved our way through the crowd towards the loos. I had a pee, emerging to see Esme, face right up to the mirror, staring at herself. Not so much checking her make-up, more peering into her own eyes, as if trying to see inside.

'Hey, you never did tell me about that girl,' I said.

Esme's eyes swivelled to mine. 'What girl?'

'You know, that Latvian performer, the one that disappeared.'

I'd been thinking about her on and off since Esme told me they were seeing her parents. I couldn't say why it bothered me so much, but it did. The idea of them being so desperate, coming all this way to find her. Discovering what she'd probably hidden from them all along.

Her guilty secret.

Maybe I just wanted to believe my parents would care that much, if I went missing. Maybe it was simply the constant nagging guilt of everything I was concealing from Mum and Mike.

Though no doubt they already knew.

'Nothing to tell – which was pretty much all we could say to her parents.' Esme's mouth drooped. 'It was really depressing, actually. She's their only child. They'd spent all their money getting over here, had barely anything left for food, were sleeping on the floor of a friend while they searched. Nelson gave them a hundred quid, but I felt bad we couldn't be more help.'

I shut my eyes briefly, wishing I hadn't asked. It felt like a downer on the whole evening.

'Time to cheer ourselves up,' declared Esme, reading the mood. She rooted in her bag, pressed something into my hand. I gazed down at the tiny pink pill.

'It's only E,' she said. 'It'll pick you up a bit.'

I turned it over in my palm, unsure. The coke I'd had earlier had worn off, leaving me slow and listless. Surely taking anything else wouldn't be a good idea?

'Christ, Leanne, loosen up. Live a little.'

I stuck my tongue out at Esme, then placed the pill on the back of it and swallowed it with a scoop of water from the tap.

'Happy daze,' she grinned, downing her own dose, before checking her make-up in the mirror.

We emerged into the boom of the music. As we headed towards the dance floor someone seized my arm. I turned to face him. Stocky, with grey-flecked dark hair.

Shit. It was that man who'd been at Pulsar. The guy who'd sniggered at my 'accident'.

I tried to pull away but he held on. Tattoos along his forearms, thick silver rings on every finger. He grinned, revealing a large gold filling in one of his back teeth.

'Esme,' he said. 'Who's the little friend?'

'*My* little friend.' She grabbed my other hand and tried to drag me away but he wouldn't let go. His grip on my arm tight, almost painful.

'Sweet little thing, isn't she?' He looked me over then back at Esme, like I was her pet or plaything. 'Can I borrow her?'

'No, Victor, you can't. She's with us.' Esme prised his fingers from my arm, pulling me into the mass of dancers.

'Who is he exactly?' I shouted above the trance track booming through the speakers. 'You said he's a director.'

Esme cupped a hand over my ear so I could hear. 'Gonzo stuff mainly. Victor Gomez is a cunt, Leanne – you don't want to get involved with him. But he's a well-connected cunt. A lot of people owe him favours, so it's best not to piss him off either.'

She lifted her gaze to the lights strobing the dance floor, abandoning herself to the music. I let my own body start moving, picking up the beat, feeling it pulsate right through me with a sudden, blissful rush of heat. Esme turned and smiled and when I smiled back it felt like my face was as hot as the sun, radiating warmth and life and energy.

The thumping house track segued into a remix of iiO's 'Rapture'. 'Oh God, do you remember this one?'

screamed Esme, looking entranced as the music morphed into something silky and smooth. 'I love this song SO much.'

She closed her eyes and swayed her hips in time to the beat. She'd changed from her sundress into a pair of tight cut-off jeans and a bikini top, and the lights bounced off her perfect breasts as she twisted and writhed, her expression euphoric.

Esme was spellbinding. Impossibly beautiful, attracting glances from all the men around us – and half the women too.

I shut my eyes as well, letting my hips pitch and roll as I merged with the music. I was feeling ... everything ... yet numb at the same time, almost anaesthetized, as the ecstasy and booze began to party in my system.

Anything was possible.

Anything at all.

As if in answer, I felt Esme's lips on mine. She pushed down a strap on my dress, one hand on my breast, the other pulling me into her.

Always the performer.

A second later her tongue was in my mouth and I could smell her skin, her perfume, as intoxicating as the chemicals in my bloodstream.

Then she drew back, laughing, exposing that little gap between her front teeth, so achingly sexy that it made me want to clasp her head in my hands and squeeze it very tight.

I knew I was grinning too because my cheeks ached, but I couldn't feel it somehow. I felt distant from myself, as if none of this was real. It was a sweet, magnificent feeling, like all my problems – Mum, Mike, everything – were nothing but a mistake.

Easily rectified. Just as easily forgotten.

Then Nelson was beside us, shirt off, sweat beading on his lush brown skin, his veneers gleaming under the strobe lights. Nelson was here and the song melted into another insistent refrain and we were off again. We danced for hours. We danced for weeks and months and years. We danced till I was so lost in the music I didn't know if I was dancing or dreaming, or suspended somewhere in between.

A hand on my shoulder. I turned, and there you were, and I wondered how long you'd been here, watching, and I was so happy to see you I felt my heart might ignite, might actually burst into flames. I flung my arms around your neck and hugged you.

'Steady on.' You laughed as you peeled me away. 'I'm only offering you a drink.' You mimed necking a bottle of beer to Nelson and Esme. They both gave you the thumbs-up.

I couldn't let you go. I followed you to the bar and stood there while you ordered four Peronis. Nelson and Esme joined us five minutes later, grabbing the beer and gulping it back, their skin slick with sweat.

'Oh shit, there's Marcie.' Nelson grimaced as a pretty girl with dark hair and skin-tight black jeans made her way towards us.

'Who's she?' I asked him.

'She's slept with Felix Santiago. You know, the dude who presents that music programme on Channel Four.'

'Felix Santiago?' Esme tossed her a sceptical look as Marcie inserted herself into our circle. 'How come?'

'Client,' said Marcie nonchalantly.

Esme's face darkened and she looked away. 'Fucking hookers,' she muttered, but not low enough.

Marcie fixed her with a deadpan stare. 'You got a problem with that?'

'Hey, cool it.' Nelson held up both hands, one finger grasping the neck of his beer. 'Esme didn't mean anything by it, did you, babe?'

Marcie ignored him, giving Esme another hard stare, her expression contemptuous. 'Like you've never done any privates? Yeah, sure.'

Esme's eyes narrowed and her fingers curled into fists. I saw the tension in her face and neck. If Marcie noticed too, she didn't care. She took a step forward, getting right into Esme's space.

'You porno girls think you're so fucking superior,' she spat. 'You reckon you're some kind of star because you screw in front of a camera.'

Esme's mouth twitched. 'Better than selling yourself to any man with thirty quid in his pocket.'

'Make that five hundred,' Marcie sneered. 'For an *hour.* Which is more than you're paid, isn't it, *sweetheart*?' She said the word with a drawl of contempt, then licked her lips.

I glanced round, caught Nelson eyeing the pair of them nervously.

'You reckon the fact that some sleazy guy is filming you makes all the difference, don't you?' Marcie wrinkled her nose in disgust as she took another step closer to Esme. 'You know what, it just makes you a mug, sweetie. I've seen the stuff you do. It's degrading, humiliating. Double anal. Throat-fucking. Fisting. I'd never do shit like that, no matter how much any man offered me. I'd tell him to fuck off, but you' – she jerked a finger at Esme's face – 'you lap it up like a little dog. And *you* think *I'm* a slut.'

Esme looked stunned, like Marcie had actually

slapped her. She stepped back and I gripped her arm, pulling her towards the exit before it kicked off into something more serious. We stood outside, dazed by the blast of sea air, the bass still pounding behind us.

Then Esme wrenched herself from my grasp, stumbling over to the railings separating the beach from the promenade. She slumped against them and began to cry.

I stared at her. I couldn't think what to say. I had no idea what was the matter.

'Bitch,' Esme sobbed. 'That nasty skanky bitch. I know she slept with Nelson.'

I bent down to look at her. 'Esme, don't take any noti—'

'Fuck off, Leanne,' she screamed in my face. 'You have no fucking idea.' All at once she became hysterical, tears streaming down her cheeks, snot running from her nose. 'I'm sick of it,' she shouted. 'I can't take another fucking *minute* of this.'

She took off, heading along the seafront. I tried to follow, but she pulled off her shoes and started running, fast, in bare feet. I stopped. I felt suddenly unwell, dizzy and sick. I'd never catch her up in heels, and no way was I taking them off with all the broken glass around.

I'll go back to the club and find Nelson, I decided. Get him to track Esme down.

'Don't worry,' said a male voice behind me. 'She's always pulling this shit. Did it to me on a shoot once.'

I spun round. Saw that man, Victor, the orange tip of his cigarette glowing in the dark.

'She's off her head.' He dropped the butt, grinding it with his heel. 'Usually is.'

I stared at him for a few seconds. Then everything

began to disintegrate. I could barely stand, like my legs were about to collapse from beneath me.

I needed air. Space. Rushing over to the beach, I stumbled towards the sea. Took deep breaths, dropping to my knees, crouching on all fours, the pebbles hard and sharp.

Fuck. I inhaled, dragging fresh air into my lungs. I needed to go back to the hotel.

'Here.'

Victor was standing in front of me, holding out a tissue. I took it, wiped my mouth. Tried to steady my breathing, the salty, bracing smell of the sea beginning to clear my head a little. My ears were ringing, but I could hear the waves breaking against the shingle, the distant boom of the music back in the club.

'Thanks.' I looked up at Victor. It was hard to make out his expression in the darkness, but I sensed he was smiling.

'You girls. When will you ever learn?'

I ignored the jibe and clambered to my feet. I had to get Nelson. As soon as he found Esme we could all go to bed and sleep this off. But as I went to pass Victor, his hand shot out and circled my wrist. 'I've been looking out for you since I saw you at Pulsar. How come we never bump into one another?'

'We have now.' I shrugged, trying to pull away.

He grinned, a smile like a hyena. 'Not properly.' He pushed me back on to the pebbles, which dug into my spine with a flare of pain. In a flash he was on top of me, his mouth on mine, the sour taste of whisky and cigarettes on his breath.

I twisted away. 'Get off!' I shouted, pushing him, but he leaned in, pinning me to the beach. I brought my right knee up, aiming at his balls, but he was too quick, using his bodyweight to wedge himself between my legs.

'Get the fuck off me!' I yelled again.

'C'mon, baby.' He bent his head and whispered into my ear. 'Be nice. I like the look of you. I think we could do some good stuff together.'

Using one hand to pinion my wrists against the stones, he slid the other up my dress and into my knickers, jamming a couple of fingers inside me. I cried out in pain, beginning to panic.

'Fuck off!' I tried to scream again, but his free hand shot up and clamped my mouth and my words came out muffled.

'Leanne?'

A voice. Somewhere in the dark.

You.

'Joe!' I shouted, and seconds later felt Victor's weight lifted from me. I scrambled to my feet in time to see you punch him in the guts, Victor doubling over with a grunt. Before he had a chance to recover, you grabbed his shirt and pulled him upright, hitting him in the jaw with an audible crack, then shoving him backwards on to the stones.

'Jesus,' he groaned. 'What the fuck was that for? We were just getting to know each other.'

I dragged my gaze from Victor to you. Your face wore a murderous expression, your features hardened by disgust. It shocked me, that look. In that moment, you seemed a whole other person.

'Leave her the fuck alone, Gomez,' you hissed, then turned to me. 'You all right?'

I shook my head. I was crying so hard I couldn't speak.

Victor heaved himself to his feet, raising his hands in

112

a gesture of surrender. 'Back the fuck off, man. I wasn't going to hurt her.' His mouth, which was bleeding, curled up in contempt. 'Have fun with these crazy bitches,' he called as a parting shot, before staggering towards the club, hand pressed against his bloodied lip.

You came straight over and put your arm round my waist, supporting me. 'You hurt?'

I shook my head again. Tried to pull myself together. 'What happened?'

'He jumped on me,' I sobbed. 'I came out with Esme, then she ran off, and the next thing he was here and . . .' I stopped. Tried to calm down.

'Esme,' I said. 'I've no idea where she's gone.'

'Probably back to the hotel.' You searched in your pocket, pulled out a handkerchief. A proper one, made of cotton. It suited you somehow. Old-fashioned, but in a good way.

'Here, I think it's clean. And don't worry about Esme – she just needs to get it out of her system. I'm more concerned about you. Are you sure Gomez didn't hurt you?'

All I wanted in the world was to crawl into bed and sleep off the feel of that man, the smell of whisky on his breath, the sensation of his fingers inside me. I needed him out of my head.

'I'm fine,' I lied. 'Can we leave? I've had enough for one night.'

Of course, if I'd known then what I know now, it would all have been different. If I'd had a clue what sort of person Victor Gomez was, I wouldn't have let it go so easily. I'd have told you the truth and let you deal with him there and then.

And none of what followed would ever have happened.

14

HMP Brakehurst

Wednesday, 2 March 2016

'Hello, Kitty.'

Darryll Crocker grins at his favourite joke. His standard greeting – even now, nearly a decade on.

I let it go. I've pretty much given up trying to get him to use my real name.

He's put on weight since he last came to the prison – several years ago – his hair longer, though he's still dyeing out the grey. The same ferrety look about him, eyes darting around the visiting room at the other inmates, like he's afraid someone will whip out a razor blade taped to a toothbrush and cut his fleshy old throat.

The stupid fuck.

But beggars can't be choosers. Any visit is a link to the outside world, and a welcome interruption to the monotony of Brakehurst. And there's been no one since Maxine a couple of months ago.

'What brings me the pleasure?' I ask Darryll. 'Something urgent you need me to sign?'

Usually he sends in the paperwork, though it can

take an age to make it through the system. Despite my being banged up, Darryll continues to work for me – running my website, squeezing money out of my DVDs and other tatty bits of merchandise.

The Kitty Sweet brand – still a bestseller after all this time. Nothing like a little notoriety to keep people interested.

'It's good to see you,' Darryll says, brow creasing as he scrutinizes me. I probably look older; more likely he's thrown by my lack of make-up – I couldn't be bothered to borrow any for his sake. 'So how are you, Kitty? It's been a while.'

I get a blast of aftershave. The same crap he always used, cheap and heavy. I glance around, breathing through my mouth. A few feet away, Laura from the cell next to mine is talking urgently to a young man, her voice low, almost a whisper.

Her son, I'm guessing. The one shacked up with a Polish girl in Clapton Pond.

'Why are you here?' I ask bluntly. I can't be arsed to go through all the chit-chat with Darryll. It's not like he gives a shit. Me landing up in Brakehurst is probably the best thing that ever happened to him, giving my stuff a shelf life he could only have dreamed of.

My agent sighs. 'Don't be like that, Kitty,' he wheedles, like I'm being difficult and he's the soul of patience.

'*Leanne*,' I say, mine having just run out.

'Sorry, Leanne. Leanne,' he repeats, as if trying to imprint it on his mind, running his hand over his chin. It's baby smooth, I notice – he must have shaved before he came. And he's wearing a suit; the jacket gaping at his stomach.

I should be flattered he's gone to so much effort. He must want something pretty badly.

115

'Um . . . here's the thing.' Darryll leans forward, clears his throat, his eyes shifty. I can tell he's trying to find a way to break bad news.

Jesus. Can't anybody ever tell me anything good?

I consider calling it a day. Leaving him to it. But decide to hear him out – after all, it's not like I've anything better to do.

Next to us, Laura's voice grows louder, more anxious. Her son is frowning, running a thumbnail along a groove in the table. He feels my gaze, looks over.

I swing my eyes back to Darryll. 'OK. Spit it out.'

'Well, it's like this . . . someone's writing a book on you.'

'What do you mean?'

'This journalist. He's been in touch and asked me for an interview. For background, he says.'

'Tell him to fuck off.'

'That's the thing . . . I wanted to talk to you about. It might be better if we . . . I cooperate. Put your side of the story, so to speak. Otherwise, what's to stop him making it up?'

'I've no idea,' I snap. 'There's laws, isn't there? Against inventing things about people and putting it in print?'

'Sure, libel law,' Darryll sighs. 'But the thing is, Kitty—'

'*Leanne*,' I growl through gritted teeth. 'We must be able to do something to prevent him?'

'Don't see how. There's no law against writing a book about someone else. It's called an . . .'

'Unauthorized biography,' I cut in. 'Yeah, I know.'

Darryll looks surprised. Clearly he thinks I'm an idiot. But then if you're an ex-porn star, no one expects you to have brains, or a mind of your own.

Actually, I only know cos Tanya mentioned it the other week, when she claimed Tom Cruise was gay and I didn't believe her.

116

'Listen, Leanne,' Darryll continues, undeterred. 'It could be good for us. A chance to put a different spin on things. Counter some of the shit they wrote about you in the papers. It'll boost your brand too, give it a new lease of life.'

No wonder he's smartened himself up. With Darryll it's always about the pound signs.

'We could do stuff off the back of it, revamp your website. Offer a wider range of products.'

'Like what?' I ask.

'I dunno. T-shirts? Get you a new signature line of vibrators, that sort of thing. Maybe even have you moulded for a doll.'

That actually makes me laugh – as Darryll intends. Like the governor would ever let someone in to cover me with latex, so a bunch of sleazebags could fuck me by proxy.

I picture Sharon Harding, her tired face and lank hair. I'm hardly her favourite con as it is – even before I sorted Ash. All those letters from fans and nutjobs. The amount of paperwork I generate.

Not to mention Drew. I wouldn't be surprised if Harding knows about him, even if she can't prove anything.

'Listen, Ki— Leanne. I thought it might make sense to cooperate . . . for me to talk to him, I mean. Obviously you're not allowed to be involved, unless you can persuade the governor it's in the public interest or whatever.'

Jesus, I think. Darryll has clearly been looking into this. Checking out the possibilities.

'Fat chance of that,' I retort. 'I can't imagine the life of a porn star would be in anyone's interest, can you?'

'How about what happened to those Eastern European

girls?' he suggests. 'You know, all that fuss over the dark side of porn. Maybe there's a way in there.'

I close my eyes. Blank out their faces.

'I asked a lawyer friend,' Darryll says. 'He reckoned we might be able to argue it's in the public interest – revealing what goes on, the underbelly of pornography. You could bring in what happened with Victor Gomez.'

The second he utters Victor's name, Darryll sees he's blundered. 'Sorry,' he sniffs, eyeing me warily.

I grit my teeth again, forcing myself to calm down.

'You don't have to actually do anything,' he whispers, leaning closer. 'Just give me a few pointers. You know, set me off in the right direction.'

I think of all the pages I've written for Yvonne. How Darryll would love to get his hands on that.

Pay dirt.

'Give it some thought, Leanne. That's all I'm asking.' He holds up a hand to appease me, like I'm about to have a go at him.

So I oblige. I narrow my eyes, fix them on his. 'You've already done it, haven't you?'

'Kitty,' Darryll's voice is indignant. 'Why would you think that?'

'Cos I *know* you,' I hiss.

He sighs again. 'Look, the journalist came to see me, that's all. I said you wouldn't be keen on the idea, but he's very persistent.'

'Has he offered you money?'

Darryll spreads his hands in his would-I-lie-to-you gesture. 'Honest to God, I haven't told him a thing. For fuck's sake, Kitty. I wouldn't do that.' He adds a bit of hurt to his tone.

I bend right across the table, lowering my voice. 'If I get the slightest hint that you've said anything,

Darryll – one single bloody word – you and I are over. Plenty of other agents out there who'd be happy to earn their commission.'

I sound cool and together, but my heart is thumping; the idea of someone poking around my past, writing shit about me makes me feel sick. Though you'd think I'd be used to it by now. People making money off my back – or from watching me on it.

Darryll shrugs. 'Consider it, Leanne, that's all I'm asking. It could do you good. Some folks out there reckon you should have got a fucking medal for what you did.'

Out of the corner of my eye I see Laura's son look over again. I wonder if he knows what we're talking about, who I am.

Probably not – a bit before his time.

I drag my focus back to Darryll, who's eyeballing me, waiting for my response. God, how he must love all this, hobnobbing with lawyers and journalists. Does he ditch the whole wide-boy routine when they're on the phone? I wonder. Stop dropping his consonants and sniffing at the end of every sentence?

'The thing is, Kitty, if we don't manage this, he's going to write it anyway – or someone else will.'

I narrow my eyes again. 'Like who?'

Darryll makes his I-dunno face, a little shrug with his mouth. 'Anyone. There's been others nosing around. It's all very topical.'

'What do you mean?'

He runs his tongue over his teeth. Sits back in the chair. 'Didn't you hear about that girl? The one they banged up for stabbing a male performer on a shoot? Everyone's been talking about it, in the papers, on TV.'

'I don't read the papers – or watch the news.' It's true. I've had enough crap for one lifetime. Why load my head with more?

'Anyhow,' he says, 'it's all kicked off again, the whole debate over the industry, what it does to women. Your name comes up all the time.'

I close my eyes. Christ. Why can't everyone just fuck off and leave me alone? It's as if my life, like my image, is public property.

Another thing for people to exploit.

At least I can be sure Mum won't talk to them, or Mike. They refused to speak to the journalists, right from day one. But what about my father?

My stomach lurches. Could that journalist track him down? What might he say?

Nothing, I realize. My father can't tell him anything at all cos my father doesn't know a single damn thing about me – beyond what he might have read in the *Daily Mail*.

'The answer is no, Darryll. And I don't care about the money, or selling more stuff. It's not like I'll ever get to spend a penny of it, is it?'

He rubs his chin again. I watch him calculating how to respond.

'Sure you will,' he says, sounding rather less than convincing. 'I'm stashing it all away for you, love. I told you that. It'll be there when you get out.' His eyes dart round the visiting room, rest back on me. 'After all, you'll be up for parole in what . . .' Darryll waits for me to fill in the blank.

'Six years.'

A snuffling sound. We both glance at Laura, who's crying now, one hand covering her eyes. Her son looks bored. Embarrassed.

'You honestly expect me to believe that?' I turn back to Darryll.

'Believe what?' He frowns.

'That it won't all have vanished, in taxes and fees and expenses I'll never be able to pin down.'

I picture my agent, older, fatter, sitting in some little Spanish villa he's bought off my back. 'Kitty,' he'd croon in that placatory tone he uses to make out you're being unreasonable. 'It just went here, went there – you know how it is.'

And there'd be no way to check. He'd ring off and go and sit by the pool, sipping his margarita. It'd be like everything I ever earned, flowing into other people's pockets.

Though, to be truthful, I pissed a lot of it away myself.

'C'mon, Kitty.' Darryll uses his most persuasive tone. 'Don't be like that. You can go through my records, if you want. It's all kosher. I'm not ripping you off.'

A hint of resentment creeps into his voice. 'I've come all this way to see you. A hundred and eighty miles up here from Crouch End, with the roads a bloody nightmare. And it's Sunday – I could've stayed home, watched the footy.'

Next to us, Laura's son gets up with a loud scrape of his chair. Fifty pairs of eyes follow him to the exit, while Laura blinks at the table, struggling not to fall apart.

I focus on Darryll, giving her some privacy. 'I didn't ask you to come,' I remind him.

'Jesus, Kitty,' he whines. 'I'm the one bloody looking out for you. You're in here, doing . . . whatever it is you do all day, and I'm grafting for you outside, keeping everything going.'

I snort. He makes it sound like he's doing me a favour. 'You're my agent, Darryll. It's what I pay you for.'

He scratches his nose. Thinking. 'Listen, if you're worried, I'll hand your earnings over to someone else. Anyone you like.'

My mind leaps to Mum, her illness. Would she take it? Maybe to help out Mike and the twins . . . afterwards.

No chance. Mum swore she'd never touch a penny I earned. Ever. And I can't see Mike going against her wishes – even posthumously.

I consider your parents instead, your sister Ayanna – would they accept money from me? No, I think, your face rising up again. The way you looked that moment before—

I push it away. Take a deep breath, waiting for the feeling to pass. Then turn back to Darryll.

He's looking at me. The way everyone does when they visit. Their expression a question mark – and always the same question.

Why?

Why on earth did I do it?

Why did I kill those men?

15

Wimbledon, London

Tuesday, 2 August 2005

It took the taxi nearly forty minutes to get to Wimbledon. By the time we made it through the traffic, pulling
up a few streets away from the tennis courts, the meter
had clocked up over fifty quid. I paid the cabbie and
ran through the rain into the front garden of 29 Brigden
Road.

It was like something from a TV make-over programme, full of huge sharp-stemmed plants and
artfully arranged black stone. The house itself was
modern, all steep-pitched roofs at weird angles and lots
of aluminium.

Must have cost a fortune.

The doorbell set off a series of tubular chimes. Deep
inside, a dog began to bark, and through the engraved
glass panel, a dark shape loomed towards me. A few
seconds later, the door opened.

I clocked the dog first, straining against the hand on
its collar, hackles raised, emitting a long low rumble of
a growl. Then I noticed the man restraining it.

Victor Gomez.

What the fuck? Darryll hadn't mentioned a thing about Gomez. A standard one-man, two-girl shoot, he'd said.

We stared at each other. Victor was wearing a sleeveless black T-shirt and faded jeans, and in the daylight I could see what I'd missed on that beach ten days ago: his tattoos extended right up his arms and over his shoulders, with what appeared to be the tail of a snake coiled around his neck.

'Kitty,' he purred, sizing me up with the kind of smile that made your insides curl.

I turned to leave.

'Kitty.' Victor's voice behind me. 'Hang on a minute.'

I kept walking. Out to the road, but the taxi had already gone.

Shit. I glanced around.

Not a car in sight, and no way I could walk. The nearest tube station was a mile back, and I was wearing heels I could barely stumble ten yards in.

'Kitty, please, give me a moment.' I turned to see Victor a few feet away. 'Listen, I know we got off on the wrong foot in Brighton. I'm sorry I came across a bit . . . forceful. My fault. I'd had a skinful.' He bent into a deep bow. 'I apologize.'

I stood there, hesitating. Rain beginning to soak into my hair and clothes; I hadn't thought to bring an umbrella.

'Come in and have a drink at least. I'll call you a cab if you still want to leave.'

I gazed down at the dog. It looked like a cross between a Doberman and a Staffie. A thick cord of drool hung from the corner of its mouth.

'Don't mind him.' Victor's smile widened till he was showing as many teeth as the animal. 'He's a pussycat really.'

He strolled back towards the house and I followed him

into a hallway about the size of my flat. A large glass chandelier was suspended from the high ceiling, surrounded by a series of tiny skylights that cast light across the huge space. On the white-painted walls were several large pictures, a kind of arty graffiti. One of a girl lying naked in what looked like an abandoned church. Another, a close-up of a face, only all the angles were wrong, like the cheekbones had been shattered, the features rearranged.

'Over there.' Victor heaved the dog into a side room then pointed to a door on the left.

I walked into what I expected to be the lounge, but there was no furniture beyond a desk and filing cabinet, and a large leather couch – the old-fashioned kind with dimpled cushioning. Around it, several arrays of studio lights and a couple of cameras on tripods. Where the windows should be, full-length curtains blocked out the view.

'Where's everyone else?' No sign of any crew or any talent.

'The other girl cried off with flu, which is why I can't afford you to bolt on me too or I'll have to ditch the whole shoot.'

'You mean it's only us?'

'We're it, baby. You, me and the camera. Gonzo porn at its raw-and-ready best.' Victor held his hands in the air. 'But I promise to behave, OK?'

I didn't answer, feeling edgy and uncertain what to do. If I left now, I'd have to explain myself to Darryll, and that was something I didn't relish at all. Nothing he hated more than letting down a client. I'd known Darryll drop several girls for being unreliable, leaving them high and dry and desperate for cash – rumour had it one had gone on the game.

'How long will it take?' I ask.

'Just the pair of us . . . reckon we can wrap it up in an hour.' Victor eyed me for a second, gauging my interest. 'Look, I'll pay you double. You can have that other girl's fee on top of your own.'

A thousand pounds. For an hour's work. It was certainly tempting.

'Where's the loo?' I asked, buying myself time.

He nodded back out of the room. I found it on the other side of the hallway and locked myself in. Sat on the seat and got out my phone to call Esme, to ask her what I should do. But it went straight to voicemail.

I thought about ringing Darryll. But what would I say? He knew I wasn't ill cos I'd spoken to him only this morning, to check the address.

Christ, why not go through with it? I asked myself. It was only an hour and Darryll knew I was here, and presumably who I was with.

What could happen, after all?

I stood up and leaned on the sink, peering at myself in the mirror. Kitty Sweet stared back. And she looked braver than Leanne. Someone who wouldn't turn tail and run, however scared she might be.

'Fancy that drink?' Victor asked when I returned.

I shook my head. I wanted to stay alert. On my guard.

'Sure?' He studied my face. 'You look like you could do with something to loosen you up.'

'No thanks.'

He walked over to the filing cabinet. Opened the top drawer and pulled out a litre of whisky, taking a swig straight from the bottle.

'As I said outside, Kitty, I'm sorry about our first meeting. I'd had too much to drink. But there was no need for your boyfriend to rough me up like that.'

'He isn't my boyfriend.'

Victor's face twitched into a smile. 'Good to hear. My advice would be to keep it that way.'

'Why?' I demanded, wanting him to explain. Did Victor know something about you?

But he ignored me. Took another gulp from the whisky bottle before screwing the cap back on. 'You remind me of someone,' he said. 'I thought that, the moment I saw you at Pulsar. You're the dead image of her.'

'Who?'

'Anya Viksna.'

I blinked, remembering. 'That Latvian girl? The one who disappeared?'

Victor sniffed. 'She was never terribly reliable.'

'You knew her?'

'Not well.' He took a cigarette from a packet of Marlboroughs and lit it. 'I only worked with her a few times.'

'You have any idea where she got to?'

Victor smiled as he exhaled a puff of smoke. 'What is this, Kitty? An interrogation?'

'You brought her up, not me.' I shrugged. 'I'm interested, that's all. Esme said her parents were searching for her.'

'So I heard.' There was something unnerving in the way Victor was studying me. His gaze full of intent. The man radiated bad energy. Everything about him repelled me, a negative charge that made my skin prickle with tension.

'Right.' I swallowed. 'Well, let's get it over with, then.'

Victor grinned, and I saw he hadn't expected me to go through with it. So why bring me here? I wondered.

'Yes, let's get this show on the road.' He took a last drag on the cigarette, stubbed it on the side of a metal bin. 'Strip to your underwear.'

He fiddled with one of the cameras as I undressed, then beckoned me over, pushing me to my knees. There was no carpet, only polished wooden floorboards, so it was far from comfortable.

I undid his flies and removed his cock, jerking my head back in surprise. It was unerect.

And black. Really, really black. It took me a moment to figure out why. A tattoo.

His whole cock was a mess of ink.

Victor pulled off his T-shirt, exposing his torso, which was surprisingly tanned and firm – the man obviously worked out – then picked up the other camera and pressed a button. From the corner of my eye I saw a red recording light come on, but I was too busy studying his prick, watching it unfurl, the knot of dark skin expanding into something I recognized.

I was staring at the other end of the snake, I realized, the body coiling around his waist, its mouth gaping at the head of his penis.

It was grotesque. And mesmerizing.

Almost . . . beautiful.

Victor let me admire it for a moment then pushed my head down. The serpent filled my mouth, right to the back of my throat. Gripping my hair, he began to thrust.

'So, Kitty,' he murmured, raising my chin so the camera could peer into my eyes. 'Talk to me. Talk to the guys watching this. Tell them what you want.'

I pulled my face off his dick. 'Fuck you,' I said, ambiguously.

He laughed. 'Oh, you will, baby.' He shoved himself back in my mouth. 'You will. Keep looking into the camera.'

I kept my gaze fixed on the lens rather than Victor.

There was something in his eyes I didn't want to see. I needed to finish this scene and get the hell out of here.

But his cock kept getting bigger. It wasn't that long – not like Nelson's – but it was thick. As he forced it further into my throat, I started to gag. I tried to draw back, but he gripped my head and thrust harder.

My eyes watered. I couldn't breathe. I tried again to shove him away, but he pushed deeper. I could feel him banging against my tonsils and I knew I was about to puke. So I did the only thing I could think of.

Bit down. Hard.

'Jesus,' Victor yelped, jerking backwards, almost swiping me in the face with the camera. 'What the fuck was that for?'

I took a deep gulp of air. 'You were choking me, arsehole.' I scrambled to my feet.

Victor put the camera on the floor. Recovered for a moment, his cock drooping slightly, then held his hands out to me. 'OK, OK, baby, I'm sorry. I didn't mean to be so rough. Let's start over.'

I hesitated, long enough to give Victor the upper hand. Picking up the camera, he yanked my bra to my waist, his hand darting out to grab my left breast. He squeezed it hard, forcing his tongue into my mouth as he pushed me against the sofa.

Suddenly it was like being back on the beach. The stink of whisky and cigarettes on his breath. His weight pressing down on me. I started to panic. What the fuck was I doing? Why hadn't I turned and walked away the moment I saw him?

Esme said he was a cunt – clearly she wasn't joking.

Victor seized my thong. A small ripping sound, then he chucked it on the floor.

Shit. He tore it right off.

Deep within me, something stirred. Something molten, more potent than fear. I tried to push him away but he pinned my arms above my head.

'Kitty Sweet,' he said, gazing down. 'Now there's a misnomer if ever I heard one.' Pushing my legs apart with his knees, he thrust himself inside me.

'I know you,' he whispered, as I glared back at him. 'I can *see* you.'

I had no idea what he meant, and I didn't ask. Too busy gritting my teeth as he began to pump into me, hard and fast.

Was he still filming any of this? Surely the camera angles were all wrong?

But Victor no longer seemed to care. He spun me over, my breasts squashed against the sofa cushions, his cock nudging my buttocks. 'No!' I tried to turn around. 'No anal.'

He ignored me, pulling my arms behind me so I couldn't move. 'What's it worth, Kitty? Your "virginity"?'

'Piss off, Victor.' I kept my voice steady, refusing to show I was afraid.

'Never tried it with any of your boyfriends?' His tone teasing, scornful. He jerked my wrists higher up my back and I cried out despite myself. 'Come on, baby, name your price.'

I thought of what Darryll said, about not doing everything at once. 'No,' I repeated.

Victor bent down, whispered in my ear. 'Another thousand, and we keep it between us. My own private little video.'

His grip on my wrists tightened.

That made two grand. Two grand and no one would ever know. But then, did I really trust Victor to keep that video to himself?

'No,' I said again. 'And let go of me.'

A pause before he pulled me round to face him. 'In that case, you'd better make this good.'

Victor thrust himself back inside me, pinioning my wrists in his left hand, the way he did on the beach. The other circled my throat, thumb one side, fingers the other.

'Tell me you want me,' he murmured, but he was squeezing my windpipe too hard for me to do anything but grunt. I tried to breathe, to twist away, but that made him up the pressure even more.

All the while he stared into my eyes. Searching. Prying.

He wanted me to lose it, I knew. To freak out on him. He wanted the whole thing on camera.

He squeezed harder and I began to feel dizzy. Stars exploded in my head. Lights blinking in and out of my vision. I thought of all the men who'd view this, alone, in secret – this wasn't the kind of porn you indulged in with anyone else around. I pictured their arousal as they witnessed the pain on my face, my fear, watching me gasp for breath.

Something broke loose inside me, flooding me with a calm, cold kind of rage. I imagined walking into their bedroom, their office, their living room, wherever I'd find these men hunched over a screen, their cock twitching in their hands. I saw myself picking it up – their laptop, their tablet – picking it up and smashing it into their skulls, and my whole body shivered with emotion.

Suddenly Victor released his hold on my neck. Withdrawing, he clutched his dick and came all over my face, grasping my hair to stop me pulling away.

I didn't swallow. I spat it out in disgust, but that only made him laugh.

'Nice work, Miss Sweet. I like your style.' He said it so sincerely that for a moment I thought I'd imagined the last ten minutes. That it had been nothing more than an ordinary shoot.

I didn't respond, just wiped a splash from my cheek, searching around for a tissue. Nothing. I picked my ruined knickers off the floor, used those instead, then scrambled to my feet.

I couldn't, wouldn't even look at him. This had been a mistake. I'd got in well over my head, and now I wanted out as fast as possible.

Victor checked something on the camera, then pulled on his jeans and retrieved his jacket from the hallway. He lit another cigarette as he watched me get dressed.

'Here.'

He handed me a wad of cash as I did up my blouse. I rifled through it. True to his word – there, at least – a thousand pounds, for half an hour's work.

But the most painful and humiliating half hour of my life. And the most degrading.

I stared at the money, then at him.

Victor smiled. Brought his mouth so close to mine I could feel his breath on my skin. 'Think of it as a screen test, Kitty.'

'For what?'

'Let's just say I'm recruiting. I'm looking for a very special kind of girl, one prepared to go all the way. And I think you might be her.'

I could tell he wanted to add more, but something held him back. The fuck-you look written all over my face, perhaps.

'Good luck with that.' I stuffed the cash into my bag. 'But you can definitely cross me off your list.'

16

Mayfair, London

Monday, 15 August 2005

'Congratulations, darling,' Esme chinked her glass of Taittinger against mine. 'To our fabulous new stablemate.'

Nelson unleashed a megawatt smile as he raised his glass to ours, while all around other diners shot us curious glances. 'To the best Pulsar babe in town.'

Esme stuck out her tongue, but Nelson kept grinning. I knew she wasn't really jealous – Esme had no reason to envy anyone. She was Pulsar's star attraction, one of the most popular girls in the business, riding high in the charts for several years now.

But for me, still clawing my way up, the offer from Pulsar couldn't have come a moment too soon. No more shooting five days a week to keep Darryll happy. No more sleazy sets in suburban bedrooms with guys who stank or wanted you to rim them.

No more Victors.

Kitty Sweet was a contract girl!

I took a sip of champagne, savouring its delicate flavour. Get used to it, Leanne, I told myself as I soaked up the luxury around me – the starched white table-cloth, the silver cutlery and immaculate polished glasses, gleaming with the promise of more to come.

After all, going on contract is what every porno babe dreams of – the equivalent to becoming exclusive, if you're a hooker. One client, less work, more money.

An easy life.

'Of course, this now means Pulsar basically owns your arse,' said Esme, nudging my arm. 'You'll have to take good care of it.'

She was joking, though not entirely. Being on contract did mean you had to look after yourself. The company could veto a tattoo or a piercing, tell you to lose weight, or even what to do with your hair.

But I didn't care. Contract girls were the closest it came to being a movie star in this business. Contract girls got their pic blown up big on DVDs. Contract girls got to do all the promotion. Everyone looked up to you. All the other girls envied you.

You'd made it. You were top of the heap.

'Anyway, Joe sends his apologies.' Esme poured herself another glass of champagne. 'Tied up with a shoot over in Camden.'

I smiled to hide my disappointment. I'd been hoping to see you again, had made an effort to look my best. But I kept my face deadpan; knowing, instinctively, that revealing my feelings to Esme wouldn't be a good idea.

Scared, I suppose, that she would make light of them. Or tell me you weren't interested. Or off-limits, snapped up by someone else in the intervening weeks since Brighton.

'So what are you going to do?' Nelson asked as he scanned the menu. We were lunching in one of

Mayfair's most exclusive restaurants – another place with an endless waiting list that seemed to evaporate in the face of his irresistible charm. 'You know, with the extra income?'

Five thousand a month, just for basics. And that wasn't counting what I could make as add-ons, selling stuff through my website and running other promotions.

'I'm going to move,' I said, without even having to think about it. 'Get out of that shithole flat.'

I should have done it months ago. I had enough money. One of the more positive side effects of working so hard was plenty of cash. But I was always scared it might dry up again.

'Anywhere in particular?' Esme asked.

'Not sure. Some place more central.' There was no need for me to be in the heart of London, but I wanted to feel like I could.

'Hey, how about Talisa's apartment in Docklands?' Nelson suggested to Esme as we gave the waiter our orders. 'She's moving to Berlin, isn't she? I heard she was planning to rent it out.'

I wrinkled my nose. It didn't sound very nice.

Esme laughed at my expression. 'Docklands is a very exclusive address to have these days.' She put a hand on Nelson's arm. 'Send Talisa a text. Tell her Leanne's interested.'

She turned to me as Nelson fired up his phone and scrolled through his contacts. 'Let's go shopping this afternoon. You're not shooting, are you?'

I shook my head.

'We'll get a cab into Knightsbridge. Hit Harvey Nicks.'

I hesitated. Last time Esme and I went there, we spent over a grand each. My wardrobe was crammed with stuff from Juicy Couture and Stella McCartney. I had five pairs of Jimmy Choos, half a dozen designer handbags and drawers full of lingerie from Agent Provocateur and La Perla. I wasn't sure I needed any more.

'C'mon, honey,' Esme coaxed. 'You're the face of Pulsar Entertainment now. You've got to look the part.'

I laughed. Looking the part was already taking a heavy toll on my income. Somehow I'd fallen into having my hair done every fortnight. Then there were my nails, facials and fake tan – my barely there gleam cost as much as a full-on mahogany glow. Add in gym fees, regular teeth whitening, and monthly STD tests, and there wasn't a whole lot left over.

Truth was, I'd been spending my porn pounds nearly as fast as I could fuck for them. Nothing, not even coke or ecstasy or champagne, matched the buzz of being able to walk into a shop and buy anything I liked.

But now I wanted to do something better with my money. Be more responsible. Have something to show for it at the end of it all.

'Anyway, it's a relief,' I said as our starters arrived – bite-sized portions arranged on our plates like miniature works of art. 'Getting the contract, I mean. A couple of weeks ago Darryll booked me in for a scene with that bloke Victor – you know, the one we met in Brighton?'

'Victor?' Esme's eyes narrowed with distaste. 'You did a scene with *Victor Gomez*? What the hell were you thinking? Or your agent?'

'You OK?' Nelson looked concerned.

I nodded. 'It was a bit of a head fuck. Literally. Never again.'

Nelson gave an approving nod. 'You're well out of it. My advice is steer clear.'

'I worked with him once,' Esme admitted. 'When I

started out. He offered me double the going rate and I didn't know any better. I was shaking by the time I left.'

'What did he do?'

'Nothing in particular. It was this vibe he's got. Like he really wants to hurt you . . . can hardly hold himself back.'

Yeah, that pretty much summed up my encounter with Victor. The sense that he was barely managing to restrain himself.

Nelson topped up our glasses. 'There's a rumour he killed his girlfriend.'

My eyes widened. 'Really?'

'Gabriela. She was this South American chick . . . Venezuelan, I think. Came over to work and hooked up with Victor, and one day she didn't show up at a shoot.'

'Like that girl Anya who disappeared,' I said, and caught Esme and Nelson exchanging glances.

'What?'

Esme looked at me. 'You didn't hear?'

I frowned. 'No.'

'She turned up.' Esme fingered the stem of her champagne glass. 'On a rubbish dump out in Dartford. A couple of days ago.'

'Turned up? You mean . . . what . . . dead?' I felt a shiver of shock. 'Jesus, why didn't you tell me before?'

'It was all over the papers. I assumed you knew.'

I shook my head. 'Oh God, that's terrible.' I felt winded, which was crazy – I mean, I'd never even met the girl. Though somehow, being her last-minute replacement on that first Pulsar shoot, I couldn't help feeling it gave us some kind of connection.

'So you think *Victor* killed her?' I remembered his hand around my throat, the way he pressed his thumb into my windpipe. That sense he'd been on the brink of going further.

'Who?' Nelson asked, confused. 'His girlfriend or Anya?'

'Don't be daft,' Esme sighed, smiling as the waiter brought another bottle of champagne. 'Victor didn't kill anyone. Gabriela went home. It was a stupid rumour, that's all. You know the shit that goes around.'

'So do they know what happened, then? To Anya?'

'No idea.' Nelson said, chewing his seared scallop. 'I heard the police were going to interview everyone who worked with her. Apparently they're doing the rounds of all the studios.'

'Why?' I asked. 'I mean, it was probably a boyfriend or someone, wasn't it?'

Nelson shrugged. 'Probably.'

'God, let's not talk about this any more.' Esme knocked back the rest of her glass. 'We're supposed to be celebrating here.'

'You're right,' Nelson agreed, but it made me uncomfortable somehow, the way they dismissed it so easily. Anya had been one of us. They knew her. They'd met her parents.

But then porn was like that. You could only stand it if you didn't think too hard about what you were doing. Didn't dwell on things.

Esme picked up her fork and speared a penny-sized circle of heritage beetroot. It was then I caught sight of it. There, on her ring finger. I couldn't believe I'd missed it before.

A diamond. A great fat sparkly diamond.

Esme saw me clock it and grinned. 'What do you think?' She held out her left hand so I could get a better look.

'You're engaged?' I gasped, holding her finger by the manicured tip and twisting it from side to side so the stone glinted in the overhead lights. 'When? Why didn't you tell me?'

'We were about to,' Esme laughed. 'Nelson proposed a few days ago. On set, in front of the crew. Went down on one knee, the whole works. Joe got it all on camera.'

I smiled, but inside I felt odd. A bit lost.

Left out, I supposed. I'd have liked to have been there. Could imagine it all, everyone clapping and breaking into cheers as Nelson slipped the ring on Esme's finger. I really wished I'd seen that.

I shifted in my seat, trying to hide my discomfort. It wasn't just missing that particular performance. This was supposed to be my celebration, wasn't it? Part of me felt hijacked. After all, who else could share my good fortune? Maxine? Mum and Mike?

No chance.

But it wasn't quite that either, this heaviness inside. More than anything, I couldn't help feeling that Esme and Nelson – my best friends, my mentors, almost my new family – were somehow leaving me behind.

I was a bit player, and they were the stars. Everything they did seemed to turn to gold, and none of the shit ever touched them.

It was silly, I know. But I couldn't shrug off a nagging sense of resentment. Like they were inside some fabulous building, basking in the spotlight, the glory, while I was forever stuck out in the cold, my face pressed up against the window, looking in.

17

Wiltshire

Tuesday, 6 September 2005

'You know anything about the cameraman, Joe?'

I tried to sound casual, watching you out of the corner of my eye as you fiddled with one of the lights, a group of black cows spectating from behind a wooden fence. My first contract shoot for Pulsar was at a farm, of all places. Deep in the Wiltshire countryside, it looked like something from a period drama, with its ramshackle stone barns and tracks rutted with mud.

'Why? You got a crush on him?' Vicky grinned and prodded my arm.

I felt myself blush. I suppose I had, though I wanted to think it was more than that. Something more serious.

'Whatever.' I shrugged, looking away. 'I'm just curious.'

I couldn't quite shake off Victor's warning. Telling me to steer clear of you. I felt the urge to dig deeper, find out what I might be getting myself into. My eyes strayed back to where you were standing, chatting to Eddie the director. You were wearing cargo shorts and a plain black T-shirt that emphasized your lean physique. Especially next to Eddie, who seemed to carry all his weight around his belly. You spotted me watching and waved. I waved back, trying to act like there was nothing between us, but all the time wondering, did you like me at all?

'I knew it!' said Vicky triumphantly. 'I saw you eyeing him up in the barn.'

'I so was not.' But the flush in my cheeks gave me away and Vicky laughed. 'Yeah, right. No wonder you were so hot in that scene – I knew it wasn't just the weather.'

The barn shoot had taken half the morning on a stifling September day, in what was turning into an Indian summer. Eddie was pissed off there was no actual hay in there, so insisted on tearing open a plastic-wrapped bale of straw and strewing it around the place.

What I learned – the last thing you want to fuck on is straw. It's itchy and prickly; I had tiny scratches everywhere, and a rash right across my back.

But that was porn for you. In its relentless search for something new, comfort or convenience didn't get a look-in. It was all about the fantasy that sex happened anywhere, anytime, under any circumstance. If aliens only watched adult movies, they'd think the human race was as randy as rabbits; that all we ever did was strip naked at a moment's notice and screw each other senseless.

'Well?' Vicky nudged me again, not about to let the matter drop.

'Do you know if he's seeing anyone?' I asked, giving up the pretence that my interest was casual. After all, I liked Vicky. She didn't take herself too seriously, treating porn like a fun new hobby. And she was cool and kinky, with a piercing in her clit and half her body covered in huge Technicolor tattoos.

'No idea, sweetie,' she shrugged. 'All I know is he's a

bloody good cameraman. Joe on set, and you get it down first shot. No pissing around. Everyone goes home on time.'

'Who are you talking about?' Vince flopped on the grass beside us, examining one of the wilting sandwiches the runner had picked up in the village.

'Boyfriends,' said Vicky with a leer that showed off her tongue stud.

'Really?' Vince wiggled an eyebrow. 'Tell me more.'

Vince was bisexual – or at least that's what he claimed. Rumour had it he was actually gay, but wanted to break into mainstream porn.

'Not much to tell.' I flashed a warning look at Vicky, who winked. One thing admitting my feelings to her, another entirely to broadcast them to Vince, who relished nothing more than gossip – and the porn industry was a small world.

I wanted to keep you under wraps, something to savour in private.

'Just as well.' Vicky scratched a lump on her knee that looked like a horsefly bite. 'Relationships never work, not in this business.'

'Tell me about it,' Vince sighed, running his hand over his designer stubble, so dark and perfectly outlined it was like he painted it on. 'Last guy I dated freaked out when he saw one of my movies. Snapped the fucking DVD in half, then burst into tears.'

'No way to win,' Vicky said. 'Either your career screws up your relationship, or your relationship screws up your career.'

I thought of those girls who turn up to shoots with their boyfriends in tow. Suitcase pimps were another industry hazard. Pumped full of steroids and bad attitude, they trailed after their porn-star girlfriends, lugging their Barbie-pink cases stuffed with lycra and lube, managing their schedule and their money. Watching their every move on set and making the crew nervous.

'This one guy I dated wanted me to get him into the industry.' Vicky picked up a sandwich, pulled out a piece of onion and chewed on it. 'So finally I persuaded a director friend to give him a trial and he completely flunked it. Couldn't get a hard-on, even after I gave him a pill. Walked off set and I never saw him again.'

'Should have given him a shot of Caverject.' Vince grinned as he pointed to his cock, still straining against his shorts. 'One little prick in your prick and you're hard for hours.'

Vicky grimaced. 'That guy needed an injection in the brain – it was his head that was the fucking problem.'

'It's not always like that, surely?' I asked. 'Relationships, I mean. Look at Esme and Nelson.' I thought of that diamond on Esme's finger. The triumph on her face.

Vicky rolled her eyes. 'Esme and Nelson don't count. It's different for us lesser mortals.'

'I don't see why.'

'Think about it.' Vince chucked the remains of his sandwich on to a huge pile of dung. 'You meet some guy. You tell him you work in porn. At first he thinks it's cool, but sooner or later it'll get under his skin. Not many people can watch the person they love have sex with someone else – especially if that someone is better looking, has a bigger dick and can fuck for hours.'

'And it's no easier dating another performer,' Vicky chimed in. 'The minute you start really feeling something for each other, the paranoia and the jealousy kick off. One doesn't want the other performing with someone else, so you agree to only work together and soon the shoots dry up and you're both bloody broke.'

143

She ran her tongue around her teeth, sucking them clean, and turned to me. 'My advice, honey. Do this for a few years. Make all the money you can and stash it. Don't spend it on shit you don't need or stuff it up your nose. Then get out. That way you have a fighting chance of a normal life.'

A normal life. I wasn't even sure what that was any more. Marriage? Kids? It seemed too remote to consider.

Then I remembered Maxine's latest email announcing that she and Greg were engaged. Planned to marry next spring, buying a house in Stevenage.

Esme and Nelson. Maxine and Greg. It felt like the whole world was moving on without me.

'Hey, I hear you're doing your first anal scene this afternoon,' Vicky said and Vince beamed. 'Ain't I the lucky one.'

'Yeah.' She reached up and squeezed his cheek. 'At least Kitty gets to do it with someone who's had plenty of practice.'

Luckily we got the first take in the cab of the combine harvester wrapped up in one go, though I could see you struggling for a decent camera angle. At one point you were practically in there with us, leaning over the console, trying to get a penetration shot as Vince screwed me doggy style.

I glimpsed you out of the corner of my eye, wearing that deadpan expression intended to save the performers from embarrassment – though it never worked for me. You always made me self-conscious.

Especially when it came to my anal scene.

'Vince, move round here a bit.' Eddie sounded tired and grumpy, like porn was slumming it and he was destined for better things. 'Try and put more expression into it. Like you're actually excited about this.'

'I'd be more excited if he just shut the hell up,' muttered Vince. 'Who does he think he is? Fucking Fellini?'

'You ready, Kitty?' Eddie asked.

I gave him the nod. I'd done an enema in the outside loo behind one of the barns, trying to ignore the spiders and stink of damp as I cleaned myself out. I'd also swallowed a couple of extra-strong painkillers. I was about as ready as I'd ever be.

'OK, Vince, I want you to take this slowly,' Eddie droned. 'Once more with feeling.'

'Fuck off,' Vince murmured again under his breath, before leaning in to me. 'Here we go, sweetie. Get your game face on.'

I smiled, despite my tension, despite the reek of bodies and lube, dust and farmyard, arranging my features into what I hoped resembled the heights of sexual ecstasy. But I was nervous. Really nervous. I'd never done this before – not even with Ross, though God knows he'd pestered me enough.

Not to mention it was hot as hell in that cab. Apparently it had air conditioning, but the ignition wasn't on and no one could face traipsing off to find someone who had the keys. So I was glistening with sweat, my make-up beginning to run.

I felt Vince line himself up behind and slide into me. It didn't hurt exactly, despite his size. It was a very full sort of feeling, and I had to fight my body's urge to push him straight out again.

'That's it, baby. You love this, don't you?' Vince slipped further inside me. 'Make like the earth is moving, kitten,' he whispered again. 'Let's keep old Eddie happy and then we can go to the pub and get pissed.'

I closed my eyes, trying not to grimace. Concentrated on making the right noises. I was doing all right, even getting into it, when I felt a hand on my bare heel.

I glanced over. It was you. Holding my foot out of the way of the camera.

My body stiffened. And the pain kicked in. A sharp ache, like cramp.

'Cut,' said Eddie, annoyed. 'Kitty, what's the matter?'

'I'm fine,' I mumbled. 'Just give me a minute.'

I scrambled out of the tractor, grabbing a towel so I didn't have to walk butt naked across the farmyard. Locked myself in the loo and sat with my head in my hands.

That's when it hit me, how deeply I felt about you. In a filthy toilet that stank of piss and manure.

The first time you touched me and I fell apart.

My stomach lurched with embarrassment and shame. My debut shoot for Pulsar, under contract, and I'd totally fucked it up.

A knock on the door. 'Are you decent?'

You.

And such a ridiculous question it made me laugh – given I'd spent the last hour or so starkers in front of two other performers and a crew of four.

I unlocked the door, tucking the towel tight under my armpits. You poked your head inside. 'Sorry. I put you off your stride.'

I smiled. No point pretending otherwise. 'I guess I was more nervous than I realized.'

You stood there, gazing at me, saying nothing. And I remembered again how you'd rescued me on the seafront at Brighton. How you'd looked after us that night – tracking down Esme and herding the three of us back to the hotel. Driving us home the next day, when Nelson was too hung-over to get behind the wheel.

Like you were the grown-up, and we were three over-sized children.

I liked it, though. Loved how serious and responsible you'd been. You felt like someone I could trust.

'You feel up to carrying on?' you asked.

I nodded, searching your face for clues. Did you like me? Even a little?

'No hurry,' you said. 'Eddie's taking a break. It's way too hot for shooting. Everyone's getting tense and edgy.'

I smiled again, grateful you were trying so hard to make me feel better. You were always kind, weren't you, Joe? The sort of person who liked to take care of others. Put them at their ease.

'Anyway, you're pretty much off the hook. Just a quick pop shot with Vince and I can fake in the rest. Let me know when you're ready.'

18

Wiltshire

Tuesday, 6 September 2005

'What are you having, Kitty?' Eddie asked, as he stood at the bar taking orders.

'Just a white wine. Thanks.'

I found our table in the corner of the pub garden, away from the curious stares of locals and tourists. Inside we'd been too loud and too lewd, clearly pissing off the landlord.

I sat at the end of the table, opposite you, but you were busy talking to Mia, the make-up girl. I couldn't resist checking you out again, trying to pin down what it was about you I found so attractive. Saw you laugh and put your hand on her arm.

My heart collapsed. I looked away quickly.

'It's different for men,' Vicky was saying to Vince. 'You can keep going for what, thirty or forty years? You don't even have to be good-looking, for Christ's sake.'

Vince frowned.

'I don't mean *you*.' Vicky punched his arm. 'You're bloody gorgeous, you know that. But take Ron Jeremy – the man's a fucking gorilla. Us girls, though, we have to be super-hot. And young. Most of us are washed up in a few years.'

'Yeah.' Vince sighed. 'They do seem to be getting younger. I'm starting to feel like their dad.'

'Ewwww . . .' Vicky wrinkled her nose in mock-disgust. 'But seriously, Vince, it's pretty tragic. These girls go into porn the minute they turn eighteen, believing it'll be all glitz and glamour, then get arse-fucked by the director at their first gonzo shoot. And they don't even realize it's OK to get upset about it.'

She took a swig of the beer Eddie handed to her. I flicked my gaze back to you. You were still listening to Mia, your eyes never leaving her face as she talked, her arms waving around, describing something.

'The trouble is, it sets a precedent for the rest of us,' Vicky continued. 'Directors think they can get away with anything now – it's like we've signed over our basic human rights.'

Eddie placed my wine on the table and sat next to me at the end of the bench. 'Tell me about it,' he said, picking up the conversation. 'Most girls in the industry are fucked up. If not when they arrive, certainly after a few years. But, it's worse in the States – half the women in the San Fernando Valley are on antidepressants and a dozen other drugs. Those women are *empty*. I mean, ravaged, inside and out.'

I thought of Esme. All the shit she was taking. Not to mention the booze.

'It's not good,' Vince agreed, telling us about a director he met in the US who refused to work with any girl over twenty-one.

'Yeah, in this business you're old by twenty-five,' said Vicky. 'You're fucking over.'

'You'll never be over.' Vince stroked her arm and

made a kissy face. 'You've got years ahead of you as a sexy milf.'

Vicky punched him again. 'Don't even say that word.'

'Anyway,' Vince yawned, changing the subject. 'I'm waiting for a call from Pipedream. Gonna get my dick moulded so it can go and seek its fame and fortune.'

This sent Vicky into near hysterics. 'Fifty quid says you can't sit still long enough,' she gasped. 'Honestly, you can't move for, like, two hours, while the plaster sets.'

'It's not two hours, dung brain – it's more like twenty minutes. They use this fast-setting alginate stuff. My friend Paulo had it done, said he was picking bits out of his foreskin for days.'

That just kicked Vicky off again. She was laughing so hard she could barely hold her glass.

'Guys? Want another?'

I glanced up to see you clutching a bunch of empties, about to return to the bar.

I seized my chance. 'I'll give you a hand.'

'Fancy a stroll?'

You turned to me once we'd doled out the drinks. 'I was going to have a look at the canal.'

My heart lifted as I followed you through the gate at the end of the beer garden, and down the footpath that led to the water. Was it possible you felt the same way about me? Was I in with a chance?

We walked along the towpath, taking in all the green and still and quiet, as refreshing as a long cool drink after the noise and heat of a London summer. The sun was beginning to set, tingeing the sky a deep pinky-red, making everything around us seem softer somehow, more vibrant in the evening light.

As we rounded the bend, a canal boat approached, flushing out a trio of ducks roosting under a quaint stone bridge. They swam around, quacking with indignation, as the barge chugged past. At the rear, sitting on the tiny deck, I saw the family – two parents and two kids – eyeing me with undisguised curiosity. No doubt wondering what the hell I was doing here, in my short dress and stupid heels.

The spell broke. I sat on the bank and closed my eyes. Behind my lids, your face danced like an after-image, your serious features, your deep brown eyes.

I loved you, I realized. This wasn't some crush. Nor lust. I wanted you more than I'd ever wanted anyone. All of you – not just your body.

How did this happen?

'You OK?' you asked.

'Tired.' I opened my eyes but was unable to look at you. Convinced you could read my feelings on my face. 'Long day.'

'You're shivering.' You took off your jacket and draped it round my shoulders. Always the gentleman.

And yet ... I recalled the way you laid into Victor. Hard and fast. It didn't seem possible it was the same person as the one now sitting beside me.

Maybe that's what made me fall for you. Your complexity. Your contradictions.

'I'm OK.' I pulled your jacket tighter around me and flashed you a grateful smile. I should have come better prepared, packed some boots and a jumper. Flatter shoes. I felt like an idiot.

A laughing stock.

151

'First day on location.' You sank on the grass next to me. 'You're bound to be knackered.'

I smiled again, tried to pull myself together. 'Was I all right?'

'Course you were. You were great.'

'Seriously?'

'Seriously.' You swung your gaze from the water. It was darker here under the trees, but I could see your eyes fixed on mine, their expression sincere. 'You've got it all, Leanne. A nice, fresh natural look. Nothing fake.'

I laughed at the irony. Everything about me felt fake, though I still had my own tits and teeth. I felt fake through and through. Inside and out.

'I guess I'm worried. What Eddie said, about most women in porn being fucked up.'

'Men too,' you added. 'No one gets off scot-free in this game.'

I grimaced, staring up the towpath towards the fields in the far distance, remembering that canal holiday I had with Mum and Mike, back when the twins were toddlers. Mike steered the boat, and Mum and I spent the week doing the locks, trailing Tom and Liam everywhere, making sure they didn't fall into the water.

The memory snatched at my heart, sharp as a stitch. That was the last holiday we ever took together.

Four years later and we weren't even speaking.

'Maybe I shouldn't be doing this,' I said. 'Porn, I mean.'

You sighed. 'Goes with the territory. I doubt there's a day when any of us doesn't ask ourselves that.'

'How about you?' I let my eyes drift to your face. 'Is this what you thought you'd end up doing?'

You looked away, gazing at the far bank of the canal and I assumed you didn't want to answer.

'Actually I wanted to be a physicist,' you said finally.

'A physicist?' I tried to keep the surprise from my voice. 'With stars and black holes and stuff?'

'Sort of. More quantum mechanics, matter and anti-matter – things like that.'

'OK,' I replied, though honestly I hadn't the faintest clue about any of them. 'So how come you're here, then? Doing this.'

You fell silent again. Around us the light was fading. The sense of nature settling down for the night.

'Long story,' you said eventually. 'Let's just say it didn't pan out.'

'So you're not happy, then, doing this?'

'It's, you know, work. It pays the bills. All my mates envy me. They reckon I've got the best job in the world, surrounded by naked girls every day.'

'But you don't think so?'

You wrinkled your nose as you considered this, and I tried not to stare. You looked so cute when you did that.

'At first, when you start out, you're so focused on getting it right, on getting a good shot, you barely register that half the people around aren't wearing clothes. Then, when you're more experienced, when you know what you're doing, it all feels . . .' You stopped.

'Feels what?'

'I dunno. It's hard to explain. Unreal, I suppose. Because that's what it is, isn't it? Make-believe.'

You turned to look at me again. As the sun sank behind the hill, it was harder to make out your expression, but it seemed to hold a question. Asking me to confirm something. And partly because I didn't know what it was, or what you wanted me to say, I leaned over and let myself do what I'd been so longing to do.

But you drew away the instant my lips touched yours.

'Kitty . . .' Your voice regretful.

'What?' I said, too quickly. 'You don't fancy me?'

You dropped your eyes to the ground. 'No, it isn't that. You're lovely. Christ, who wouldn't fancy you? It's just that you're . . .' You paused again.

Something disintegrated inside me. Right in the heart of me.

'Oh, I get it.' The bitterness in my tone surprising both of us. 'I'm dirty. That's it. I'm a slutty porn girl, not good enough—'

'Kitty, no . . . that's not what I—'

'You can't even remember my real name, can you?' I scrambled to my feet. 'It's not Kitty. It's *Leanne*. Leanne fucking Jenkins.' My heart was thumping and I felt myself flush with shame and anger.

You got up too, running a hand through your hair. Something I'd seen you do whenever there was a problem on a shoot. Whenever things were going wrong.

'God, Leanne, I'm sorry.' Your face was full of apology and regret, yet it only made me feel worse. Devastated. I . . . this . . . was clearly nothing more than a mistake. 'I'm so sorry. It's not you, it's—'

'Fuck off, Joe.'

I turned and stumbled back in the direction of the pub. Walked away before you could crush me further with your kindness. That's what hurt the most, draining all my fury and replacing it with defeat – the fact that you actually cared how I felt.

Tried to let me down gently.

You didn't follow me, of course. Simply waited till Vince and Vicky offered me a lift, then went home with

154

Eddie. I had to hold it together all the way to London, while Vicky and Vince bantered and bickered, sensing what was wrong and doing their best to give me the space I needed.

It wasn't until several hours later, when I got back to my flat, kicking open the front door that always stuck, then slamming it behind me, that I finally gave in and let myself cry.

19

HMP Brakehurst

Tuesday, 8 March 2016

'That must have been very painful.' Yvonne is gazing at me with the same expression of sympathy you wore that evening, and it's making me fidgety and cross.

No shit, Sherlock, I think, but just nod, not wanting to sour the session the moment we're getting started. I've actually been looking forward to seeing Yvonne again, missing her the week she was on holiday.

Or rather, missing the chance to talk about you.

It's natural, isn't it? To want to discuss the person you love, to say their name out loud, even if the relationship is over. It makes you feel like somehow they're still part of your life.

And who else can I talk to about you in here? Tanya? Drew?

Not likely.

'You mentioned that right from the moment you met Joe, you felt a strong connection. Do you think it was the same for him?'

'How do you mean?'

'Well, reading this' – Yvonne nods at the fresh pile of

notes in her hand – 'it would seem that perhaps he wasn't—'

'I'm simply telling you how it happened,' I snap. If looks could kill, Yvonne would be heading straight to the mortuary.

But she doesn't even blink. Just holds my gaze, and I notice her roots are growing out, leaving a badger stripe of grey across her parting.

'I'm only saying, Leanne, that your feelings for him . . . this realization you were in love with Joe, well, it seems very sudden. You barely knew him at this point, after all – you'd only met him, what, a couple of times?'

'Three,' I say. 'But what's so strange about that? Never heard of love at first sight?'

Yvonne's mouth tightens, emphasizing the wrinkles around her lips. I glare back at her. How could this woman understand anyway? She doesn't look as if she's ever been in love.

And to think she's supposed to be an expert on feelings.

Yvonne lets the silence linger for a moment then changes tack. 'You said in our last session that making porn was like a drug. Have you considered, Leanne, that it was a kind of addiction?'

'You mean a sex addiction?'

'Would you agree?'

I sink back in my chair and stare out the window. Nothing but light high cloud. The trees in the distance are bare, still in the clutches of winter.

'I think I was addicted to the attention.' I swing my gaze back to my therapist. 'Especially when I became better known. Directors were fighting to book me; I was working with some of the best people. And the fans – I started getting emails, letters, presents.'

157

'That must have been . . . gratifying.' Yvonne smiles.

I lift my shoulders into a shrug. 'Mostly. Sometimes it was plain creepy.' Like the guy who sent a bouquet to Darryll's office every week, inviting me to call; when I didn't, he sent lilies and other funeral flowers. Or that weird little man who somehow was waiting outside each shoot – till I threatened to get an injunction.

'It must have been hard to know who to trust. In terms of your relationships with men.'

I run my tongue over my teeth, considering this. 'I dated a bit, but it was difficult. Either men were completely freaked out by me working in adult films, or that was exactly why they were with me.'

'For the sex, you mean?'

I nod. 'I should have been thrilled, shouldn't I? After all, my whole career revolved around blokes wanting to screw me.'

'All the more understandable that you wouldn't want your relationships to be the same,' Yvonne says. 'Maybe you needed to feel that the men who were important to you weren't using you that way.'

'I guess.' I inhale, trying to release the tension building up inside.

'Do you think perhaps that was why you fixated on Joe? Because he was different? Because he wasn't simply after what he could get?'

I grit my teeth at the word 'fixated', but I'm not about to take the bait again. Instead I remember that weekend in Brighton, the way you talked to me, like I was real. Like I was worth the effort. Most blokes weren't interested in what went on in my head, but you were different. You never assumed I was stupid, even though I could have got decent A-levels and gone to university. You asked me questions, always listening to my answer,

158

instead of talking over me like other guys. And you kept your eyes on my face, never let them wander.

You were well brought up, Joe, that much was obvious. Wherever we went that weekend, you held the door open for me. And offering your jacket, down by the canal. You had manners, despite everything you'd been through.

I admired that in you, then and later, when I knew your past had been less than a picnic. I admired the way you held on to your decent, civilized self. But I can't be arsed to explain all this to Yvonne. If she can't see how being treated nicely might make you fall for someone, more fool her.

Probably she has no idea how it feels.

Yvonne smooths her hand over my notes, preparing her next question. 'And what happened to Anya Viksna . . . You mention this a number of times, that you felt a connection to her. How did it affect you? Were you concerned for your own safety?'

I give another shrug. 'I felt bad for her, obviously. But I wasn't particularly worried.'

'Were other people anxious about it? Taking extra precautions?'

'Not then,' I say, shaking my head. 'I mean, at that point we had no idea her death was connected to porn. Her killer could have been anyone – a boyfriend, someone she owed money to. A random psychopath. No one got really paranoid till later on.'

'You weren't scared?'

'Like I said, I had no reason to be. We assumed it was a one-off.'

Yvonne falls silent, thinking. Then sits up straighter as she drops in her next question.

'What about your father?' The quality of Yvonne's

attention shifts to something more watchful, alert for my reaction.

I almost laugh. She's forgetting I'm a porn star. I'm used to disguising my feelings – exhaustion, disgust, pain, boredom, all of them. I'm much better at it than she is.

Besides, I'm ready for her. I've been expecting this one.

'What about him?' I ask.

'He left when you were what . . . age six?'

'Seven.'

'And he hasn't been in contact since?'

I shake my head again. 'Not with me.'

I'm not surprised my therapist has seized on this. Dear old dad. The papers made much of him vacating my life when I was small. The blank space he left. One journalist even wrote a whole article about how many women in the sex industry had missing fathers, using me as her primary example.

It gave us permission, she concluded. Our father's absence from our lives. It left us no one to disappoint.

Though surely that's an insult to my stepfather, who filled the space a lot better than my dad ever had – and I did a bloody good job of disappointing Mike.

It's all too neat. A tidy, convenient little explanation for what happened. The porn, all of it.

Fuck that.

'How do you feel about him, Leanne? Your father?'

'I don't,' I say. 'I never think about him.'

Yvonne pauses, then carries on. 'Do you ever wonder . . .' She stops again, weighing up her words. 'I'm guessing your father didn't know what you'd been doing until the trial.'

I fist my hands behind my chair. Force myself to look

composed. 'You mean, do I ever wonder if he saw my videos?'

Yvonne nods.

'Have I considered whether my father may have inadvertently wanked off to one of his daughter's scenes? Is there any point in me actually answering that?'

Yvonne shifts in her seat, looking uncomfortable, but doesn't push it any further. We both sit in silence, listening to the usual prison sounds, muffled and more distant in this part of the wing. Finally she speaks.

'You killed two men, Leanne. Don't you feel there's a connection? Between your father's abandonment and what you did?'

In my head birds take off from the tops of trees, flapping and squawking and swooping in the sky. Then I think of you. That always calms me down.

'You pleaded guilty, Leanne. On both counts.'

Again I don't answer. I've never spoken about this, not even to my solicitor and barrister. I had nothing to say. I pleaded guilty, and that was all anyone needed to know.

They had what they wanted, after all: someone to blame, someone to punish. Another tidy, convenient little explanation for what happened.

And I had the truth. A secret, hidden in my heart.

My silence.

My final gift to you.

20

Docklands, London

Friday, 11 November 2005

'Wow!' Esme exclaimed, eyes scanning my new flat. 'Like fucking WOW!'

She dumped the cake box on the glass-and-aluminium coffee table, heading straight for the huge picture windows overlooking the Thames. Studied the view for a minute or so, the river and the apartment blocks of Canary Wharf, then turned her attention to the living room.

'This all Talisa's stuff?'

'Most of it. She took some with her.'

'Nice.' She nodded approvingly.

It was. The whole flat looked like a show home, lots of exposed brickwork and patterned oak flooring. Talisa had left the bulky furniture – leather sofas and armchairs, a huge wooden dining table – along with all the crockery and kitchen stuff I could ever need. Good quality too; tasteful, not the sort of crap I was used to. I was almost scared to touch anything, though God knows my deposit was large enough to cover any kind of damage.

Esme sank on to one of the sofas. 'So how's it going, hun? Long time no see.'

We hadn't met up for a month or so. I'd been busy with the move; Esme was off doing several shoots in France. It took an effort not to feel jealous. Esme got the glamour of Paris; I got a farm full of cowpats, and a lumber yard in Crouch End.

'It's all good.' I put a happy smile on my face. 'At least, I love it here.'

A couple of weeks on and I could still hardly believe this was my new home. I woke up every morning, thinking I must be dreaming.

Leanne Jenkins, living in a place like this.

The only downside was not being able to show it off to Mum and Mike. I'd have loved them to see the flat, to be proud, rather than ashamed. But Mum was continuing to blank me, and any hope that she might accept what I was doing had dwindled to a bleak acceptance.

I had toyed with the idea of going to visit, forcing her to talk to me, but I knew that would only make things worse. And the truth was I couldn't face it. If I stayed away, I didn't have to hear what she had to say. Didn't have to see the disappointment, the disgust on her face.

'Gus told me you're doing well at Pulsar,' Esme said. 'Your farm shoot was their top download last month.'

'Really?' I tried to sound pleased. I should have been overjoyed. But even the mention of it brought on a rush of humiliation, as I remembered what happened with you.

Esme caught my expression. 'What's up, babe? I thought you'd be over the moon. That's a big deal.'

'Sorry. I'm tired, that's all.'

She eyed me steadily. Reading my mood. 'I saw Joe the other day. He was asking after you. Said he hasn't seen you much.'

I shrugged. 'He's been around – at shoots, I mean.' Though we'd barely spoken in the two months since that evening by the canal. At work I'd avoided eye contact, rushing off the minute the camera stopped rolling.

'He seems to think you're avoiding him.' Esme's gaze didn't leave mine.

I inhaled. 'Yeah, maybe.'

'You going to tell me why?'

I sighed. Bit the bullet. 'OK. I made a fool of myself. With him.'

Esme's expression remained neutral. 'What happened?'

'I threw myself at him, after that Wiltshire shoot. He wasn't interested.' An actual pain in my chest as I say this. Nothing I'd done since eased the sting of your rejection – not even screwing other men.

'Oh Lord, why didn't you say anything?' Esme got up and wrapped her arms around me. 'So you're keen on him, then? I guessed as much in Brighton.'

I flashed back to Esme watching me, in that club. Assessing.

'Whatever.' I shrugged again. 'It's clearly not recipro-cated.'

Esme made a sympathetic movement with her mouth. 'What we need here is cake.' She grabbed plates and forks from the galley kitchen, opening up the Kon-ditor & Cook box to reveal a large, elaborately decorated chocolate gateau.

'It's not that he doesn't like you, Leanne,' she said, cutting us both a slice. 'It's more that Joe's . . . complicated.'

'How do you mean?'

'He has . . . you know, a lot of history . . .' She searched for the right words.

'History?'

164

Esme examined the cake, falling silent for a moment or two. 'Just stuff. Joe's tougher than he looks. He's been through some real shit.'

Tougher than he looks. I remembered again the way you dealt with Victor. Swift and unhesitant.

I could believe that.

It should have put me off, I know, but somehow seeing that not-so-gentle side of you made me like you more. The kind of person you'd want watching your back.

'And he's been burned,' Esme added, 'in the past.'

I assumed she meant your ex, the one that went off to America.

She handed me a fork and my slice. 'You know his family's from India, don't you?'

I nodded, though in truth I hadn't known. I mean, it was obvious your parents weren't European, but I'd never asked about it.

'His real name is Arjun.'

'So how come everyone calls him Joe?'

'I'm not sure. I think it was a nickname, at school or something.' Esme cut a chunk of sponge with the side of her fork, leaning over to scoop it into her mouth. 'Anyway, his family's Muslim and Joe struggles with that. His father's very traditional. His sister too – she wears a headscarf and everything.'

'Do they know what Joe does?'

Esme shook her head. 'He's terrified they'll find out. You never noticed his name isn't credited on any of our films? It's in his contract, that they don't mention him.'

I took a bite of my own cake, but the sweetness was overpowering. 'So why does he do it? If it would upset his family so much.'

Though God knows I was a fine one to talk.

'Money,' shrugged Esme. 'He helps them out a lot

and Pulsar pays him a packet, much more than he'd get doing anything mainstream.'

She finished her slice, then collapsed back on to the sofa, hugging her knees as she stared out at the view. On the far side of the river, the trees were beginning to shed their leaves. November already, I realized, which meant it would be Christmas soon.

Would I be spending it on my own this year? The thought made my spirits plummet. The idea of Mum and Mike and the twins, opening presents and having Christmas dinner without me.

'Shit.' Esme turned back to me. 'Nelson and I should have sold our flat and nabbed this place for ourselves. It's fabulous.'

I abandoned my cake, putting the plate back on the table. 'I'm grateful you didn't. Seriously. Thank you.'

Esme grinned. 'My pleasure.' She eyed my plate. 'You don't want that?'

'Sorry. I'm not hungry.'

She picked it up and tucked in. 'All I'm saying is, don't take it to heart, Leanne,' she mumbled between mouthfuls. 'Joe's not like other guys. He's cautious around people, you see? Maybe . . .' She hesitated. 'Is there anyone else in the picture? Any other blokes you fancy?'

I frowned. Was Esme warning me off?

'How well do you know him, then?' I asked, ignoring her question. Remembering what she'd told me before, about meeting Joe before she got together with Nelson. He was like family, hadn't she said?

'God, we've known each other for ages, ever since I got into the business.'

'So you and he never . . .' I stopped. Did I even want to know the answer to that?

Esme laughed. 'Don't be daft, Leanne. I told you, we're friends.'

She put down my empty plate and brushed a crumb from the front of her jumper. It looked expensive. Cashmere, a beautiful shade of pea green. Everything Esme wore seemed designed especially for her. It was a spell she cast, not just over people, but clothes too.

'Actually, you're not the only one whose love life sucks right now.' She licked chocolate from her top teeth.

'How do you mean?'

'Oh, Nelson and I have had a huge blow-up. Got to the point where I even threatened to move out.'

'Why?' I gazed at Esme with concern. I thought she and Nelson were rock solid. Christ, they'd only been engaged a few months.

But inside, I'll admit to a small flicker of pleasure, ignited by this crack in their relationship. A little tarnish on their perfect veneer. It made me feel less inadequate somehow.

'Someone told him I was on the books with Star Turn.'

I frowned. 'Who are they?'

Esme inspected the floor, bending to run a finger along the groove of the parquet. 'They, well . . . you know . . . set people up with clients who want to meet a porn star.'

My frown deepened. 'Meet as in *screw*, you mean?'

Esme's mouth curled a little, but she didn't deny it. 'Yeah, OK, I used to do privates – now and then when I was starting out.' She held up a hand, as if warding off something I might say or think. 'It was mostly before I met Nelson. I needed the money, had run up a load of debt on my credit cards. But I forgot to tell the agency to take me off their books and so my name and picture are still on the website. Nelson found out and went ballistic.'

Jesus, Esme did *privates*? I tried not to look shocked. I mean, I knew lots of porn girls did a bit of escorting on the side – it was hardly a secret – but somehow I'd never imagined Esme resorting to anything like that. Was that why she'd reacted so badly to that girl Marcie at the club in Brighton?

'But then, fuck, Nelson's in no position to criticize,' Esme sniffed. 'He's still on the books with a couple of agencies.'

'He is?' I felt my eyebrows lift again. 'But don't you—?'

'Don't I what, Leanne? Nelson fucks women for a living; what do I care whether Pulsar pay him or some desperate middle-aged socialite?'

'Right.' I could see her point. Maybe.

She glanced out the window again, before turning back to me. 'Leanne, can I tell you something?'

'Sure,' I said. 'What?'

She examined her fingernails, painted in high-shine pale lilac polish. 'I'm thinking of getting out. Of the business, I mean.'

My stomach grew heavy, like I'd eaten the whole cake. 'Get out? Esme, *why*? You're doing so well.'

Esme chewed her bottom lip. 'It's more Nelson. He wants me to jack it in. He's freaked out by what happened to Anya. Says it's not worth the risk and we can live on his income.'

I frowned again. 'But we don't know if her death had anything to do with porn, do we? I mean, it could have been anyone. Her boyfriend. Some random pervert.'

'Yeah,' Esme sighed. 'I've told him that, but he's still worried.'

168

'It's not like you're taking risks, though, is it? You work for Pulsar, with other actors and a crew. What could possibly happen with all those people around?'

'You try telling Nelson that. He's convinced Anya's not the first. Keeps going on about Gabriela disappearing. And other girls.'

'Other girls?'

'Yeah. There's been a few, especially Eastern Europeans. They do a couple of shoots then simply vanish. No one ever hears from them again.'

I thought this over for a minute or two. 'But that doesn't mean anything, does it? They probably went home.'

'I know. I keep telling Nelson that, but once he has something in his head you'd need a bloody crowbar to shift it.' Esme looked tired, the skin around her eyes taut and shiny. Like she'd been up all night arguing.

'What are you going to do?' I asked. 'You're not really leaving, are you? Would Pulsar even release you from your contract?'

Esme shrugged again. 'Nelson can sort that.'

She pulled a tissue from her bag, wiped her fingers. 'It's not just what happened to Anya. I'm always ill, always picking up some cold or bug from the other talent. And I'm lousy in bed – too tired and sore to make an effort. I get home and the last thing I want is to act the porn star in my own bedroom. I'm usually desperate to go to sleep.'

'Surely Nelson feels the same way? He must be knackered too.'

Esme snorted. 'Nelson is a bloody machine, Leanne. Seriously. He's like the Duracell bunny – he can fuck for ever.' She turned down the corners of her mouth. 'He says I'm lazy, and he's started getting jealous of the other guys on shoots. But it's only work, for Christ's sake.'

'Always?' I narrowed my eyes. 'Do you never enjoy it?'

Her mouth twists into a smile. 'Sure, OK. Sometimes. You know how it is, occasionally you're in the horny part of your cycle and you get into it. But it's mechanical, isn't it? Like someone pressing the right buttons. Doesn't mean a thing.'

But there was a tinge of red on her cheeks. As if there was something she wasn't telling me.

'So what are you going to do?' I asked.

Esme flopped back, shutting her eyes. 'Fuck knows, Leanne. I keep hoping if I ignore it, he'll stop. Then other times, when I've had a rough day on set, I start thinking perhaps he's right.'

I tried to come up with something reassuring to say, but the truth was I was shaken. I thought of what Vicky said on that farm shoot, about Esme and Nelson being the exception. If they couldn't make things work, what hope was there for the rest of us?

'Hey.' Esme opened her eyes again and started to giggle. 'You won't believe what happened last week. Remember that gig I did in that abandoned church? Jason Rutter was supposed to co-star, but he got sick at the last minute, so Gus called some other guy he knew.'

She laughed, clearly picturing it in her head. 'This bloke turns up absolutely plastered in fake tan – you could smell it on him, you know, sweet like honey. But he'd forgotten to reach between his buttocks. I could hear Mark and Joe sniggering when he was on top, then they showed me the footage afterwards.'

Esme was crying with laughter now, dabbing her eyes with the tips of her fingers. 'All you could see was this white crack down the length of his arse, and a pair of orange balls dangling underneath. They had to chuck the whole scene.'

I grinned, despite another pang at the mention of your name. 'Priceless.'

Esme got to her feet. 'I need a pee,' she said suddenly, disappearing into the bathroom. I took the plates and the rest of the cake into the kitchen, wondering whether I could freeze it. No way I'd ever eat all this on my own.

Then I heard it. The sound of retching, followed by the flush of the loo.

'Did you just throw up?' I asked the moment Esme reappeared.

She looked a bit startled. 'Um . . . yeah.'

'Deliberately?'

'What's the big deal? I only do it now and then, Leanne. Half the girls I know are at it – or live on laxatives and coke.' She walked up and squeezed my waist. 'We're not all skinny little minxes like you. Some of us have bigger bones – we have to be more careful.'

'Jesus, Esme, who tells you this shit? Nelson?'

Esme pulled a face. 'I watched the scene I did on that Paris shoot. You could see my stomach bulging as I was blowing this guy.'

'Your stomach is completely flat,' I said, but Esme ignored me.

'The camera adds pounds, darling. You end up looking like a blob even if you're super skinny.'

I was about to protest when Esme's phone broke into a jingle. She pulled it from her bag and read the text. Her mouth dropped open, forming a large O of surprise.

She turned to me, eyes huge.

'Oh. My. GOD!'

'What?' I asked. 'What is it?' For a second I thought

something terrible had happened. That she'd been sacked, or Nelson had been run over by a bus.

'It's an email. From Jane, the booker at Pulsar.' Esme made a 'squeee!' sound, jumping up and down while clutching her phone. 'She says we're both nominated in the AVNs!'

My jaw dropped too. The Adult Video News awards. The Oscars of the porn industry.

'Both of us?' I asked, incredulous.

'*Both of us,*' shrieked Esme, grabbing my arm. 'Me for best oral sex scene, and you for most promising newcomer.'

Now it was my turn to look amazed. 'You're shitting me.'

'I most certainly am not.' She was grinning so hard it must have hurt. 'Pulsar will be totally psyched!'

Esme pulled me into a hug. 'Christ, Leanne, that's really good, honey. Best newcomer – win that and it'll take your career to a whole new level – more money, you can call the shots about the stuff you do. Merchandise. The works.'

I studied her. I could tell she was genuinely thrilled – for me as well as herself.

'I can't believe it.' Esme clutched my arm again, punching the air with her free hand. 'We're going to Vegas, baby. We're off to Sin fucking City!'

And I felt myself grinning too, gripped by happiness and excitement, carried along with the moment. The three of us, off on a big adventure.

No idea then, of course, that only two would ever make it home.

21

Heathrow Airport, London

Tuesday, 3 January 2006

'High five!' squealed Esme as we made our way into the first-class lounge. 'What did I tell you, Leanne?' She grabbed Nelson and gave him a big fat kiss. 'You're the best.'

Nelson beamed. *'De nada, señoritas.'*

In truth his performance should have been up for its own award. How he'd talked that snooty cow on the check-in desk into upgrading us from business class to first was definitely worthy of one.

'You wait till he hits the cabin crew.' Esme leaned into me, laughing. 'Last flight he had them eating out of his hand.'

'The male crew or female?' I quipped.

'Duh,' said Nelson. 'Both.'

I grinned, letting Esme drag me off to the loos, even though her bouncy, too loud, too excited routine was already wearing thin. My nerves over this whole trip were building to a crescendo, and I had no energy for Esme in one of her manic moods.

'Christ, I could really do with a line.' She sighed,

pouting at her reflection in the mirror. 'Do you think any of the crew bring stuff on board?'

'Not if they want to keep their jobs.'

'Gawd,' she huffed. 'Flying's no fun if you have to do it straight.'

I looked at her. How much was Esme taking these days? Over the last few months her habit seemed to be sliding from normal-for-porn to borderline problem.

And she looked thinner, too, must have dropped half a stone since I caught her throwing up in my loo. Though I'd not seen her do it again, even during the boozy, bingey Christmas I'd spent at their place ten days ago. Perhaps she'd had the sense to pack it in.

'I guess I'll have to wait till we get to LA.' Esme wiped a smudge of foundation from under her chin. 'Nelson will know who to call.'

Back in the airport lounge, we found him reading a broadsheet newspaper, a cup of black coffee in his other hand. Esme frowned. Like most of us, Nelson hardly bothered with current affairs. We were outsiders – what did it matter what was going on with the rest of the world?

'Camouflage,' he explained as we sat down. 'Check them out. Three o'clock.' He nodded discreetly towards the corner of the room. I glanced over casually, but Esme spun round and stared.

'Shit!' she mouthed, twisting back to Nelson. 'It's Ruella and Martin!'

The co-stars of a recent big-budget Hollywood movie. Unmistakably them.

'Crap film,' Nelson declared, then started browsing the sports pages. Esme and I ogled the movie stars and their entourage until our flight was called. For me at least, it helped take my mind off what was coming.

So it wasn't until we were seated on the plane that I began to fall apart.

'What's up?' mouthed Esme, from across the aisle. I was next to a middle-aged man in a sharp suit who looked me over as I took my seat. The movie star couple were near the front, ignoring everyone.

'Nothing.' I made myself smile. I didn't want to admit I'd never flown before. It seemed ridiculous, in this day and age. Embarrassing.

A pretty air hostess, wearing more make-up than I ever had on set, offered me a glass of champagne. I was too wired to enjoy it, so sat there, seat belt tight round my waist, watching the tiny bubbles rise in columns as the plane jerked, then advanced towards the runway.

The noise was unnerving, a mounting engine throb that sounded like it was building to an explosion. As we taxied into position, there was a pause, then a high-pitched hysterical mechanical whine as we began to pick up speed. I felt my body grow heavy as we rushed forward, the scream of the engines growing louder. I watched the ground through the little porthole window, blurring past, faster and faster. Then, with a barely perceptible lurch, we left it behind.

My stomach cartwheeled.

We were lifting into the air.

Impossible.

I clutched the armrest. Oh, Jesus. We were rising into the sky, everything turning to toy town below. All of a sudden the plane tilted, and I let out an involuntary yelp of terror.

'You OK?' asked the man beside me.

I gazed at him, wild-eyed with panic. 'Never done this before,' I admitted.

He stared back. 'You're kidding, right?'

175

'Nope. Just never happened.'

After my father left, there hadn't been enough spare cash to fly us anywhere. While other kids holidayed in Spain or Florida, Mum and I drove to Paignton or Tenby. When Mike joined us, the twins arrived soon after, so the closest I ever came to a plane was driving past Heathrow on the way to somewhere wet and windy.

I peered out the porthole again. Clouds had engulfed the view. We were climbing through what felt like heavy fog. Then suddenly, miraculously, we broke through, and the dull grey day turned blue.

I almost gasped with the wonder of it. I'd never realized, would never have guessed that up here was another world. A brighter, bluer, sunnier world, like something out of the twins' old picture books.

A chime as the seat-belt signs went off, then the stewardess reappeared and offered us another drink.

'Go on,' said my neighbour. 'You look as if you need it.'

I turned, took him in properly. About forty, clean-shaven. Nice-looking too.

'David.' He held out a hand for me to shake. 'What should I call you?'

I hesitated. 'Leanne.'

David examined my face for a moment. 'That's strange.' He screwed the corner of his mouth into a smile. 'I could have sworn your name was Kitty.'

I felt myself blush. I hated it when people recognized me. Esme was always flattered, but it left me feeling exposed, like there was nowhere I could hide.

'Don't worry.' David angled his head towards me. 'I'm not a stalker or anything. I used to do some production work for Nebula.' Nebula was Pulsar's main

176

British rival, specializing in fetish and BDSM. 'So I guess you're flying out for the AVNs?'

I nodded. 'I'm up for an award, actually. Best newcomer.'

He gave me an appraising look. 'Hey, that's tremendous. You'll have a great time. I went once, the whole thing is completely insane.'

I knocked back half of my champagne and allowed myself to relax a little. The engine noise had waned, the plane horizontal now, and steadier.

'You know, I've watched a couple of your films,' David said. 'You're a natural. You should think about branching out.'

'Into what?'

'Get yourself a decent website for a start. Set up your own brand.'

I wrinkled my nose. Only the very top girls got to do that; I definitely wasn't there yet.

But you're a contract girl now, I reminded myself. Maybe I should give it some serious thought. Speak to Darryll.

David beckoned over the stewardess and ordered more drinks. 'We'll probably regret it,' he whispered conspiratorially, 'but what the hell. It's not every day I get to fly with a veritable movie star.'

I narrowed my eyes. 'You taking the piss?'

David laughed, then nodded towards the Hollywood couple. 'Take it from me, Leanne – you look a whole lot better naked than she does.'

Two hours in. I was half watching a film about an alien invasion, half looking out the window – though there seemed nothing below us now but endless sea. The Atlantic, I supposed.

Nelson was playing a video game, Esme dozing beside him, seat reclined. Next to me David was reading a newspaper and as he turned the page something caught my eye. A picture of a girl with light brown hair and a serious expression, as if posing for a passport photo. But it was the headline that snagged my attention.

SECOND BODY FOUND ON LANDFILL

I shifted in my seat so I could read the lines below, my sense of unease increasing as I scanned the words.

Waste management staff at a landfill site in Essex discovered the body of a young woman last Friday. The Metropolitan police have identified the victim as Tula Kask, a 21-year-old Hungarian who worked in various Soho strip clubs, as well as performing in low-budget adult films. She was reported missing two weeks ago by a flatmate.

Four months ago Latvian porn star Anya Viksna (above) was found in another landfill in Kent. It's not yet known if this second victim had any connection to Viksna, whose parents alerted the police after their daughter failed to keep up regular contact.

David caught my eye. 'Gruesome, huh?'

I swallowed. Read the article again, remembering that conversation with Esme. Nelson's conviction that there'd been others. 'You think there's a connection?' I asked.

'Between this girl and Anya Viksna? Seems likely, doesn't it?'

'But why would someone kill them? Because of the

porn?' I felt my stomach contract. A precarious feeling that wasn't simply about being suspended high in the sky in a long metal tube.

'Who knows?' he said. 'Might be. Or it could be money. Lots of girls run up debts in this business, despite earning a lot by most people's standards. They take out a dodgy loan and can't pay it back. Some girls are trafficked, especially those from Eastern Europe – forced to shoot porn and hand their earnings to whatever gang brought them over.'

I frowned. 'Why don't they run away?'

'I guess these gangs must have some kind of hold over them. Debt, maybe, or possibly they threaten the girl's family.' He closed the paper. 'I don't know, I'm only speculating. I'm not saying Anya was trafficked or anything, but she struck me as someone with a lot of weight on her shoulders.'

I thought about this for a while, feeling tired and scared. All of a sudden I wanted to go home, back to my flat, crawl into bed.

There but for the grace of God . . .

'You know,' David pointed to the picture of Anya, 'she looks a lot like you.'

I didn't respond. It seemed a pretty tactless thing to say, though Victor had mentioned it too and even I could see the resemblance.

I shivered, trying to chase off how that made me feel.

'Did you know her?' David asked.

'Anya?' I shook my head. I didn't mention I'd been brought in to replace her on that very first shoot with Pulsar. The connection still troubled me, an invisible line in fate that felt like a jinx.

'I met her several times. She did a few scenes for

Nebula, came out for a drink afterwards. She was a cool girl, very bright and very kinky. It's a fucking shame.'

I didn't comment. What could I say? She'd been murdered by someone who might well be targeting porno girls.

That seemed a whole lot more than a fucking shame.

'Anyway, let's forget this morbid stuff.' David signalled to the stewardess, requesting two more glasses of champagne. Though I was hardly in the mood now for bubbly, I needed the alcohol, so downed it in a couple of gulps.

'So how about it?' he asked, turning to face me with a roguish expression. 'Be quite something to join the mile high club on your first flight.'

'The what?'

'Mile high club – you know, screwing at thirty thousand feet. Not got that on your bucket list?'

'Is that how high we are?' I felt an aftershock of vertigo. Like I'd forgotten to be scared.

David leaned towards me. 'I'll make it worth your while,' he whispered.

My first instinct was to tell him to piss off. Then I thought twice. I could do with something to take my mind off the flight, off those girls, and whoever had dumped their bodies like that.

Like they were garbage. Just so much rubbish.

I eyed him. 'How much?'

'Two k.'

'Two thousand pounds?' I tried to keep the surprise from my voice. Was he serious?

'Dollars,' David added, a tad too quickly.

Still, two thousand dollars for a quick fuck. Why not? I asked myself, remembering Esme's own revelation about privates. Then I thought about you. What if you found out?

But why would you? And so what if you did – it wasn't like there was anything between us.

Not to mention this guy was clearly well connected – keeping him sweet might pay even larger dividends than two grand.

'OK.' I swallowed. 'Where?'

David winked as he got up from his seat. 'Don't worry. I'll sort it.'

Five minutes later he returned, beckoning me to follow. We squeezed ourselves into the tiny airplane loo, David locking the door behind us.

'Won't the cabin crew know we're in here?' I asked.

'I've offered them a little something to turn a blind eye.'

He tilted his head and kissed me, pushing me against the washbasin. With two of us crammed in such a small space, there was barely room to move – it was worse than the cab of that combine harvester.

David, however, was undeterred. His hand dived under my skirt and straight into my knickers, while the other unbuttoned my blouse. He pulled aside my bra from one breast, planting his mouth on my nipple. I could feel his erection pressing against my leg.

'Kitty,' he breathed, moving his lips back to my face. 'You're so gorgeous. I can't believe I get to do this.'

Unzipping his trousers, he let them drop to his ankles, hoisting me on to the washbasin. It was really uncomfortable, but I had a feeling I wouldn't have to endure it for long.

A second later he was inside me. Another second after that I remembered he wasn't wearing a condom.

Shit. He could have anything.

181

'Pull out.' I tried to push him away. 'I'm not on the pill.' A lie and a crap excuse, but all I could think of without insulting him.

'Don't worry,' David murmured into my ear. He thrust a few more times, then withdrew. Pulling me back off the basin, he pushed me to my knees, his erection slapping my cheek.

I closed my eyes, took him into my mouth. He was small – at least by porn standards – so it wasn't difficult, but I had to suppress an upsurge of disgust. What the fuck was I doing?

How had it ever come to this?

'Jesus,' David groaned, thrusting deeper. 'Kitty . . .'

I thought of you. I didn't want to, it only made me feel worse, but I thought of you and how much I'd rather it was us doing this, a mile in the sky. I thought of you and suddenly it was all I could do not to cry.

A minute later, David shuddered. Semen, hot and sour flooded my tongue. I swallowed quickly, then got to my feet, washing out my mouth with a scoop of water from the tap.

I rested against the sink, my back to David, averting my eyes from my own reflection. We stood like that for a minute or so, both breathing heavily, then I bent to retrieve my knickers, smoothing my skirt before I faced him.

'Here.' David removed his wallet and counted off a wad of one-hundred-dollar bills.

I stared down at them. 'Forget it.'

'On the house?' His smile was wide. Like I'd told him I'd loved every moment.

'Put it down to a mistake.'

I let myself out of the loo. Esme gave me a quizzical look as I returned to my seat, while Nelson flashed me a thumbs-up. I found the blackout mask in my welcome pack and dipped into my bag for the sleeping pills Esme had given me for jet lag. Taking two, I put on the earphones to drown out everything around me.

I didn't wake until the wheels of the plane touched down in LA.

22

Los Angeles

Wednesday, 4 January 2006

A buzz, somewhere at the edge of my mind. Loud and insistent, breaking through my dreams.

My phone.

'Leanne.' Nelson's voice on the other end of the line. '*Leanne.* Open the fucking door.'

I stumbled across the room and flung it wide. Flopped back on to the bed.

'Leanne, come on.' Someone shaking me. I prised my eyes open again, the lids fat and heavy.

'Wake up!' Nelson's face hovering over mine. 'You've got to get up.'

He was standing next to me, dressed in slouchy jeans and a skinny T-shirt. 'Esme's sick,' he said. 'You have to go and do her scene for her. Stratos need you at the studio in half an hour.'

I groaned. Bits of memory shifted and slotted into place. Plane. Hotel. Walking along the street somewhere in Los Angeles – *La la land!* – feeling cold because it hadn't occurred to me that it wouldn't be warm here in January and I'd left my jacket in my room. Tequila in a bar somewhere near Venice Beach. The three of us laughing and laughing after we ate those marijuana cookies we picked up at a dispensary.

'Legal dope!' Esme kept scream—

'Leanne!' Nelson was shaking me again. 'Come on, babe. You have to go do the scene. Esme's completely out of it.'

Me too, I thought, swallowing down a flash of resentment and groping my way from under the duvet. My head felt muggy and floaty, my stomach hot. I stood up, the room spinning, my limbs draggy and limp.

'Where is she?' I mumbled.

'Sleeping it off.'

'She all right?' My voice slurry, full of lag.

Nelson shrugged. 'I guess it all caught up with her. You know Esme – candle, both ends.' He went into the bathroom and turned on the shower. Steered me into it, handing me a razor from my wash bag. 'C'mon. They've got a car waiting downstairs.'

I pulled my mind into focus. Quickly washed and conditioned my hair. Balancing on one leg, ran the razor over my labia. Thank God I'd done this so many times, could do it with my eyes shut, could do it in my sleep.

Fucking Esme.

Wrapping my head in a towel, I found fresh clothes in my suitcase. Would they have stuff I could wear at the studio? I had no idea. I grabbed my carry-on bag and shoved in a pair of heels and a dress. Picked out my best underwear and pulled it on. Dragged jeans and a T-shirt over the top and slipped on my boots, making it down to the lobby in ten minutes flat.

Thankfully the journey to the studio took nearly half an hour, giving my hair time to dry in the warmth of

185

the car. The driver had the radio on, country music playing, a song about a woman with a broken heart. They're always about a woman with a broken heart, I thought, remembering you.

I was thirsty and hungry. I felt hollow and sick, my blood sugar hitting empty. I prayed there'd be something to eat at the studio.

But when I arrived, there was nothing. Just a glass of water, grabbed from a cooler, before I was whisked straight into make-up. I felt sorry for the girl doing my hair. Even in the hung-over, jet-lagged core of me I could see it was a mess. My face looked thin and sallow, and there were dark circles under my eyes even youth couldn't hide.

A runner came in with a clipboard to check how much longer I'd be. 'Any chance of something to eat?' I croaked as she turned to go, and she gave me a look that said everything and nothing, returning five minutes later with a banana, an apple and a small pack of sushi.

I gulped down the fruit. As the girl ironed my hair straight, I tried the sushi. It tasted like the sea. And I remembered the Pacific Ocean was here, close, and promised myself I'd go before we left – last night we'd got no further than the bars along the promenade. I'd find the beach and lie on the sand – sod the fact that it was winter – and I'd close my eyes and listen to the sound of the waves, and let everything be very, very far away.

'Kitty Sweet?'

A plump woman was standing in front of me. At least forty. Pissed-off looking.

'Make-up,' she said, taking me into a neighbouring room, where she sat me in the chair and gave me a once-over, her mouth a tight line of disapproval. 'You girls,' she muttered, in an accent I couldn't pin down. 'Why do you do this to yourselves?'

'Sorry?' I blinked as she picked up a tube of foundation and smoothed it over my skin.

She scowled back at me. 'Playing Russian roulette with your whole future. Has it ever occurred to you that your life isn't simply going to end at thirty?'

I wasn't sure if she actually wanted an answer. It seemed more like a speech, something she'd been bottling up, rather than anything to do with me, but it reminded me of those girls. Their discarded bodies.

Something I'd been trying to forget since I arrived here. Was that what we were all doing now? I wondered. Playing Russian roulette? Waiting for someone to pick us off and throw us away?

I shut my eyes, forcing it out of my head.

'What are you going to do when this is all over, huh?' the woman's voice continued as she smoothed eye shadow across my lids. 'When you're washed up in a couple of years?'

I opened my eyes and stared at her open-mouthed, some part of my brain finally sobering up. Was she really allowed to say this stuff?

The make-up artist glared back, her gaze hard. 'You know, I have a daughter your age – I pray to God she never ends up like you.' She looked like a woman on the edge, someone unable to keep her mouth shut any longer.

It occurred to me to reach out and slap her. Instead, I clenched my jaw, hard.

No way I needed this shit right now.

'You're finished,' she said after a few more minutes, and for a moment I thought she was still telling me off, but as I opened my mouth to protest I realized she meant I was ready. This was obviously the express make-over.

I glanced at my reflection. I'd pass. Just.

I followed her directions to the set. Got the paperwork out of the way, then the director – a crazy-looking dude in a cowboy hat and Pimpster T-shirt – introduced me to my co-star: Rhett LaStade, tall and tan and completely hairless, a supersized Action Man doll.

Not that I gave a shit what he looked like, as long as he didn't smell or have a bad attitude. Or turn arsy if he couldn't get wood. I prayed he didn't eat the kind of junk diet that made his spunk taste foul – the food I'd swallowed felt precarious in my stomach, like it might resurface at any moment.

All I wanted was for this to be over so I could crawl into bed and sink back into oblivion.

'Hi, Kitty.'

I turned to see another guy – older, craggier, with a near-white goatee and long grey sideburns. I'd assumed he was one of the crew.

'Psyched when I heard I was doing a scene with you,' he said. 'Loved that whole farm gig you did.'

Oh fuck, *two men*? Nelson hadn't mentioned anything about that. Normally I wouldn't mind, but right now I barely had the energy for one.

'Call me Daddy.' The old guy offered me a lopsided smile as he stuck out his hand.

Daddy? My head reeled. I stared back at him, feeling giddy, then reminded myself this was America, and there was no trace of England in his accent.

'You OK, Kitty?' The director was eyeing me dubiously. 'You seem kind of wasted.'

'Jet lag,' I mumbled. 'I'll be fine.'

The director looked unconvinced. I closed my eyes again, trying to stop the room from spinning.

'Right,' I heard him say. 'We'll do a soft, then stills, then hard, three positions, pop shots, then it's a wrap and we're out.'

What that added up to was a lot of fucking. *A lot.* When we reached the hardcore, Action Man and Daddy worked me over like a rag doll, passing me backwards and forwards between them. It got so I was hardly aware which one was inside me – though often it was both.

'You good for DA?' the director asked, after a break to retouch my make-up and administer more lube. I felt close to tears. We'd been at it for over two hours; all I wanted in the world was to get back to the hotel and my king-size bed.

I nodded, unsure what he meant but desperately wanting it over. Action Man lay down on the divan, pulling me beside him. I put my hand on his leg to steady myself and it felt like wax, smoother even than mine.

Revolting.

Too late, those initials finally made sense in my head. DA. Double anal.

Too late to object.

Too late to take any painkillers.

And it seemed to go on for ever, Action Man grunting, sweat forming a sheen over the shaven skin of his chest. I closed my eyes again. One more minute, I told myself. One more minute and I'd say I'd had enough.

Screw their footage.

'C'mon, Kitty,' the director coaxed. 'Show us how much you're enjoying this.'

If I could have reached, I would have hit him. Or spat in his face. I clenched my fists harder, trying to distract myself from the pain.

Fucking Esme.

Fucking, fucking, fucking Esme.

And Nelson too. Did he know, I wondered? Did he know what they wanted for this scene? Did Esme simply bottle out?

I'd murder them both when I got back.

I turned my mind to you, letting your face fill the space behind my eyelids. 'You can get through this, Leanne,' you said. I thought of England, and you in it, and suddenly I was crying.

'For fuck's sake,' I heard the director mutter. 'Keep her head out of shot.'

But it was hopeless. I was sobbing. Great choking gasps that made my whole body tremble. 'Cut,' the director called in a weary voice.

Both men pulled out at once. I rolled off Action Man and leaned over the side of the divan, throwing up the food I'd eaten earlier.

'Jesus,' swore Daddy, swiping something off his leg. 'Stupid fucking bitch.'

I got to my feet and grabbed the white dressing gown the runner was offering me. I could see something in her eyes. Horror or sympathy – it was hard to tell. I snatched up my bag, stumbled towards the toilets. Crouching in the stall, I threw up again into the toilet bowl.

As I flushed the loo, leaning my head on my arm, I saw it. What that runner probably noticed back then.

I was bleeding. Not like before, when I came on during my first ever shoot. This was bright red and fresh, running down my thigh. As the nausea passed, the pain took over. I felt suddenly woozy, like I was about to pass out.

I sat on the loo seat and rooted through my bag till I found my mobile and called Nelson.

'Leanne?'

I couldn't formulate the words, was crying again, into the phone.

'I'll come and get you,' he said, without hesitation. 'Hold on tight.'

I stayed there, in the stall, till Nelson arrived and got the crew to rustle up some painkillers. They must have been strong, because I fell asleep in the taxi on the way back to the hotel, a sanitary towel wedged in my knickers to soak up the blood.

23

HMP Brakehurst

Tuesday, 15 March 2016

'Why, Leanne? Why did you go through with it?'

An obvious question. I've been waiting for Yvonne to ask it ever since the session started. She's got her palm pressed against the pages where I wrote it all down, what happened in America.

She looks visibly upset, though God knows I spared her most of the gory details.

'What choice did I have?' I shrug. 'You walk off set, especially when you're under contract, and it's game over.'

'But you weren't under contract, were you, for this scene?' Yvonne counters. You were a substitute for Esme.'

Fair point. The truth is it seemed easier to go along with it. All the way down the line, that was my problem. Always too compliant, willing to go with the flow.

'No one likes porn girls who whine and complain, or act like divas,' I say in my defence.

Yvonne frowns. 'I hardly think you'd be seen as a diva for not agreeing to something like that?'

You reckon? I smile back at her, but it's laced with

frustration. What the fuck does she know? Most women go through their lives in a bubble of respectability, with no clue what it's like to be on the other side.

'There's a reason we're paid a lot of money,' I explain. 'It's to put up and shut up.'

Yvonne purses her lips but doesn't comment. 'Did Nelson know?' she asks instead. 'Did he realize what he was getting you into?'

I don't reply. That's the million-dollar question, isn't it?

For which I have no answer.

'Did you ask him?' presses Yvonne.

Nelson's expression floats into my head, when I tackled him in the taxi back to the hotel. The earnest way he looked at me, his forehead furrowed with concern. 'Honestly, babe, I had no idea.'

But there was something too practised, too sincere in his denial.

'Leanne?'

I gaze at Yvonne, my expression blank. Giving nothing away.

She stares me out for a moment, then changes tack. 'How do you feel about it now, Leanne. Would you say this was a turning point in your life?'

A turning point.

I guess she's right. It was, in so many ways. The beginning of the end.

I can see that now, see from that moment, everything was blighted. Trashed.

That there was simply no way back.

24

Las Vegas

Friday, 6 January 2006

I have no fucking idea what we're doing here.

It's warm in the winter sunshine, and we're stumbling along the Vegas street, literally *in* the street, because there's no pavement – or *sidewalk* as Nelson reminds me – and there's the roar of traffic and a car hooting and someone jeering at us and Esme is sitting down, on the sidewalk that isn't there, only baked mud and weeds and bits of litter, and Nelson picks her up and carries her into the bar.

Good girls go to heaven and bad girls go everywhere. Did I read that? Or just invent it?

And I still have no idea what we're doing here, in this bar, in this country that feels familiar and yet so strange. So I go for a wee and my pupils are huge in the mirror, puppy eyes, big and brown, and the lights are blurry and I can't focus properly. But I'm still bleeding, the pad in my knickers red with it – like a period now – and I wonder if I could use a tampon instead, then I'm thinking I should see a fucking doctor and *do I even have health insurance* and how come Esme and Nelson don't seem to give a shit, but then I'm back sitting at the bar with the pair of them and I forget all about it. We're in a bar in Vegas and we're talking to some dude who says he's an actor and so are we – *ha ha!* – and we tell him the names of some of our films and he laughs so hard he nearly falls off his stool, but he comes with us, he drives us, we're in his car and it's a proper *Mustang* and we're speeding across the desert – *look, cacti!* – and then we're in the chapel, only it's not a real chapel, it's all white and gold and tacky and I remember then forget then remember again why we're here.

Esme and Nelson are getting married!

But Esme is off her face and I'm finally sobering up a bit and she's laughing and I've got the ring and I'm beginning to think this is a bad idea – shouldn't we talk about it first? – but Steve, that's the guy's name, the actor, had a small part in a Ben Affleck film, Steve says this is *fucking fabulous*, so I'm clutching the ring Nelson picked up in that giant mall – a *huge* platinum ring with a string of little stones – *rhinestones?* I've got the ring, though Steve should have it because he's the best man, so I give it to him and they get married, Esme in the beach dress she bought – yesterday? – and Nelson in shorts and a Hawaiian shirt but of course they both look *fucking amazing* and Steve laughs and slaps them on the shoulder and we drive back to the city and go to a casino and Nelson blows a thousand *bucks* rolling dice and then we're in another bar and Steve's talking to me and he's got his hand on my bum and I'm feeling very tired and like *I want to go home*, only we're so far away, like a million miles away, light years away, and then we're in the flat Pulsar rented for us, this amazing high-rise *apartment* with a view right over the Strip where all the crazy lights are flashing and we do some more lines – *where did Steve get all these drugs?* – and then we go to bed and we fuck. Me and Steve and Esme and Nelson, like a game of *Twister with cocks*, the four of us in every possible combination, except not my arse – no way is anyone touching my arse – and Steve says we're *awesome* but all I can think is *this is completely fucked up* and I'm crying again and Steve hands me another pill and suddenly I'm gone.

25

Sands Expo and
Convention Center, Las Vegas

Saturday, 7 January 2006

My feet were killing me.

I'd been standing there, in six-inch platform stilettos, for over five hours and still the Expo Center in Las Vegas was heaving. *Heaving.*

I'd never seen anything like it. The place was cavernous, and full of bars. People were staggering around drunk. House music boomed from the speakers, while above our heads hung enormous promotional posters for the various studios.

The girls here were unreal. Giant Barbies with pneumatic boobs and overblown lips, dressed in tiny skirts or skimpy bikinis, teetering in impossible heels made of transparent plastic, taking slutty to a whole new level. Acting like they loved each other, grabbing each other's arses and touching tongues, talking in their annoying whiny voices.

Always, always performing.

'Zero talent, no taste, no style, no sophistication,' muttered Esme wearily, eyeing yet another girl pouting and posing to the flash of cameras. 'Christ, it'd be more interesting screwing an inflatable doll.'

She sat down and slipped off her sandals, rubbing the balls of her feet. Esme wasn't wearing her wedding ring, I noticed, and only a thick layer of make-up masked her hangover. So far, she hadn't even mentioned last night. The ceremony. The foursome in the apartment.

'Honestly this place is taking years off my life,' Esme complained, her voice rough from talking to fans and inhaling the recycled air in the Expo Center. 'It's a fucking temple to fakery. Christ only knows how anyone could find this erotic.'

She flashed a smile at another man approaching our booth, signed a photo, practically shoving it back at him. 'You should take a walk around,' she said to me. 'It's mental. There's a girl in the next aisle charging five bucks for a feel of her boobs – right by a studio specializing in Japanese *eel fucking*.' Esme pulled a disgusted face. 'I swear to God I never want to have sex again.'

'No thanks,' I laughed. 'I'm staying put. I had three blokes try to grab my tits on the way to the loo – the security guards had to drag one of them off.'

I straightened my pile of eight-by-ten-inch glossy photos, showing me in what was rapidly becoming my signature pose – finger in mouth, with bunches each side of my head and huge geek girl glasses. My fans couldn't get enough of them.

Fans. I still wasn't used to the idea that I had any. Since Darryll stuck my profile on his website I'd had a bunch of weird emails and comments – most too random or filthy to bother with – but I'd never thought of them as actual people. Especially as no one ever used their real names.

198

But here I was – and here they were. Men in all shapes and sizes and ages. Some seizing my hand and shaking it, gazing into my eyes like they'd lost something precious and hoped to find it there. Others shy, more withdrawn; taking the photo I'd signed and turning away.

And not all of them were men. A woman approached the Pulsar booth, middle-aged, worn-looking, with a girl beside her wearing hooker heels and a cropped T-shirt that left nothing to the imagination. She didn't look a day over sixteen.

'Kitty!' The girl's eyes widened and she hugged me like a long-lost friend. Then hung on to my hand, staring at me like I was something new and amazing.

'Susie's your biggest fan,' the woman said. 'She's been just dying to meet you – been talking about nothing else for days.' She held out a mottled hand for me to shake. 'I'm Yolanda. Susie's manager.'

'Actually she's my mom,' Susie giggled, still ogling me. 'But she's my manager too. She wants to be in charge of my career . . . y'know, make sure I don't get exploited or whatever.'

I gazed back at them with something like horror on my face, but neither seemed to notice. 'That's really nice,' I said, as behind them a guy caught my eye and smirked. I signed a photograph and handed it to Susie. 'Good luck!'

The man pushed forward and reluctantly they conceded their place. 'Name's James,' he said, in an accent I guessed was Texan – mainly because he was wearing a huge cowboy hat. 'Your number one fan.'

'Apart from them,' I quipped, nodding at the departing duo.

'Yeah, that's sure messed up,' he grinned, picking up a picture for me to sign.

To James, I wrote, *with love, Kitty*, putting a heart over the 'i' the way we used to in school. Because half an hour in this place and you understood that being a porno girl meant acting like an overdeveloped, not-very-bright child.

'Cute,' said James, refusing to budge from the front of what was becoming a small queue. 'Actually, Kitty, I was wondering if you'd like to hang out tonight?'

'Sorry.' I simulated a smile. 'I'm completely tied up.'

'How about Skype, then?'

'It's against my contract,' I lied. Christ, the guys here were creeps. They made my fucking skin crawl.

James treated me to a last lingering look then gave up, wandering across to the toy stall opposite, featuring the largest selection of silicon genitals I'd ever seen. Vibrators and dildos in every colour, size, shape and material you could possibly imagine – and plenty you couldn't.

'See her?' Esme asked when we'd finally got rid of the punters. She pointed towards the end of our aisle where a girl in a tiny red tartan skirt and matching bra was preening and posturing for photographers and fans. 'Missy Dixon. Spent $40,000 getting her tits done so they'd look better in HD.'

I checked them out. They seemed the same as the breasts of most girls in here – like someone had blown them up with a bicycle pump. But behind her, over by the Kink stand, I glimpsed a face I did recognize.

Kirk Clark, porn's very own teen heart-throb. He looked tired and preoccupied, flanked on each side by girls wearing silver lipstick and tiny black latex shorts.

I was about to point him out to Esme when I saw someone even more familiar. Standing by the Wicked booth and looking straight at me.

200

Victor Gomez.

He gave me a sarky little wave, wiggling the tips of his fingers. 'See you later,' he mouthed, then laughed and turned away.

I flashed back to the sensation of his hand around my neck, the feel of him inside me, and shivered despite the fug of heat in the exhibition hall.

'You OK?' said a voice. 'You kinda blanked out there.'

'Sorry.' I pulled my gaze from Victor to the short fat man in front of me. 'Miles away.'

'I gotta say, Kitty Sweet, you're even sexier in the flesh.' He grinned, showing gappy, misshapen teeth, as he inspected my breasts in the push-up bra and the tight spandex top Esme had lent me.

'Thanks,' I said absently, glancing back towards Victor, but he'd gone.

'Nuttin' to say?' the man drawled, edging closer. There was sweat on his top lip, like dew. He leaned in, his smile morphing into a leer.

'So tell me, Kitty. You feelin' horny today?'

26

The Venetian, Las Vegas

Saturday, 7 January 2006

'Go on, take it.' Esme pressed the pill into my hand. 'A little pick-me-up to see you through tonight.'

My first instinct was to refuse, but I was exhausted from the hours on the Pulsar stand; frankly, I needed all the help I could get. I downed the pill with a glass of water, and wriggled into my black satin gown.

Low on the back but not revealing too much skin at the front, it was classy but cute, showing off what curves I had without shoving them up your nose.

'Lovely,' Esme said approvingly, then gave me a twirl of her own dress. She'd gone for a full-length silvery number that caught the light whenever she moved. She was gorgeous, her dark hair curled into loose ringlets that perfectly framed her face.

I had to admit we both looked pretty hot. Thanks to the girl Esme had hired to come to the apartment to do our hair and make-up, we appeared dewy and fresh despite the non-stop partying. A miracle what a nice frock and a bit of well-applied slap could achieve, I thought, as we collected Nelson and piled into the limousine.

As we headed towards the Hard Rock Hotel, I was feeling better. Better than better. I was looking forward to tonight, I realized. The AVN awards were the biggest event in the world of porn – and I was on a shortlist.

Way to go, Kitty Sweet!

'Blimey,' Esme gasped when the limo drew up in front of a horde of fans and photographers. 'Look at them all.'

I stared at the crowd while the chauffeur came round to open our door. When I glanced back at Esme, her jaw was tight.

'Here goes,' she said, stepping down on to the red carpet. 'See you on the other side.'

'*Pasha! Pasha Steele!*' called the mob of photographers as Esme advanced, striking a pose in each direction, blowing kisses to her fans. No trace of her nerves now. Nelson followed right behind in his tux and bow tie, watching and smiling, looking as handsome as I'd ever seen him.

'*Kitty!*' a voice rang out to my side. 'Kitty Sweet! This way!'

I turned to see a news reporter holding a mike. He beckoned me over, a cameraman and sound engineer filming my approach.

'Kitty Sweet, one of the nominees in the Best Newcomer category, all the way from merry old England,' the reporter intoned to camera before turning to me. 'So tell me, Kitty, are you feeling confident about your chances of walking away with an award tonight?'

Oh God, I thought, as he brought the mike to my lips. Was I feeling confident? To be honest, I had no idea how I felt. The four days since we touched down at LAX hadn't left room for anything much beyond survival.

'Well, I know I'm up against some stiff competition,' I improvised. 'So, fingers crossed, and may the best girl win.'

The reporter laughed. 'Such a cute British accent. Wishing you all the luck, Kitty!'

He turned away, letting me rejoin Nelson and Esme as they made their way into the ballroom. The huge space was already packed with glossy, air-brushed people, the men in black tie, the women in an assortment of dresses and gowns, many barely the right side of obscene. Everyone strutting around like this was the Oscars, not a glorified get-together for some of the trashiest human beings on the planet.

We were seated at a table with the head of Stratos, plus several of the contract stars and crew. Esme and Nelson were on my left; on my right, a director who introduced himself as Larry. A weathered, once-handsome man in his fifties, sporting one of those little goatees you saw on most of the porn guys out here.

'Hey, look,' he exclaimed, pointing towards a good-looking guy with dark hair, wearing a black T-shirt under his tux. He was chatting to a group near our table.

'Who's he?'

Larry laughed. 'Tom Traynor. America's most notorious rent boy. If you get a chance, check out his tats.'

'Rent boy? You mean he's an escort?'

'Allegedly. He was on this reality TV show about male prostitutes. You should watch it. Very entertaining.'

I stared at the people clustered around the other tables. I'd never seen so much glitz and cleavage. Half the men were beefed up like they'd been mainlining steroids.

'More silicon than in the Valley,' Larry sighed,

following my gaze. He glanced down at my tits. 'Those all yours?'

I nodded.

'Good girl.' He patted my knee. 'Leave them alone. You don't want to end up looking like a sex doll.' He nodded towards an older blonde woman with breasts so large they looked like they might burst at any moment.

'Gotta hand it to 'em.' He rolled his eyes as the woman squealed and flung herself around a balding guy in a white tuxedo. 'No one in the world can party like a bunch of coked-up porno peeps.'

The awards took for ever. There were dozens of categories, glorifying everything from the best oral and anal sex scenes to threesomes, foursomes, cum shots and even gang bangs.

That bloke on the plane had been right – it *was* insane.

'Bloody surreal,' Esme muttered, as one actress sobbed at the podium. 'Imagine crying cos you're the fucking anal starlet of the year.'

Best Newcomer went to an eighteen-year-old from New Mexico with straw blonde hair and a laugh that made you want to kill yourself.

'Never mind.' Larry patted my knee as I applauded. 'Life at the top is overrated – the air's thin, and it's getting mighty crowded up there.'

While I didn't win an award, Esme did, rising to accept it with all the grace and poise of a genuine Hollywood star. I glanced at Nelson as she thanked everyone at Pulsar. Saw him watching her – his *wife* – with an expression nothing short of adoration.

He'd do anything for her, I realized. Anything.

I closed my eyes, pushing it all down, opening them again as Esme, beaming, returned to her seat.

'I can't believe I won an award for something as absurd as fucking.' She bent to give Nelson a kiss before sitting back down to examine her 'Woody' – a transparent Perspex block, with an engraving on the front that looked vaguely like a couple embracing.

Up on the stage the compère was moving on. 'OK, folks, we've come to the award for Best Gonzo Film,' he declared, reading out the list of nominees.

'Jesus,' Larry snorted. 'So now we're giving prizes for making utter shit?'

Some porn dude I'd never heard of emerged from the wings, clearing his throat and surveying the audience before announcing the result. 'And the winner is . . .' he proclaimed, leaving the obligatory extended pause . . .

'. . . . . *Victor Gomez.*'

Esme and Nelson exchanged glances, and Larry gave another grunt of disgust. 'Would you fucking believe it? Dozens of directors out there who actually care about making the best films they can with a limited budget – and they give an award to that sleazy punk.'

All the little hairs stood up on the nape of my neck as I watched Victor make his way to the stage from the back of the ballroom. He stepped up to the mike, a lazy sneer on his face.

'I'll keep this short.' He examined his award then brandished it like a trophy. 'To everyone who voted for me tonight, I want to offer my sincerest thanks.' Victor made an ironic little bow. 'And for the rest of you, I'd like to say this . . .'

He gave the audience the finger as he walked off the stage.

'Wanker,' Esme said loudly as everyone around us applauded.

Larry grinned. '*Amen* to that.'

An hour later we were sitting in the main bar at the Hard Rock Hotel, several bottles of Moët et Chandon lined up between the four of us.

'To Esme, reigning champion of blow jobs.' Larry raised his glass to chink with ours. 'And I hear further congratulations are in order,' he added, turning to Nelson. 'You, my son, are one very lucky man.'

'I'll drink to that.' Nelson tilted his glass to Esme. 'To my lovely and most talented wife,' he declared, before downing the champagne in one go.

Esme shrugged. 'Nothing to it. Basically I just lie around and get screwed.'

'You talking about your movies or your marriage?' quipped Larry, making us laugh. All except Nelson, whose smile was muted, and I remembered what Esme had told me a few months ago, about being too tired to bother.

'Anyway.' Esme twisted round to give me a hug. 'It'll be your turn next year. Or maybe we should try and get ourselves nominated for the best girl/girl scene?' she added flirtatiously.

'Now, *that* I would like to see.' Larry rose to refill our glasses, and out of the corner of my eye I spotted Victor walk into the bar, flanked by a couple of girls in dresses that might easily be mistaken for underwear. He glanced around, then clocked our group.

'Wanted to offer my congratulations,' he said as he strolled over, conspicuously eyeballing Esme's cleavage.

Nelson glared up at him, but Victor acted like he hadn't noticed, turning to me instead. 'And commiserations to you, Miss Sweet. That award had your name on it – clearly the idiot who presented it couldn't read.'

I forced a reluctant smile.

'What's up, Leanne?' he whispered in my ear, so close I could feel his breath on my cheek. 'Not sulking, are we?'

I drew away, glaring at him, my skin crawling from his proximity. His smell – sweat and aftershave – spinning me back to the sensation of him inside me, the pressure on my neck. That sense he wanted to throttle the life out of me.

I narrowed my eyes. 'Why don't you just fuck off, Victor?'

He smirked and straightened up. 'Toodles.' He gave us a little wave as he strode off, trailed by the scantily clad girls he'd brought with him.

'That guy' – Larry's gaze followed him all the way out to the bar – 'that guy is everything that's wrong with this industry.'

'How do you mean?' Esme raised an eyebrow.

Larry drained the rest of his glass before settling back into his seat. 'Basically, that piece of shit wins an award because porn is running out of ideas, because it's all *escalating*. You can't do a threesome any more, it has to be four, five, six men drilling a girl. Fucking moresomes, man. *Morgies!*'

'Yeah,' Nelson agreed, signalling to a waitress for another bottle of champagne. 'Once upon a time there was a bloody storyline. It used to be about acting, at least a little bit, but more and more it's all strip and fuck, no preliminaries.'

'Christ, punters don't even have the patience for that any more,' Larry sighed. 'Now we have compilations of *cum shots*.'

208

We all refilled our glasses when the fresh bottle arrived. 'Look at his movies.' Larry drained half his champagne in one go. 'Gomez, I mean. It's all hardcore action, nothing but brutal sex, pure fucking hatred. And everyone's lapping it up. It's like we don't want to see men actually talking to women any more, we don't want any kind of *dialogue*, we only want to see girls getting nailed. Or rather, being abused.'

Abused. The word resonated through me. I thought of that scene at Stratos two days ago. When it had all tipped over the edge from work to . . . what? Pain. Degradation. That sense of being used . . . yes, *abused*.

Something worthless and disposable.

'There's this massive disconnect, don't you see?' Larry continued, slugging more champagne and warming to his theme. 'Men claim they want romance, they want a *soul mate*, to get married and have kids, live happily ever after – yadda, yadda – yet what do they do the minute they're on their own?' He gazed at each of us in turn, like we might have an answer.

None of us did.

A gleam of sweat broke out on Larry's forehead and he started poking the air as he spoke, his movements reflecting the energy in his voice.

'I'll tell you what they do. They're watching the crap Victor and others like him pump out, day after day. And it's not the least bit romantic or loving. It's five men fucking a woman till she's limp. It's three men ramming their cocks up her arse at the same time. It's ten men coming on a woman's face. It's rape scenes and near-strangulation and anal prolapse, *on screen*. If the girl is puking or bleeding or plain hysterical, that's *gonzo gold*, man. And this stuff is *mainstream* now. We're handing out fucking *awards* for it.'

I glanced at Nelson, gauging his reaction. But he was simply twirling his glass in his fingers, listening to Larry's tirade.

'We've got men saying they want one thing, but jerking off to another. It's like "I love you, darling, I want to marry you, but underneath I want to fucking *kill* you, you bitch, I want to screw you till you're dead."'

Till *you're dead*.

I didn't look at Esme or Nelson, but I knew what they were thinking. What we were all thinking about, though never voicing it out loud. As if never discussing it would somehow keep us safe.

Anya Viksna and Tula Kask.

It had been a front-page story, even over here. On the TV news too, whenever we happened to catch it. The hunt for the London Landfill Killer, as everyone was now calling him.

Targeting vice girls, as one newspaper put it. Like it was all our fault. Like we were the problem, not the victims.

Like we deserved it.

'Bullshit,' Esme exclaimed suddenly. I turned to her, surprised to see she was close to tears, her eyes shining, her lovely mouth trembling. She was staring at Larry with a look that should have shut him up in an instant.

'Oh yeah?' Larry frowned back at her. 'So, we have all this stuff that's deeply nasty and damaging and we tell ourselves it's OK, cos it's, what, "*made up*"?' He raised a brow at Esme as he formed little speech marks with his fingers. 'So we're all colluding in it now? Let's face it, if we had a shred of decency left we'd walk out of this place and refuse to ever come back.'

'Screw that,' Esme sneered, eyeing the waitress clearing

210

the table next to us. 'What's the alternative, Larry? I mean, who wants to be fucking *ordinary*?'

Larry eyeballed her for a moment, then laughed. A hard, bitter laugh. 'You think that's bad, do you, Esme, being ordinary?' He shook his head in a despairing sort of way. 'Christ, you should be so lucky.'

'Lucky?' Nelson appeared genuinely curious.

Larry cast his gaze around again, his expression gloomy, and with it all the atmosphere of celebration seemed to drain away. 'People like us, we're cursed,' he said, his voice weary now. 'We're the fucking *damned*, doomed to wander the earth like vampires. We can't stomach anything conventional, anything average, anything *ordinary*, can we? So no chance we'll stick out a marriage for forty years because, fuck, man, we're too *special*.'

He leaned forward, poured himself another glass and raised it in a mock toast. 'So here's to us: a bunch of sexed-up, restless little kids who can't say no. Face it, there's no temptation we can resist. If we're not wielding our sexual power over someone – seducing or being seduced – then we feel like we're *nothing*.'

He paused, fixing his gaze on Esme. 'So good luck with that when you're older.'

Esme's cheeks reddened, like Larry had reached over and slapped her. Nelson laughed. A short bark of a laugh that told me this man was beginning to get under his skin.

Certainly he was getting under mine. I felt it growing, the feeling that had been building ever since I set foot in this country.

That I was coming loose.

That I'd been pushed too far.

Finally, Larry caught up with the mood around the

211

table. He nodded to Esme. 'I apologize, my dear. I shouldn't be spoiling your big night. But that guy ...' he closed his eyes briefly, as if trying to get a grip on himself, then nodded in the direction Victor had disappeared. '. . . that guy . . . I hear stuff about him. None of it good.'

'Like what?' I sat up, wanting to know more. Sensing this was information I needed.

Larry got to his feet, straightening the trousers of his tux then picking up the bar bill from the table. 'I think I've done enough damage for one evening,' he said, then turned to me. 'Believe me, Kitty, it's nothing you want to know – and sadly nothing I can ever prove.'

Maybe Larry was the reason we got so fucked up again. After he left, Nelson, Esme and I partied like people needing to drown a whole sea of sorrows. I lost count of what we did, what we took. Esme was off her head on a blend of E and coke and speed and alcohol, grinning so hard her face looked like a death mask – you could almost see the skull beneath her skin. Nelson got more and more hyper, filled with a manic kind of energy, as if desperate to shrug off all trace of Larry's sermon.

And me. Feeling dead inside.

Or dying.

But it was our last night in America and we were making the most of it, partying like we were never going home.

And of course, one of us never did.

27

HMP Brakehurst

Tuesday, 22 March 2016

'I don't want to talk about it.' I cross my arms in front of my chest and glare at Yvonne, daring her to look away. But she holds my gaze, and in the end it's me who breaks the deadlock with a glance at the clock on the wall.

Still half an hour to go.

I've had enough of this session, reliving what happened when I stood in for Esme on that LA shoot. Don't want to think any more about the whole car crash that was our trip to America.

'All right, Leanne. Obviously you're under no obligation to tell me, but don't you think it's important? It must have been very difficult to deal with.'

I shake my head. Say nothing. Stare out the window at the March rain, slashing on the glass like someone pissing against a wall.

'This isn't an interrogation, Leanne,' Yvonne adds another minute later. 'The idea is that you have space to talk to somebody in confidence about the things that happened.'

'In confidence?' I turn back to her.

She nods. 'As I've said before, nothing you say in these sessions will be passed on without your permission.'

I digest this for a minute, though of course she'd told me that already. But it doesn't hurt to be reminded.

'What do you want to know?' I watch my therapist smooth her hand over the buff file where she keeps my notes. Not for the first time I wonder what else is in there, what she records when our hour is over. Yvonne never writes anything while we're talking.

'You don't actually say what happened to Nelson Garvey, in the account you gave me.'

I keep my expression deadpan. 'Is it relevant?' How does she know about him? I wonder. After all, none of this came up in court.

Yvonne cocks her head to one side. 'He was a close friend, Leanne. His death must have had a huge impact on you.'

I inhale as I consider how best to deal with this. Simpler, maybe, to play along. Perhaps Yvonne's right. Perhaps it would be good for me to get it off my chest.

So I let my mind drift back to Nelson, try to conjure up his face, but it's yours I see instead. Your expression when . . . I pinch off the thought at the roots.

'We'd had a pretty heavy night,' I say. 'We were really fucked up. It's hard to remember exactly.'

I'm lying, though. Despite all the booze, all the pick-me-ups and put-me-downs, despite the accumulated exhaustion of jet lag and four nights on the town, it's all crystal clear in my head. I can recall every single detail.

'It must have been very distressing,' Yvonne agrees, and I ask myself again what she knows.

My eyes prickle. Truthfully, I've never got over that

214

night – not really. Arriving back at our apartment block, Esme so drugged and drunk she could hardly stand, Nelson and me either side of her, dragging her into the lift.

It was then I noticed Nelson was sweating. His pupils were huge, like pennies, and there were dark patches on the armpits of his shirt.

Esme must have felt it too, the heat coming off him. 'You all right?' she slurred as the lift doors opened and we almost fell out on to the landing.

A scream from somewhere. I jump, snapping back to the present, to the prison. Another wild screech from nearby. Suki, I realize, the girl who murdered her baby daughter when she had PMT. Every month, around her period, she goes mental, crying and freaking out till the screws get fed up and stick her in isolation.

Never a dull moment.

'So that's when you first noticed Nelson was ill?' Yvonne asks, ignoring the commotion outside.

I go through it all. How we unlocked the door and took Esme into her bedroom and tipped her on to the bed. As Nelson straightened up, I saw how pale he was. His brown skin turned sallow, almost yellow.

'Excuse me.' He stumbled into the bathroom. I heard the sound of him retching.

'I assumed it was the booze that made him sick,' I tell Yvonne. 'I thought he was throwing up from all the alcohol.'

'That's understandable.' She interlinks her fingers, resting them on my file. She never puts it down, and that bugs me. What is she afraid of? That I'll snatch it up and look inside?

'So at what point did you realize there was something wrong, Leanne?'

I take a deep breath. 'Nelson came out of the bathroom and made straight for the balcony. Muttered something about needing fresh air. I was talking to Esme, checking she was OK, and when I looked round, he was lying on the floor, half in the room, half outside, like he'd collapsed on the way back in.'

Esme yelped with alarm. I'd never seen someone sober up so fast. It was like a switch flipped in her brain. Instantly she was by his side, bending over him.

'Nelson,' she yelled, as if shouting would somehow restore him. *'Nelson!'*

'I don't feel so good, babe.' He opened his eyes halfway, as if even that was too much effort.

'What's the matter?' Esme shook him like he was falling asleep. 'Chest hurts,' he groaned.

His breathing was funny, sort of raspy and irregular. I knelt by his other side, using my fingers to search for a pulse in his wrist, but really I had no idea what I was doing.

'Call an ambulance!' Esme said to me.

'But . . .' I stared at Nelson. We were all off our heads. If we took him to hospital, they'd be bound to run tests and he could end up in all sorts of trouble. We all could. We were in America, for God's sake – what would they do if they caught us with a ton of drugs in our bloodstream?

I hesitated, wondering whether to say anything, but Esme was crying now, tears streaming down her face. Nelson looked in real pain. Squinting, his breathing laboured.

'What are you waiting for?' she sobbed. 'Call the fucking ambulance *now*, Leanne!'

I rummaged in my handbag. Found my phone. Shut myself in the bathroom where I could focus.

'So you rang the emergency services?' Yvonne has her eyes fixed on mine, but there's nothing in her expression.

'I called 999, but it said "number unrecognized" or something, and then I remembered that was wrong, it was a different number over there. And that's when I started panicking. Even with the door closed I could hear Esme crying and calling Nelson's name over and over, and I couldn't think what I was supposed to dial. So I ran outside and asked a passer-by what the number for the emergency services was.'

'911,' says Yvonne.

'Yes, 911. As soon as they said it, I remembered it was 911. But I was in such a state because it was clear there was something very wrong with Nelson and I was still feeling so fucked up.'

'Who was it? The person who gave you the number?'

I blink at Yvonne. 'I don't know. Some guy walking down the street. Does it matter?'

'It sounds like a very stressful situation,' she says, which doesn't strike me as much of an answer.

'It was.' I bite my lip. 'It really was.'

'So you rang 911?'

'I rang them and told them what had happened and they said they'd send an ambulance straight away. So I went up to the apartment and waited with Esme.'

Nelson looked awful. His breathing was ragged. His chest rising and falling erratically.

'So what happened next?' Yvonne's voice asks, but I barely hear her. I squeeze my eyes shut and I'm back there, with Esme, her arm cradling Nelson's head.

'Where are they?' She looked terrible, terrified, her mascara streaked from crying, lipstick smeared across her cheek.

217

'They're coming. They said they'd be here soon.'

'But it's been twenty minutes already,' she wailed, glancing at the digital clock on the TV. 'It's been fucking twenty minutes, Leanne. They should be here by now.'

'Maybe they got stuck in traffic.' I edged round Nelson, on to the balcony and peered at the street below.

No ambulance. But I spotted a couple of taxis cruising past. 'C'mon,' I told Esme. 'Let's get him into a cab. It'll be quicker.'

I could see the fear in her face. The desperation. But she didn't argue. Somehow, between us, we got Nelson to his feet and into the lift and out on to the street.

'Leanne.' I look up and see Yvonne offering me a box of tissues. I take one and blow my nose. Tears are running down my face and my throat feels blocked.

'So you got him into a taxi? Because the ambulance didn't arrive?'

I nod.

'Do you have any idea why it didn't turn up, Leanne?'

I frown at her. 'You tell me. Maybe I got the number of the apartment wrong. I don't know.'

Yvonne seems about to say something, then pauses. 'So you went to the nearest hospital?' she asks instead.

I nod again. 'But he was dead. By the time we got there Nelson was dead.'

His eyes rolled back into his head and he passed out and Esme started screaming again and calling his name over and over and the taxi driver was yelling at her to calm down, saying he was going as fast as he could. But Nelson had stopped breathing. When we arrived at the hospital Nelson still wasn't breathing and they couldn't get it started again.

'Heart failure,' confirms Yvonne.

'A bad reaction to the coke,' I sniff, trying to pull myself together. 'He was unlucky.'

I shut my eyes again and Yvonne disappears. I'm no longer in that room, in the prison, I'm sitting there, in the emergency department of some Las Vegas hospital, in the waiting room – all muted pastels and soft muzak and the faint lemony smell of disinfectant – and I'm holding Esme's hand and listening to the doctor telling her all the clichés – '. . . did everything we could . . . no way to save him . . .' – and Esme isn't screaming any more, she's gone quiet. She's so pale and her hand is trembling in mine and I remember thinking.

This is going to be the end of her.

28

Las Vegas

Monday, 9 January 2006

Then you were there.

Esme begged me to fetch you, so I rang not long after Nelson died and you caught the next flight, arriving at the apartment that evening. It felt like a miracle, and not a moment too soon. Twelve hours of Esme, hysterical – and I'm not using that word lightly. Screaming hysterical, ever since we got back from the hospital – without Nelson. Yelling and wailing and sobbing so much her face swelled up. She looked like those pictures you see of women a day or so after plastic surgery, all bloated and red and puffy.

Unrecognizable.

When you walked in, she hung round your neck like a dead weight, like an anchor, and you had to carry her back to the bedroom, had to sit her down on the bed, grabbing her arms and talking to her in that calm, soothing way you have. Over and over.

Eventually Esme shut up. Then lay back and fell instantly asleep.

'You all right?' You turned to me. Almost the first words you'd spoken to me since you arrived.

I nodded.

Your look lingered. 'Jesus, Leanne. What a fucking mess.'

That was all you ever said about it. You never asked me what happened. Didn't press me to go over it all, for which I was – am still – immensely grateful.

Some things you should only have to live through once.

Your arrival marked a turning point in Esme. Even when we got home and made all the arrangements and had Nelson's body flown back to the UK, she barely reacted. She didn't cry at the funeral, just sat at the front of the crematorium, dead-eyed, staring at the white coffin – who the *fuck* decided Nelson should have a white coffin? – with a bemused expression like this was all made-up. Something we were acting for a shoot. Like anyone would make a porno in a bloody crematorium.

Scrap that. Chances are, someone has. Some dude somewhere, some sick sad cunt of a director has decided that's the neatest location he's ever come up with.

Someone not unlike Victor, perhaps.

Of course, Esme was doped up to the eyeballs on whatever she'd managed to persuade that private Harley Street GP to prescribe. More of the Xanax we got hold of in America, I'm guessing.

'I don't know how I'd manage without you,' she repeated, every time she saw either of us. Once she grabbed my hand, pulling me towards her, breathing into my ear as she squeezed my fingers so hard it almost hurt.

'Leanne, Leanne. Seriously. What would I do without you? How could I ever survive?'

29

Pulsar Studios, Hackney, London

Monday, 10 April 2006

I was on a shoot when I heard. In the middle of a fucking shoot with some German guy called Super Hans who had red hair and gave the length of his dick in centimetres. Twenty-one, I seem to remember.

With Esme out of action, and Nelson gone, I'd been working twice as hard in the weeks following our return to the UK. Life went on. Men still needed to wank, which meant the rest of us had to carry on making crap to help them.

I was there in body, but not in spirit. Going through the motions, with plenty of lube.

Fake. All of it.

Alive, but dead inside.

Hans had me pinioned over the back of the sofa, screwing me doggy style. He was really getting into it too, I could tell by the way he kept grunting, when out of the corner of my eye I saw Irene, the new runner, come up and tap Ron on the arm.

Ron was my favourite director at Pulsar, constantly cheerful and upbeat, the kind of guy who seemed overjoyed to be making porn. He was like a scout leader or something, always a smile on his face, cheering us on. Whenever the action was going well, you'd hear him in the background, crooning 'oh yeah' and 'that's great'.

So I saw Irene come in and whisper to Ron. He was still smiling as he followed her to the back of the set, signalling to the cameraman to continue. Not you today, but that new bloke, Roger. Hans carried on pummelling me, grunting, until Ron returned a minute or two later.

No smile on his face. The first time I'd ever seen him without one.

He appeared to be wondering what to do. He kept glancing at me and at Hans, who I could tell was getting close to the pop when Ron held up his hand.

'Hey . . . err, guys . . . why don't you take a break?'

Hans stopped mid thrust. He looked at Ron. 'Are you sure? Something is not right?'

Oh God. Not again.

I assumed they'd found another one. Another girl, dead. Dumped on landfill.

For a moment I thought by the look on Ron's face that it was Esme.

Ron stared back at us helplessly. 'I need to have a word with Kitty.'

I frowned at him. Why only me?

Why not tell us both?

'There's been a call from Pulsar head office.' He swallowed. 'There's something you should see.'

I felt myself go cold. Hans withdrew, fondling his dick to maintain his erection while Irene handed me a tissue. I wiped myself and grabbed a dressing gown.

'What is it?' I asked Ron. He was still gazing at me, his expression indecipherable.

He didn't answer. Led me into the little office at the back of the main set. On the desk was a laptop, the screen dark. He pressed a key and it fired into life.

'I'd sit down, if I were you.' He pulled back the chair.

I did as he suggested, studying the website in front of me. PornBuzz. 'All the juice on the jizzbiz' it said underneath.

Below that, a headline, capitalized:

PORN ACTOR FAILS HIV TEST
STRATOS CALLS HALT TO PRODUCTION

'*Scheisse*,' I heard Hans mutter behind me. He must have followed us into the office. 'That is not good.'

I turned and Hans saw my expression. Put two and two together. 'You mean you are *working* with that guy?'

His face paled. His cock, despite the Caverject, started to hinge downwards like a drawbridge. I'd never seen a man lose his erection so fast.

'*Scheisse*,' he said again. 'Shit . . .'

His words tailed off. Ron put a hand on Hans' shoulder, but he was looking at me as he spoke.

'I think we'd better call it a day.'

30

Central London

Monday, 10 April 2006

You came to the studio as soon as I called, though I think you'd heard already. Everyone at Pulsar knew by the time the taxi arrived. No one could meet my eye.

You took me home and sat with me while I freaked out. Then you dialled the clinic.

'They can see us in an hour.'

Us. The first time you ever used that word.

You bundled me into another taxi. I couldn't speak the whole journey, just looked out the window as we cruised from Hackney over to Harley Street, barely registering the glorious April sunshine, the fat buds of leaves on the London trees.

'Leanne?'

You led me into the private sexual health clinic, through a discreet doorway on New Cavendish Street. Inside, it was all plush carpets and tasteful décor. A cultivated air of calm.

You watched as I filled out the form at reception, then sat next to me as I waited to see the doctor.

I wanted you to hold my hand, but I didn't dare ask; not after what happened between us before.

No way I could deal with that again, not on a day like today.

We sat there in silence. I was grateful you didn't try to make small talk. Didn't try to pretend everything was OK. When my name was called, I asked if you could come with me; I was beyond taking in anything. I held my arm out, barely aware of the prick of the needle, just watched the syringe fill with my blood, rich and red.

I couldn't take my eyes off it. Wondering what might be lurking in there. Right then, porn felt like a death sentence, one way or another. You end up as landfill, or your blood poisoned.

You choose.

'Should have the results by six.' The nurse placed a little round sticky plaster over the hole in my skin.

'Leanne?' you asked again, when I didn't move. Then took me gently by the arm and led me away.

Six o'clock.

When we stood outside, blinking in the sunlight, that was all I had taken in.

We walked for miles, from Harley Street to Oxford Circus and Piccadilly, and on down to the river. I don't think either of us spoke the whole way – what was there to say?

By now I knew the risks. Most studios wouldn't shoot with condoms – they made the work harder, they didn't feel good, and they looked shit on camera. Anyway, they didn't fit most male performers – not even the extra-large.

So we all relied on screening. But even with monthly

tests, it only took one person to screw a civilian, or do a shoot somewhere like Brazil where monitoring was lax, and a serious disease could enter the talent pool. There was no mention where Action Man might have caught it, or when.

But I'd had anal sex with him, and bled copiously. I knew my chances weren't great.

We headed west along Millbank, the Thames almost blue in the bright spring light, little waves rippling the surface in the breeze. 'Leanne, listen to me,' you said eventually. 'There's a good chance that guy wasn't infected when you performed with him. It was nearly fourteen weeks ago – he could have contracted it after that.'

I nodded, but we both knew it was a long shot.

'And even if the test does come back positive, it's not the end of the world.' You took my hand and made me stop. Pulled up my chin so I was forced to look you in the eyes. 'There are drugs to control it these days – HIV is no longer a death sentence.'

I managed a smile, but you and I both knew it went way beyond that. A lifetime on medication. The end of my career – and any chance of a normal love life.

I closed my eyes. Was this punishment? I kept wondering. For failing to help Nelson?

It felt like it somehow. It felt like a judgement. A conviction.

His face flashed up inside my head. The way he looked, so pale, his breathing so laboured, audible even under Esme's moans of anguish.

I should have done more, I kept thinking. Should have acted faster.

I should have saved him.

*

227

You took me to that gallery by the river – the Tate. I don't know why. It's not like I cared much about paintings.

But you did. Would it be wrong to say that surprised me? That a guy filming people who screw for a living should be interested in art?

You led me through the galleries and showed me your favourites. You liked the Turners, but I found them dull and gloomy, so you led me to the Pre-Raphaelites, stopping in front of that painting of Ophelia drowning in the river.

'Millais made the model pose in a basin of water for over four months,' you told me. 'She got ill and nearly died.'

'How do you know that?'

You shrugged. 'I guess I read it somewhere.'

I studied the girl, her long brown hair floating amongst the weeds. I knew how that model must have felt. It was like the kind of shit I had to do – boring and deeply uncomfortable.

And dangerous.

'Poor Ophelia,' I said, more to myself.

'She was a character in Shakespeare's—'

'*Hamlet*. Yeah, I know. I did it for A-level.'

'You did?' This time it was you who looked surprised.

' ". . . as one incapable of her own distress",' I quoted, then stopped. 'It's the only line I can remember – just as well I chucked it in.'

Still, you were impressed. I could sense you revising your opinion of me as we traipsed from room to room, stopping occasionally to gaze at pictures that caught our eye.

And when we were tired and our feet ached, we found the café and you bought me soup and spread the roll with butter and made me eat the lot. Both of us silent, in a place beyond small talk.

I was so scared, but it was Nelson I kept seeing in my mind. His expression, as he lay dying. Bewildered, like it was the last thing he'd ever expected.

And I remembered Brighton, me and Esme, hair flying in the wind as we sped down the motorway. We were riding high. Invincible. Infallible.

How had it come to this?

How had we made such a mess of our lives?

'It'll be OK, Leanne,' you said, breaking into my thoughts. I looked at you, trying to believe it, but I knew your words were empty.

Before we left, you took me to view some of the modern stuff. I spotted one called *Venice Beach*, which reminded me I never did get back there, like I'd promised myself – and then I felt sad as well as scared.

But I liked the paintings by David Hockney. I stood and stared at *A Bigger Splash*. There wasn't much to it, really. A flat house with a swimming pool, out in LA, a plume of white water where someone had just dived in. Two tall skinny palm trees in the background.

It was bright and sunny, though, and the brilliant blue sky reminded me of that world above the clouds. And somehow, in that space the picture created in my mind, I managed to forget what was coming for me.

Until my phone rang.

And then, like people in a painting, we stood there, my head buried in your shoulder, your hand stroking my hair while I broke down and cried.

31

Central London

Monday, 10 April 2006

We ate in that posh Chinese restaurant up on Goodge Street and you showed me how to use chopsticks and we got drunk on cocktails made with baijui and lychee juice. Much too sweet, but I didn't care. I was basking in happiness, high on relief.

I had dodged a bullet. One with Kitty Sweet engraved on the casing.

I was clear. I'd need another test in a few weeks to make sure, but in all likelihood I was fine.

You made me laugh, spinning your chopsticks like cheerleader batons, cracking jokes with the waiters, who seemed as enchanted by you as I was. I studied your face as you spoke to them, asking about their families, their dreams.

I liked that about you. Nelson would always treat the people around us – serving in restaurants, hotel staff, the minions at Pulsar – as opportunities to showcase his charm. It was different with you. You talked to them because you were interested, saw them as real, not simply bit players in our lives, taking care of our needs.

And it gave me an opportunity to study you. Your perfect brown skin. The way your eyebrows almost met in the middle. The first shadow of stubble appearing on your chin and cheeks after a day without shaving.

As I said, not classic handsome, but somehow all the more heart-breaking for that.

You smiled as you caught me studying you, and there was promise in that smile. We had turned some sort of corner, and the feeling lifted me as we took a taxi back to your flat in Herne Hill. The cabbie had the radio on and as we sailed over Vauxhall Bridge I let the music fill me. I felt reborn. Released. Like nothing would ever touch me again.

'I love this song,' I said.

' "Hoppipolla",' you replied.

And I was tired and drunk and thought you said Happy Polar. Had visions of white bears with big grins on their faces. Big white bears bounding across the ice, deep in the frozen north.

And this made me laugh, then as the taxi drew up outside your flat, it filled me with all the joy in the world.

'Come on.' You paid the driver and guided me indoors. Your flat was on the ground floor. Nothing special. A living room, one bedroom, a kitchen and a tiny bathroom. But out the back, through a door in the kitchen, you had access to a small patch of garden, just grass and a concrete path, a few bushes either side.

I went out and sat on the lawn, looking up at the sky. It was chilly but dry, the grass only slightly damp beneath my jeans. I lay back, resting my head on my arms. I couldn't see much, just a few stars, dotted around like dust on a windscreen, the crescent of the moon hovering behind the tower blocks across the road.

'Shame about the light pollution.' You handed me a mug of tea, then sat down beside me, taking a packet of cigarette papers from your pocket and a small zip-locked bag of weed. 'This would be a good night for star-gazing.'

'Light pollution?'

'Skyglow.' You pointed into the distance, the horizon beyond the neighbouring rooftops. 'It's that orange haze visible over towns or cities, from all the streetlights. It stops you being able to see anything up above.'

I watched you roll a spliff, neatly, careful not to spill any of the weed. 'Chances are, if you've lived round London most of your life, you've never really seen the night sky. You need to go somewhere more remote.'

I was tempted to suggest we jump on a train and head out of town, go right away, to anywhere we could revel in the naked starlight. Scotland, maybe. Or even Wales. But I was afraid you'd say no, afraid of spoiling this new mood between us.

You lit the spliff, making the tip glow in the darkness. More light pollution. You inhaled deeply, then passed it to me; I took a long drag, waiting for the sweet buzz to hit my brain.

I was all right. I hadn't been infected.

Everything was going to be fine.

'So what's out there?' I asked, passing the spliff back and peering up into the sky again. 'What am I missing?'

'Stars. Planets and galaxies. Lots of space in between.

In total, matter makes up only 4 per cent of the universe.'

'So what's the other 96 per cent, then?'

You took a drag, held your breath for a moment. 'We're not sure. Physicists used to think it was nothing. Emptiness. A vacuum being the universe's default space.'

'Nature abhors a vacuum,' I said, quoting Mike, who came out with it whenever he was hungry.

'Aristotle. *Horror vacui.*'

'Well, he was right,' I said, feeling a little high. 'Men do abhor vacuums. They see a hole and they want to fill it.'

You laughed, and that set me off giggling. 'Seriously, though.' I lay back on the grass. 'You're saying, what . . . that most of the universe is empty?'

'Even the stuff around us. You ever heard that explanation of an atom? You know, the one with a football pitch?'

I shook my head. 'I was rubbish at science.'

You lifted my left hand, drew an oblong on the palm. 'Everything is made up of atoms, right?'

I nodded.

'So imagine an atom blown up to the size of a football stadium. The nucleus – the centre of the atom – would be the size of a pea in the middle of the pitch. The electrons would be whizzing round the outer stands.' You drew a circle around the edge of my palm to illustrate your point. 'Everything in between is empty space.'

'So how come I can't see through my own hand,' I asked, my skin prickling in the wake of your touch. I stared at my palm – it seemed so solid.

You wrinkled your nose. 'To answer that properly I'd

have to go all quantum on you. Basically ... it's complicated.'

I laughed. 'It always is.'

'Forces, electrons, something tricky called the Pauli exclusion principle.' You took a last drag on the spliff and stubbed it on the lawn, resting back on your arms. 'Actually, we now know if you look harder, closer, you find that what appears to be empty space is teeming with fleeting virtual particles or quantum fluctuations. A kind of dark energy.'

I gazed up towards the stars again, wondering how the ground was solid enough to support me. You leaned over, studying my expression, then bent your head to kiss me, and I imagined all the atoms in your lips brushing against mine.

Or maybe not. It was impossible to fathom.

'Leanne,' you whispered, withdrawing from the kiss and caressing my hair. 'So lovely.'

'But I'm empty.' I smiled up at you, at the tiny stars beyond, feeling the earth spin beneath me. 'Nothing inside me but dark energy.'

'Ha,' you laughed. 'A little learning is a dangerous thing.'

And then you kissed me again.

When it became too cold to stay outside we huddled on the sofa, drinking hot chocolate that tasted deep and sweet and insanely delicious because we were stoned. Sitting side by side, legs touching, but still fully clothed. Neither of us in a hurry to make a move.

And I remember thinking that this was the difference – the difference between this and our other life. If this was a scene in a porn movie, you'd have been fisting me by now.

234

'Why did you stop?' I asked.

'Stop what?'

'Studying. Why didn't you carry on, with your atoms and quantums and stuff?'

You took a sip of your drink, put it down on the table. I sensed something in you, in your energy. A resistance.

'I went to prison,' you said finally.

The silence that followed was anything but empty. It teemed with questions, with all the things I needed to know, but knew better than to ask. At least now.

'I went to prison, and when I got out, everything had changed.'

'Prison,' I echoed. The word seemed new, somehow, in the context of you. Alien and impossible.

'Young offender institution, to be precise.'

'What was it like?' This wasn't the vital question, of course. What I really wanted to know was *why*? What the hell had you done to land yourself in a place like that?

You looked mournful, and I instantly regretted asking even this. Worried I'd ruined the mood.

'Hell on earth,' you said quietly. 'I'd rather die than ever go back there.'

I put my hand against your cheek. You let it rest there for a moment, then got up and switched on the TV. Put a disk in the DVD player and the screen snapped into life, a burst of classical music pouring through the speakers.

'What's this?' I looked at you.

'I thought we might watch a film.'

'OK.' I tried to hide my disappointment. Had I annoyed you? Asked too many questions? 'What's it called?'

235

'*Brief Encounter*,' you replied, and for a horrible moment I thought you were putting on some porn, but as the titles rolled and the piano music built to a crescendo, I realized it was an old black-and-white film.

'Why are we watching this?'

You looked at me. 'An antidote,' was your reply.

On the screen an old-fashioned steam train hurtled past a platform. A man and a woman sat in the station café; everyone around them talking in that fast, clipped way they did back then, though God knows why.

The camera panned in slowly on the woman. She had the saddest face I'd ever seen.

Gradually, despite myself, I was sucked into the gravitational pull of the story. A story where nothing, and yet everything happened. A story with all the passion and heartbreak you could ever imagine. I was lost, in the swell of the music, the emotion, and as the closing credits rolled I turned to you with such a choking in my throat I could barely breathe.

'So that's it?' I asked, my voice breaking. 'They give each other up? They never see each other again?'

I couldn't believe it. It was awful. Unbearable. I didn't want to even think about it.

You nodded, not looking at the screen but my face, and something burst inside me and I started crying. Terrible wrenching, heaving sobs, like I was broken. And you held me. You held me till eventually I stopped.

And then, when you kissed me this time, I understood. I understood why you played that film. An antidote to all the crap we'd ever made, had ever seen. An antidote to sex without meaning.

I never needed you more than in that moment, Joe, when you showed me to myself.

Stripped down to the core.

And afterwards, when we finally went to bed, it felt like a miracle. As you moved inside me, I thought about what you'd said, about atoms and electrons and empty space, and knew what held us together, what stopped your flesh from simply sliding through mine, missing it by miles and miles.

The most powerful force in the whole universe.

Love.

32

HMP Brakehurst

Friday, 25 March 2016

It's cramped in the store cupboard, barely room for two amongst the mops and brooms and other bits of junk. I'm kneeling on a flat-packed cardboard box, a corner digging into my left knee.

But hell, I'm a porn star. I'm used to it.

'Mmmm ...' Drew moans as I take him into my mouth. His cock twitches and stiffens and I stretch out my neck and pull my lips over my teeth and let him deep-throat me for a minute or two. He's not that large, so it's easy work. I don't even gag.

'Jesus, Leanne,' he gasps as I swirl my tongue around the head of his prick – guaranteed to send any man over the edge in seconds. Right on schedule, Drew shudders and shoots into my throat. I chase it down with some saliva as he pulls me to my feet.

'That was nice,' he murmurs. I can tell from his voice that he's smiling, though it's too dark to make out his face. 'I'll get you those tampons. And another notepad, you said?'

'Yeah. Thanks.' I ponder whether there's anything

else I need. Paracetamol, perhaps? A new pack of knickers?

No end to the perks of screwing a screw. The little things that make life in here more bearable.

'How's it going with that therapist?' he asks, opening the door a crack so he can see my face.

'OK.'

'You still writing it all down?'

I frown. How does Drew know that? I've never mentioned it, have I, what the notebooks were for?

But hell, as Tanya always says, no such thing as a secret in this place. Or maybe he guessed. I catch him watching me sometimes, when he thinks I'm not looking. Watching and wondering, trying to suss me out.

'Yeah,' I tell him. 'I've nearly finished.'

Though that's something I don't want to face. Writing has filled the endless hours of lock-up, given them meaning. The thought of finishing leaves me feeling hollow.

More than that. Getting my story on paper has helped me join the dots. Shown how one thing led to another. At the time it all felt random, but now I can see that was because I hadn't yet discovered the connections. How Nelson's death led to what happened to Esme. How that dragged me into confronting Victor.

How I landed up in here.

As I write each episode, I can see everything so much more clearly: that shoot in LA, Nelson's death, the HIV scare – all marking a watershed in my life. The point at which I started to take things into my own hands, not allow someone else to dictate my future.

Otherwise I'd have been screwed, one way or another.

'You going to let me read it, then?' Drew chuckles.

'What?'

'Your life history.'

Jesus. I'm tempted to reach down and give his balls a good hard squeeze. He's as bad as Darryll, expecting it to be fucking *erotic*. Like titillation is the only possible interest my life could offer. Like everything I say or do should help some tosspot get his rocks off.

Screw you, arsehole.

I bite back the words as I bend over and dust off the knees of my jeans, glad Drew can't see my expression as he stands there, stroking my hair.

It's at that moment we hear footsteps in the distance. Another guard, probably, the footfall hard and heavy; most prisoners wear trainers that barely make a sound.

Shit. Who is it? No one except the cleaners uses this part of the building, but they've all gone off duty.

Drew's body tenses beside me. 'Oh Christ,' he mutters as the footsteps draw nearer, his voice anxious. After all, he's got more to lose than me. If we're caught, Drew would get the sack. No chance he could bluff his way out of that one – Harding would have him out on his ear.

All I've got at stake is losing my privileges again – and possibly the chance of early parole. And of course my little arrangement with Drew, though it would be more inconvenient than disastrous. That new guard, Everett, might be a balding, loose-fleshed bottom feeder, but he's definitely up for an exchange of favours.

As the footsteps draw closer, I'm struggling not to giggle. I'm not sure why. I guess the idea of Drew being caught with his pants down – literally – in a broom cupboard strikes me as hilarious.

'Shhhhhh,' he says, but I can't stop myself. I'm almost convulsing with the need to laugh. I grit my teeth together but a squeak leaks out, loud enough to be heard outside.

240

'*Shut the fuck up, Leanne!*' Drew hisses, covering my mouth with his hand. We both hold our breath, waiting.

The footsteps pass on by, retreating along the corridor. Finally the clank of the door closing at the other end.

Drew exhales, sounding relieved. 'We're OK,' he whispers as he retrieves his trousers. 'No thanks to you. What the hell were you playing at?'

'Sorry,' I say. 'Couldn't help it.'

He opens the door and sticks his head out, checking the coast is clear. Then turns back to me, his expression caught between annoyed and bewildered. 'Honestly, I sometimes wonder about you. What goes on in your fucking head.'

'Yeah?' I allow myself an open smirk. Drew will never dump me. He's addicted, that much is obvious, though he'd probably use another word. He's quite the closet romantic, I think, my own pun making me giggle again.

Drew looks annoyed. Then his expression softens. 'Can I ask you something, Leanne?'

'You can ask,' I say, checking I haven't got spunk on my clothes – no point advertising what we've been up to.

He clears his throat. 'I've been wondering . . . did you really . . . you know?' He pauses, gazing at me. Giving me *that* look.

Everyone wants to know the truth. It lingers there, in their eyes, in the words they swallow back, always on the tip of their tongue.

I sigh, feeling exasperated now. 'Did I really *what*, Drew?'

'Your conviction. Did you do it? Did you kill both those guys?'

241

I almost laugh again. He sounds more like a kid than a screw with ten years' experience under his belt.

Poor old Drew. He really does have it bad.

I let silence fill the air between us. Only the sound of us breathing. Mine a little faster than usual.

'Listen.' I bring my face up to his. Close enough so he can smell his semen on my breath. Drew's short for a guy, barely an inch or two taller than me, so I don't even have to stand on tiptoe.

'Listen,' I repeat, whispering in his ear, 'what you need to ask yourself is this . . .' I sense his anticipation, his desire to peer inside me. To expose whatever he imagines lies within. 'Why do you even want to know?'

I raise my hand and trace the stubble along his jawline, feeling the tiny hairs prickle beneath my fingertips. 'After all, does it really matter?'

Before he can respond, I push past, into the daylight, then turn back to face him.

'You decide, sweetheart,' I add, giving him a pat on the cheek. 'Your call. Just pick whatever answer suits you best.'

33

Herne Hill, London

Thursday, 25 May 2006

'What the fuck?'

My mouth dropped as I opened the door to your flat. Outside, leaning against the wall, was Esme.

She looked awful, dishevelled, eye make-up smudged, hair lank and messy. Worst of all she had several deep scratches running down the side of her face. One crusted over, the other still weeping a thick ooze of blood, the tissue she was clutching covered in red stains.

'Leanne!' Esme started, as if surprised to see me.

Her left eye was swollen, I noticed, the surrounding skin beginning to bruise.

'Could you pay for the taxi?' she stammered, waving a hand behind her. 'I can't find my purse.'

'Joe,' I called, and a few seconds later you appeared. 'Jesus Christ,' you exclaimed, taking in the state of Esme.

'Go sort out the cab.' I nodded at the taxi hovering by the kerb, then steered Esme into the living room. Made her sit on the sofa, then turned off the telly.

'What the hell . . .?' I couldn't take my eyes off the

wreck of her face. It looked like she'd been in a car crash – or maybe some kind of fight.

Esme swallowed and winced. 'Have you got a drink?'

I frowned. Judging by the lag in her speech, she'd had enough already, but I went into the kitchen and got a bottle of vodka and some Diet Pepsi from the fridge. Loaded it on a tray with three glasses.

I returned to find you kneeling in front of her, holding her hand while she sobbed. 'Who did this to you, Esme?' Your voice tense and angry.

Esme pulled her hand away and wiped a trail of snot and tears from her cheek. Then shook her head miserably.

'You have to tell us,' you growled. 'For fuck's sake, what happened?'

She looked down. Picked at something on her jumper. 'Victor,' she said, so quietly I almost didn't catch the name.

'*Victor Gomez?*' I stood there, holding the tray, staring at her.

Esme nodded, and I caught the look on your face. Fury mixed with what . . . disgust? Desperation?

'What the fuck, Esme?' I said. 'What were you doing with Victor Gomez?'

I put the tray down and poured her a drink. Esme sniffed, smiling gratefully as I handed it to her. 'Pulsar cancelled my contract,' she said. 'I needed the money.'

Pulsar sacked Esme? When?

I glanced at you, but your expression was as shocked as mine.

'Why?' I gasped. 'Why would they do that?'

Esme took a gulp of vodka and Pepsi. Winced, like her throat was sore. 'Why d' you think?' She shrugged.

244

'They can't get rid of you because of Nelson,' I said. 'You're allowed time off to grieve, for God's sake.'

Esme inhaled. Stared at the contents of her glass. 'It wasn't only that.'

'What then?' But truthfully, I already knew. The situation wasn't hard to read. The drugs. Turning up to shoots half smashed. I was guessing the post-Nelson meltdown had been the final straw.

Not that it made it all right. Pulsar could have cut her more slack. Given her a chance to get her life back on track. Then again, Esme was pushing thirty – perhaps this was simply the excuse they needed.

'Esme . . .' Your voice trailed away. Like you had no idea what to say, where to begin. You sat on the edge of the coffee table, your fists clenched, jaw tight with emotion.

'I know I shouldn't have done it,' Esme murmured, and I realized she was talking about Victor. 'But I've got debts to pay off. I needed the cash.'

I poured myself a drink and sat in the armchair, things beginning to add up. Debts? Drugs, probably. Every time I'd seen Esme since we got back from Las Vegas, she'd been off her head. Mainly on the pills her doctor gave her – or so I'd thought.

'You could have come to us for help.' You were frowning at her. 'You didn't have to resort to Gomez.'

She shot you another grateful smile. Shrugged again before finishing off her vodka.

'So what happened?' I asked.

Esme set her glass on the floor, then dropped her head into her hands and started crying, a horrible jagged sound that reminded me of that night we lost Nelson. I got up and sat beside her, put an arm round her shoulder. Beneath her perfume I caught a whiff of something else. Something sour and unpleasant. Stale, like she'd been really sweaty and it had dried on her skin.

'What did Victor do?' I asked again, more softly this time. Coaxing.

Esme lifted her face and the anguish on it made my stomach clench.

'I ran into problems with my dealer, and the next moment Victor was calling me, offering to get hold of stuff. Nothing much – tranx, that sort of thing. You know, to help me through.'

'But your doctor—' you started.

'My doctor wouldn't prescribe any more pills,' said Esme, sniffing again. 'They get their knickers in a twist about dependency or whatever.' This was said with a bitterness that suggested she thought addiction was some made-up thing.

'How did Victor know you needed them?' you asked.

'No idea.' Esme pulled a face. 'He started calling me up, getting me to hang out over at his place. He was kind of charming.' She glanced at me, a look full of apology. 'I thought maybe people had got him all wrong, what with the rumours over his girlfriend. He has this way about him, sort of convincing. Like he's OK, just misunderstood.'

'But you knew what he did to me,' I said. 'I told you. And in Brighton. You know what he's like, for God's sake. You warned me off yourself.'

I shuddered, remembering the pressure on my throat as he peered into me.

I can see you.

Esme blinked. 'I wasn't thinking straight and he was there and you . . .' She paused, eyes darting between both of us. 'You two had other things on your mind . . .'

I felt my cheeks redden. It was true. I hadn't seen Esme for several weeks, not since you and I had got together. I'd been meaning to get in touch, kept nearly picking up the phone and calling her number, then something would distract me and I'd put it off for another day.

'Esme,' you said, your voice heavy with emotion. 'Tell us what happened.'

She slumped back on to the sofa and inhaled. Seemed to be steeling herself for whatever was coming next. 'He called me last night, suggested we meet up at his studio. Some place out in Barking.'

Barking? I thought his house was in Wimbledon.

'It turned out to be a warehouse, on an industrial estate.' Esme shut her eyes briefly. 'Fuck. I mean, I should have known the second I got there. Should have realized . . .' She broke off. Gazed at me. 'Can I have another drink?'

I poured her a shot of vodka, filling the glass up with Pepsi. Esme gulped down half of it in one go.

'There was this other girl there,' she continued, after a minute or so. 'Very quiet. It wasn't till later I realized she could barely speak English. Victor was giving us booze, and some gear . . . coke, a puff of weed. He was going on about Nelson, asking how he died, interrogating me almost . . . wanting to hear every detail, even asking about you—'

'Me?' I frowned. 'What about me?'

Esme rubbed the side of her temple, as if her head hurt. 'What you were doing, where you were when . . . when he . . . and I was getting fed up, getting pissy, then his phone rang and he disappeared. Next thing I know, there were two other blokes and I . . .' she falters, her voice choking out.

'Who were they?' you asked.

'I've no idea.' She started shaking. 'One of them sounded Eastern European. Russian maybe. The other had a Scottish accent, I think, but not strong. They didn't say much. Just sat there, staring at me. And her.'

'Then what?'

Esme didn't reply, sat gazing into her drink. I felt the hairs on my skin stand to attention. All at once I had a very bad feeling about this.

'Esme?' you prompted.

'Then ... then it all went hazy. I mean, I'd been drinking, had a few lines of coke, but suddenly it turned seriously weird. I can't remember most of it. Only snatches.' She glanced again at both of us. 'I think maybe Victor spiked my drink.'

Shit. I looked at you, but you were busy staring at Esme, all your attention focused on what she was saying. 'Just tell us what you can remember.' You sounded calmer now, but I could see from your expression that you were as freaked by all this as me.

Esme gulped down the rest of her vodka, her hand trembling so violently the glass clinked against her teeth. 'He ... they ... you know, they were filming. And all three of them ... At first I thought that's all it was going to be. A standard gang-bang scene, but then ...'

Without warning she began to cry again, only it wasn't really crying it was wilder, more desperate. A kind of hysteria.

You grabbed her wrists. 'Esme,' you said, shaking her. 'Esme.'

You stared down. Where you'd rucked up the sleeves of her jumper there were several large bruises running

248

the length of her arms. 'You have to go to the police – look at you!'

'I can't . . .' she stuttered, gasping for air. 'I can't . . . he made me do it . . . oh God . . .'

'Esme!' you repeated, more fiercely, holding her wrists up in front of her face. But she kept her head lowered, refusing to see.

Jesus. What the fuck had Victor done to her?

'Joe, let's get her into the bedroom,' I suggested, helping you pull Esme to her feet. We led her through and sat her on the side of our bed. She was still crying, but the fight had gone out of it and she flopped back on to the duvet, curling into a ball. You unzipped her boots and pulled them off. Got a blanket from the cupboard and laid it over her.

We both stood there, watching, for a minute or two. Eyes closed, Esme's terrible, hiccupping sobs gradually subsided, until her breath slowed into the rhythms of sleep.

'Leave her for a while,' I said, pulling you away.

I went back into the kitchen and made us both a mug of tea. When I returned to the lounge, I stopped dead in the doorway. You were pacing the length of the room, fists clenched. Your face a grimace of fury.

'Hey.' I walked over and put the mugs on the coffee table. Stopped you as you reached the window. You wouldn't look at me, carried on staring out at the street-lights and shadows in between.

I waited for you to speak.

'That fucking cunt.' You lifted a fist and banged the window frame, making the glass rattle in the sash. I stepped back in surprise. I'd never seen you so angry;

even when you laid into Victor that time in Brighton, you weren't like this.

You looked desperate. Murderous.

'Joe . . .' I put my hand on your arm. You twisted round and hugged me, burying your face in my neck. 'I'm sorry. It's just . . .' You stopped.

'Just what?' I asked gently.

You released me, turning back to the window. Outside, a couple were highlighted by the street lamp, pausing while their dog stretched into a pee.

'What is it?' I asked again. 'Do you think we should do something? Go to the police?'

I wondered if we could, without Esme. Wouldn't she have to make the complaint against Victor? Besides, we weren't even sure what exactly he'd done.

You didn't speak. I let the silence drag out for a minute or so.

'Joe?'

You turned back to face me. But you still wouldn't speak.

'What is it?' I asked, taking a step towards you.

'I've never told you about Ayanna.' Your tone was quiet. Solemn, like someone breaking bad news.

'Your sister?' You'd only mentioned her in passing, and I hadn't pursued it. Like me, you clearly didn't relish talking about your family.

You sighed. Closed the door, then led me to the sofa. I could feel your hand trembling. Pulling your wallet from the pocket of your jeans, you removed a photo and handed it to me.

It was you, standing next to a beautiful Asian girl with soft features and a serious, earnest expression. She wore a black headscarf, wound tight around her head, covering her hair.

'So are all your family religious?' I asked.

'Not exactly.' You inhaled, letting the air out as a sigh. 'My father more than my mother. Ayanna only got into it after ...' You stopped. Gazed at the picture.

'After what?'

You replaced the photo in your wallet, tucking it back in your jeans. 'Amit, my older brother—'

'You have an older brother too?' Neither you or Esme had ever mentioned him.

You shot me a guilty look. 'Two years older than me.'

'Right.' I felt sort of squashed inside, but tried not to show it. Why had you never told me this before? Didn't you trust me?

'Anyway, Amit got mixed up in some trouble, back when I was still at school. He fell in with this gang. Nothing serious. Petty drug stuff, a bit of fencing.'

I frowned. 'Fencing?' For one insane moment I thought he meant sword-fighting.

'Handling stolen goods,' you explained, seeing my confusion. You clenched your fists again and pressed them into your forehead. I didn't speak. I had a feeling that, if I interrupted, you'd clam up then I'd never find out what this was all about.

'There was this rival gang, based over near Southall. Mainly they stayed out of the way, but occasionally there was a clash over territory. There'd be a skirmish, some kind of reprisal.'

'Reprisal? Like what?'

You glanced back out the window, though from this end of the room it was impossible to see much. 'Ayanna's a year younger than me. She was still a teenager when it happened. Only fifteen.'

You swallowed. This was obviously very difficult for you.

'It was all over a consignment of weed, apparently. They reckoned Amit and another guy had stolen it from one of their suppliers.' You closed your eyes for a second, allowing yourself to remember something you'd clearly prefer to forget.

'Anyway, a couple of the Southall lot waited for Ayanna to come out of school. They bundled her in the back of a car and took her to this empty house near the park.'

'This happened to your *sister*?' I felt a chill of foreboding.

You opened your eyes and looked away, but not before I saw them shining. 'They ... you know ... Three of them. One after the other.' Your legs were shaking now; I could feel the vibration through the sofa cushion.

'Oh Christ, Joe ...' I hugged your shoulder. 'Why? Why didn't you tell me all this before?'

I'd only asked you once about your spell in prison, a few days after we got together. 'A long story,' you'd said, making it clear you'd rather not get into it, and I hadn't pushed any further. I assumed you'd been done for nicking stuff. Joyriding, perhaps.

But this was way more serious than I'd imagined.

You dragged your gaze back to mine, your expression fierce. Then your face collapsed. 'I don't know, Leanne. I'm sorry. I meant to tell you, but it's all so ... complicated.'

Complicated. The same word Esme had once used. Was she aware of all this?

'How?' I persisted, desperate now to hear it all. 'Complicated *how*?'

You groaned. Seemed to come to a decision. 'That wasn't the end of it, Leanne. Amit found her – they'd left her to make her own way home. He found her and made her promise not to tell our parents. Said it would kill them . . . the shame . . .'

'Shame?' I frowned. 'But it wasn't her fault.'

'You don't understand, Leanne.' You sighed with frustration. 'It's different . . . there's this whole thing about family honour. Even in a family like ours, westernized, it still matters. And although it wasn't her fault, people would know . . . they'd talk. Her chances of making a decent marriage would be over.'

'But that's ridicul—'

You held up a hand to silence me. 'I don't want to debate it now, Leanne. I agree it's wrong, but that's the way it is.'

I bit the inside of my cheek to stop myself protesting. 'So what happened?'

'Amit said he'd deal with it himself. *We'd* deal with it.'

'We?' I felt a bit queasy. Suddenly I wasn't at all sure I wanted to hear any more.

You nodded. Wouldn't quite meet my eyes.

'He told me when I got home from college. Told me what they'd done to Ayanna. Wouldn't even let me go upstairs and see her. We got straight in the car and drove over to the house of one of the ringleaders, Ranjit Sayed. Ayanna had described him to Amit, him and the other two. My brother knew who he was looking for.'

A faint noise from the bedroom. Like a cat mewling. Esme.

'I'll go and check.' I got up and popped my head round the bedroom door, but she was fine. Or at least she was breathing OK. Heavily, almost snoring, though she'd kicked off the blanket. She must have whimpered in her sleep.

I walked in and pulled the blanket back over her. As

253

I did I caught sight of the marks on Esme's stomach, where her jumper had ridden up while she slept.

I froze. Those fucking bastards. An image of Victor rose in my mind. I could smell him, my face buried in his pubic hair. All at once I felt dizzy. I rushed into the bathroom, scared I might be sick. Gulped water from the tap until the sensation had passed.

'Leanne?' I heard you calling from the living room. I rinsed my face then went back in, closing the door.

'She's OK.'

Your eyes searched mine as I sat beside you, trying to act like nothing had happened. 'Go on,' I said.

You leaned forward, elbows on knees, head hanging. 'We headed to Sayed's house, a few streets away from where they'd taken Ayanna. Amit went straight in. I ran after him, tried to stop him, but Amit caught Sayed by surprise. He barely had time to register what was happening before Amit decked him with the bat.'

You stopped, your voice cracking with emotion.

'He *killed* him?' I stammered. 'Your brother killed the guy?'

You cleared your throat, forcing yourself on. 'Not killed, no. But he was badly hurt. In a coma for nearly a week. They arrested us the next day. A woman across the road witnessed the whole thing, made a note of Amit's number plate.'

'Jesus . . . so what happened?'

'Amit was over eighteen. He got life.'

'He's in prison?'

'Stanmore.'

'Christ.' I tried to take this in. 'But you . . . why did they prosecute *you*?'

'Accessory,' you said simply. 'They claimed I was fully aware of my brother's intention when we went over

254

there, that I didn't do anything to prevent him. I got two years.'

You sighed, rubbed the palm of your hand over your chin. 'It screwed up my A-levels, my chances of going to university. And when I was released, I had to work. Mum and Dad were broke, from all the legal bills. And no chance that Ayanna would ever be off their hands, not after it was in the papers.'

I rubbed my forehead, trying to process all this. Thought of Amit, in prison for life. For avenging his sister, his family. Their honour.

I grabbed your hand again, squeezing it. 'What was it like?' I asked. 'In there.'

You exhaled, bracing yourself. 'Like I said, Leanne, hell on earth. Fighting, assaults . . . I was only a kid, and a nerdy kid at that. I didn't stand a fucking chance.'

I swallowed. Tried not to let the pictures form in my mind.

'I never want to go back,' you repeated. 'As long as I live I never want to get near another place like that again. I can't even go with my mother when she visits Amit.'

You were trembling as you said this. Quivering with the force of the memories. The guilt. So I lifted my fingers and touched your face. Held them against your cheek, to let you know that none of it mattered – at least not to me.

'I'm sorry, Leanne.' You shook your head, as if in despair with yourself. 'I should have told you all this before. I know it was wrong to keep it from you . . . I was afraid, I guess. Afraid of how you'd react. What you'd think.'

I gazed back at you. And there it was. Another fork in my life. Another crossroads. I could have upped and gone. I could have walked away. Left you to that whole sorry mess before the past seeped into our present and poisoned all of it.

Instead I chose blindness. I chose love.

I chose you.

34

Herne Hill, London

Friday, 26 May 2006

'No police.'

I gazed at Esme, huddled in our bed, hands cupped around the mug of coffee I'd brought her.

'Why not?'

She shook her head, slopping coffee on the duvet cover. I tried not to mind, but I was exhausted. I hadn't got back to my flat till two this morning, leaving Joe to spend the night on the living-room sofa. Neither of us had wanted to disturb Esme; nor leave her on her own.

I took the mug from Esme's hands and placed it on the bedside table. Sitting beside her, I grabbed her wrist, twisting it round so she was forced to face the bruises. Properly livid now, a dark purple tinged with yellow. Both scratches on her cheek had crusted over, but still looked deep enough to scar.

'It's nothing.' Esme snatched her hand away. 'I don't want to report it.'

I thought of what you had told me last night about Ayanna and Amit. How all that could have been

257

avoided if you'd gone to the police instead of allowing your brother to take things into his own hands.

'So you're going to let him get away with this then?' I said. 'Victor and those other two blokes?'

Esme closed her eyes, her mouth beginning to tremble. 'You don't understand,' she murmured, tears leaking down her cheeks. '*I can't*, Leanne.' Her words dissolved into a whimper and she clutched her knees, burying her head in her arms.

'Why, Esme?' I stroked the back of her hair. 'Tell me why.'

'Leanne, *you don't understand*,' she wailed again, lifting her head, her eyes raccooned with lingering smudges of eye make-up. 'I can't tell anybody. *Anybody*.'

I stared at her. Something occurring to me now. 'This hasn't got anything to do with them, has it – those girls, I mean? Anya and that other one?'

Esme blinked. Her jaw tightened and she inhaled. Seemed to pull herself together somehow, straightening her shoulders and getting out of bed. 'Don't be absurd, Leanne.' She started looking for her things. 'Just leave me alone. I'm not going to talk to any—'

At that moment the sound of the front door being opened then kicked shut – you, returning from the corner shop. Your face appeared at the bedroom door, forehead creasing with concern.

'What's going on?' You gazed at me, then at the mess that was Esme.

'I was trying to persuade Esme to go to the police. To report Victor.' I stood up, my voice rising with frustration. 'Look what he's done to her, Joe. He shouldn't get away with stuff like that.'

Or worse, I thought, but didn't say it. After all, there was no proof. We didn't even know what had happened.

Last night, alone in bed in my flat, I'd lain awake, replaying that encounter with Victor. I'd never admitted to you that I'd worked with him. In truth, I didn't want anyone besides Esme to know. I was desperate to erase it from my mind. The thought of him, inside me, in my mouth, anywhere, made my skin crawl.

Victor had wanted to hurt me. Really hurt me. I'd never been so sure of anything in all my life.

I walked into the hallway and took the bag of shopping, leaving you to try and talk some sense into Esme. In the kitchen, I unloaded the bread and milk. Outside the distant blare of a siren, rising then fading as it disappeared into the capital.

Someone else's emergency.

I stuck a couple of slices of bread into the toaster. Somehow I knew Esme wasn't going to talk to me or anybody else. She seemed terrified. Broken. Whatever Victor and those other men had done, it had obviously scared the life out of her.

He made me do it.

Esme's comment last night niggled away at the back of my mind, like a headache you couldn't quite ignore. *He made me do it.* What had she meant?

And why not tell us? What could possibly be so bad she couldn't even confide in her friends?

259

35

HMP Brakehurst

Tuesday, 29 March 2016

'So what did you do,' Yvonne asks. 'About Esme.'

She has her hands folded over my most recent stack of pages, placed on top of my file. I had to stop last night, the battery giving out on my torch. Never got to what happened next, and I can tell by the look on my therapist's face that she's gagging to find out.

'Joe rang her brother,' I say, dredging up the memory of searching through the contacts on Esme's phone, after you'd persuaded her to stay and she'd dropped back off to sleep. 'It was the only family we could locate.'

Not that Esme's brother was exactly keen on taking her in. Said he'd have to clear it with his wife. It was two hours before he called back and agreed Joe could drive her to their house in Bristol.

'So Esme never went to the police?'

I shook my head. 'She flat refused.'

'And you never found out what happened to her?'

'Not then.'

Yvonne studies me for a minute or so. 'Did you have any theories?'

I sigh, slump back in my chair and examine her outfit. A thick khaki fleece that must be way too warm in here, and black jeans, feet cased in those ugly plastic shoes that have come into fashion while I've been inside – the kind you might wear gardening or to the beach.

'I thought Victor and those other guys had roughed her up,' I say. 'Probably the other girl too. I had no idea why Esme was protecting him though, except he'd obviously made her do something she was too ashamed to admit.'

'But you didn't do anything about it?'

'What the fuck could I have done?' I snap. 'Drag her into a police station? Force her to make a complaint?'

'You could have alerted them,' Yvonne replies evenly. 'Told them you believed Victor was hurting people.'

I frown at her. Is she serious?

The psychologist holds my gaze. 'I'm not criticizing you, Leanne. What interests me is how you chose to deal with it. You mentioned a couple of sessions ago that this was the incident that prompted you to get out of porn.'

I nod. It was. I spent the whole time you were in Bristol alone in your flat, mulling it over. The stuff Larry had said after the AVN awards running on a loop through my head.

We just want to watch girls getting nailed . . . being abused.

What happened to Esme felt like a warning. Another I shouldn't ignore.

After all, there's only so many bullets you can dodge.

One way or another I'd started to feel that bolshy make-up woman in LA had been right. That I really was playing Russian roulette. That the longer I stayed in porn, the less life I'd have left afterwards.

Maybe none at all.

'It seemed the right time,' I say to Yvonne.

'I'm assuming you were worried, Leanne. About what happened to Anya Viksna and Tula Kask?'

I look at her. 'Of course I was worried. We all were – the female performers, I mean. But life goes on. We had to keep working, assume the police were handling it, though several girls started getting escorted to and from shoots. But that struck me as stupid. It wasn't like someone would bump you off in the middle of filming, was it?'

Or so I thought then.

'So leaving porn had more to do with Joe?' Yvonne raises an eyebrow into a question mark.

'I guess. It was hard for him, being with someone whose work involved sex with other people. Especially after the AIDS scare. We both knew that was always going to be a risk – I didn't want to put him through that any more.'

'Was he ever jealous?'

'Not really. He understood it was my job, that it didn't mean a thing. If anything, it was me. I felt guilty if I got turned on during a shoot – it felt like . . .' I search for the word.

'Like a betrayal?'

I nod again.

Yvonne says nothing, simply waits for me to continue, sensing there's more. My mind flits back to that first scene at Pulsar and what Rhian had said as she did my make-up, about becoming the character you create. About losing pieces of your soul with every shoot.

'I was scared,' I add. 'Not in the way you think. More that if I carried on I'd lose myself – and Joe.'

Yvonne's expression lifts, and I realize she's pleased. Like we're finally getting somewhere.

I try not to let this irritate me.

'Were you shocked, Leanne, about what Joe revealed that night?'

'Shocked?'

'Yes. What happened to his sister. What he and his brother did afterwards. Did you believe his account? Did you look into it any further?'

I glare at her. 'Check up on him, you mean? Why would I do that? I trusted Joe absolutely.'

This isn't entirely true, of course. I did try to find out more, while you were driving Esme to Bristol. I searched online for information, but turned up nothing. So I googled the young offender institutions, trying to guess which one you'd been in.

Randhurst, probably. It had a terrible reputation, according to several articles I came across. Reading them made me cry, the idea of you, at sixteen, having to endure all that. And worse – the racism must have been terrible.

I'd wondered what had happened to you in there. Did they simply taunt you, or beat you up? Were you raped? Abused?

'So you're saying much of the reason you left porn was for Joe's sake?' Yvonne asks, circling back.

'Yeah.'

'I mean, giving up a successful career must have been a big deal. He meant that much to you?'

'Joe meant everything to me. He was a decent man who loved me.'

'And you hadn't experienced much of that before in your life, had you, Leanne?'

Too right. Every man I'd met up to that point had

263

screwed me over one way or another. Except, I guess, for Mike.

I wait for Yvonne to bring up my father again, but she doesn't. She lifts her gaze to the corner of the room, thinking. I like that about Yvonne, how she takes her time. Never rushes things, even though our sessions only last an hour.

'So did you talk it over with Joe?' she asks. 'About leaving the industry?'

I gaze outside. Blue skies today, little wisps of white cloud visible through the upper window. A couple of rooks streak past, like miniature fighter jets. Where are they off to? I wonder. What goes on in their tiny bird minds to make them take off like that?

Finally I shake my head. 'I didn't want him to talk me out of it. I wanted it to be my decision.'

I remember you arriving home from Bristol, hours late. Traffic on the motorway, you said, kissing my cheek. And stupidly I blurted it out, there and then, told you I'd emailed Pulsar and resigned. That I'd phoned Darryll too, enduring his half-hour lecture on how I was throwing everything away.

I'd told Darryll I didn't care, but watching your expression as I related this, I thought I'd made an awful mistake. Though I had it all worked out. How I could move in here with you, pay half the rent with the money I'd saved. I could redecorate, till I found another job. Cut the lawn and buy some plants to cheer up the back garden.

But you seemed stunned by my news. Not pleased at all. 'So what are you going to do? For money?'

'I don't know.' I shrugged. 'I'll find something.' I could see how tired you were, your face drawn from the drive and dealing with Esme. I should have waited, I realized, should have told you after you'd had a chance to sleep.

But I was too excited. Too apprehensive. For the last eighteen months my whole life had revolved around porn; walking away felt like a step into the unknown. Who was I, if I wasn't Kitty Sweet?

I'd been hoping you'd have the answer.

'What about your flat, Leanne?' you asked several minutes later. 'The rent's nearly two grand a month.'

I stared at you. Felt the bottom drop out of my world, an actual sensation like falling. Was that all you cared about? The money?

Besides, I spent most of my time at your place. It'd be no hardship to give up mine.

I looked away, blinking back tears. My hopes collapsing. My silly little dreams. Why had I ever imagined I could have a normal life?

I remembered, then, what Esme had said in America at the AVNs. *Who wants to be fucking ordinary?*

Me. That's exactly what I wanted. Me and you, leading an ordinary life.

A *normal* life.

'Leanne?' You stepped forward, pulled me into you. 'I'm sorry,' you breathed. 'Leanne, I'm so sorry, I didn't mean that. Of course you can move in with me.' You rested your forehead against mine. 'It was just a bit of a shock – you know, on top of everything – but I'm glad, really I am. It's for the best.'

I gazed up, seduced by your smile, your hand stroking my hair. And let myself believe you.

But I don't tell Yvonne any of this, though she's sitting patiently while I sift through my memories. 'He was pleased,' I say simply, and she nods. Doesn't press me any further.

Me leaving porn meant commitment – I got that, my love. No one needs to know you had doubts, even if it was only for a little while. What do they call it, the nerves people get before a wedding? The jitters?

A touch of the jitters.

Why would I hold that against you?

36

Farringdon, London

Thursday, 6 July 2006

The lobby was huge, probably larger than our flat. The
front a glass wall, covering the whole building; inside
high ceilings and arty steel chandeliers. The reception
desk a sleek sweep of polished granite, two large vases
of flowers perched on each end.

Lilies. And those exotic orange blooms that looked
like the heads of tropical birds.

I gave my name, was directed to wait in an area flanked
by leather sofas. Above, a big flat-screen TV on the wall,
tuned to a news channel; the sound was turned off, but
subtitles ran underneath.

I sat on the furthest sofa and sized up the receptionist, her long blonde hair pulled into a sleek ponytail.
Was she the one leaving? You'll be in a team of three,
the job ad had said, managing reception. Though it was
so calm in here, so pristine, I couldn't imagine there
was much to manage – it seemed more like a church
than a thriving company.

I inhaled, trying to steady my nerves. I could hardly

remember a time when I'd been more anxious – not even that first photo shoot, baring everything but my soul.

Stripping for the camera had nothing on this.

I glanced down at my outfit. A dark-grey skirt and jacket I'd bought a few days ago, convinced the clothes I'd worn to those other interviews were the reason I'd been rejected. Everything I put on felt too short, too low-cut, too revealing – though it was all from ordinary high-street shops.

Today I was worrying about my blouse. I'd arranged a small scarf to cover my cleavage, to appear more demure, but it gaped open every time I bent forward.

So much for proving I was more than just tits and arse.

A low buzz. The girl on reception answered a phone hidden behind the front panel of the desk, then said something to the black security guard manning the lobby, the one who'd been giving me occasional appreciative glances.

I ignored him, raising my gaze to the TV. Pictures of a helicopter hovering over the White House, soldiers in camouflage running across a battlefield somewhere in the Middle East. I was about to turn away when a single photograph filled the screen. A girl, in her early twenties perhaps, though it was hard to tell from this distance. Small, unassuming features. Staring into the camera without smiling.

Subtitles unravelling underneath:

Woman's body found on a Haringey building site. Police suggest link to the landfill murders.

A heaviness in my stomach. Oh Jesus. Another one? But wait . . . there was no mention of her working in porn.

268

It could be anybody, I told myself. *Anybody.*

'Ms Jenkins?'

I looked round at the receptionist.

'Mr Anderson said to let you know he'll be down in a minute.'

I nodded. Glanced back at the screen, the camera panning in on the crime scene, red-and-white tape roping off an area out of shot.

Initial tests confirm the girl was killed between six to eight weeks ago. Detectives are as yet unable to identify the victim.

I felt sick. Suddenly I wanted to go home. Abandon the interview and buy a bottle of wine and try to wipe all this from my head.

Because something about this was bothering me. Something I couldn't quite pin down. An itch in my mind. A warning.

He made me do it.

Six weeks since Esme went to Bristol, and I'd heard nothing, despite ringing her mobile half a dozen times. She never picked up; nor returned the messages I left her.

Gone to ground.

I fished out my phone, went to dial her number again.

'Leanne.'

I raised my head to see a suited man smiling down at me, arm extended. 'Julian Anderson.'

Too late.

I got up and shook his hand. 'This way,' he said, leading me into a corridor surrounded by various suites of offices. Julian directed me towards one at the end,

269

closing the door then sitting behind the desk, indicating the seat opposite with his hand.

'Thanks for coming today, Leanne.' He smiled again, tapping a couple of keys on his open laptop.

'Thank you for offering me an interview.'

I tried to keep my voice steady. That TV report had me rattled, making it hard to focus on why I was here. I felt queasy and tired. Really tired, like everything was suddenly too much.

While Julian Anderson checked something on his screen, probably the covering letter and CV I sent in two weeks ago, I gave the room a quick once-over. Four walls, painted cream. A modern art print with plain blocks of colour dominated the area behind the desk, the only other distraction a whiteboard in the corner, scrubbed clean. All very much like the set Pulsar built for that first shoot with Esme and Nelson.

I pushed the thought from my mind. Before this started to feel like the prelude to a porno.

Julian swivelled his eyes back to mine. 'So, Leanne, you've applied for the position of junior receptionist?'

'Yes.'

'It says here that your last job was working for a film production company?'

I swallowed. 'Yes,' I repeated. It was the closest you and I could think of without actually lying; after all, I was familiar with the environment.

Julian Anderson said nothing, and I saw I needed to be more specific. 'I was a runner,' I added. 'Making tea, chasing up the talen— actors. Photocopying, that sort of thing.'

'What kind of films?' His gaze never left my face, and I noticed an odd twitch in his right cheek. Some kind of tic. He didn't seem aware he was even doing it.

'Corporate stuff. Mainly for the advertising market.'

'Sounds interesting.' Julian leaned back in his chair, his eyes flicking to the screen again before resting on me. 'So tell me why you gave that up?'

'Money,' I shrugged, before realizing that was exactly the wrong thing to say. 'I mean, the money wasn't great in my old job.'

So much for not lying.

'I wanted to get into something steadier,' I went on. 'And I'm interested in business, of course.'

'Right.' Julian Anderson's gaze dropped for a moment, lingering a little longer and a little lower than it should. 'So what sort of qualities would you say you could bring to this . . . err . . . *position*, Leanne?'

There was something in his tone, the way he said my name and emphasized the word 'position', making it sound dirty. I shut my eyes briefly and tried to focus. 'I'm very flexible,' I said, but that only made it worse. I scrambled to remember the things you'd suggested. 'I have well-developed communication skills, and good attention to detail.'

Julian Anderson gazed back, his face impassive, then pressed his lips together as if mulling something over. I had a feeling this wasn't going well. Shit, I thought, my confidence plummeting. Would I never get a normal job? Seems I hadn't the first idea how to sell myself without taking my clothes off.

'Can I ask, Leanne? Are you aware what kind of company we are?'

I frowned. Was that a trick question?

'Management consultancy,' I replied. I'd checked again last night. Genned up as much as I could on the organization and the industry. 'You help other companies become more efficient?'

It came out as a question. I felt like an idiot. A fraud. Like I'd arrived from another country, fresh off the boat, and had no idea how to talk or behave.

'Yes, we're specialists in change management.' Julian Anderson gave a brief overview of the job. I tried to focus on what he was telling me, but I was so nervous I kept tuning out.

'. . . you'd be taking calls, allocating meeting rooms, dealing with incoming and outgoing mail, travel arrangements for our consultants, managing stationery and other supplies.' He stopped. 'Would you say that's within your remit?'

'Absolutely,' I agreed. In truth it didn't sound too difficult.

'So you're familiar with Office?'

'Sorry. Where?'

I caught the look on his face. The barely suppressed smile, and saw I'd blown it. Whatever had been the right answer, I hadn't given it.

'Well, it was a pleasure to meet you, Leanne,' he said, getting to his feet. 'I'll discuss your application with my colleagues and we'll come back to you shortly.'

He held out his hand again. As I shook it, something in his expression, the intensity of his gaze gave him away.

He'd been playing me all along.

Julian Anderson knew exactly who I was. Probably recognized me from the photo I sent in with my CV. This whole thing had been a farce, a set-up. I wasn't really being considered for the job; he just wanted to see what I looked like.

In the flesh.

I blinked, steeling myself not to cry, then made for the door, Julian Anderson following behind. As I

272

headed towards reception, I saw a woman approaching, dressed in a short skirt and high black stilettos, carrying a smart leather briefcase. Her blood-red lipstick the same shade as her tight-fitting blouse.

Exactly like Esme back on that first Pulsar shoot.

Her eyes widened when she saw me. And there it was, a twitch in her lips as she glanced at Julian Anderson. I whipped round, in time to catch his smirk.

She was in on it, I could see. They *both* knew who I was. They'd got me in here for what? Curiosity? Shits and giggles? Something to liven up a dull Thursday afternoon?

'Hey,' I called out, as the woman strode past, clearly trying not to laugh. She paused, looked round.

'Yes, you.' I took a couple of paces towards her. 'Fancy explaining what's so bloody amusing?'

Surprise on her face, then she arched an eyebrow. 'Excuse me?'

'*Excyooose me*?' I repeated sarcastically, mimicking her posh-school accent. 'Don't pretend you don't know what's going on here.' I took another step forward and she flinched, like I might leap on her.

'Miss Jenkins, if you—' I heard Julian Anderson's voice behind me.

'Fuck off,' I said loudly, without bothering to look at him. I kept my eyes fixed on the bitch in front of me. 'Think this is funny, *do you*?'

'I've no idea what—'

'Let me tell you something, Miss Whatever-your-name-is.' I looked her up and down, letting my contempt show. 'I'll bet I was earning twice . . . three times whatever you make in this dump – and I never had to pull this kind of crap to brighten my day.'

In the background, Julian Anderson's voice calling

for security. I stepped right up to the woman executive, watching her shrink back against the wall.

'You think you're so fucking superior, don't you?' I hissed. 'You think porn has nothing to do with you, but take a look at yourself, in your six-inch heels and your teensy little skirt. You're more slutty than half the girls I ever met on set.'

I leaned in, getting right into her face. 'And I bet you shave your pussy too, don't you? Go for a Brazilian once a month, to please the boyfriend. So, tell me, what's the difference between you and me, *sweetheart*?'

Behind me I heard the security guard pounding up the corridor. 'I'll tell you what the difference is, *Ms Toity*, the difference between you and me is I got paid for what I did, and I did a damn good job, while you're a fucking stuck-up tart who thinks that dressing like a porn star will speed up her next promotion.'

A hand grabbed my arm. As the guard hauled me towards the exit, I turned my head, relishing the shock on Julian Anderson's face. I wiggled my little finger at him. 'As for you, *Mr Anderson*, I'm willing to bet everything I ever earned that you've got a really, really small dick.'

A few seconds later I was propelled out the fire exit, avoiding the main reception area. The guard marched me twenty yards up the street before releasing my arm.

I turned to face him and saw that he was grinning. 'Nice one,' he said as we stood there, the wind buffeting along the street and messing up my hair.

'You reckon?' I frowned, rubbing my arm.

'What you said to that bitch in there.' He nodded back towards the building. 'That was a cheap trick they played on you.'

My frown deepened. 'How do you mean?'

He looked down. Despite his dark skin, I could tell he was blushing. He had a nice face. Mid-thirties, I reckoned; from South London, if his accent was anything to go by.

'Everyone knew,' he said. 'I heard it from Macey on reception.'

I felt the heat of shame seep from the soles of my feet right up to my scalp. It was all I could do not to burst into tears.

The guard caught my expression. 'Hey, forget it.' He looked like he wanted to pat my shoulder or stroke my hair or something. 'Fuck them. You're best off out of it. The whole company's going down the pan anyway, what I heard. With any luck, they'll all be out of a job soon.'

I managed a smile, and his face turned serious. 'Do you mind if I say something?'

I nodded.

'I hope you won't take this the wrong way, but I just wanted you to know . . . well . . . your stuff rocks, Miss Sweet. You were always one of my favourites, and I'm sorry you've given it up, but I really hope you find whatever it is you're looking for.'

Whatever I'm looking for.

What was that, I wondered, as he turned and headed back. I felt shaken. Devastated. My small victory inside that office block feeling increasingly hollow.

I was trapped, I realized. I'd never get away from porn. From my past.

I leaned against the wall of the next-door building as hope drained away. I should have listened to Rhian, on that first shoot for Pulsar, back before it all began. Didn't she warn me not to mix them up? Your real self and your alter ego, the one you create for the screen.

275

The minute the two begin to merge, that's when you need to get out.

Advice I should have taken to heart. It was too late, I knew that now. Leanne and Kitty were fused together.

Forever.

And nothing would ever prise them apart.

37

Romford, Essex

Sunday, 9 July 2006

'I'm not sure I can do this, Joe,' I said, as we stood outside the station, gazing down the street in the direction of the pub. Traffic kept getting in the way but I could make it out in the distance, near the corner of the intersection with Victoria Road.

'C'mon.' You took my hand and gave it a tug, but my feet were rooted to the pavement. So you turned and folded me into a hug. 'You *can* do this, Leanne.'

I still couldn't move. 'They won't want to see me,' I repeated, for what felt like the hundredth time since we visited your parents a fortnight ago. When you got this idea into your head.

'But they've already agreed. Why do you think we're here?'

It was true. You'd persuaded me to send Mum and Mike an email, saying we'd like to come and see them and the twins. To my surprise, I'd had a reply.

If you could call it that. Barely more than a time and a date.

Today, 2 p.m.

But here, now, with ten minutes to go, I was having second thoughts.

'Listen, we've been through all this,' you said. 'We'll give it a try. Take things slowly. It might not be as bad as you imagine, Leanne.'

You were always so persuasive, weren't you, Joe? Working on me until the idea began to thaw in my mind. Somehow managing to convince me that it would be the best thing to do. That we could be normal. That everything would turn out OK.

You infected me with your optimism. Blinded me to everything that could go wrong.

Right up until the end.

'So you're living together?'

There was no joy in Mum's voice. She was staring at me, stony-faced. Had been pretty much from the moment we arrived, though at least she'd let us in; all the way here I'd been afraid she'd have a change of heart, would simply slam the door in my face.

'Yes, at Joe's place.' I knew my cheeks were reddening. I felt sick again, like my stomach was bearing the brunt of everything that had gone bad in my life.

'So you've been together how long?' She glanced from you to me, her expression a shade away from hostile.

'Mum. Don't be like that, please.'

'How long?'

'I don't know.' I tried not to sound irritable. 'Three months or so, but we've known each other for well over a year.'

Mum raised an eyebrow.

'To be fair, Sally,' Mike cut in, 'it wasn't much longer than that before I moved in.' His tone was weary.

Conciliatory. Though he'd hardly met my eyes since we arrived.

They knew about the porn, obviously. How could they not? But it wasn't until I was sitting here, upstairs in the pub, that I realized how part of me had been clinging on to the ridiculous hope that somehow, just somehow they didn't. That those blokes at Mum's party had kept schtum. That no one else had blabbed it to them. That our estrangement for the last year was down to something else entirely.

Something that could be mended.

'Well, Leanne, I have to say you've plenty of nerve.' Mum straightened up and inhaled, her features tight. She kept her eyes on Mike, as if waiting for him to confirm her sense of outrage. 'Turning up out the blue to announce you're living with some bloke we've never even met.'

'I'm sorry,' I said, meaning it. Suddenly I had no way to explain my behaviour. Why hadn't I tried harder? Come home and confronted this sooner?

But of course we all knew the answer to that. I was a coward. As long as I didn't see them, I wouldn't have to witness their disgust. Wouldn't have to deal with the embarrassment and shame.

'So what do you do, Joe?' Mike asked, changing the subject.

You cleared your throat. 'I drive a taxi.'

Another lie we'd agreed upon. That you'd taken a share in your cousin Ashad's taxi business. I watched your face as you said it, smoothly, without a ripple of guilt. You were good at this, I realized. Had a talent for deceit.

Mum, however, wasn't convinced. 'So how long have you been doing that for, then?'

279

'A year or so.'

'And what did you do before that?'

'Does it matter?' I snapped, unable to hold myself in any longer. 'Did you care about Mike's job when you met him?'

Everyone fell silent. I clutched the mug of tea Mum had made when we arrived. All that was on offer, it seemed – a far cry from the lavish meal your parents had laid on. Lots of different home-cooked dishes, delicious and nothing like those greasy, lurid-coloured takeaways Mum and Mike get from the Indian round the corner.

Mike coughed, but everyone remained silent. We appeared to have run out of small talk. I wished the twins were here, could distract us from this stand-off. But Mum had said they were on a birthday outing, some kid in their class.

I wasn't sure I believed her – more likely Mum wanted them out the way, had asked a friend to mind them.

She didn't want me near them. My own brothers. Like I'd contaminate them or something.

The thought made my eyes hot and I looked down to hide my face. Examined the carpet, even more worn and tired-looking than I remembered. The tangle of wires round the back of the TV. I saw the games console was different to the one I'd got them the Christmas before last. They'd probably ditched it, I realized, along with the earrings and anything else I'd bought them with the money I'd earned.

I inhaled, trying not to let it get me down, but the contrast with the visit to your parents made everything feel worse. Even the setting. Your parents' home wasn't large – an ordinary semi in Brent, crammed with sofas and armchairs, padded velvet footrests and little side

280

tables. The walls were covered in prints and paintings, the mantelpiece crowded with ornaments, carved wooden elephants, china figurines, a pair of ornate glass candlesticks.

But it was immaculate. Everything lovingly cleaned and cared for. None of the dinginess and air of neglect of these rooms above the pub.

'You should have told us,' Mum said without warning, her voice low.

'I just have,' I sighed. 'That's why we're here.'

'I don't mean about your relationship.'

The atmosphere in the room seemed to shift. Mike fidgeted in his chair; even seated, you could read the strain in his posture.

'You should have told us, Leanne, not left us to find out via a bunch of squaddies. Not left us to look like a couple of bloody *mugs*, everyone knowing, everyone talking behind our backs.'

Mum was glaring at me now, fury filling her eyes with tears. 'How could you, Leanne? How could you do that? Christ, the flack Mike's had to take in the pub. People cracking jokes all the time, laughing behind his back. In front of him, even. He came in once and found one of your DVDs playing on the screen in the games room. Can you imagine what that was like, Leanne? What Mike *saw*?'

She eyeballed me, jaw rigid with emotion. 'Then you roll up here telling us you're living with somebody and this is the first time we've ever met him.' She spat out the words like they tasted bad, then turned to you.

'I'm assuming you know ... what she does. I'm assuming she hasn't been pulling the wool over your eyes too.'

You nodded. 'Yes. I know. I always knew.'

281

'Right.' Mum bit her lip, gazing out the window. Clearly fighting back tears.

'The twins, Leanne,' she said quietly, after a minute or so. 'Did you never give a thought to your brothers?'

Tears stung my eyes too. I nodded miserably, unable to speak. This was worse than I'd imagined, though God knows, I'd run through this whole scenario in my head a thousand times.

'Well, since you ask, they don't know,' she added, bitterly. 'At least, I don't think so. They've never said anything, but it's only a matter of time, isn't it? How long till some kid at school spots you online? That stuff, it's all over the bloody Internet. Anyone can see it.'

Her voice broke off. Mike leaned across and put his arm around her. 'Sally, come on. This isn't going to help.' He still wouldn't look at me.

But Mum wasn't finished. She'd obviously been waiting a long time to get this off her chest. 'And what about *your* kids, Leanne?' She glanced at me, then you. 'I'm assuming you'll both want children one day. What about them? What are you going to say when their friends find out? Or their teachers? What will you tell *them*?'

I felt my stomach churn again. Mum was right, of course. I hadn't looked far enough ahead. Didn't appreciate back when all this started that I'd be a different person in five or ten years' time. That I might want different things.

Shit, what a fucking mess I'd made of everything.

'I hardly know who you are any more, Leanne. Impossible to believe you were ever any part of me.'

I glanced at you, but your gaze was trained on the floor. Were you regretting this, I wondered. I thought back to the reception we got from your parents, your mum all smiles in her best pink sari, your sister Ayanna so lovely, even with that black headscarf covering her hair.

'I'm sorry,' I repeated, watching the clock on the mantelpiece tick off the seconds as I flailed around trying to find something to say. How could I possibly make this better?

'I was in such a state after Ross—' I broke off. What was the point of excuses? I couldn't explain it, not when it came down to it, not even to myself. How I'd wrecked my life with one advert, one stupid decision. How I didn't think any of it through until it was too late.

'I'm sorry,' I whispered again, wishing I hadn't come. This was hard. Too hard. Mum voicing all the things I was most afraid of – and could no longer change.

'What about those other women, Leanne?' Mum's voice was beginning to crack. 'Ever thought about them? They reckon he's targeting girls in porn. Is that how you want to end up, dumped in a rubbish tip somewhere?'

I nearly laughed. Ever thought about them? They were always there, shadowy figures lurking at the back of my mind. At the back of all of our minds.

My thoughts flashed to Esme, wondering if that was why she'd disappeared off the radar. I'd assumed it was because there was nothing left for her in London, what with Nelson gone, along with her career. That she'd cut it all loose – us, the city, this whole episode in her past.

But maybe she was just frightened. Wanted to keep herself out of harm's way.

Another silence. Then Mum cleared her throat, building up for one final assault. 'Your father,' she said slowly, like the words were poison to her. 'Your father knows. He wrote to me a few weeks ago. Seemed to think it was *my* fault.'

Suddenly the room ran out of oxygen. I stood up. So fast my tea slopped on to the carpet and you seized my mug as I moved towards the door. I crossed the landing, barely making it to the bathroom before I threw up.

Oh God. Oh God, oh God, oh God, oh God.

I closed my eyes, still kneeling on the grubby bathmat, gasping for air. My breathing laboured from the effort of being sick.

Jesus, why had I come here today? How had I ever imagined it would be a good idea?

I forced myself to my feet and flushed the loo. Splashed water on my face, avoiding my gaze in the mirror. Went back into the living room.

'Let's go.' I turned to you, not looking at Mum or Mike. Neither spoke as we picked up our jackets and left. No one even said goodbye.

That's haunted me, these last ten years.

I never said goodbye. I was too desperate to get out of there. Too shocked and humiliated by what I'd heard about my father.

But then, how could I have known it would be the last time I'd ever see my mother?

38

Herne Hill, London

Thursday, 13 July 2006

Four days later there was a ring on the doorbell, right after I'd stripped for a shower. I pulled on your dressing gown, unable to suppress a rush of hope that it was Mum. That maybe she'd had a change of heart, had come round to patch things up.

But it was Esme I found standing outside. Bare-faced, pale, and drenched – caught in the heavy rain that had set in that morning, the kind you get after a run of dry weather.

'Esme . . . *Jesus.*'

I stared at her. How long had she been out there? Water was dripping from her hair, and her clothes were soaked. 'Come in, for God's sake. Let me get dressed.'

I darted into the bedroom, wriggling into jeans and a cotton jumper. But when I returned to the living room, she wasn't there. 'Esme?' I checked the kitchen and bathroom, but there was no sign of her. I went back to the front door. It was still ajar.

Peering out, I caught sight of her retreating down the street.

'Esme!' I shouted, but if she heard she ignored me. I slipped on a pair of boots and ran outside. 'Esme!' I yelled again, but she kept on going. I sprinted after her, splashing through puddles, and grabbed her arm, forcing her to turn and look at me.

'Esme, what the fuck? Why are you running off like this?'

Out here in broad daylight, I could see her properly. She looked terrible. I mean, truly, truly terrible. Her eyes were ringed with shadows, dark as bruises, her hair even greasier and more tangled than the last time she was here. And she was swaying slightly.

Off her head, I realized.

'Esme, what the hell is going on?'

She stood there, gazing at me. But not quite meeting my eyes.

'Come on.' I pulled on her arm. 'Let's not stand out here. It's freezing.' Rain was beginning to soak into my scalp, into my clothes; another minute and I'd be as wet as Esme.

My friend resisted for a moment or two, then let me lead her back to the flat. I sat her on the sofa and perched on the armchair opposite. I'd have offered her a cup of tea, but I was worried she'd run off again the moment I turned my back.

'What's going on, Esme? I thought you were in Bristol.' I couldn't stop staring at her, at how thin she'd become, how much older she looked. She'd changed so much in the last six weeks I could barely take it in.

'Esme,' I asked again. 'How come you're back in London?'

She shrugged. Gazed down at her hands. Her nails, once neatly manicured, were chipped and flaking. 'My brother threw me out.'

'Threw you out? Why? When?'

She didn't answer. Simply lowered her head and groaned.

'Esme, what's the matter? What's happened?'

She was drunk again. I could smell the alcohol on her breath, sweet and heady. But when she looked up, I saw her pupils were wide as saucers. She'd clearly got hold of more than booze.

'Where's Joe?' she asked, her voice slurry.

'On a shoot.'

'At Pulsar?'

I shook my head. 'Some manor house out in Berkshire.' The studio had hired the place for a couple of days and was shooting several scenes back-to-back. 'He left early. He's not home till tonight.'

'I wondered where he was.' Esme sniffed. 'I mean, when he wasn't at work.'

'You went to Pulsar?' I frowned. Why would she do that? 'Were you looking for Joe?'

She shook her head. 'Not really ... I ...' Her voice drifted off. Like she'd forgotten what she was saying.

'Why did your brother kick you out?' I asked again.

Esme stared around the living room as if seeing it for the first time. Her gaze fixed on that carriage clock I'd bought from Selfridges, on a shopping trip a lifetime ago. My CDs stacked on top of yours. The little bits and pieces I'd brought from my flat.

'So you've moved in?' There was something in her expression I couldn't read.

I nodded. Wondering if all this was about Nelson, about the reversal in our fortunes. Esme, alone and single again. Me, shacked up and happy.

'When?' she asked suddenly.

'A couple of months ago.'

She ran a hand across her face, digesting this. 'After I'd gone to Bristol?'

'Yeah. When I left Pulsar.'

Esme sniffed again. 'I heard about that.'

'I told you about all of it,' I insisted. 'Left you half a dozen messages on your phone.'

She didn't respond. Just glanced around, as if thinking something over. 'I have to go,' she said suddenly, lurching to her feet.

'No, Esme, stay.' I pulled on her wrist and she slumped back on to the sofa. 'Tell me what the matter is. Is it Victor? Has he hurt you again?'

She laughed. It was an awful kind of laugh, more desperate than amused. Then her head dropped into her hands and she started crying.

'I'm fucked,' Esme sobbed. 'Everything, Leanne. I'm totally screwed.'

I took her hand in mine. 'Of course you aren't, Esme. You're simply going through a bad patch. That shit with Victor . . . and Nelson, it's bound to take a while, you know, to get over it all. But you will. You'll get back on your feet, start working again.'

Esme snorted. 'Are you kidding, Leanne? Who the fuck would have me now?' She shook her head, as if at my stupidity. 'I can't even look at my face in the mirror, let alone perform.'

'OK,' I conceded. 'But there's other things you can do.'

'Yeah?' she asked, almost aggressively. 'How's that working out?'

I gazed at her, puzzled. I hadn't told her I was looking for a job. Had someone at Pulsar mentioned it? But who knew, besides you?

'Come on, Esme,' I said, my tone soothing. 'Don't be so down on yourself. You're beautiful. You'll meet someone new. This is a horrible phase in your life, that's all.'

'Really?' My friend's expression was mocking. 'Who wants an ex-porn star for a wife, let alone have kids with them? It's like having a virus, Leanne, like HIV or herpes – you've got it for life. We'll never be rid of it, what we've done.'

Mum's words echoed through my head. Hadn't she said much the same thing?

'You know, when I went into it, I thought porn was a ticket to a better life.' Esme's voice was full of exhaustion and bitterness. 'I imagined it would be all money and glamour.' She stared at the window, watching the rain hurl itself against the glass. 'And it was, for a while. But then it all catches up, and you realize you've screwed up everything that matters.'

She closed her eyes for a couple of seconds, brushing a strand of wet hair from her cheek. That was when I noticed Nelson's rings were gone.

She caught my gaze. 'Pawned them,' she said. 'Needed the money. Anyway, they were only making me feel worse.'

I had no idea what to say to any of this. I could feel my mood spiralling down, a terrible weariness creeping over me. I glanced around for my mobile, wanting to ring you, see if there was any chance you might get away early.

Perhaps you'd know how to handle this.

'I rang my mum,' Esme blurted, and the coincidence jerked my head back to hers. 'In Portugal. She told me to fuck off and put the phone down.'

Jesus. I guessed I should thank my lucky stars mine was still speaking to me. Just.

'What about your dad?' I nearly asked, then

remembered Esme told me he was dead, back when I discovered I had herpes. We'd rarely mentioned our families since. It was no-go territory, an exclusion zone. Something we'd rather not dwell on.

Your father. Your father knows.

My stomach clenched again as I recalled Mum's words. My father. His disgust, his disappointment, mirrored in my mother's expression.

I forced my attention back to Esme, trying to think of something comforting to say. 'I'm sorry about your mum. That's rough.' Though God knows, things had hardly gone better with mine.

Esme began to sob again, her lips twisting with emotion. 'I still miss him, Leanne. All the time.'

I assumed she was talking about Nelson, and I didn't know how to respond so I stroked her hand. 'What about your brother?' I suggested, hoping I could get Esme to tell me why he'd chucked her out. 'Can't he speak to your mum? Explain what's happened?'

Esme swallowed and I felt her hand trembling. Low blood sugar probably; I mentally scanned what food I had in the kitchen.

'My brother won't do anything for me. Not now.' She said this so quietly it was barely a whisper.

'Why not?' Surely things can't have gone that bad between them. What had Esme done to piss him off so much? Got plastered and puked up on his carpet? Shagged someone in his marital bed?

'He knows,' she said, eyes averted from mine.

I frowned at her. 'What do you mean? I thought he already knew what you did.'

My friend swallowed again, visibly steeling herself for whatever she was about to say. 'Not that, Leanne. I'm not talking about my work.'

'What, then?'

A pause, before she answered. 'What happened with Victor.'

'But that's not your fault, what he did.' I squeezed her fingers to emphasize my point. 'Why would your brother hold that against you?'

More tears rolled down Esme's cheeks. She looked desperate. Like someone on the edge. That itch in my mind again, more insistent now. Closer to something I'd rather avoid.

'He knows what Victor made me do, Leanne. I broke down and told him – after I saw that girl on the news.'

'What girl?' But the moment I asked, I knew. 'You mean the one they found in Haringey?'

Esme nodded, and the ache in my gut hardened to actual pain. 'Was she the other girl, that evening with Victor and those men?'

She nodded again.

I let a few moments pass before speaking. Outside a siren blared past in the road parallel to ours.

'Esme,' I said, exhaustion turning to dread, 'tell me what happened.' But some part of me already knew. It was like I'd always known somehow. That I'd just managed to keep it at the margins of my thoughts, never quite allowing it into focus.

He made me do it.

My friend gazed at me. A look on her face I'd never seen on anyone before – or since. Desperate. Despairing. It was even worse than when Nelson died.

'I . . .' She stopped. Unable to bring herself to say it.

'You did it, didn't you? You killed her.'

I'm looking for a special kind of girl. One prepared to go all the way. Wasn't that what Victor had said, when I did that shoot with him?

291

Esme gazed back at me, eyes swollen with fresh tears. Then she nodded.

A tiny movement. But it was there.

I let go of her hand, my mouth gaping with shock. My brain refusing to take it in, though the weight in my stomach told me it was true. She doesn't mean it, said a voice in my head. Esme has no idea what she's saying, has screwed with so many drugs, so much alcohol, she's completely lost her grip on reality.

All of this was some kind of mistake. It had to be.

Then I remembered those scratches on her cheek. Those bruises, on her arms, on her belly . . . like someone had been fighting back, someone panicking, someone . . .

I stood up, trying to shut down the images that rose in my mind.

Esme leaned forward, grabbed my hand again and I had to resist the urge to pull it away. 'He made me do it, Leanne. I swear.' Her voice urgent, frantic even. 'It would have been me if I hadn't. It was her or me. That was the deal.'

I swung round. 'Esme, what the fuck are you talking about? How could Victor possibly make you do that? Why?'

My voice was rising. I felt shaky. Like I was going to throw up again. I didn't want to hear any of this, deal with any of this. I tried to move away, but Esme kept a tight grip on my hand, refusing to let go.

'It *was her or me, Leanne.* The client wanted another girl to do it this time. So it was her or me.'

'Esme,' I said, my voice wavering. 'Esme, what did you actually *do?*'

Then my phone rang, from somewhere in the kitchen. I knew from the ringtone that it was you.

292

'I have to go.' Esme jumped up, as if released from a spell. She placed both hands around my face, and bent to kiss me, briefly, on the mouth.

'I'm sorry,' she repeated, resting her forehead against mine for a second before stumbling out the door.

This time I let her go.

39

Herne Hill, London

Thursday, 13 July 2006

I went to the supermarket after Esme left. That sounds crazy, like I wasn't devastated by what she'd told me, but I couldn't think what else to do. I couldn't face sitting around the flat, churning over her confession.

Besides, we needed some food.

I grabbed a sandwich for lunch – one I knew I wouldn't eat – a packet of fresh ravioli and a pot of tomato and basil sauce for later. Stood waiting at the checkout, numb with shock.

Could it possibly be true? Did Esme really kill that girl?

I'd left you a message, after she'd gone, asking you to come straight home. Said it was urgent though I didn't give any details. I wanted to tell you face-to-face. Work out together what on earth we should do.

Even so, I was surprised, as I let myself back into the flat, to hear you in the living room, talking on the phone. I dumped the shopping in the kitchen and ran myself a glass of water. I still felt tired and trembly, all the stress of the morning taking its toll. Your voice, barely audible in the lounge, sounded strained, though I couldn't make out what you were saying.

Five minutes later you stood beside me as I unloaded the food into the fridge. When I got up and caught your expression, I saw how anxious you were. Was that Esme on the phone? Had she rung to tell you what she'd already confessed to me?

'What's up?' I asked, searching your face for clues.

Your mouth twitched in response. There was a pause before you replied, a moment where you were clearly considering whether to lie or tell the truth.

'It was my father.'

Your father. I flashed back to our visit to your family home. The way he observed us quietly, wearing an awkward half-smile that looked like it hurt his face. How he watched you, all the time, like someone hungry, faced with food. As if he could never get enough of you.

'Is everything OK?' I asked.

'It's nothing.' You stared out the kitchen window at the garden. At the lawn I still hadn't cut and the flower-beds I still hadn't planted, and I felt a pang of regret that it all looked so dreary and neglected. 'He wanted to discuss something.'

I let that hang in the air for a minute. But as you turned back, your face was sad. It made my heart curl into itself, seeing you like that.

'Joe,' I said, tired of trying to guess what was going on in other people's heads. 'I don't believe you. Tell me what the matter is.'

You returned my gaze, knowing I had you sussed. 'Dad's lost his job, Leanne. He's been off with a bad back for six weeks and they've sacked him. It looks like they might have to sell the house.' You closed your eyes briefly, as if that was unthinkable.

Mine widened. 'Why, Joe? Surely it won't come to that.'

'Money,' you sighed. 'They took out several loans when me and Amit . . . you know, to help pay legal costs and other stuff. And the bank is threatening to foreclose.'

'How much?'

'Fifteen thousand. They have to find three grand in the next week to head them off.'

Fifteen thousand? Shit, your poor parents. I'd no idea things were so bad. 'Didn't you get legal aid or anything?' I asked. 'When you and Amit . . .'

'Yes and no.' You exhaled, sitting down at the tiny kitchen table where we ate our meals. 'Dad wanted to make sure we had the best representation. And he took loads of time off work, and then Mum was made redundant after the trial. It all built up.'

'Fuck.' I sank on to the other chair. Thought of that little house. All that furniture. All those things. 'Where will they go? If they have to sell.'

'It's not going to come to that.' Your voice fierce, as if by refusing to believe it could happen you could somehow head it off. 'I'll think of something. Maybe get an extra job. Ask Ashad if I really can do a few shifts with the minicab.'

'But that's not going to come anywhere near—'

'It'll have to,' you snapped, and I could see you were hovering on some kind of brink. 'What other choice do I have, Leanne? Ayanna's at university, but now she's threatening to leave . . . No way I can let her do that.'

'I'll go back to work. I'll call Darryll tomorrow.'

Your eyes locked on mine. Your expression tight. 'No, Leanne. That's not the answer.'

'It makes sense, Joe. Think about it. I'm simply hanging around the flat all day—'

'There's other jobs. Other things you can do.'

'What? Stack shelves in the supermarket? Sweep the bloody streets?'

'Why not?'

I glared back at you. I felt insulted. Was that all you thought I was worth? And how come you cared so much anyway? I asked myself, remembering your initial reaction when I told you I was leaving porn. The uncertainty in your face.

I looked at you now. Your head turned away, but I could tell you were upset. A few minutes passed where neither of us spoke. Both locked into our own private thoughts.

'So, what's going on?' You were first to break the silence, but the shutters had come down; it was clear you no longer wanted to discuss your family, or what we should do. 'Why did you need to speak to me so urgently?'

Esme's face rose in my mind. Her anguish. Her terrible admission. I tried to think how to tell you, to find the words, but now wasn't the time. I could see you'd had more than enough for one day.

Fuck. I felt my exhaustion deepen, dragging me down as I tried to come up with an excuse, some way of stalling, till tomorrow. Could things get any worse?

As if in answer, your phone rang again.

40

HMP Brakehurst

Tuesday, 5 April 2016

'That must have been terrible, Leanne. When you heard.'

Yvonne is gazing at me, her expression sympathetic. Again I'm wondering how much of it is sincere. I'd arrived early this morning, caught her reading through what I'd written, pencilling notes on a separate piece of paper.

Questions? Doubts? It made me uncomfortable, the thought of being evaluated like that.

'Yes, it was horrendous,' I say in answer to her statement, though my words sound hopelessly inadequate. How to begin to describe it? I recall your face as you listened to Gus from Pulsar breaking the news. The way your skin paled. How you pressed your lips together to stop them trembling, but your hand shook as you held the phone to your ear.

'OK,' you said finally. 'Leave it with me. I'll speak to her brother.'

You ended the call and tipped your head back, blinking at the ceiling.

'What is it, Joe? What's happened?'

Slowly, as if time had stretched and sagged, turning seconds into what felt like hours, you twisted round to face me. The shock on your features was awful to see. I watched your struggle to bring something under check before you spoke.

'Esme's dead.'

It was like someone had kicked me in the stomach. I slumped on my chair, winded.

Esme was dead.

It wasn't possible.

'But she was here,' I whispered. 'Only hours ago. She was looking for you.'

You didn't reply. Simply opened the back door and walked out into the garden. It wasn't dark yet, but the rain clouds made it gloomy. I watched you standing there, facing the railway line, as if waiting for something. Or someone.

'Leanne?' Yvonne's voice snaps me back to the present. I stare at her, like I've forgotten who she is and why I'm here.

'Are you OK, Leanne?'

I wipe my cheek on my sleeve and nod.

'How did Esme die?' she asks.

'A neighbour found her body in her flat. Syringe by her side. She'd taken an overdose.'

'An overdose?'

'Heroin.' I clear the lump in my throat. 'That was half the shock of it – we didn't know she'd been injecting. Hadn't seen any evidence. No needle marks on her arms or anything like that. I mean, Esme was often high, sometimes completely off her face, but never in withdrawal. She was into drugs, yeah, but she wasn't an addict.'

'There's a difference?' Yvonne crosses one leg over the other. She's wearing thin cotton trousers and a short-sleeved T-shirt; it must be warm outside as well as in here.

'She didn't use needles – I guess that's the difference.'

'All the same, this must have come as an awful shock.'

It had. You stood there, in the garden, for what felt like forever but was probably more like ten minutes. When you came in you were shivering, even though the rain had stopped and you were still wearing your coat.

'Are you going to ring her brother?' I asked. 'Do you want me to do it, Joe?'

You shook your head. Went into the bedroom and closed the door. A minute later I heard you speaking on the phone.

'What about you, Leanne?' Yvonne's question drags me back again. 'Esme was your friend. Your mentor too, as you said. How did this news make you feel?'

I blink.

I'm still not sure I know the answer to that.

I never saw Esme's body – not in real life, but I did in my sleep. She visits me, even now. At first, in the mess she was towards the end, drugged and bewildered.

'What happened, Leanne?' she asked once, turning up in my dream like an uninvited guest. 'What happened to me?'

These days she looks happier. More like that weekend in Brighton. Elated. Carefree, as if nothing could ever touch her. It's like she's reliving her life – only backwards – and now she's arrived at the good bit, while I'm stuck in here, in Brakehurst, counting off the hours.

So I never saw her dead, though you did. You waited for Esme's brother to arrive from Bristol. It was gone eight when he stood at the door of our flat, still in his work suit, his face pudgy, his hair receding so much he was virtually bald on top.

I studied him but couldn't see a trace of Esme. As if she'd got one half of the gene pool, him entirely the other.

'Don't wait up,' you said as you left. 'I've no idea how long this will take.'

What did you imagine I was going to do, Joe? Have a bath and an early night? It was like Esme's death had nothing to do with me, that it was your business, and yours alone.

I assumed you were protecting me. Acting like your father, taking all the burden. All the responsibility.

So I never saw Esme's body – you spared me that. Though I did go to the funeral, in a church in a small village in Somerset. Which was crazy, because Esme hated the countryside; she was as far from a mac and wellies kind of girl as you could get. No doubt her brother had hoped it would keep her porn friends from turning up.

He was wrong. The place was heaving. Practically everyone from Pulsar was there, even the runners and the editing crew. And what looked like most of the performers she'd ever worked with, standing out a mile in their make-up and showy clothes.

It made me proud, actually, seeing the way their eyes flitted over the other mourners, daring them to react. 'Fuck you' written right across their faces.

Esme's tribe.

I counted the wreaths before we left. Fifty-three, to be exact. Several had photos of Esme attached. In the centre of the largest – the one from Pulsar – was her bestselling DVD – 'Love, Lies and Cream Pies' – surrounded by a mass of white lilies and blue forget-me-nots. Stratos, the LA film company, had sent over a gold plaque, engraved with the words 'Pasha Steele', and displayed it next to Esme's AVN award.

I never did work out how they got hold of that.

I watch Yvonne's expression as I'm telling her this, filling in all the stuff I couldn't bring myself to write down. Alert for signs of disapproval.

But she sits there, her face unmoving. Not giving anything away. Not speaking until I mention the inquest. 'You're saying you didn't believe Esme's death was accidental?'

I shook my head.

'So what was your theory, Leanne?' She leans forward, like she can't quite hear, though I'm talking at a normal volume.

'I assumed it was suicide.'

'You thought she killed herself?'

I nod. 'It made sense. She'd lost everything. Nelson. Her job. Her livelihood. What did she have left to live for?'

'And how about what Esme told you just before she died? About Victor. What he made her do. Why didn't you go to the police. Leanne?' A trace of real emotion, finally, in Yvonne's voice. A crack in that neutral front she maintains.

'Yvonne,' I say, as patiently as I can. 'What proof did I have? Nothing. I had absolutely no evidence besides Esme's confession.'

'So did you tell Joe? What she said?'

'Not right away, but later, a few days after the funeral. He was too . . . Esme's death hit him hard. They'd been friends a long time.'

'And what was his reaction?'

I replayed it in my mind. Your disbelief when I disclosed what Esme claimed to have done. You kept shaking your head, like I was making the whole thing up. You wouldn't accept it. No way Gomez could get away with anything like that, you concluded. Esme had been confused, too drunk and drugged to have a clue what she was saying.

You were convinced. Convincing. Eventually I believed it too.

'So Joe never suggested going to the police either?' Yvonne asks.

I shook my head. 'Like I said, what evidence did we have? An alleged confession from someone who was no longer around to confirm it. Someone who was emotionally unstable, and a long-term drug user to boot.'

The therapist purses her lips, but doesn't argue. She leans further forward, resting her forearms on her knees. 'Can I ask you something, Leanne?'

I shrug. 'Go ahead.'

'Up to this point, you've kept this version of events to yourself. You pleaded guilty to both counts of murder and refused to give any details to anyone. So why tell me all this now? What's changed?'

I think of you. How you were in those last few weeks we had together. I think about you and what happened and I get a feeling about the past, a sense that it was inevitable. Unavoidable. That somehow things were always going to turn out the way they did.

Like I was the actress in that film, sitting in the station café, waiting for the train that would separate us for ever. Unable to do anything to change the script.

I shrug again, looking Yvonne head on. 'Maybe we all need someone who knows the truth.'

41

Kingston, London

Tuesday, 1 August 2006

'Come on, Darryll. You must have something.'

My agent sighed. 'I told you, Kitty. It's tricky at the moment. Everything's gone on hold since that last girl died. I've had to turn down stuff cos I haven't the time to go and check people out – I can't just send girls off who knows where. Not with things how they are now.'

I made a pleading face, hating myself for sinking so low. Darryll ran his tongue over his teeth while he thought. 'I guess you could stand in for Tara North.'

'Tara?' He had to be kidding. She was the kind of porn actress that made street hookers look classy.

'One of my best earners these days.' Darryll's expression told me he hadn't forgiven me yet for dumping him, that he wasn't about to make things easy now I'd come crawling back. 'She was supposed to do a scene this arvo for Gavin Stockland out in Walthamstow, only she's gone and broken her bloody ankle.' He said this as if Tara had done it purely to annoy him.

I narrowed my eyes. 'How come you didn't offer me that job first?' I felt a flare of indignation. Jesus. Three months ago I was his star performer – his cash cow – and now I was a stand-in for a cheap tart like Tara?

I'd been back on the books for a couple of weeks, telling you I was temping on the admin side, fixing up girls with jobs, that sort of thing. Made Darryll promise to back up my story if you ever checked.

Fuck admin. This was what I was good at, pleasing men. And I'd missed it more than I anticipated. Feeling in the limelight. The centre of at least someone's attention.

All the same, I was sticking to low-key stuff – if I'd done scenes for Pulsar or any of the main studios, word would have got straight back to you. Ideally, I'd have preferred sex phone work – even webcam stuff – but Darryll didn't have much in that line; low profile for him meant gonzo, the bottom of the porn food chain.

'OK, I'll do it,' I said, swallowing my pride. I was desperate. We needed the money. My income allowed us to take out a small loan for your family – enough to keep the bailiffs off their doorstep. Between your job at Pulsar, my work and the extra night shifts in your cousin's taxi, we could keep up the payments and cover our bills. Just.

'Darryll?' I prompted, when he didn't reply. I watched as he squirmed in his seat, adjusting the collar of his shirt like it was tight, though the first few buttons were undone.

'Don't look at me like that, Kitty. I'd have offered it to you first, but . . .' He paused, looking shifty.

'But what?'

Darryll cleared his throat, something he always did when he anticipated a difficult conversation. 'The thing is – and I don't want you to take this the wrong way, darling – well, I'm having a job getting you bookings.'

'How do you mean?' I frowned.

'What I mean is, we can't use any of your old contacts, can we? And you won't work bareback any more, so that rather narrows the field.'

'OK, I get that. But surely there's other stuff?'

Darryll sat back, sucked his teeth. 'I'm gonna level with you, Kitty,' he sighed. 'It's like this . . . I've had one or two complaints.'

'*Complaints*? What about?'

He sighed again, like all this was more than he should have to handle. 'How shall I put it? That you've let yourself go a bit. Chubbed out, sweetheart. Maybe you should think about going on a diet.'

I stared at him, horrified. I had? But you hadn't mentioned anything, and I could still get into most of my clothes.

Glancing down, I saw it was true – I had put on a few pounds round the middle. I'd cancelled my gym membership in Canary Wharf cos it was costing two hundred quid a month and I wasn't even living there now; I'd meant to join somewhere cheaper, but there never seemed to be time.

I put a hand on my belly. Jesus. Was I that out of shape?

'I'm not saying you're fat, Kitty.' My agent eyed me warily. 'More perhaps you need to tone up a little.'

He shrugged, like this wasn't something he agreed with. He was only passing on the bad news. The messenger I shouldn't shoot.

I closed my eyes. Made a resolution. I'd fix this. Go on a diet. Check out the local leisure centre tomorrow, look into classes in zumba or aerobics. Start swimming perhaps.

Whatever it took.

*

I fretted all the way to Walthamstow, checking out my reflection in the windows of the tube train, standing sideways and sucking in my stomach.

It wasn't that bad, was it?

I thought of Esme, throwing up that cake in the loo. Maybe I should give it a try. But the idea of making myself sick made me feel . . . well . . . sick. Anyway, I hadn't been eating that much, had I? No more than usual. Perhaps slightly less, the stress of Esme's death and the last few weeks taking its toll on my appetite.

So it wasn't until I was walking out of the station, up into the sunlight of Hoe Street that it hit me.

I stopped in the middle of the pavement. Breath tight in my chest.

Shit . . . surely not?

I headed into the first chemist I could find.

Gavin answered the door in jeans and a dressing gown, a fag hanging out the corner of his mouth like he was a character in a sitcom.

'Kitty,' he grinned, extending a hand.

I shook it and stepped inside. Christ, what a dump. Boxes and plastic bags piled up in the hallway, filled with books and clothes and other pieces of junk. The wallpaper grubby with hand marks, peeling and torn at the edges. In the living room the curtains were drawn, leaving a couple of bare light bulbs to brighten up the place.

'Can I use your loo?'

'Sure.' Gavin nodded upstairs.

The bathroom was filthy. You could tell this bloke lived on his own. The sink looked like it hadn't been cleaned for months, rimmed with scum and ancient globs of toothpaste, and the bath had a tideline right round the inside.

The whole place reminded me of home, above the pub.

I peered into the loo. It was so black with scale I couldn't see much, which was probably a blessing. I wiped the seat then sat down, taking the box from my bag, ripping it open and removing the instructions. Peed on the stick as directed. Closed my eyes and counted to sixty.

Opened them again.

Saw the words highlighted in the little plastic panel.

And did the only thing it was possible to do – vomited into the sink.

I sank back on to the loo, dabbing my mouth with some toilet roll. Fuck. How had this happened? I was still on the pill. Almost never forgot to take it.

'Kitty?' Gavin's voice.

Oh God, how could I go through with the shoot? My mind whirred, then I reminded myself how much we needed the money. Man up, Leanne, I told myself. It's only a couple of hours, then you can go home and think this through.

'Sorry,' I called downstairs. 'Just getting changed.'

'You OK?' Gavin asked, when I finally reappeared. I'd put on my heels and a short skirt, but felt so shaken I was worried I'd throw up again.

I nodded. 'Needed to freshen up. Got a bit sweaty on the way over.'

'Been a fan of yours since you signed with Pulsar,' he said, prepping the camera while I concentrated on breathing through my nose, trying to keep the nausea at bay.

'Thanks.' I smiled.

'I was gutted when I heard you'd quit the business. Thought I'd never get the chance to do a scene with

309

you.' He left a pause, presumably hoping I'd fill in some detail.

I didn't oblige. I wanted this over and done with, so I could go home and work out what the fuck I was going to do.

'Right.' Gavin glanced around, adjusting the lights he'd set up on each side of the narrow room. 'Thought we'd maybe start on the sofa.'

Outside, beyond the curtains, I could hear a couple of kids squabbling in the street, their mother telling them to keep quiet. It wasn't making me feel any better. Suddenly, I wasn't sure I could go through with this after all.

'Gavin, I . . .'

'Gav,' he said. 'I hate Gavin.' He grinned again. 'I can't believe I get to work with the lovely Kitty Sweet. You've made my day.'

I gave up. Easier to get on with it. I went through the motions for the whole scene. Classic gonzo – straight on my knees for the blow job, sparing punters the effort of fast-forwarding through any preliminary dialogue. Gav was different to Victor though, careful not to bump me on the head with the camera while he filmed me going down on him. When he stripped off and fucked me, sticking the camera on a tripod, he was almost tender about it; in another era, another genre, Gav might have been quite the romantic.

I tried to focus on what I was doing, throwing in a few appreciative moans as he went to work on my nipples, sucking at them like a . . . I cut off the image with a shudder, but my mind raced off again. How had I even got into this situation? Did the pill have a failure rate?

I guess it did. I remembered reading somewhere that no method of contraception was 100 per cent effective.

What in God's name were we going to do? I asked myself. Renting a flat. No money, no prospects. And if I couldn't work, how would we keep up the loan repayments?

Round and round it all went, as Gav turned me over and screwed me from behind, occasionally slapping my arse for good measure. But you could tell his heart wasn't in it. There was nothing vicious about Gav; he exuded none of the menace of Victor.

'I worked with a friend of yours once, you know the one that overdosed,' he said after we'd done the obligatory pop to the face. 'Heard she was mixed up with that Victor Gomez.'

'Esme?' I wiped my chin and stared at him.

'Don't make the same mistake, Kitty. Keep away from that fucker, that's my advice.'

'Why?' I asked. 'Why are you saying that?'

'Cos I like you. You're a good girl. And you'll make a good mum.' He leaned over and patted my stomach.

I groaned. 'Is it that obvious?'

'I was married, hun,' Gav smiled. 'Three kids. Women's bodies change, though it's often their men who notice first.' He pointed to my breasts. 'Your veins are more prominent. It's a sure sign.'

I glanced down at my boobs. True enough, I could see, right beneath the skin, a network of blue lines. How could I have missed those?

All through the scene I'd been trying to work out how many weeks gone I was, whether it was too late for a termination. Why on earth hadn't I realized sooner? But I'd still been bleeding, now and then, and my periods had never been regular. It simply hadn't occurred to me.

'Bloody shame about Esme.' Gav pulled on his jeans

311

and flopped on to the sofa. 'I heard she got really fucked up when Nelson died. You reckon that's why she started on the heavy stuff?'

'Who knows,' I sighed, reaching for my clothes.

'I often wonder if it was deliberate – her overdose, I mean.'

I frowned, my mind whirring. So I wasn't the only one who'd come to that conclusion?

Gav sniffed. 'Jesus, this industry is going to shit. Another death and guys like me will have to close down. It's getting harder and harder to get girls to come out here. Every bloke involved in porn is now a suspect; I keep waiting for the police to knock on my door.'

'What do you know about Victor Gomez?'

He gave me a sharp look. 'Why are you asking?'

'Darryll said he wanted to book me,' I lied. 'I'm just checking him out.'

Gav sniffed again, smoothing the hair on his belly the way you might stroke a cat. 'Nothing definite, Kitty, but you hear stuff. Rumours. I used to work with a lot of Eastern Europeans – give them a drink or two and they'd talk. Some said they knew several girls who'd worked with Gomez, then simply disappeared.'

I thought of Anya. Tula Kask.

And that girl who did the scene with Esme, her body still not identified.

'Why didn't they go to the police?'

Gav pulled a packet of cigarettes from his pocket and lit one, careful to blow the smoke away from me. 'Some are here illegally, and don't want trouble from their pimps.'

'What? You mean they're trafficked?'

He nodded. 'Brought over by gangs, tricked with promises of well-paid hotel or bar jobs, then find themselves cut off from their families, their friends. No access to a phone, locked indoors when they're not working. Most are coerced into prostitution, but quite a few end up in porn – or both.'

He took another drag from his cigarette, tapping the ash into an empty mug he'd wedged between his knees. 'I stopped booking any of them after one told me she'd been forced to come here against her will. I only go through proper agencies now. But it's tough. Guys like me, we're being squeezed by the low-end gonzo stuff coming out of Asia and Eastern Europe. Those girls were cheap, helped keep overheads down.'

I considered what he'd said. 'So you think Victor may be mixed up in this? In trafficking?'

Gav cocked an eyebrow at me. 'Or worse.'

'Worse how?' I returned his gaze, making a conscious effort to breathe.

He sighed. 'All I'm saying is, you don't need money that badly, Kitty. I'd steer well clear of Gomez, if I were you.' He stubbed out his cigarette, dropping the butt into the mug, then sat back, eyeing me thoughtfully. 'Bit of a comedown for you, this, isn't it?'

I didn't answer. What could I say?

'But if you think this is bad, believe me, you'd be mistaken,' he added. 'I make cheap porn for normal guys who want to get their rocks off without any pissing about, but there's plenty of men with tastes way more hardcore.'

He rubbed his chin with his palm. The faint rasp of skin against stubble. 'There's a whole subset of people out there who enjoy things rough. And I mean violent, nasty, sadistic sex – the kind Gomez is happy to cater for.'

'OK,' I said, though of course it wasn't. I left a space for

Gav to carry on talking. He studied me for a moment, saw I really needed to know.

'My point is, Kitty, these girls they've found, I reckon that's not all of them. Like I said, there's others ... women who vanish. Vanish, as in never seen alive again. People assume they've gone home, back to wherever, but I'm not so sure.'

I remembered what Esme had said. About Nelson being convinced there were more.

I stared at Gav, my breath stalling. 'So you what ... you think Victor Gomez is making *snuff* movies?' I felt winded. Jesus. Could it be true after all, what Esme had told me?

Gav held his hands in the air. 'I'm not saying anything, Kitty, all right? You didn't hear any of this from me. Draw your own conclusions.'

'So you've not seen any, then? These films.'

He shook his head. 'I haven't looked. No way I want to encounter that shit, but I've no doubt it's out there. Not on the Internet, I mean the standard web. But you've got the dark web—'

'What the fuck's the dark web?'

Gav wrinkled his nose. He seemed edgy, really uncomfortable. 'It's totally anonymous – you use a portal like Tor so you can't be traced. The irony is the dark web was invented to protect people – you know, dissidents hiding from totalitarian governments and so on – but it's ended up a refuge for every kind of shady activity you can think of: drugs, assassins, and merchants of some seriously nasty porn.'

He sniffed again, wiping his hand over his mouth. 'It's a bloody nirvana for rich perverts; whatever you can imagine, you can find some cunt to film it for you. Makes my stuff look like kids' TV.'

314

I closed my eyes. What had Esme said?

It was her or me, Leanne. The client wanted another girl to do it this time. It was her or me.

Oh God . . . maybe it really was true. Maybe Esme hadn't been crazy, and my instincts about Victor had been right all along.

'But aren't . . .' My voice cracked and I had to clear my throat. 'Aren't the police aware of this? Why don't they put a stop to it?'

'Why don't they put a stop to drug cartels or arms smuggling or paedophile rings?' Gav's laugh was hollow. 'It's practically impossible, sweetheart. Stamp out one dodgy website and another mushrooms up overnight. And like I said, it's anonymous out there, making it very, very difficult to track these people down – particularly if they're operating overseas.'

He blew out a long breath then got to his feet. 'You want to know what I really think?'

'Yes.'

'My guess is Gomez's legit stuff is a cover for something darker, and far more lucrative. But that's all it is – a guess. I don't have a shred of proof.'

'Shit,' I said, more to myself than to Gav, fighting down another swell of nausea. Suddenly this was too much to stomach. Everything – my whole life – had become more than I could possibly handle.

'I have to go.' I grabbed my jacket and made for the door.

'Hey, hang on a mo.' Gav walked over to the TV cabinet and removed a little black box. Opening the lid, he took out a wodge of cash. 'You nearly forgot this.' He counted out a bunch of twenties and handed them to me.

His eyes lingered as I stuffed them into my bag.

315

'You're a nice girl, Kitty, and I know you were good friends with Esme.' Putting a hand on my arm, he held me back for a second. 'Don't get me wrong, I'm over the moon about working with you, but if you want my advice, luv, jack this in, once and for all. It's not worth it. Not for the money, not for anything.'

He glanced down again at my stomach. 'Have your baby, marry your man, and put all this behind you.'

'Thanks,' I replied, standing on tiptoe and kissing Gav on the cheek.

But thinking, *If only it were that easy.*

42

Herne Hill, London

Tuesday, 1 August 2006

You found me later that evening, standing in the bay window of our bedroom. Crying.

'Hey, Leanne, what's the matter?'

I pointed to my laptop. I couldn't speak. I watched you fire up the screen and click on the open video. Then I walked out of the room. I couldn't bear to see or hear any of it again.

I'd spent ages hunting it down. An hour to download Tor and get into the dark web: amazing how vast it was – five hundred times bigger than anything you could access using Google. Which is probably why it took me so long to find what I was looking for.

I discovered myself first. That scene with Victor. Almost impossible to watch, equally impossible to look away.

The other I stumbled across pretty much by accident. Not all of it, not by a long chalk. Nothing as bad as Gav had implied – and what I was now sure was out there.

But I had found Esme.

Drugged up. Five men. In what looked like a warehouse – nowhere I'd ever seen before.

She was in a circle, surrounded. Five men taking their junk out of their trousers and smacking her around the face until they were hard. Calling her names.

Whore.

Bitch.

Slut.

And then it all went mental, an orgy of throat-fucking and fisting, slapping and pinching and punching. Esme looked drugged, nearly unconscious, but even so, you could tell she was in a lot of pain. She was moaning, and crying, almost hysterical.

It must have hurt like hell.

The light was minimal, and all the men wore balaclavas. In the background a voice, egging them on, a non-stop track of quips and insults, venomous, oozing malice.

Victor.

I only saw him once, when he got up, leaving the camera rolling. Just a glimpse. That tattoo. A snake winding round his torso, curving down to its gaping mouth.

And you could see it, in his right hand. Unmistakable.

A syringe.

I pressed stop. I couldn't watch any more.

When I came back into the bedroom, it was getting dark, and the room was dim. The rain had eased up, but the sky was still cloudy. You were lying propped up on a pillow, your eyes shut, my laptop closed beside you.

'So you think they killed her?' you asked.

I sat on the end of the bed. 'I think they couldn't afford for her to disappear, like the others. So they made it look like an accident. Or suicide.'

'What do you mean, the others?' You opened your eyes, but they wouldn't meet mine.

318

I inhaled. 'Anya Viksna, Tula Kask, and the body they haven't identified – that girl they found on the building site. Probably others no one's ever discovered.'

'Jesus.' You looked shell-shocked. As if I'd detonated another bomb in your life. You stared at the laptop, even though it was off. When eventually you spoke, your voice was quiet. Subdued.

'Leanne, how come you knew where to look?'

A long silence as I tried to think what to say. Then I decided.

No more lies.

'Gavin told me.'

'Gavin Stockland?'

I nodded.

'When you were sorting out a booking? He told you this over the phone?'

'I was over at his place. We were talking.'

You gazed at me, eyes widening. 'What the fuck were you doing over in Walthamstow?' You paused, held up a hand to stop me from answering your question. 'Leanne, you weren't . . .?'

I nodded again.

'Christ.' Your face went rigid, your hands clenched. 'I knew it. Jesus, what is it with you? You quit without telling me, and now you're working again behind my back?'

'I thought you didn't want me to give it up in the first place,' I snapped, unable to keep my frustration to myself.

You massaged the side of your head, like it was aching. 'That was different, Leanne, and that was then. I didn't want to rush things, that's all. It all seemed a bit . . . sudden. We get together, then you want to stop work and move in, and now you're back doing scenes again without even discussing it first.'

319

'We needed the money,' I said flatly.

'But you were temping for Darr—' The penny dropped. '*Fuck.*' You smacked your palm against your forehead. 'Fuck, Leanne. Fuck.'

You looked so angry I started crying again. I thought you were going to walk out on me. I thought you'd never forgive me for deceiving you.

'I did it for you,' I sobbed. 'I did it so your parents wouldn't have to sell up. So Ayanna wouldn't have to leave uni and get a job.'

'*Bullshit, Leanne!*' You leapt to your feet. 'Don't you dare use them as an excuse. You did it for yourself. You couldn't leave it behind, could you? The adulation, the lifestyle. You couldn't handle being ordinary. Being with me.'

'Joe.' I was crying harder now. 'Joe, that's not—'

'Fuck off, Leanne.' Despite the fading light I saw you were actually shaking, and I wondered, was this all about me? About what I'd done?

Or something else?

'I don't trust a word that comes out of your mouth any more,' you hissed.

'I'm not lying,' I said, as calmly as I could, but you glared at me. An awful expression on your face.

'Are you sure, Leanne? Are you sure you really know the difference? Sometimes I'm not convinced. You say one thing, then do another. It's getting so I never know where I am with you, whether you mean anything you say.'

It was possibly the most hurtful thing you ever said. All these years, I've played those words over and over in my head. Wondering if you really meant them.

'Joe.' I reached out, put my hand on your arm. You didn't shrug it away. I could feel it trembling under my fingers. You were upset, in shock. Your anger with me was just a symptom, I told myself.

As if on cue, you suddenly burst into tears. 'Oh Jesus, look what they did to her, Leanne. What are we going to do?' You stood up and looked at me. 'We have to go to the police.'

I let the silence hang in the air. 'Do you think they'd believe us?'

'Why not? We've only got to show them this.'

'How will that help, Joe? This isn't evidence. Even if they could link it to Victor, he'd simply claim they were acting, that it was just a shoot, that they were faking all of it. There's no proof they murdered Esme.' I leaned over and stroked your hair. 'Think about it. Dozens of people can testify that Esme was dabbling in every kind of drug. And dozens more could make a convincing case that she committed suicide.'

You went mute. Thinking this through. 'What about those other girls?' you asked finally. 'There must be more videos. If we could find them, the police would have to believe us.'

'I doubt we'll ever find them. Victor's not stupid enough to leave those floating around, even on the dark web.'

'So why these? Why leave these online?'

I shrugged. 'His shop window, maybe. Something he can direct people to, like a sample.'

'Or perhaps he's doing this for his own kicks?' you suggested. 'Not selling them on.'

I shook my head, remembering Esme's words. *The client wanted another girl to do it this time.* 'I reckon Victor makes them to order. Made-to-measure porn.'

'Bespoke films? Who the hell for?'

'Anyone with tastes like his. Anyone with enough money to make it worth his while.'

'Snuff movies?' you said, still incredulous, but in the silence that followed I knew you were facing the truth of it. And I remembered Victor's words again, after that shoot I did for him.

Let's just say I'm recruiting. I'm looking for a very special kind of girl.

I was guessing he didn't find her, so he did the next best thing. He gave Esme a choice – kill or be killed.

She murdered that girl, the one they found in Haringey. And that's why she wouldn't go to the police – because even if they managed to unearth that film, she was the one who did it. Esme would have been implicating herself.

And no doubt Victor edited it to look like she'd done it willingly. Out of choice.

But Esme was no natural killer. She was fragile. Flimsy. She was falling apart, starting to let things slip.

Victor couldn't run that risk, that she might crack. That someone might believe her.

Not that I could prove any of this. Not yet. But I had a plan, and as the room grew dark around us, I explained it to you. How we might tackle Victor once and for all.

Stop him ever doing this again.

To anyone.

'But how?' you asked, your face shadowed by dusk and indecision. 'How will we get him to book you without being suspicious?'

'That's easy,' I said. 'Tell him I'm pregnant.'

43

HMP Brakehurst

Tuesday, 5 April 2016

'So how did Joe react, Leanne?' Yvonne is gazing at me with a puzzled expression, like there's something she doesn't understand. 'When you broke the news that you were pregnant.'

I glance at the clock, another thirty minutes to go. I'm tired. Was up half the night, unable to sleep. Reliving all this has caused a tsunami in my head. Memories and images flooding in, threatening to engulf me.

'Your account stopped there. At the point you told him about the baby.' She nods at the notes in her hand.

I pull my eyes to hers. 'I didn't feel like writing it down.'

That's true at least. I hit a brick wall. Had sat in my cell, holding my pen, incapable of going any further.

Some stuff you can't commit to paper.

'I have to say,' Yvonne continues when I don't speak, 'this struck me as rather an odd time to tell Joe you were pregnant. On top of what you'd discovered about Esme.'

'I had to.' I try to keep my voice even. 'I had to tell

323

him then because it was the only way I could think of to get to Victor. Besides, I was worried Gavin might let the cat out of the bag – I didn't want Joe finding out from someone else.'

Yvonne nods, accepting my explanation. 'But I'm still not sure I understand why your pregnancy would be of any interest to Victor Gomez.'

I sigh. Has she listened to a single thing I've told her? How to explain porn to a woman like Yvonne? 'Men always want something new, something different. Like I said, the whole industry is running out of ideas, so catering to any kind of fetish is a bonus.'

Yvonne pulls a face, her expression full of distaste. Decides not to pursue it. 'So, what about Joe?' she asks instead. 'How did he react when you told him about the baby?'

How did you react, my love? Your face looms in my mind, and I'm tempted to get up and go. Walk out of the session, leaving my therapist to draw her own conclusions.

But of course I can't. We're locked in; I'd have to get one of the guards to let me out.

'Leanne?' Yvonne's voice is gentle. 'Tell me why you're crying.'

I swipe a hand over my cheek. Sure enough it comes away wet.

'Joe was fine with it,' I lie, too fiercely to be believed. 'He was delighted, OK?'

But there you are, surfacing again. The pair of us standing in that bedroom, me watching the shock slide across your face.

'Oh, fuck.' You sank on to the edge of the bed, looking stunned, your eyes fixed on my stomach. 'Are you sure?'

'I did a test, Joe. It's 99 per cent accurate. I can show you if you want.'

You shook your head and my heart contracted. I could see this was the last thing you ever expected. Probably the last thing you ever wanted.

'How, Leanne? You're on the pill.' You raised your face to mine, your eyes narrowed. 'You *are* still on the pill, aren't you?'

'It's not fool-proof,' I said, but I could tell you didn't believe me. Could see you biting back the words: had I done this deliberately?

But when you spoke, it was a different question. The very last I expected.

'Are you sure it's mine?'

How, Joe? How could you ever ask me that?

Did you really doubt me that much?

'Leanne, are you OK?' Yvonne is looking at me with concern, and I realize I'm shaking. 'Do you need to take a break?'

'I'm fine,' I insist, then carry on telling her what happened. Jumping ahead, right over that terrible thing you asked me. Deleting it from my mind like it never happened.

Moving straight on to Victor.

44

Notting Hill, London

Monday, 7 August 2006

It was a shock to see Esme's flat so bare. Someone had packed most of her stuff, stacking the boxes three high in the spare bedroom. They'd tidied up and stripped the bed, leaving the mattress and frame. I peered in the fitted wardrobes. All her clothes had gone.

'I've put the key back,' you said, joining me in the bedroom. 'With any luck no one will realize we were ever here.'

I knew you were uncomfortable with the idea of using Esme's place, but you didn't want to invite Victor to our flat, so this was our only option. Though you knew where she'd hidden the spare key, it still felt like we were trespassing.

Which of course we were. I wondered who the flat belonged to now. Her mother? Her brother? Had Esme ever got round to making a will?

Somehow I doubted it.

'I suppose this place is being sold.' You glanced around, your face tense and worried. Like you half expected Esme to show up any moment and demand to know what we were doing here.

'Joe.' I placed my hand on your arm. 'It'll be OK.' You hadn't been the same since Esme's death. In a state of shock. Barely talking, lost somewhere in your head.

I wondered if you felt you should have saved her somehow. Wondered if it reminded you of what happened to your sister.

'I still don't like this, Leanne,' you said, your voice tight. 'In fact I think it's fucking insane. We should go to the police, let them deal with it.'

I sighed, exasperated. 'We've been through this, Joe. Time and time again. We've got nothing on Victor, nothing concrete. They won't take us seriously.'

'I don't agree. They'll look into it. Girls are getting murdered out there. They'd have to investigate at least.'

'Yeah? And what are they going to find? Even if they arrested Victor, there's no proof he was involved with Esme's death – or any of the others. Unless we get it.'

You rubbed your eyes. You were tired, I could see that. Knew you'd hardly slept these last few days. 'I just think it's too risky, Leanne. There must be some other way.'

'Like what, Joe?' I could feel myself getting frustrated. I wanted to do this. It was our best chance to nail Victor, and I wanted that very, very badly.

I'd been through it all in my head, over and over. Why I needed to do this. Maybe it was simply the thought of those girls, of Esme.

How it could have been me.

Or perhaps it was the way I knew it would all get buried – no one in this business wanted to face anything. Dead girls. Disease. Everybody wanted things to disappear as fast as possible. Get back to business as usual.

Fuck that. This time someone had to pay.

'Joe,' I pulled you into a hug. 'I promise I'll be careful. Let's get it over and done with.'

I got myself ready while you set up the hidden camera in the centre wardrobe, placing it so the tiny lens viewed the bedroom through the crack between the doors. The microphone you wired across the top of the left-hand door, taping it discreetly in place.

'How did you get hold of this stuff so quickly?' I asked, admiring your handiwork. As I'd anticipated, Victor had leapt on my invitation – giving us only a few days to prepare.

'The Internet.'

'You can buy this shit online?'

'God, yeah. You can buy cameras hidden in clocks, air fresheners, smoke alarms – even teddy bears.'

I swept my eyes around. 'Maybe we should have got the air freshener. Belt and braces.'

'I thought about it, but you need Wi-Fi to pick up the signal – I wasn't certain the router would still be on.' You closed the doors of the wardrobe gently to make sure everything stayed in place. 'This'll be fine. And if there's a problem with the camera, we've got audio backup.'

'But what if he looks inside?'

You pulled the door open again and pointed to the large shoebox where you'd stashed the equipment. 'Nothing to see . . . just an old pair of boots.'

I nodded, but it was my turn to feel nervous. This had been my idea, but now we were here I was aware how much could go wrong. I tried to push the thought from my mind.

This would work. I had to believe that.

'All right. Well, I guess we're set.' You gazed at me helplessly. 'Please, Leanne. I'm really worried—'

'There's no other way, Joe,' I said in my firmest voice. 'I can handle myself, and this is our only chance.'

You didn't look convinced. But you'd given up trying to argue me out of it ten minutes ago after I'd threatened to go ahead on my own.

'Right. Well, you know where I'll be.' You nodded towards the café over the road. 'Remember I can hear everything with my headphones on. If anything, *anything* kicks off, say my name and I'll be here in seconds.'

'You sure they work?' I nodded at the headphones. Truthfully I *was* scared, the idea of being left alone with Victor starting to freak me out. Though I was careful not to let it show.

'I've checked it half a dozen times. It works fine.' You ran a hand through your hair. 'But remember, the first hint of trouble, you call for me. No heroics, OK?'

'OK.' My smile was weak. 'Right, then . . . Leave me to it.'

You gave me a resigned look, clearly still unhappy about all of this. 'Don't forget to whistle or talk to yourself for the next few minutes,' you said. 'So I can double-check the sound equip—'

A loud buzz filled the apartment, making us both jump. The intercom.

You frowned. 'What time did you tell Victor?'

'Nine,' I said, panicked. 'I said that was when you started your taxi shift.'

'Jesus.' You glanced at your watch. 'It's only half eight. What the fuck—'

The intercom sounded again. 'Shit, shit, shit.' Your eyes were wild with alarm. There was no rear exit out of

329

the building, no way for you to slip out without Victor seeing you. 'We'll have to call it off. Don't answer the door.'

'No.' I grabbed your arm. 'No, Joe. We can do this. Hide in the spare room.'

You stared at me, incredulous. 'But what if he goes in there? We can't take that risk.'

I swallowed. 'I'll keep him out.'

'I can't hide in the flat, Leanne. It's fucking ridiculous.'

No time to argue. I went to the door, as the buzzer rang a third time.

'Leanne . . . this is absurd. It won't—'

I picked up the receiver.

'Where the fuck have you been?' Victor's voice, tinny and pissed off.

'On the loo. And you're early.'

'In the area,' he said, nonchalantly. 'Buzz me up.'

45

Notting Hill, London

Monday, 7 August 2006

Victor strolled into Esme's flat, backpack slung over his shoulder, hands thrust into the pockets of his jeans. He was wearing a dark-grey suit jacket over a white T-shirt, only the middle button done up.

'Why are you so early?' I asked. 'I only got here ten minutes ago.'

Victor looked pleased I was put out. 'Like I said, Kitty. In the area.' He didn't offer any more information, simply gazed around him, surveying the near empty flat. 'They haven't wasted much time, have they?'

I walked straight into the main bedroom, praying he would follow. 'So you've been here before?' I tried to keep my voice natural.

Victor narrowed his eyes. 'Why d' you ask?'

'Just wondered.' I shrugged.

It was true. I *had* wondered. How had Victor got Esme's body up here without anyone noticing? Was she still alive when he dumped her on the bed? Maybe he'd pretended she was drunk or stoned – God knows, if the neighbours saw, they wouldn't have been suspicious.

It'd hardly be the first time Esme had been carried in practically senseless.

But then, how had Victor got in at all? Like us, I suppose – Esme must have told him where she kept the spare key.

I watched as he checked out the bedroom. If it brought back any bad memories, he certainly wasn't letting on. Victor looked relaxed, even cheerful.

'So, Kitty . . . or should I call you Leanne now?' he said, and I mentally flinched. I didn't like him using my real name.

'Kitty will do.'

'Well, either way, this is an unexpected pleasure. I must admit I didn't think I'd ever hear from you again.' He grinned, showing that glint of gold in his back tooth.

I smiled coyly. 'I've been biding my time.'

'Really?' Victor cocked an eyebrow. 'That's curious. I got the distinct impression you no longer wanted to work with me.'

'Who from? Esme?'

He eyed me steadily. 'No, Kitty. From you. That wasn't exactly a friendly reception you gave me at the AVNs.'

I didn't answer, thinking the less I said, the better. Let Victor wonder a little about my motives. Also, I was sure he liked a challenge.

'Selling the place, are they?' He sloughed off his backpack and laid it on the bed, sitting beside it.

'Looks that way.'

Victor beckoned me over. Pulled the neck of my blouse open with his index finger and gazed at my boobs. 'Now that's something I'd liked to have seen – you and her, getting it on.'

'Check out the Pulsar website.'

'No,' he said. 'I mean properly, not play-acting.'

I took a step backwards and he released my blouse. 'You knew Esme well, did you?'

'A little. We used to go out drinking sometimes, after Nelson died. She was a mess. I wasn't surprised when I heard.'

'What about?'

'Her death.' Victor looked at me like I was stupid.

I stood there, hoping all this was recording. Were the camera and microphone already on when the doorbell went? I couldn't remember.

I pulled my focus back to Victor. 'Esme never got over Nelson dying. He was everything to her.'

'You were there, weren't you? When he died.'

'Yeah.'

'That must've been pretty traumatic.' Victor sounded almost genuine as he said it. For a second I wondered if I'd got it all wrong about him. Misjudged him entirely.

Esme had been right. Victor had a knack for making you doubt what you thought you knew.

Then I remembered that video. His voice in the background, egging them on.

'Do you want a drink?' I asked. 'I've wine, or beer, or vodka.'

'I'll have wine.'

I went into the kitchen and poured him a glass. Saw my hand was trembling. It was one thing planning all this out in my head, but now it came to it, I didn't have a clue what I was doing.

And that effect Victor had on me. The fear and disgust. I was thanking God now that you were close by.

I took a couple of deep breaths then headed back to the bedroom. 'You not having one?' Victor asked as I handed him the glass. He had a cigarette in his mouth, was fishing in his pocket for a lighter.

'Like I said, I'm pregnant.'

'A fag, then?' He laughed as he proffered the packet in my direction.

I shook my head.

'Wow, you're all the fun, aren't you?' He inhaled, blowing out a plume of smoke as he sat back on the bed. 'So you're planning to keep it, then?' He nodded at my belly.

I didn't reply. It was none of his business.

'Shame,' Victor said, undeterred. 'I was watching one of your scenes the other night, that farm shoot with Vince Able and Vicky Queen. It's a pity you didn't have more ambition. You really had something about you.'

I didn't react. Just let him continue.

'Not hungry enough,' he concluded.

'What do you mean?'

'You. Not enough greed, enough passion, Kitty. Not enough *need*. Bit of a disappointment, really – I had you down as someone who'd go far.' He beckoned me forward again, put his hand to my chin, forcing me to look at him. 'I thought you had *potential*.'

'For what?'

His mouth was a smirk, but there was something serious in his expression. 'Most girls are bland. Nothing inside. I prefer women with more . . . of an *appetite*.'

The way he looked at me was starting to freak me out. Again that sense that he could peer right into my head. That he recognized me somehow, could see things no one else could see.

He was trying to bait me, I realized. Victor had to assume control of any situation. He wasn't sure why I'd brought him here; this was his way of getting the upper hand.

'So why did you call me?' he asked, as if reading my

334

mind. 'You after work?' He looked me up and down. 'You sure, in your condition?'

'I need the money.'

'Why not get Darryll to fix you up? There's a good market for girls . . . how shall I put it . . . in the family way.'

'Too squeamish,' I said. 'Seems he draws the line at pregnancy porn.'

Victor chuckled. 'Who knew Darryll had a line to draw?'

I stared him out. 'So what's yours?'

'What's my what?'

'Your line. The one you wouldn't go over.'

His eyes narrowed again, his mouth crooked into a smile. Sizing me up. 'You're very inquisitive, all of a sudden.'

I felt myself flush. 'I'm simply curious, that's all.'

Victor's smile widened. 'Good. As I said, Kitty, I thought you had . . . potential.' Unzipping his rucksack, he removed a camera and a tripod, set them up in front of the bed.

'Take your clothes off,' he ordered, finishing his drink then stubbing the cigarette into the glass. I could see his erection poking against the denim of his jeans. I felt sick again. Unwell. I should put a stop to all this now.

'Victor, I'm not sure I can—'

'Take them off, Kitty. I only want to look at you.'

I removed my blouse reluctantly, aware of you in the other room – could you hear us? All at once this seemed like the very worst idea in the world.

Victor stood in front of me. Without warning he grabbed my hair, yanking my head back and staring into my eyes. 'Don't play fucking games with me, Kitty, OK? I don't like it.'

'OK,' I repeated, and he bent to kiss me. Less a kiss really, than a kind of assault, a raid on an enemy stronghold. Then he pulled away. 'So you want to work with me, do you?'

I nodded again, screwing up my courage to carry on. I wanted to nail this bastard. Badly.

'I still can't help thinking that's something of a U-turn,' Victor said. 'You must really have fallen on hard times.' He released my hair, but shoved his hand into my bra, squeezing my left breast hard.

'Why do that, Victor,' I yelped, swatting him away. 'Why fucking hurt people?'

He raised an eyebrow. 'On camera, you mean? Or in general?'

'At all,' I said, with a burst of fury as I thought of Esme.

Victor ran his tongue over his teeth. 'What I do in private is none of your business. But on camera, that's easy to answer.'

He lit another cigarette, taking a drag and blowing the smoke right into my eyes. 'It's more authentic, more ... believable. Mainstream porn is all fake orgasms, all *acting* – it's not very convincing, let alone erotic. Pain, on the other hand ... that's at least an honest response, one you can capture on camera. That's what my fans enjoy.'

I thought about it. He was right, in a way. It was easy enough to fake pleasure – all of us did, pretending we were loving it when really we were wondering what to have for supper or whether we'd paid our electricity bill. It was simply a question of making the right noises.

But hurt someone, and there was no need to fake a reaction. Your pain was genuine.

Victor brought his face right up to mine, so close I

could smell the fags and alcohol on his breath. 'You know what the French call an orgasm, Kitty? *La petite mort.*' He lifted his hand and grasped my breast again, not quite so hard this time. 'The little death. Makes you think, doesn't it?'

Was he on to me, I wondered? Had he guessed why I'd invited him here? I sensed him teasing, daring me to give voice to something.

'What happened with Esme?' I blurted before I could stop myself. Or rather, I realized I'd never manoeuvre Victor into incriminating himself – better to ask him outright.

Victor took another drag then dropped the cigarette on the floorboards, stubbing it with the toe of his boot. He grinned. 'I wondered how long it would take you to ask me that.'

So he'd guessed – at least part of it. Hopefully he had no idea he was being filmed.

'So what did she say, the lovely Esme?' Victor asked. 'Did she tell you anything about me? About what I enjoy?' He nodded at my bra, instructing me to remove it.

I unclipped the clasp at the back. Let it drop to the floor, leaving Victor's question hanging.

'I didn't hurt her,' he added. 'If that's what you want to know.'

'Then who did? I saw the bruises, Victor.'

'That's the question, isn't it?' Victor undid his flies and pulled out his cock, rubbing it absentmindedly as he studied my breasts, pregnancy having given them a fullness they lacked before. Then he slid his eyes back to mine, never moving them away as he pulled me down beside him.

'She was into it,' he crooned, close to my ear. Like this was some kind of seduction. I thought of that video

337

again, of Victor's voice in the background. I was shaking, I realized. My legs actually quivering.

Fuck, I needed to get a grip.

'Into what?' I kept my breathing steady. 'What was Esme into?'

Victor lifted a hand and stroked my cheek. 'Being roughed up. And more.'

'How do you mean?' I tried to keep the quaver from my voice. 'I asked her what happened with you, and she said she couldn't remember.'

Victor laughed again. 'Did she now? How very convenient. Esme had a nice line in selective amnesia.'

He glanced at my bottom half. 'Chop-chop, Miss Sweet – we haven't got all night.'

I stood again and unzipped my skirt, letting it drop to the floor. Victor scratched his chin as he examined the gentle swell of my belly. 'Well well, Joe really has left you high and dry, hasn't he? No wonder you're having second thoughts.'

'I'm not—'

'So why are you here then, Kitty?' He seized my wrist. 'The truth. Don't give me all this money bullshit.'

My head reeled. Victor had me cornered, always a step ahead. He pulled me forward until I was standing over him in my heels and thong, then put a finger in the elastic, pinging it against my skin. 'Not terribly appropriate, would you say, for a mother-to-be? Are you going to take them off or is this some kind of prolonged striptease?'

I did as he said. What choice did I have? The minute I refused, I had no doubt he'd up and leave. I'd promised you I wouldn't let him actually do anything – that was your condition to agreeing to this – but getting Victor to talk was proving harder than I'd anticipated.

338

'I have a child, actually.' Victor trailed a finger from my breast, down over the curve of my tummy where my belly button was beginning to flatten out. 'I was married once, back in the ice age. I know what it does to a woman's body. Pregnancy. Birth.' He lifted his gaze to mine. 'Stretch marks, saggy breasts, your pussy will lose all its elasticity.'

I shut my eyes, tried to tune him out.

'And that's just for starters, before the little bastards really get their teeth into you. The nappies, the bawling, the sleepless nights. The endless whining. I'm surprised you've opted for all that, Kitty. Wouldn't have thought it was your style.'

I opened my eyes again and glared at him. 'Why are you telling me this?'

Victor grabbed my wrist and yanked me on to the bed, pushing me on my back. He leaned over. 'Is it worth it, Kitty? Seems a high price to pay, losing your looks, your livelihood, to carry the child of that cheating bastard. What was it – afraid you wouldn't be able to tie him down, otherwise? Was he playing hard to get?'

My eyes widened, my breath stalling in my throat. 'What the fuck are you talking about?'

Victor squinted with amusement. 'Dear little Joe, such a sweet romance. Guess you've not heard all the rumours, then?'

'What rumours?' I stammered.

Victor sniggered, clearly enjoying my reaction. There were other ways of hurting people, I now understood. Of torturing them. Ways you couldn't capture on camera.

'The rumours about Joe and Esme,' he said it slowly, savouring my reaction. 'Their affair.'

'Don't be ridiculous.' I pushed him away and sat up, my head beginning to spin.

'So I'll ask you once more, Kitty. How come we're here, then?'

My mind whirled. Could it be true? *Could it possibly be true?* But I'd have known, surely? Would have noticed, would have worked it out.

'There was nothing going on between Joe and Esme,' I insisted, hearing the vehemence in my voice. *'Nothing.'* Some part of my mind wondering again if you were listening to this.

Victor raised his hands in mock surrender. 'Whatever you say, my dear.' He stood and picked up the camera. 'Let's start with the usual.'

I gazed at him, my mind in freefall. I'd lost track of what I was doing here. Were you and Esme really sneaking around behind my back?

Or was Victor fucking with me? Messing with my head?

He pulled me off the bed and on to my knees. 'Why don't you remind me exactly what you can do with that sweet little mouth of yours.' He thrust himself into my face, holding the back of my head, pushing deeper despite my resistance.

I gagged. Tried to shove him away, my nails clawing at his skin.

'Careful,' he growled, pulling out. 'You were the one who started this, so play nice.'

I took him back. He tasted of soap and something earthier. He was rock hard now, but I knew he was nowhere near orgasm. It was going to take a lot more than this to get him off.

Desensitized. Wasn't that the word they used, when it took more and more of something to provoke a reaction?

If anyone was desensitized, it was Victor.

'I can't do this.' I jerked my head away. 'I've changed my mind.' I wanted out. Wanted to walk away and forget the whole thing.

Fuck Esme. Fuck those girls. Fuck all of it.

Victor seized my wrist, and dragged me to my feet, getting his face right up to mine. 'He was seeing her while she was in Bristol.'

'What?'

'Joe, he was visiting Esme at her brother's.'

'How do you know that?'

'How, Kitty, do you think I know? Esme told me.'

I shuddered. Felt tears begin to sting. Christ, could it possibly be true? Were you really having an affair with Esme?

'When?' I stuttered, everything collapsing inside me.

'When did she tell me?' Victor shrugged. 'A few nights before she died.'

'No. I meant when were they . . .' I couldn't say it. I didn't even believe it.

'Oh, you mean before Nelson? Or before you?' His smile hardened. 'All along, sweetheart. All the fucking way.'

I punched him. So hard that I gasped in pain, snatching back my hand.

Victor's fingers went up to his nose, and came away bloody. His expression incredulous, half a sneer, half a grin. 'Why, you fucking crazy little—'

He lunged towards me. I jumped backwards, crashing into the wardrobe. The noise resounded around the empty flat.

Seconds later, you stood in the doorway.

Victor turned and saw you. 'What's this?' he laughed, blood dripping from his nose. 'The fucking cavalry?'

You took a couple of steps forward. 'You're a vicious

341

lying cunt,' you hissed. 'I know what you did to Esme, Victor. I saw that video you made. Do you get that? *I've seen it*. We've got proof.'

'Proof of what, ladyboy?'

'You killed Esme,' I said. 'I saw the syringe in your hand. You killed her then you dumped the body here.'

Victor rolled his eyes and guffawed. 'You think those videos are real? Christ, you're both more stupid than I thought.' He glanced at me, then back at you. 'It's fantasy, you fuckwits. *Make-believe*. Exactly like you provide to those unwitting punters. All those fake moans, and orgasms. We go a bit further, that's all.'

'So what were you doing with that syringe?' I repeated.

'Giving it to her.' Victor shrugged again. 'That was the deal. She did the scene and I provided the gear.'

I stood there, mind reeling. 'What about those other girls? Anya. Tula. The one they found in the building site. You saying you had nothing to do with them either?'

'What is this?' Victor spat. 'A fucking *cross-examination*? For your information, I've already spoken to the police, cleared myself out of the frame. If you must know, I've never set eyes on Tula Kask. And the last time I saw Anya Viksna she was walking out of my studio. Alive and well.'

He pulled a tissue from his jacket pocket and dabbed his nose. 'OK, maybe not well. You work with these bitches, they say they're fucking into it, then all they do is complain when they get a bit roughed up.'

'So who killed them?' you asked. 'Anya and the others? Who killed them, then?'

He frowned. 'How the fuck should I know? Might be anyone. These girls, they come and go like flies on shit. Easy prey for any pervert.'

I gazed at him. Could Victor possibly be telling the truth?

No, I thought, catching another smirk on his lips. He was playing with us. Actively enjoying this.

'She told me,' I said. 'Esme confessed she killed that girl, the one they found in the building site. She told me you made her do it.'

Victor snorted. 'Esme was off her fucking head – she didn't know her cunt from her arse. I've no idea what crap she spun you, but I can assure you I didn't—'

'You expect us to believe that?' you shouted, moving closer. 'A man like you? You expect us to believe a fucking word that comes out of your mouth?'

Victor's laugh was a bark. 'You're a fine one to talk, Mr Mistry. Already banged up for GBH. Or are you still pretending your brother decked that bloke?'

I spun round to face you, my jaw slack with shock. I thought you said it was Amit who hit that guy. After all, he was in jail for it . . . wasn't he? I realized I didn't know. Wasn't sure about any of it.

I'd never managed to check.

'That the line he fed you, Leanne?' Victor's voice inside my head, mincing and mocking. ' "I didn't do it, it wasn't me, darling, it was my brother . . ." '

I glanced at Victor, my head reeling, then turned back to you. I felt sick again, unsteady. Like I no longer knew which way was up, which was down. I closed my eyes, trying to orientate myself.

'You should watch yourself,' I heard Victor say. 'Esme told me about your cute little sister . . . what's her name . . . Alma? Ayanna? She said you—'

A dull, sickening crunch. I swung round, alert again. Saw Victor on the floor. His left cheek looked strange, sort of caved in around the temple. You were staring down at him.

You'd hit him with the camera. A heavy bit of kit, with sharp corners.

And you'd hit him hard. Hit him very hard.

My mind formulated the words, but they had no meaning. I gazed at you, eyes wide, vision blurry with tears. Then dragged my focus back to Victor. He shifted, one arm twitching, as if trying to raise it to his damaged face. A second later, a muffled choking, then blood trickled from the corner of his mouth, and he went completely still.

Oh shit.

I looked at you.

You, the love of my life. My one and only.

'Joe . . .' I said quietly, so quietly it was like I imagined it. 'Joe,' I asked, 'what the fuck have you done?'

46

Brakehurst Women's Prison

Tuesday, 5 April 2016

Yvonne is staring at me. She has dropped the impassive expression she's maintained through most of our sessions. The shock clear on her face. 'So you're saying what . . . you're now telling me it was actually Joe – Arjun Mistry – who killed Victor Gomez?'

I nod, ignoring the frown creasing up her forehead.

'So you lied under oath, Leanne?'

'Not really.' I lift my mouth into a shrug. 'I pleaded guilty. I didn't say anything under oath.'

The lines in my therapist's brow deepen as she tries to take in everything I've told her. 'But *why*, Leanne? Why plead guilty to something you're now saying you didn't do?'

I inhale. Think of your face. Your horrified expression as you stared down at Victor's body.

At what you'd done.

The answer to that is so simple, I'm amazed Yvonne even has to ask.

I did it for you, Joe. Despite everything.

It was only ever for you.

47

Herne Hill, London

Tuesday, 8 August 2006

We were sitting in your cousin's taxi outside our flat. It was gone two in the morning but finally we were ready to go, after several frantic hours packing everything we could think of – clothes, toiletries, various pairs of boots and shoes. It seemed to take so long – finding our passports, picking up the car, a dash to the cashpoint.

Time we didn't have.

But now, after all that frenzy, you didn't seem ready to leave. You sat in the driver's seat, flexing your palms against the steering wheel, then spoke in a weary voice. 'Leanne, listen, I'm not sure this is the best—'

'Yes,' I said, squeezing your arm. 'Yes, it is.'

'We should think this through a bit more—'

'No,' I cut in again. 'No, we have to go.' But I didn't move. Couldn't move, or urge you on until I'd asked the thing I hadn't been able to banish from my head. Asked it now, while I still had a chance to change my mind.

'Did you do it, Joe?'

'Do what?'

'Hit that guy? The gang bloke who raped your sister.'

You clutched the steering wheel, knuckles whitening. 'I told you the truth, Leanne. Think about it. Why is Amit still in prison, not me?'

But how could I be sure he was? He could be anywhere, for all I knew. Hell, how could I be certain any of your story was true? Maybe no one was raped or assaulted. Maybe you made the whole thing up.

Though fuck knows why you would.

I gazed at you, trying to suss whether or not you were lying. There must be some way to check, I thought. Something online, somewhere. I closed my eyes briefly, wondering when I'd get a chance. Enough time alone.

Of course, that wasn't really what was bothering me. Round and round my head it went. Victor's voice. That taunting, sneering look on his face.

Guess you've not heard the rumours, then?

A thump on the window made me jump. Your fist. 'Jesus, Leanne! I can't fucking believe this is what's worrying you. After you . . . after everything that's happened.'

You stared at me, your expression anguished. Your features haggard with tiredness, and something else. Something like desperation.

For a moment, everything threatened to collapse inside me. All my new plans, the revised future I'd quickly constructed. My faith that it would all be OK, that we could somehow salvage a life for ourselves.

You were right. I had to pull myself together. For my sake, for our baby's sake. And for yours.

So I did my best to believe you.

To believe *in* you.

'Let's go.' I rested my hand on my belly, reminding you of the life inside. Kept my tone flat and calm. 'We can't stay here any longer.'

347

You didn't reply. I glanced over and saw tears on your cheek.

'We have to go. Now,' I repeated, praying we hadn't left it too late.

We dropped down towards the M25, then headed east, picking up the motorway to Dover. The traffic was light this deep into the night, but you refused to hurry, always keeping well within the speed limit.

It was frustrating, but I understood why. The last thing we needed was to be pulled over.

As it was, we only saw one police car, cruising along the slow lane. You kept your eyes fixed on the road, overtaking at a steady sixty-five. I could see your knuckles tighten as you gripped the steering wheel, could sense your breathing become more rapid and shallow.

It stayed that way till we were several miles past.

At Leeds Castle services, we stopped for twenty minutes while I went to the loo and you knocked back a double espresso, to keep you alert. We stocked up with water and sandwiches, bought crisps and muesli bars for later. I don't know why; it wasn't like they'd be short of food in France, but we were fugitives and somehow it felt the right thing to do.

All the way to the tunnel I was calculating how much time we'd got. With any luck, no one would return to Esme's flat for several days, possibly a week or more – though I guessed eventually the smell would alert the neighbours. Even so, unless things really went against us, we'd have plenty of time to get down to the cottage, plan our next move.

Hell, even if they found Victor tomorrow, how could they pin it on us? It would take them ages, surely, to do the forensics? And I'd been careful. Gone through the whole flat, checking we hadn't left anything incriminating, wiping everything we'd touched. I was pretty sure there was nothing to link us to the crime.

I'd done all this while you sat sobbing in Esme's kitchen, drinking neat vodka from the bottle. You wouldn't speak, or even look at me. Just sat there, drinking and crying.

I'd let you neck an inch or so before I took it away.

'Hey.' You made a grab for it but I swung it out of reach. 'You have to be in a fit state to drive.'

I poured the rest down the sink, then pulled up a seat and told you my plan. About the cottage in the south of France that belonged to Mike's friend Tony. A place he hardly ever used, now he'd remarried.

You didn't argue. I don't think you had the strength.

And it wasn't like you had any better ideas.

After you'd bought a ticket for the tunnel, we drove through Customs. I found I was holding my breath, terrified they'd stop us.

In the boot was Victor's camera – though I'd cleaned off all the blood – and the surveillance equipment I'd removed from Esme's wardrobe, hidden in my washbag. I'd planned to ditch it from the ferry, dump it into the English Channel, but then we'd decided the tunnel would be quicker and less risky.

I'd have to deal with that stuff later.

Customs didn't stop us – two officials waved us through with barely a glance in our direction. We drove straight on to the next train, sitting in silence as the car swayed its way under the sea. I was starting to feel desperately tired, and you looked half dead, hung-over, resting your head against the side window, your eyes closed. But I could tell from your breathing you weren't asleep.

How could we ever sleep again?

'What are we going to do, Leanne?' you whispered as the train pulled into Calais. Still unable to look at me.

I reached over and squeezed your hand. 'Trust me, Joe, it will all work out fine. It's going to be all right.'

We pulled into a rest stop a few miles beyond the port. It was getting light now, the outlines of lorries visible amongst the trees. We went to the toilets, then returned to the car and lowered the backs of our seats. I did manage to sleep, though only for an hour or so. I was dreaming. I was at Venice Beach, finally, and it was sunny and warm and deserted, only the sound of waves breaking on the sand. A perfect day.

And all of it was familiar somehow, and in my dream I remembered how much I'd wanted to go there, and then realized I never could.

Not now.

My face was wet when we were woken by the sound of someone rapping on the back windscreen. A male voice saying something neither of us understood. It might have been French, but I didn't think so; seemed more like Spanish or Portuguese.

You sat bolt upright and stared outside, but there was no sign of anyone. You looked awful in the dawning light, scared and bewildered, your skin grey and greasy.

Though I doubted I looked much better.

'I'm going to clean my teeth,' I said, grabbing my bag of toiletries. When I returned, you were gone. I sat in the car for ten minutes, trying not to let my mind spin off into panic.

Where were you?

Fuck, what would I do if you never came back? Maybe you were hitching a lift to London this very minute. Shit. I should have stayed with you, should have made sure you didn't do anything stupid.

You turned up five minutes later, your hair wet, as if you'd washed it in one of the sinks. And you'd shaved; a rough, quick scrape that left the skin on your cheeks red and raw-looking.

You avoided my gaze as you got into the driver's seat.

'Did you ring Ashad?' I asked.

You nodded. 'I left a message. Told him it was an emergency.'

The biggest flaw in my plan was the car – and delaying the inevitable moment when your cousin reported us for nicking his taxi. In the meantime I reckoned we could fob him off for a day or two; by then, hopefully, we'd be long gone.

You rubbed your eyes, picking up the French road map we'd bought at the shop in Dover and finding the right page.

'So where exactly are we going?'

48

HMP Brakehurst

Friday, 8 April 2016

'Leanne?'

I glance up to see Drew standing at the entrance of my cell. Pull off my earphones so I can hear him.

'Sharon Harding wants to speak to you.' He shifts on his feet, looking uncomfortable, not quite meeting my eyes.

'Now?' I ask, wondering what I've done to put myself in the firing line this time.

'Yeah.'

I fix the cap on my pen and tuck my notebook under my pillow. It's my last session with Yvonne in a few days and I've been trying to tell the rest of my story.

But the closer I get to the end, the harder I'm finding it to write any of this down. Everything started accelerating, things happening so fast it's difficult to get them all straight in my head. Remember the exact order of events.

I follow Drew to Harding's office, ignoring the curious stares from the other inmates. Keep my eyes forward, walking past Ash without so much as a fuck-you on my face.

'Sit down,' Harding says, dismissing Drew with a nod.

I lower myself into the chair opposite her desk. It reminds me of Darryll's – a big oak number with sturdy units either side. The kind of desk Darryll imagines gives him status, but only works for people like Harding.

She studies me for a second or two, her lean face expressionless. 'So, how are you, Leanne?'

I shrug. 'All right.'

The governor leaves a pause, as if she has her own opinions about my wellbeing. 'You've been working with Yvonne Conway, haven't you?'

No need for an answer, though Harding leaves another gap, like it somehow requires confirmation.

'I hear things have been calmer, since you started with this therapy,' she says eventually. 'Do you think it's helping?'

I shrug again. 'I guess.'

Harding sighs, steeples her fingers as she scrutinizes me. 'Do you understand the concept of informed consent, Leanne?'

'Sure.'

'I'd like to ask Yvonne Conway to provide an overview of her work with you, which will be retained in your file for any future parole board to take into account.'

She removes her glasses, polishing them with a tissue from her pocket before perching them back on her nose. 'You'll be up for parole in six years and this might help your case, Leanne. You don't have to agree, of course. As I am sure Yvonne has explained, everything you told her was in confidence, but I think it would be a good idea if you agreed to her giving me a general report on your sessions together.'

My first instinct is to say no, no way. But then I give

it some thought. Harding is right. I have been in better spirits since starting with Yvonne. Since I fessed up, got things out into the open.

I've felt more relaxed. Lighter. *Happier.*

And after all, what have I got to lose? Don't I want people to know the truth? I remember that journalist Darryll mentioned, the one poking around my life, threatening to write my story.

Perhaps it would be better to get my version on record. For people to know what really happened.

After all, who would it hurt?

No one now. No one that matters.

'OK,' I say.

49

Troyes, France

Wednesday, 9 August 2006

'Shit.'

I was staring down, alerted by a sensation of dampness between my legs. 'Oh God, Joe. Pull over.'

'I can't. We're on the motorway. Can you hang on?' You sounded irritable, like this was the last straw.

'Just pull over.'

You dragged your gaze sideways, hearing the anguish in my voice. And saw it. The dark, damp stain of blood expanding across the crotch of my jeans.

'Fuck . . .' you gasped, taking your foot off the accelerator and pulling on to the hard shoulder. A couple of seconds later we slid to a halt.

'Christ, Leanne.' You peered at the blood in horror. I could see the desperation in your face. The dread. 'We need to get you to a hospital.'

I stared back at you, wild-eyed and frantic. 'We can't, Joe. We can't take the risk.'

'But—' You stopped, closed your eyes, resting your forehead against the steering wheel. We sat like that for a minute or two, the car shuddering as other vehicles sped past, buffeting the air around us with surprising force. I watched you pushing through your exhaustion, trying to think.

We were both so tired. We'd stopped again to sleep in a layby beyond Paris, you flattening your seat as far as it would go, me curling up in the back. We'd managed a few more hours, but woke feeling worse somehow. Stomachs hollow, eyes filled with lead.

'It might stop.' I tried to sound hopeful. 'I read somewhere you can bleed in early pregnancy, that it's not uncommon.'

'But you're thirteen weeks gone.'

I blinked. Inhaled. 'I'll pick up some pads in the next service station.'

'No, Leanne, we need to get you to a doc—'

'It won't make any difference,' I fired back, on the very edge of tears. I turned to face you. 'It won't help, Joe. Whatever's happening, no doctor can stop it.'

You gritted your teeth. I could see that you, too, were on the verge of breaking down. You did care, I realized, despite barely mentioning the pregnancy since you made that dreadful accusation.

Though you'd never again suggested it wasn't yours.

Suddenly all the hope drained out of me. It was madness. This whole trip. This getaway. What had I been thinking? I gazed at you and felt defeat seep into every corner of my mind.

I turned to look at the expanse of fields around us, the line of wind turbines in the distance, blades glinting as they rotated slowly in the late afternoon sun. I watched them for a moment, mesmerized, then shook myself out of it.

'Let's keep going. We should be there by this evening.

I can rest when we arrive.' I tried to smile. 'Maybe it will ease off.'

You closed your eyes. Blocking me out. 'How do you know, Leanne? How can you be so sure this place will be empty? What if we can't find the key? What then?'

It was obvious these questions had been playing on your mind all the way down through France.

'Joe.' I touched your arm. 'It's going to be all right. I promise.' I said it like I meant it, trying to convince myself as much as you.

But you didn't respond. Just stared at the road ahead, the cars disappearing round the bend in the distance.

'C'mon,' I urged. 'We need to get out of here, before the police pull over to check what's wrong.'

You sighed, turning the ignition. Revving the engine, we edged back into the flow of traffic.

50

Near Lyon, France

Wednesday, 9 August 2006

'I have to rest.'

I checked out your face. It looked terrible. Drained of energy and expression.

'I'm stopping at the next services, Leanne. I can't carry on driving in this state. I need an hour or so of sleep or we'll end up in an accident.'

I nodded. 'OK.'

It was another twenty kilometres to the nearest *aire*, as the French called their motorway services. We parked well back from the garage and shop, underneath the trees.

'I'm going to clean up,' I told you, getting out of the car. I needed a wash, hadn't had time for a shower before we left London. I was hungry too, desperate for something decent to eat after the crap I'd had since breakfast – a limp sandwich oozing mayonnaise, a bag of peanut-flavoured crisps.

You nodded. Didn't speak. It was like we'd agreed not to discuss our predicament any more than we had to.

I hobbled into the small service station, legs stiff and wobbly as I made my way to the loos. Locking myself in the furthest stall, I peeled back the wad of tissue I'd shoved down my pants, hoping to protect the clean jeans I'd wriggled into while you were driving. The tissue was nearly soaked through, though the blood loss seemed to have eased off a bit.

Maybe. It was hard to be sure.

I had a pee, then took fresh loo paper from the dispenser and tucked it into my knickers. Went into the shopping area and found a pack of sanitary towels. It wasn't till I got to the cashier that I realized – I'd forgotten to bring any of the euros we'd picked up at Dover.

Shit.

I didn't want to go back to the car and wake you, but I needed those towels, and fast. Now I was on my feet and moving around, I could feel more blood leaking down – it wouldn't be long before I ruined another pair of jeans.

Nothing else for it. I paid with my credit card, then rushed back into the toilets.

Fuck. The blood had turned from a deep rust-brown to fresh red.

And there was more of it. Much more.

I felt suddenly dizzy. Leaning my head against the side of the stall, I squeezed my eyes shut, trying to banish the sight of Victor, blood oozing from his ruined face, seeping across the floorboards.

A gagging sensation in my throat as I held back a whimper. I ripped open the pack of sanitary towels, sticking one on to the gusset of my pants. Added another for good measure. There were only eight left – I'd need more, I thought. Several packets.

I made my way back to the shop. Past the bank of coffee vending machines and the shelves of French novels. And that's when I saw it.

On the screen above the seating area by the café.

Victor. His face, leering at the camera. A photo, taken at the AVNs, his finger raised in that 'screw you' gesture, the other hand clutching his award.

Underneath, text scrolling in French. *'Réalisateur de porno Victor Gomez,'* I caught, *'a été retrouvé mort dans l'appartement d'une actrice porno. La mort est suspecte, selon des sources policières.'*

Mort. I felt my stomach go cold. That meant 'dead', didn't it? I scrambled to remember the French I'd done at school. Tried to figure out the gist.

'Director of porn Victor Gomez . . . dead in the apartment of a porn actress.' I was pretty certain that was right.

So they knew. They'd found him already. And the *'mort'* was *'suspecte'* . . . Suspicious? It had to be. Hell, it wasn't like anyone could think it was an accident.

Shit. *Shit, shit, shit.*

A pain in my chest. My legs began to shake again. How was it even possible? They must have discovered the body almost straight away.

Choking down a sob, I turned and headed out of the building. The sun was fading, the air warm and sticky, clinging to my skin like a damp flannel.

Oh God. They'd found Victor. They knew he'd been murdered. But that didn't matter, did it? They couldn't possibly have pinned it on us.

How could they?

We're fine, I told myself, repeating it like a mantra, trying to breathe evenly and calm my racing heart.

We're fine.

Everything was going to be just fine.

51

Near Lyon, France

Wednesday, 9 August 2006

I didn't tell you about Victor. As I approached the car, as quietly as I could, I saw you were awake, your mobile pressed to your ear.

What the hell were you doing? We'd agreed we shouldn't use our phones unless it was unavoidable. That it was too risky.

'Sorry.' You cut the call as soon as you saw me. 'It was my dad. He left a message.'

I frowned. 'OK.'

You gazed back at me as if you needed to say something. I sat still, waiting.

'Let's go,' you mumbled finally. Sounding as exhausted as you looked, the skin around your eyes dark with fatigue.

I put my hand on your arm. 'Let me drive, Joe.'

You shook your head. 'You're not insured.'

Like that mattered now. But I didn't argue and we set off towards Lyon in silence. When you handed cash over at the *péage* for the motorway toll, I nearly told you not to bother. Too late to cover our tracks – I'd already used my credit card in the shop. If they were looking for us, they'd know we were in France. Might even have a good idea where we were heading.

But they weren't looking for us, I reminded myself. Why would they be? There was nothing to link us to Victor's death, not directly. They'd find out we knew Esme, sure, but how did that implicate us in any way?

We were fine, I kept repeating in my head, over and over, as we sailed past fields of fading sunflowers and endless clumps of woodland, the sun sinking ever lower in the sky.

It was all going to be just fine.

You drove slowly and carefully, notching up the miles as the light faded into darkness. I checked the map. We should be there soon. If we came off the motorway at Orange, then headed over towards Travaillan, we could take the back roads to the village near the River L'Aigue.

I was sure I could remember how to get to the cottage, though it was years since I'd been there; the twins were still babies. Mike's friend Tony had bought the place in the days when you could pick up old buildings in the south of France with small change; his new wife, however, preferred hotels with heated pools, so now it sat empty, gathering dust.

What I recalled most clearly from the week we spent there was its location, half a mile from the nearest hamlet. Back then, that annoyed me. I was bored and restless, pestering Mum to take me into Orange or Avignon for a bit of life. Now it was a blessing, well away from prying neighbours. We'd be safe, at least for a few days. Until we decided where to go next.

And where would that be, asked a nagging voice in my head? What exactly *were* we going to do?

Change our names, I supposed. Get new passports. How hard would it be to find someone who could do that? Hell, you could probably order them on the dark web.

We'd set up new identities, a brand-new life. Get married. Have children . . .

My mind snapped back to the bleeding. Now I was sitting, it seemed to have slowed again, but I'd got through four pads already.

Don't think about that, Leanne, I told myself. *It'll be OK.*

I forced myself to focus on the future. I'd dye my hair, I decided. Change my appearance so no one would recognize me. We'd learn to speak French, or maybe Spanish – we could head further south, live in one of the Costas, work in a bar or hotel. Rent a house perhaps.

It's all going to be OK.

'I need to take a leak,' you said, flicking on the indicator when you saw signs for the next *aire*. You parked the car in an unlit area away from the services. No one else around. It was then, as you turned off the engine, that we heard the sirens in the distance.

We both froze. Sat there, barely breathing, waiting for them to pass.

It was completely dark now. This corner of the car park, bordered by large pines, felt deserted, like we were in the middle of a forest. We were invisible, surely? Nothing could touch us here.

The wail of the sirens drew closer. I clenched my jaw, willing them past, chasing some drunken motorist. Rushing to the scene of an accident.

It'll be something. Anything.

Not us.

The din grew louder, deafening now, and headlights flooded the tarmac, dazzling through the windscreen. I stared at my wing mirror. Counted half a dozen vehicles forming a semicircle behind our car, some fifty metres back. Lights flashing from their roofs, casting a hectic, almost hypnotic swirl of blue that radiated around us.

Police.

And that noise. That screaming, synthetic wall of sound. But when it stopped, the silence was even worse.

You turned to me, blinking fiercely. You didn't say anything. You didn't utter a word.

No need to. It was all there in your look.

We were at the end of the road.

I wondered how they knew it was us. I must have overlooked something in the flat, left some clue. Maybe Ashad had turned us in, guessing immediately we'd stolen his taxi.

But how had they found us so quickly? Had they traced my credit card? Were they monitoring our phones?

Or perhaps it was the number plate, I thought, remembering those CCTV cameras at the toll booths – I should have used tape or marker pen to disguise it.

'I'm sorry, Leanne,' you said, finally.

I turned to face you. Your expression was awful. The resignation plain to see, like you had no fight left.

Something rose inside me, a desperate, choking sensation. 'Joe,' I stammered. 'We can still make it. Let's head for the trees.' I reached for my door handle, but you grabbed my arm.

'No.'

'C'mon, Joe,' I said fiercely, gazing out at the pines, illuminated now by all the headlights. There was a fence round the car park, but it didn't look that high. If we could get to the trees, we could hide. I mean, it wasn't like they'd shoot us or anything.

Was it?

'Leanne, *no*.' You gripped my arm tighter, refusing to let me go.

I twisted my head to look at you. Felt your hand trembling where you held me.

'Joe . . .' Your name came out as an animal wail, like something howling. I couldn't do this. I couldn't just sit here while my life fell apart.

Behind us, the sound of car doors opening, slamming shut. Then someone speaking through a megaphone. In English, with a thick French accent.

'This is the police. Stay in your vehicle. Repeat, stay in your vehicle.'

Part of me wanted to laugh. It sounded so ridiculous the way they said it. *Vay-hi-cyuuule.*

'I'm sorry.' You closed your eyes briefly, before fixing them on me. 'I can't go through with this, Leanne. I'm so sorry.'

I swallowed. Let go of the door handle. 'It won't come to that, Joe. We'll get a lawyer, we'll tell them about Victor. They'll applaud us for what we did. *They'll give us a fucking medal.*'

I reached over and held the palm of my hand to your face, and you smiled back at me. Though it was the saddest smile I'd ever seen. Like everything had come to a close. Like you were that man and I was that woman, sitting in the train station, knowing our life together was over.

Moments ticked by, one by one. If only I could stop them, I thought, fleetingly. Pause them like a film. If only we could stay here forever, freeze-framed, in this car, in this instant.

It would be enough.

'Wait here.' You opened your door and got out.

'STAY IN YOUR VEHICLE' boomed the voice through the megaphone. I saw you raise your hands as you stood and faced them.

'Joe!' I screamed after you. 'JOE!'

'THIS IS THE POLICE. RETURN TO YOUR VEHICLE IMMEDIATELY.'

I watched you walk round to the front of the car. I twisted in my seat, and for a second you looked back, and through my tears, through all the blinding, flashing, swirling lights, I saw your face. I saw your face, the pleading in your eyes, and I remembered what you'd said about that hellhole they put you in.

I'd rather die than go back there.

I didn't stop to think about it. I knew if I did, I'd lose all courage. I'd let you down.

Heart thumping, I squeezed into the driver's seat, feeling for the keys. Still in the ignition.

I started the engine.

A rush of blood soaked into the towels wedged between my legs.

'THIS IS THE POLICE,' boomed the voice. 'RETURN TO YOUR VEHICLE. YOU ARE SURROUNDED.'

How? I asked myself as I released the handbrake. *How* did they know it was *us?*

I spun the car round, then reversed it, fast and hard, looking over my shoulder. Felt the tyres freewheel for a second as they hit the grass beyond the tarmac, then bite the ground again. Back and back I went, until the bumper slammed against the perimeter fence and I stopped.

Blinding lights. Words blaring from the megaphone. But I wasn't listening now. I took the gear out of reverse, revved the engine, never taking my eyes from your back as you walked towards the police cars, hands raised above your head.

Then I did it.

I did what I knew you wanted.

Despite everything, your doubts and mine, I did the right thing.

And I did it for you, Joe.

I did it all for you.

52

HMP Brakehurst

Tuesday, 12 April 2016

Yvonne is studying me, her lips clamped between her teeth, trying to absorb what I've just said. I hadn't written it down. Opted instead for telling her face-to-face.

Our last session. The end of my story. It seemed more appropriate somehow.

Yvonne looks shocked, but I don't care. I don't give a fuck what anyone else thinks.

They weren't there. They don't *know*.

'Are you telling me Joe asked you to do that, Leanne? Did you actually hear him say it?'

'He didn't have to.' I hold my therapist's gaze. 'He didn't have to put it into words. I knew he'd rather die than go back to prison. *He said so.*'

She doesn't argue. Just clamps her hands together, thinking.

Finally she speaks. 'I'm confused, Leanne. You admitted to Victor's murder, took the blame anyway. So why would Joe have gone to prison?'

I look at her like she's insane. 'One conviction already for being an accessory to a serious assault – you reckon he'd have stood a chance of staying out of jail? Even if he didn't break down under interrogation, admit to killing Victor.'

You weren't as strong as me, were you, my love? Could never have held out, or survived all this time inside.

Yvonne mulls this over. I close my eyes, tired now, and suddenly I'm back there. Foot on the accelerator. The lurch of the car as it rushed forward.

You must have heard the engine rev, the squeal of tyres on tarmac as the car sped towards you, but you didn't flinch or try to get out of the way. Didn't look round.

Didn't make me see your face.

Thank you, my love. Thank you for sparing me that.

'Are you sure, Leanne?' Yvonne asks again, her voice low, controlled. Clearly choosing her words carefully. 'Are you absolutely certain it was what Joe wanted?'

I open my eyes. Inhale, trying to calm myself. 'Why else would he get out of the car? They told us to stay put, and he got out. You tell me why he did that.'

I watch Yvonne grasping for an answer. But there isn't one – God knows, I've spent enough time going over this myself. Searching my memories for clues.

Always coming to the same conclusion.

'So, in effect you're saying it was a mercy killing.' The therapist rubs her forehead, like all this is too difficult to contemplate. 'Nevertheless, Leanne, that still makes you guilty of murder.'

I shrug. 'I've never disputed that.'

'Double murder,' she adds. 'Since the CPS claimed it was in fact you who killed Victor Gomez, and that you ran down Arjun Mistry to stop him testifying against you.'

369

I laugh, genuinely amused. 'That would be a bit stu-pid, wouldn't it? Bumping someone off in front of a dozen armed witnesses, to stop him dobbing me in.'

'Yes, Leanne, but it was enough to convince your solicitor and barrister that you should plead guilty.'

I grit my teeth, suppressing another surge of frustra-tion. 'They didn't have to convince me of anything, Yvonne – the plea was my decision. I never even told them what happened. They said the evidence against me was overwhelming and advised me to plead guilty, but they didn't have to *persuade* me.'

Yvonne blinks. Glances at the clock on the wall, then turns back to me.

'I've read your file, Leanne. They found your finger-prints on the camera that killed Victor – the one that was in the boot of the car. Only *your* prints.'

I sigh. 'Like I said, I cleaned them off. Obviously I didn't do a very good job of it.'

'And specks of Victor Gomez's blood on your skin and in your hair.'

I don't say anything to this. I was there. I was stand-ing right there when it happened. Of course I got his blood on me. Jesus, I was covered in Victor's DNA – if they'd done a fucking throat swab, they'd have found plenty inside me as well.

Yvonne twists the corner of her lip, still thinking. 'You were aware, weren't you, Leanne, that an admis-sion of guilt would result in a lighter sentence.'

I can't tell whether Yvonne's asking or simply making a statement, so I don't answer. Make no effort to break the silence that follows.

I leave the therapist to draw her own conclusions, while I listen to the silence. We're in a different room today, over in F block – one of the few places where you can get away from the constant noise of four hundred people living on top of one another.

'OK, Leanne,' Yvonne sighs after a couple of minutes have passed. She sits up straighter, uncrossing her legs. 'I'm just trying to get my head around all this. Make sure I understand your perspective. So perhaps I can ask about Joe. Did you ever have doubts about him? Over his loyalty to you?'

The question ignites in my head. Bright as a flare.

Did I ever doubt you, my love?

Did I ever imagine you'd phoned the police – not your father – telling them where to find Victor's body? Letting them know we were in France?

Did I ever think that Victor's revelation about you and Esme wasn't so far off the mark?

Of course, I found out later that it wasn't true, at least the bit about turning me in. The police, apparently, had been monitoring Victor all along, had seen him go into Esme's apartment and never emerge. Had clocked us leaving the scene, managing to trace us to Ashad's car.

But you can forgive me, can't you, Joe, for a few moments of doubt?

A touch of the jitters.

After all, I forgave you for yours.

'Leanne?' Yvonne's voice drags me back. 'You are aware, aren't you, that Sharon Harding has asked if I would report to her on our work together. How much progress I think we've made.'

'Yeah, she said.'

'So . . . I guess what's still puzzling me is why you didn't tell the police all this from the very beginning?'

I look past her, at the sunlight beyond the window. No sign of the rooks today, but over in the trees, a fuzz of green emerging as the leaves unfold into spring. I feel a brief lift at the prospect of summer, though it barely counts in here.

It's not like we ever do much sunbathing.

'Can you explain again,' prompts Yvonne gently, 'why you are now changing your story?'

I shut her off. Shut her out. Let her words dissolve in my head as I focus on you. On us. Like I do, every day, every night, back in my cell. Sit and think about the two of us, waiting in the car in that far off corner of France, at that moment when the blare of all the sirens seemed to fade away and there was only you and me.

Forever.

I like to think I did it for you, Joe. That I took the blame for Victor to save your family more grief, more shame, more turmoil. But truly? I did it because it made no difference to me. I didn't care any more. You were dead. I'd lost our baby. I had nothing left to live for.

One murder, or two. What's the difference?

'Leanne?' Yvonne puts my file down on the coffee table, then leans forward, fixing her gaze on mine. Her voice soft. 'I read in your notes that you were put on suicide watch, while you were in Holloway – after you tried to hang yourself.'

I nod, fighting back tears, determined not to cry. I've done way too much of that already.

'You must have been very distraught to attempt that, Leanne.'

No shit, Sherlock. I missed you, Joe. I missed you so much I no longer wanted to live. What was the point of life, without you in it?

And I was sorry, too, for ever doubting you. For losing faith.

Yvonne picks up the box of tissues that always sits on

372

the table. I give in and take one. Wipe my face, then scrunch it in my hand, surprised I still have tears left – I thought I'd cried them all out years ago.

'Leanne,' Yvonne says, slow and soothing. 'I've listened to everything you've told me. And I can see you sincerely believe all this to be true . . .'

Believe? She thinks I'm lying, I realize, with a stab of hurt and anger. Making it up. All these weeks, explaining what really happened, and she still doesn't believe me.

I should have known, I think, remembering that day in court, the place heaving with journalists and gawpers, everyone gathered to see me sent down.

Like the AVNs all over again – but with me the only nominee.

What was it that po-faced judge said, right before she issued the sentence? What did she call my life? A morality tale. Only the next morning, one of the papers had twisted it round. *Life for Kitty Sweet: An Amorality Tale* read the headline.

An extra letter; a world of difference.

'Leanne?'

I tune Yvonne out again, listen instead to the voice in my head. You're wasting your time, it says. Nobody will ever believe you.

But I'm sick of people assuming the worst. Assuming I'm fucked up, or some kind of monster.

Though, really, why should I care? I'm in no hurry to leave this place. It's not the same for me as it was for you, Joe; prison suits me. I get my meals, even my own cell. I'm safe. No men staring at me, no one taking my picture. No one after another little piece of my soul.

Except maybe Drew and Tanya, but that's a small price to pay.

It's peaceful here, despite the noise. I get a lot of time to think.

And dream.

Every night, after lights out, I lie in my bunk and let it all play out in my mind. Imagine that we got away, that we're living in a house by the Mediterranean. Taking walks together on the beach. Meals out with our child – calamari, perhaps, or local fish. Warm nights, full of the rhythmic buzz of cicadas.

Sometimes though, I remember that old black-and-white film you showed me, replaying it in my head. The man and the woman, sitting in the station café, waiting. Her in a hat, hair in neat waves. Him in a suit and overcoat, like all men wore back then. Only in my version, it's in colour, and they both get on the train. They get on the train and go off and start a new life together.

And nobody has to be sad.

Maybe I'm wrong, to twist the truth like that. But my version is so much better, don't you think?

After all, doesn't everyone prefer a happy ending?

Epilogue

HMP Brakehurst

Wednesday, 27 April 2016

Dear Ms Harding,

Further to your request, I am writing regarding the eight sessions I have been working with Leanne Jenkins. She has given her consent for me to discuss my broad opinions of her case and her mental condition, but as you are aware, I cannot disclose the content of our sessions in any detail.

Most of our time together has been spent exploring the incidents leading to her imprisonment. One of the most notable things about Leanne has been her marked reluctance to step away from these events and engage in any deeper examination of childhood issues, and how they might have impacted on her history. Although she mentioned her father several times in passing, she has resisted every attempt to get her to consider his role in her life – or rather, his absence from it. This has been somewhat disappointing. I had hoped we might make better progress with this element of her history, and indeed, her relationship with her mother.

As you are also aware, Leanne has been writing down her version of what happened in the run-up to her imprisonment. This has made for interesting reading; Leanne has a natural flair for narration, being both expressive and insightful.

However, one thing that most struck me about Leanne's account is a certain 'fanciful' quality to the incidents she relates. I sometimes had the feeling Leanne said things simply for effect. While her story follows a logical progression, some of the events she described lack credibility. Victor Gomez, for instance, is presented as someone entirely sadistic, almost a one-sided caricature of 'evil'.

Unfortunately, his untimely death means it is now impossible to establish with any certainty whether Gomez was indeed the 'Landfill Killer', as the police also suspected. Leanne seems blithely unaware – or at least to ignore – the knock-on effects of Gomez's death, although I understand she was told Scotland Yard had him under surveillance.

She has not, however, ever acknowledged how his death effectively stifled the police investigation into the murders of Anya Viksna, Tula Kask and Heidi Wiemann, along with any hope that Gomez might lead them to the other members of the Russian trafficking gang thought to be involved. Indeed, I get the sense Leanne sees Gomez's murder as rather heroic – or at any rate justifiable.

While I can't go into detail, I think I should

point out that, despite pleading guilty, Leanne is now disclaiming responsibility for Gomez's murder – at least to me. That said, I am confident her conviction would still stand. Her motive for killing him seems clear. The fact he made violent and sadistic pornography has never been in dispute, and in general I believe Leanne's vivid descriptions of his persona and abusiveness, though sometimes, as I mentioned, I felt the accounts were exaggerated for effect.

However, with regards to the death of Arjun (Joe) Mistry – for which she still admits responsibility – Leanne's motives appear more complex. She asserts that it was a kind of 'mercy killing', something Mistry wanted her to commit. My personal feeling is her actions were largely motivated by the rumoured affair between Esme Donaldson and Arjun Mistry. While the truth or otherwise of this affair has never been corroborated, the fact that Leanne mentioned it on several occasions confirms that – at least in her head – she believed it might be true. Indeed, her own account of Gomez tormenting her with the rumour would provide more than enough motive for both killings.

That Leanne had a complex relationship with Esme Donaldson is also evident. The pair were sexually involved, if only within the context of work. I believe Leanne was likely battling deep-seated feelings of jealousy and abandonment when Esme married Nelson Garvey.

This subconscious desire for revenge may well explain why Leanne murdered her lover, and would also provide a motive for the possible manslaughter of Nelson Garvey. I was particularly intrigued by this aspect of Leanne's case, after reading in her initial psychiatric reports that Sonya Garvey, Nelson's mother, had contacted the US emergency services regarding their apparent failure to respond to the 911 calls. Unfortunately Mrs Garvey was unable to obtain any confirmation from the Las Vegas Metropolitan Police Service as to whether those calls were ever made.

Although the CPS decided not to pursue this – given there was no certainty that the timely arrival of an ambulance would have resulted in Mr Garvey's survival – I have questioned Leanne several times about the events leading up to his death; her written account, while consistent, revealed a somewhat telling lack of detail. Leanne, however, insists she did make those calls, and that it was her idea to transport Garvey to hospital in a taxi when no ambulance arrived.

In terms of Leanne's suitability for parole and rehabilitation, I find this difficult to answer. I am sure Leanne sincerely believes her own version of events; that does not, however, mean they are true. Working in the sex industry is mentally and physically arduous, and feelings of loneliness and despair may be amplified. While for many, drugs and alcohol kill those emotions – for a short time, at least – incarceration limits access to both, and I believe Leanne's principal way of coping with the prison environment and a life sentence is largely to escape into a world of fantasy.

Indeed, there are various inconsistencies in Leanne's story, and several of her assertions do not match the facts. Although she described a visit to Mistry's family, I note they claimed never to have met Leanne before the court hearing. Similarly Leanne's account of Arjun Mistry's former imprisonment seems confused. She claims Mistry told her his brother Amit assaulted a rival gang member, whereas in reality both were convicted of grievous bodily harm.

It is hard to discern whether Leanne is lying, misremembering events (which after all happened some time ago), or simply indulging an urge to 'revamp' her own history into a more palatable or dramatic version of the truth – one she finds easier to live with.

To conclude, I have read the psychological assessments made prior to Leanne's sentencing, and broadly agree with the diagnosis of borderline personality disorder. However, I believe she also presents with a high degree of fantasy and narcissism; both traits that would have been compounded by her choice of career, given make-believe and self-gratification are the stock-in-trade of the pornography industry.

It is well established that many people use sex as a way to cauterize emotional wounds; in Leanne's case it provided a source of income as well as admiration. As Leanne herself stated, being watched, being desired, made her feel 'seen'. Yet pornography precludes any kind of real emotional intimacy, and 'Kitty Sweet', Leanne's 'porn persona', became someone she could effectively hide behind.

Had Leanne not been drawn into an industry that is clearly destructive for many young women,

I feel sure her life would have played out differently. For a personality as unstable as Leanne's, however, porn was the 'perfect storm', undermining an already vulnerable psyche.

In conclusion, Leanne Jenkins, I believe, suffers from a very fractured sense of self, and it is wholly conceivable that in times of high emotion and stress she could succumb to extreme feelings of rage and violence that she might later suppress, possibly forgetting entirely. It is interesting to note that even though Leanne now denies killing Victor Gomez, she has never once suggested her conviction or sentence was unfair, or should be reconsidered.

In the light of this, I would recommend Leanne undertake further psychological assessment and rehabilitation before any consideration of parole. Indeed, I am not sure she sees early release as desirable, having displayed no interest in returning to the outside world. She appears to have adjusted well to prison life; although, as has been previously noted, her existence here relies on a certain level of coercion and manipulation – Leanne's attractiveness and amenability to sexual favours being as useful within prison as without.

Leanne has, however, expressed a desire to take an Open University degree in creative writing, having gained confidence through relating her own story for our sessions. I have no doubt that, should she pursue her studies, she will be successful, as Leanne has a well above average IQ and is very articulate, despite the somewhat abrupt end to her education.

I am hoping this decision is a sign of Leanne's progress, and that the violent episode sparked by the news of her mother's illness will not recur. Indeed, I understand there is a general consensus from the staff that she is more settled, and I am optimistic this will carry forward into the remainder of her sentence.

With best wishes,
Yvonne Conway
DClinPsych MBPsS

Acknowledgements

Many thanks to my agent Mark Stanton and editor
Frankie Gray, and the rest of the team at Transworld.
And all my lovely crimey friends, especially those who
valiantly read and reported back on earlier drafts. You
know who you are.

Untouchable
Ava Marsh

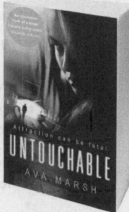

'If you start feeling anything for a client – and it *does* happen – count the money. That always brings you back down to earth.'

Stella is an escort, immersed in a world of desire, betrayal and secrets. It's exactly where she wants to be. Stella used to be someone else: respectable, loved, safe. But one mistake changed all that.

When a fellow call girl is murdered, Stella has a choice: forget what she's seen, or risk everything to get justice for her friend. In her line of work, she's never far from the edge, but pursuing the truth could take her past the point of no return.

Nothing is off limits. Not for her – and not for them. But no one is truly untouchable.

'An evocative thrill of a book . . . unlike anything I've read before. I loved every word'
Elizabeth Haynes, author of *Behind Closed Doors*

'A gritty, no-holds-barred thriller, with a flawed, uncompromising heroine – it had me racing through its pages'
Ruth Ware, author of *In a Dark, Dark Wood*